THE
TRANSCENDENT

THE
TRANSCENDENT

SALINA B BAKER

Inquiries should be addressed to the Publisher
Culper Press
Austin, Texas

First Printing 2020

This is a work of fiction. Some events and places are real and some are products of the author's imagination.

ISBN: 978-0-9987558-3-0

Printed in the United States of America

"We see the light of those who find
A world has passed them by
Too late to save a dream that's growing cold"

— Queensrÿche

Prologue

June 1847

F ather Cochrane stood in the chancel at St. Mark's Episcopal Church preparing for his first administration of the Holy Baptism rite. His lips moved in silence as he read the Baptismal Covenant and the liturgies from *The Book of Common Prayer*.

"It is time to ready the font," Bishop Howe said as he finished the arrangement for the Eucharist.

Father Cochrane laid the book on the lectern. He turned to walk through the nave, paused, and then looked at Bishop Howe. "The parents' names are Aron and Freya Walesa. We will be baptizing their infant son. Is that correct?"

"Yes, that is correct."

Father Cochrane nodded and then proceeded through the nave. A moment before he reached the sanctuary, he thought he heard murmuring. He looked back at the altar. Bishop Howe was gone. The doors to the sacristy and the robing rooms stood open. He saw nothing out of the ordinary. The church was silent.

He entered the sanctuary. The font was in a recess to the left of the church's magnificent red front door. A flagon of water was poised on the font.

Father Cochrane removed a small unlighted baptismal candle from the pocket inside his cassock and placed it on the font. The murmuring returned.

The doors to the sacristy and robing room slammed shut. A hand touched his shoulder. He gasped and whirled around.

"I apologize if I startled you," Bishop Howe said. "It is time for the service."

"Did you hear that?"

"Hear what?"

Father Cochrane listened. All was quiet. He felt foolish as he hurried to the altar.

Bishop Howe opened St. Mark's front door to a beautiful Sunday morning in St. Louis, Missouri. Blue skies and bright warm sunshine embraced him. He drew in the morning air as he greeted his waiting congregants.

Aron and Freya Walesa entered the church accompanied by their son's baptismal sponsor.

Bishop Howe peered at the bundle in Freya's arms and said, "So this is our tiny candidate. Such a beautiful baby! His eyes are *so* blue. If I may say— he looks just like you, Mrs. Walesa."

"You are very kind, Bishop," Freya said as she smiled upon her son's face.

The service lasted an hour, then, a deacon asked the Walesas to rise from their pew. They followed Father Cochrane. He spoke a short litany during the procession to the font.

At the font, Father Cochrane asked the Walesas if they renounced Satan, evil powers, and sinful desires.

The Walesas said in unison, "I renounce them."

"Do you turn to Jesus Christ and accept him as your savior?"

Each Walesa said, "I do."

Father Cochrane took the infant from his mother's arms. He looked into the baby's blue eyes and said, "I baptize you in the name of…"

He heard the voices of a thousand lost souls begging for a human life. A single voice whispered, "You are not allowed to touch him in that manner."

Father Cochrane's heart stopped, and he collapsed. The infant boy slid from his arms.

A year and a half later, the day after the Walesas left Missouri to travel the Oregon Trail, cholera waged war on St. Louis. It killed more than four thousand people. Bishop Howe was one of its casualties.

I
The Catalyst

Chapter 1

August 1872

J anek didn't feel the pain of those he loved leaving their earthbound lives. He was drunk and distracted. He had just completed his accounting studies at Willamette University in Salem, Oregon and was attending his graduation party.

His friend, Attorney Patrick Bright, handed him a shot of tequila and said, "You're twenty-five years old and finally done with your education. You'll need a wife, and she'll have to come from accepted social circles."

Janek gulped the shot of tequila. "I can't think about marriage. I have obligations to my family. I haven't seen them in six months, and I'm going home tomorrow."

"Do you suppose your father expects you to work the farm after the sum of money he has invested in your education?"

"Of course he doesn't! He knows my position at the accounting firm is advancing from a few hours per day to eight hours or more."

"Well then, I have it on good authority that Senator Williams' daughter, Sarah, wants to dance with you tonight," Patrick said. "She would make a perfect marital match."

Janek poured more tequila into his glass and said, "Must you continue?"

As Patrick had warned, Sarah Williams approached Janek Walesa with her empty dance card.

At dawn, Janek awoke in Sarah's bed with a hangover and a vague memory of fervent sex.

He returned to his apartment in downtown Salem, grabbed his packed bags, and then ran to the depot. The stagecoach was departing when he arrived. He threw his bags on top of the coach, jumped on the running board, and managed to get into a seat.

The stagecoach stopped in Albany, Oregon; a town nestled on the confluence of the Calapooia River and the Willamette River in the Willamette Valley. From there, Janek caught a ride on a farmer's wagon. The farmer let him off at the lane to the Walesa's farmhouse. The August afternoon sun blistered the dirt lane. Dust stirred beneath his boot heals with each step he took. As he neared the house, he sensed something was wrong.

Chickens and geese and cats wandered around the dooryard. The dogs were absent. His father often worked the far fields with the hired hands, but his mother and sister stayed in or around the house. There was no detectable human movement nor the perpetual aroma of food cooking. The house windows stared out in dark disbelief.

An unexpected breeze huffed in the dooryard and ruffled Janek's blond hair. Laundry drooping on the clothesline trembled in the current. There was a vile quality to the breeze, which made him shudder.

He was startled by his closest neighbor's sudden appearance in the dooryard. George Wilkerson pulled a handkerchief from the pocket of his bib overalls and mopped the dirt and sweat from his face.

Repugnant fear molested Janek. He dropped his bags and ran to the house. George intercepted him before he reached the front porch steps.

"Janek, before you go in the house, we need to talk."

"Move out of my way!"

"Not until you listen…"

Janek shoved George.

George grabbed Janek by the wrist. "Listen to me!"

Janek wrenched his wrist from George's grasp. He threw open the front door and ran down the hall to the kitchen. His mother and sister were not there. There were no simmering coals in the stove's firebox. No sign of food preparation. Dirty dishes were piled in the sink. Muddy streaks and dusty footprints covered the floor as if inept dancers had waltzed around the kitchen. Filthy towels and bed linens were piled on the back porch beside the screen door. Flies crawled and buzzed on the screen.

Janek felt his gorge rise. Terror flayed every nerve in his body. He wanted to call his mother's name, but he was afraid she wouldn't answer.

George and his wife, Edna, walked into the kitchen. Edna said to Janek, "Look at me."

He couldn't rip his eyes away from what he realized he was seeing. The rancid towels and bed linens where soaked in blood and human excrement. Edna went to Janek and cupped his cheeks with her hands. His blue eyes shifted to her face.

"Your ma and sister died yesterday. Your pa died this mornin'. He came to us for help when your ma got sick. It was cholera. There's been an outbreak in the valley. I tried my best, but you know how quickly cholera can kill. We had to bury them right away. I'm so sorry."

Janek gaped at Edna. *My entire family is dead and buried? Oh Jesus, last night while my mother and sister lay dead, and my father lay dying, I was drinking and fucking...*

I don't believe you," he whispered, although he knew she was telling the truth.

Edna stroked his cheeks with gentle hands and said, "They're in the backyard."

Janek jerked Edna's hands from his face. He fled the kitchen and ran upstairs. The hushed bedrooms mourned their dead occupants, and they begrudged the sound of the floorboards creaking beneath his boots as he walked.

His mother's silver mirror reflected the shadow of his tall figure when he walked past her dressing table. His father's shaving brush and razor lay waiting to be rinsed beside the bowl on the washstand. His sister's books were piled on the floor in a corner of her bedroom. Janek picked up the book laying on her nightstand. She had been reading *Jane Eyre*.

He dropped the book. Without glancing at his bedroom door, he went downstairs to the parlor. The mantel clock ticked dolefully. This was the room where his family gathered at the end of a long day; where they decorated their Christmas tree and sang carols while his mother played the piano; where he sat as a five-year-old boy listening to his mother's cries as she gave birth to his little sister.

The family Bible was cradled in a small book stand on the sideboard. He opened the Bible and leafed through the book until he came to the pages filled with his mother's delicate handwriting.

Aron Gwidon Walesa born September 1, 1823 in Byczyna, Poland and emigrated to St. Louis, Missouri in October 1843 at twenty years of age.

Freya Lange Walesa born August 27, 1825 in St. Louis, Missouri.

Aron and Freya married June 9, 1846 in St. Louis, Missouri.

Janek Aron Walesa born April 14, 1847 in St. Louis, Missouri.

Liv Marie Walesa born July 1, 1852 in Albany, Oregon.

Am I expected to record their deaths in the Bible? The answer was horrifying. The mantle clock continued its doleful ticking. Janek was stalling. He was certain he would lose his mind if he went into the backyard, but they were there waiting for him. He had to tell them how much he loved them and beg for their forgiveness because he failed them. He had to face the truth.

Janek went into the kitchen and opened the screen door. He stepped onto the back porch and walked to the edge. Their bleak graves haunted the backyard where, in years gone past, a boy and his little sister played. Mother would open the screen door and call the brother and sister in for dinner. Father would bow his head and say grace before the meal was served. Life was hard, but it was good.

He wiped sweat from his forehead with the back of his hand and struggled to control his breathing. The urge to dig their bodies from their graves made him feel insane. He walked to the back corner of the yard and collapsed in front of the graves. Anguish swooped down upon him like a monstrous bird of prey. Its horrible talons shredded his self-control, and his grief unleashed itself.

><><

The sun was setting when Janek left the grave site. The Wilkersons were waiting for him on the front porch.

He fought to subdue his emotions when he said, "Why didn't you send for me? I would have come home right away."

"Aron didn't want you exposed," George said.

"But Father knew I was coming home today. That doesn't make sense."

"None of this makes sense. Aron asked us to look after you. It's not safe for you to stay here. You'll be comin' home with us tonight."

"Where are the dogs?" Janek said.

"Our nephew Jess came and got them yesterday. They're at the house. Come on now, we need to get goin'. It's near candle-lightin'."

Janek didn't want to go home with the Wilkersons, but he had no choice. Edna and George would be lucky if they didn't contract cholera after caring for his dying family.

><><

In the morning, Jess Wilkerson arrived to take Janek back to the Walesa farm. The Wilkersons walked him out to Jess' waiting wagon.

"I'll never be able to thank you enough for what you've done," Janek said. "I won't keep the farm after…this. Please take the livestock and the cats as well. They'll need a home."

"That's kind of you," Edna said. "You're a kind person, Janek. Your parents were so proud of you going to the university. We're going to miss you and your family very much."

Janek worked for a minute to keep his tears at bay before he said, "I will miss you both."

"If there's anythin' else we can do, let us know," George said. "And remember, this isn't your fault. You couldn't have done anythin' if you'd been here. You most likely would've died right along with them. Aron wouldn't want you to be carryin' that burden of guilt around the rest of your life."

Janek climbed into the seat beside Jess. Shedding his burden of guilt would be impossible.

At the Walesa farm, Jess and Janek spent several hours caging the fowl and the cats, and loading them in the wagon.

"I'll be back tomorrow to round up the livestock," Jess said as he closed the back of the wagon. "My kids'll be happy about keepin' your dogs. I don't mind lookin' after the place until you figure out what you're gonna do with it. That's if you don't take too long. I got my hands full at home."

"I appreciate that, but it's not necessary. I talked to one of my father's hired hands last night. He's going to watch over the place for a while. I don't know how long it will be until it's safe for humans to live here."

"Take care of yourself, Janek."

"You do the same, Jess."

When Jess was gone, Janek beheld the surrounding landscape with profound love. The mountains of the Cascade Range to the east and the Oregon Coast Range to the west cradled the beautiful serene valley. Wheat swayed in the breeze. Sheep grazed on the gentle rolling hills. He couldn't continue to live in the Willamette Valley. It would persecute him forever.

He went in the house and packed the meager remains of his belongings and the family Bible. In the barn, he fed the pigs and let the cows into the near pasture. Afterward, he hitched the horse to the wagon and loaded his bags.

Twenty years had passed since the Walesas had settled in the Willamette Valley. Now Janek was alone. He climbed into the wagon, and without looking back, said an eternal goodbye to the life he knew and the family he loved.

Chapter 2

The solitary ride back to Salem devastated Janek. He stayed in his apartment, slept little, ate nothing, and drank excessive amounts of tequila. Death wasted his days and exhausted his sanity. When he did sleep, he dreamed of flies crawling on rancid dead bodies rotting on the back porch. When he was so drunk that he couldn't stand up, he sobbed until his throat hurt and his eyes burned. Eight days later, he realized that he had to decide what to do with his life.

He arrived at the office of his employers, Doyle and Stromburg, at ten o'clock in the morning. Before he went inside, he dissembled his grief and put on the guise of his profession.

"I've come to discuss your generous job offer," Janek said when he was seated in Thomas Doyle's office.

"You have come to turn down the position. Am I right?"

"Yes."

"I thought this might happen after your family passed."

Janek was surprised to hear his family's death was common knowledge. No one had come to his apartment to offer condolences.

"Are you thinking of leaving Salem?"

Janek nodded.

"Have you a destination in mind?"

"No."

"I can recommend some accounting firms in San Francisco that are looking for good people. It might do you good to get away from here."

Janek stared at Thomas. *San Francisco?* That seemed drastic.

"I have to settle my parents' estate and sell the farm."

"Those things can be handled by correspondence. Your friend Patrick Bright is an attorney. He can take care of everything."

Janek looked at the floor and said nothing.

"I know this is a dreadful decision, and I know you are suffering. You have as much time as you need to think things over."

"I don't…have time. I can't stay here."

"Then it is settled."

Janek looked at Thomas.

"I will have the appropriate letters drawn up today and delivered to your apartment. I *am* sorry about your family. No one should have to endure such a tragedy. Stay in touch and let me know how things work out for you. There will be a position here for you if you decide to return."

Thomas' compassion touched Janek's despondency. He wiped at a rouge tear. "Thank you. I won't forget your kindness."

On Tuesday, August 20, 1872, with two carpetbags and the letters of recommendation from Thomas Doyle, Janek Walesa boarded a train on the Oregon and California Railroad. The train took him to the end of the railway line in Roseburg, Oregon. He wrote letters to Patrick Bright and the Wilkersons saying he was going to San Francisco and would be in touch. He mailed the letters at the train station in Roseburg.

From there, he paid for passage on a merchant wagon train bound for Eureka, California. The wagon train turned westward at the California state line, then south down the coast. Janek talked to no one unless it was necessary. Guilt and grief demanded his attention. They were his sole companions until shame pointed out his weaknesses and taunted him for leaving his dead family behind in graves few, if anyone, would visit.

His mind wandered.

"Come here and see your baby sister," his mother said. She held what seemed to five-year-old Janek to be a bundle of blankets in her arms. He wasn't sure what to think about a baby sister.

"Look, Janek! I caught a butterfly!"

He looked at his four-year-old sister's out stretched hand. A small yellow butterfly rested on Liv's palm. Its delicate wings were still.

"Be careful not to crush it."

"I will!" Liv said and laughed as she skipped away to a place Janek couldn't see.

Aron handed him a hammer. "This is why you'll go to college son."

"What does this have to do with…Father?"

>⌒⌒ ⌒⌒<

The wagon train arrived in Eureka, California on the morning of Friday, September 6, 1872. Eureka was a bustling lumber town on the coast, near Humboldt Bay. Clipper ships and schooners filled with people who were looking for investments or work arrived at the docks daily. Eureka and the surrounding areas offered opportunities in mining, logging, and fishing. Cruise ships originating in Portland, Oregon docked in Eureka on their way to points south.

Eureka's ebb and flow of teeming hordes made Janek uncomfortable, and he heeded his urgency to escape. The next stagecoach departure was scheduled for Saturday morning. The overnight wait was more than he could bear, so he went to the harbor in search of another means of transportation. The only vessel offering passage was a schooner preparing to sail south to a small town called Ferndale. Janek leaned against the rail on the schooner's stern and watched the blue water rush by.

Suddenly, he heard someone say, "Where're you headed?"

He turned and saw a man, smiling. The man appeared to be the same age and height as Janek. He had green eyes, and his long dark hair was pulled back into a ponytail at the nape of his neck.

"Are you speaking to me?" Janek said.

"Aye."

"San Francisco."

"Never been. I'm Evan O'Malley, the first mate on this schooner." He thrust a hand toward Janek.

Janek shook Evan's hand. "Janek Walesa."

"Where're you from?"

Janek didn't want to have a conversation with this man, but etiquette required an answer. "Oregon."

Evan nodded and grinned. "I've been to Portland many times. There's plenty to do there if you know what I mean."

Janek had no idea what Evan meant. He remained silent.

"What kind of work do you do?"

"Corporate accounting."

Evan whistled and let out a little chuckle. "You went to college?"

"Yes."

"I don't like math. It takes too much concentration."

Janek supposed a response was required, but he was given a reprieve when the captain called for his first mate.

Someone shouted, "Arriving in Ferndale!"

Janek saw a rocky shoreline ahead and the mouth of a river to his right. The schooner slid in silence up the Eel River toward a dock where several smaller boats were moored. After he disembarked, he stood on the dock and wondered how he was going to get to Ferndale.

Evan jumped onto the dock and said, "Follow me."

Janek picked up his bags and fell into step beside Evan.

Ferndale was more settled and prosperous than Janek expected. Main Street was lined with businesses as well as a post office and city hall. Dodd's General Mercantile Store was one of several ornate storefront buildings.

Janek said, "I need somewhere to stay tonight."

"That's where we're going," Evan said. "I have a friend who runs a boarding house."

They entered a neighborhood east of Main Street. Janek noticed a church steeple protruding above the roof tops. He kept glancing at it. Evan stopped and opened a gate in front of a large white house with a widow's walk on the roof and a sign on the door that read:

The Old Virginia Home

Lise Anders

Proprietor

Evan entered without knocking. Janek remained on the front porch. He heard Evan calling for someone inside the house. A feminine voice answered, and then a woman in her early thirties opened the door.

"I'm Lise Anders. Evan tells me you need a room for tonight. Come in and I'll get you settled."

Evan was standing in the entryway when Janek followed Lise into the house.

Janek said, "Thank you for your help, Mr. O'Malley."

"It's my pleasure, Mr. Walesa," Evan said as he opened the door to leave. "Oh, a southbound stagecoach comes through here tomorrow afternoon. I thought you might want to know."

Lise Anders led Janek into the parlor. "Please sit down."

Janek sat in a chair in front of a small desk and watched Lise unlock a desk drawer. She was average height and small boned, but her slim waist accentuated the curve of her hips and full bust line. Her soft features and blond hair and blue eyes reminded him of his mother.

Lise removed the registration book and a key from the drawer. She opened the book and slid it across the desk to Janek. "Write your name and home address," she said, handing him a pen.

He stared at the book. *Is this what I have been reduced to—a homeless man?*

"Is something wrong? Surely you can write."

"I have no home address."

"Well then, just write your name. The room is one dollar a night, which includes breakfast and dinner."

Janek paid Lise.

She led him upstairs to his room on the second floor. "Dinner is at six o'clock in the dining room. Will you be eating with us tonight?"

"No."

"Breakfast is served between seven and nine o'clock in the morning. I'm sure you'll be hungry by then. If you need anything in the meantime, you can find me in the kitchen."

When Lise had gone, Janek stripped off his clothes and lay on the bed. His familiar companions—guilt, grief, and shame—joined him. Loneliness consorted with this miserable group. He wondered what his real motive was for leaving home. Sorting through his emotions with his companions interjecting their opinions was exhausting. He dropped off into a dreamless sleep.

Chapter 3

September 1872

After breakfast the next morning, Janek walked to the stagecoach depot. He read the arrival and departure schedules written on the chalkboard behind the ticket counter. He started to purchase a ticket on the southbound run scheduled from Ferndale and asked, "The coach departing this afternoon only goes as far south as Mendocino?"

"Mendocino is an overnight stop. If you pay for fare all the way to San Francisco, you can stay with that stagecoach. The fare is three dollars."

Janek took his purse from his inner coat pocket and frantically rummaged through it several times. The purse contained exactly three dollars. *How odd*, he thought. *When I paid Lise Anders for my room last night, I had at least three hundred dollars.* "I'll have to wait to buy the ticket," Janek said. "I apologize for taking your time."

He left the depot and tried to remember what he had done after he arrived in town. He didn't want to believe he was robbed while he slept. The purse was in his coat, and his coat was draped over the foot of his bed. He was certain he had not dropped it on the way to the depot. *I'm letting my grief distract me,* he thought.

As he crossed Main Street, he felt a sensation likened to delicate fingertips brushing his chest. His mind lost focus and he began to black out. With great effort, he measured his breathing until his thoughts were clear. He shook his head to chase away the residue of the episode, and then continued to cross the street. On his walk back to the boarding house, he approached the Palace Saloon and went inside.

Although it was only eleven o'clock in the morning, there were already several customers. He stepped up to the bar and ordered tequila. The bartender plunked a shot glass on the bar in front of him and filled it with tequila. Janek heard someone call his name.

"Mr. Walesa! Come join me."

Evan O'Malley was standing at the other end of the bar, smiling and waving his hand.

To Janek's surprise, he was glad to see Evan. He joined him.

"I didn't expect to see you in here. You're going to get a bad reputation patronizing the Palace before noon," Evan said, laughing. "But I guess it doesn't matter since you're leaving this afternoon."

"I'm not leaving. I can't afford the stagecoach ticket."

"What are you going to do?"

"I'm going to have to earn the money. Do you know where I could get short term work?"

"I don't, but Guthrie might know." Evan shouted at the bartender. "Guthrie, do you know anyone who needs someone to do odd jobs? My friend here needs to earn a few dollars."

Guthrie sauntered to the end of the bar. He examined Janek from his frock coat with silk facings and braided binding on the collar, to his white cambric shirt beneath a double-breasted vest that revealed a gold watch chain.

"Old man Bixby died last night. I reckon Reverend Arnold will need someone to dig that grave."

The thought of digging a grave repulsed Janek. He felt his mind begin to lose focus, but the feeling passed.

Guthrie continued to eye Janek and said, "You look soft for a job like digging graves. You think that kinda work is gonna suit you?"

"I assure you I'm capable of manual labor."

Guthrie snorted in response.

Janek ignored him and said, "Can you take me there, Mr. O'Malley?"

"Aye, and by the way, it's Evan."

"Alright then; it's Janek."

As they walked to the church, Evan explained that he was the oldest of four children and the only son. "I'm twenty-six and Margaret, the oldest of my little sisters is sixteen. Ellen and Eliza are thirteen-year-old twins. I had three little brothers die before my sisters were born. It was hard on my mom.

"My family raises dairy cattle. Our farm is a mile outside of town, which is where I live when the schooner isn't running up and down the coast."

He went on to say that he hated farming much to his father's disapproval.

"I went up to Eureka a few years ago just to see what it was like. I spent two days wandering around, getting to know the town. I saw a schooner anchored in the harbor. There was a help wanted ad at the harbor office for a deckhand on that very schooner. I didn't have any sailing experience, but I could read and write so they gave me the job with potential to become first mate."

Janek's worries dissipated as he listened to Evan.

"My father had a conniption when I told him what I'd done. He made it seem like I'd betrayed the family. He still hates what I'm doing even though I was promoted to first mate over a year ago. So where's your family? All you told me was Oregon."

Janek didn't want to talk about his situation, but wondered if saying the words aloud might begin the healing process. He was uncertain if death was an appropriate topic for casual conversation.

"I'm from Albany, Oregon in the Willamette Valley. My family has a farm there."

"Farming doesn't agree with you either?"

"My father sacrificed a tremendous amount to put me through school. I would have continued to help out on the farm after graduation."

"So why didn't you?"

The fingertips returned to wisp across Janek's chest. He blacked out before he was aware it was coming. Without his conscious knowledge, he told Evan his family was dead. He spoke of his shock and guilt, and his profound regret that he had not been there to care for them or say goodbye. When his confession was through, his world brightened, leaving him with no memory of the blackout.

><<><><

The First Congregational Church of Ferndale stood on the southeast side of town. The clapboard New England-style rectangular structure with rows of long windows lining each side was built in 1850. The steeple towered above the small front stoop. The front and side yards were narrow and the grass was mowed. The back door opened onto a cobblestone courtyard. Several mausoleums were nestled in the steep hillside on the far side of the courtyard. Stone steps climbed the hill to a cemetery.

Janek looked up at the steeple with uneasiness as he and Evan walked through the tall arched gate with FERNDALE CEMETERY lettered in the iron work across the top.

They entered the courtyard, and a man approached them. "Evan, it's good to see you!"

"It's good to see you too, Reverend. How's the church renovation going?"

"It's nearly finished. Lise is inside cleaning the floors. I see you brought along a new face."

"This is Janek Walesa. He's looking for odd jobs. Guthrie said you might need a grave dug."

The reverend turned to Janek and said, "I'm Reverend Niklas Arnold."

Janek reached to shake the reverend's hand. "It's nice to meet you, Reverend."

"What brings you to Ferndale, Mr. Walesa?"

"I'm passing through."

"Where are you headed?"

"San Francisco."

Reverend Arnold raised his eyebrows. "You embarked on such a long journey with no money?"

Janek mentally sighed. He was a stranger, and he supposed these people had a right to ask him questions. On the other hand, his money was lost or stolen in Ferndale, and he didn't know whom he could trust. It wouldn't help matters if he accused someone of robbing him at the boarding house.

"The situation is embarrassing."

"What happened?"

"I'm an accountant, and I wouldn't be irresponsible with money, but I somehow misplaced mine after I arrived here."

"You're an accountant? The closest accounting offices are in Eureka, and the fees are sky high. The church ledgers need to be reconciled. We spent a lot of money on the renovations. The church council would pay for your services."

Janek preferred to earn money doing tasks better suited to his chosen profession, but he couldn't understand why the reverend would be willing to put the church ledgers into a stranger's hands. It made him feel uncomfortable.

"Reverend Arnold, you don't know me."

"I don't know the accountants in Eureka either," Niklas Arnold said, sweeping his arm as if the said accountants were standing beside him.

"I'm sure they are established and have credentials."

"Do you have credentials?"

"Of course."

"Then I see no problem."

Janek was unconvinced, but he needed money and digging graves wasn't going to pay his way to San Francisco. "When would you like me to look over your ledgers?"

"Shall we say Monday morning?"

Janek tried to look conciliated.

Lise Anders opened the church's back door and stepped into the courtyard. "Mr. Walesa, what are you doing here? I thought you had gone to buy a ticket at the stagecoach depot."

Niklas frowned and said to Lise, "You know Mr. Walesa?"

"He's staying at the boarding house."

Niklas was relieved that Lise's association with Janek Walesa was only business. He replied to her question before Janek could answer. "Your boarder has misplaced his money and is looking for work."

"Oh," Lise said. She looked at Janek. He looked away in embarrassment.

"I have to get going," Evan said. "Mom has a list of things I'm supposed to pick up for her, and I haven't started. See you all."

Reverend Arnold said to Janek, "The burial site is on the south end of the cemetery and marked in chalk lines. Tools are in the shed. I'm going to walk Mrs. Anders home."

Janek was left alone in the courtyard with his uneasiness. He thought of St. Mary's Episcopal Church where he and his family had worshipped in Albany, Oregon. As children, he and Liv had been relegated to the youth room where they learned Bible verses and the liturgy. It was a comforting memory from a time when life held abundant happiness.

Perhaps, there is solace to be found in this simple church, he thought. He went inside through the back door and found he was in a vestibule. Coat hooks and benches lined the walls on his left and right. He opened the vestibule's inner door and stepped into the church.

The inside of the church was as plain as the outside. The pulpit was to his left. A large crucifix hung on the wall behind the pulpit. A long aisle, flanked by thirty rows of shining wooden pews, ran through the middle of the church from the pulpit to the front door. The long windows gleamed and flashed as he walked down the aisle.

He sat in the pew nearest the front door and closed his eyes. A spiritual presence lured him into darkness, and the feeling of the wooden pew beneath him receded.

Evan O'Malley returned to Main Street. He loaded his wagon with supplies from his mother's list and drove home. As he rode, he thought of the painful admission Janek had made on the way to the church. Janek's facial expression and the tone of his voice exuded desolation. Experiencing intense emotion from another man was foreign to Evan, and in his opinion, repeating those tormented words to anyone would be profane.

He knew the majority of people in Ferndale, but he was close with only a handful of people whom he trusted. He preferred Eureka with its saloons, and the ladies who frequented those saloons. The ladies loved Evan's lean muscular body, his charm and attentiveness, and his sparkling green eyes. He and his schooner mates were known to spend entire days in a saloon, drinking, carousing, and sometimes getting into brawls. After a day like that, without exception, he continued drinking with a woman or multiple women, who appreciated his stamina to fuck them most of the night.

Despite all the drunken sprees, Evan had the wisdom to forge relationships with businessmen and politicians who patronized the saloons in Eureka. He envisioned owning a schooner one day, and he would need professional backing to reach his goal. As a result, he built a reputation for discretion, sitting in the saloons, drinking with bankers and lawyers who were liars and cheaters, and listening to their woes without comment.

Thinking of Janek on his ride home, he discovered something he knew little about: sympathy. His father, William, was a hard-hearted Irishman with no patience for emotional displays. Sympathy was a rare commodity in the O'Malley household.

Evan resolved to keep Janek Walesa and William O'Malley from meeting.

Chapter 4

Reverend Niklas Arnold's wavy light brown hair was brushed back from his strong handsome face. At six feet four inches tall, he towered over Lise Anders as he walked her home from the church. He was in love with her. Fear of rejection paralyzed his daily resolve to speak the words. He was thirty-five, and it was time to marry and have children. If he couldn't gather the courage to tell Lise he loved her, he would have neither.

Niklas was from a large family whose ancestors emigrated from Germany to Pennsylvania in 1757. He grew up on a rural iron plantation near Carlisle, Pennsylvania where his father was the iron master of a large iron furnace and forge complex.

The youngest of eight children, he was a spoiled child who viewed religion as self-serving. After graduating from seminary school, he left Pennsylvania and traveled to St. Louis, Missouri to join a wagon train heading west. Six months later, in October 1868, he arrived in Ferndale.

When Niklas and Lise reached the boarding house gate he said, "What do you think of Janek Walesa?"

"I think he's handsome."

"He's too young for you. You're thirty-two, and he must be Evan's age. I don't think that comment is appropriate."

"Don't be stuffy."

"You think I'm stuffy?"

"You can be," Lise said. "Don't misconstrue what I said about Mr. Walesa. He appears to be a nice young man, intelligent, and polite."

"He didn't say why he was going to San Francisco. I wonder if he's in some kind of trouble."

"I don't think so. I do think it's strange that he has no money. Maybe he was robbed, and he's too ashamed to admit it."

"He said he was an accountant. I hired him to look over the church ledgers."

"That explains why he looked embarrassed."

"Do you think I was hasty in hiring him?"

"Are you having second thoughts?"

"No."

Lise unlatched the gate. "Good."

Niklas followed her through the gate to the porch. His daily effort to rally the courage to say *I love you, Lise* failed. Like a faithful puppy, he waited for her next move.

She turned and smiled and touched his hand. Love was written on his face, but as long as she grieved for her dead husband Christer, there would be no vacancy in her heart.

Lise opened the door. She hesitated before going in the house and looked at Niklas. "It's baffling, but I can't shake the feeling that Mr. Walesa needs looking after."

This time she saw jealousy on his face. She went into the house and shut the door, leaving him to brood alone.

Janek sat in the church thirty minutes before he realized he was daydreaming. For a short while, his burden of loneliness was lifted. His acute grief was softened. The after effects hung on him like delicate threads of silk.

He went back to the courtyard, took a shovel and a pickaxe from the shed, and climbed the stone steps to the cemetery. He avoided looking at the tombstones for fear he would see the wretched epitaphs of broken hearts.

He wandered among the graves until he found chalk lines around the burial site. Janek didn't think he could dig the grave while the dead watched.

Think about nothing, he thought, but that task was impossible.

A cool breeze ruffled his blond hair and tousled the leaves on the trees. The afternoon sun blinked and dimmed as clouds scurried across the sky like mischievous mice.

A sweeping view of the town of Ferndale, the Eel River Valley and the Pacific Ocean was visible from the cemetery hill. His eyes roamed the vista, watching the mice clouds leave giant mouse shadows on the landscape. How different this place was from the broad Willamette Valley, where his parents and sister would sleep forever.

There would be no grave digging. He would lose his mind. He walked back to the church and encountered Reverend Arnold in the courtyard.

The reverend said, "Did you start digging that grave?"

"No, I changed by mind."

Niklas took the shovel and pickaxe from Janek's hands. "You aren't the first man to say that. Are you up to painting the front stoop?"

"Yes."

"Good. The painting supplies are in the shed. Mr. Walesa…"

"Please, call me Janek."

"Janek, may I ask why you're going to San Francisco?"

"Does it matter?"

He searched Janek's face. The only thing he saw was despair.

"You're right. It doesn't matter."

Janek was exhausted when he returned to the boarding house that evening. He went to bed without dinner. He had overestimated his stamina for manual labor after spending the last six months as a student at the university, with no time spent working on the farm.

In the morning, he woke to the smell of coffee and bacon. He dressed and went downstairs. Lise was pouring coffee for the other boarders when he entered the kitchen.

She smiled at him. "Good morning, Mr. Walesa."

Janek glanced at his paint-ruined shirt and stained hands. Lise set the coffee pot on the stove and walked into the hall. He followed her.

"The tub is on the back porch in the alcove," she said in a lowered voice. "You'll have to fill and drain it yourself. Pull the curtains for privacy. I'll save you some breakfast."

The other boarders were done with breakfast by the time Janek entered the kitchen. He sat at the table. Lise brought two cups of coffee, and a plate of bacon and toast. She sat across from him.

"How was your work at the church yesterday?"

"The work was satisfactory, Mrs. Anders."

"Please, call me Lise."

They sat in silence while he ate. She stared at him, and for the first time, she clearly saw his radiant blue eyes and refined facial features. He was the most beautiful man she had ever beheld.

Janek caught her staring. She shifted her gaze and busied herself with pouring cream into her coffee. Awkward silence hung between them. He finished his breakfast and got up to leave.

"Please, stay a moment," Lise said, fearing he would shun her after the discomforting breakfast. "Niklas told me that you're an accountant. I'd like to give you free room and board for the next week in exchange for going over my ledgers. If you're interested, I may be able to get you more accounting work. My husband...I...have business connections in Eureka and Mendocino."

Lise's altruistic behavior was unsettling. It wasn't only Lise. Everyone he met in Ferndale lavished him with offers of benefaction...except Guthrie, the bartender.

For lack of choices, Janek swallowed his apprehension and said, "I appreciate your offer. I can get my diploma and letter of recommendation from my employer in Salem now, if you like."

"I'll look them over tomorrow. I need to get ready for church. Are you coming to the service?"

"No. I'm Episcopalian...and...I have some matters..."

"You aren't obligated to tell me anything."

Their blue eyes met, and like Niklas, all Lise saw was despair in Janek's eyes. She felt his despondency, and he recoiled from her by looking at the table. Lise wanted to say she was sorry for making him feel uncomfortable, but an apology would make matters worse.

She said, "I'll be out all day. Sunday dinner for all my boarders is served at my other boarding house on Little River Street. My woman who oversees that location, Mary Kellen, does most of the cooking, so I have a little free time. If you want to join us, dinner is at five o'clock."

After Lise left for church, Janek sat in a rocking chair on the front porch. He wrote the letters needed to start the process of settling his parents' estate. The first letter was to his friend Patrick Bright in Salem. He asked him to begin the necessary paperwork and gave him the address to Lise's boarding house. The second letter was to his former employer, Thomas Doyle. He wanted Mr. Doyle to know where he was, and that he may be using his letters of recommendation in Ferndale, Eureka, and Mendocino. He informed Mr. Doyle that he was preparing to settle the deed on the farm so he could sell it.

With his correspondence completed, Janek leaned back in his chair and closed his eyes. He thought about the experience he had in the church yesterday. The sharp edges of his grief were softened as he sat in the pew. He was uncertain if it was a daydream or something more spiritual, but without an explanation, the idea was disturbing.

The hinges on the gate squeaked. Janek opened his eyes and saw Evan O'Malley walk through the gate. Janek's troubling thoughts disintegrated. Evan was a welcome sight—a tonic to keep his mind sane and in a grounded place.

"Janek! Good Sabbath to you!"

"Good Sabbath to you! Why aren't you at church?"

Evan sat in the rocking chair across from Janek. "My family is Catholic. I got tired of asking the priest to forgive me for all my many sins so I stopped going to church. My father had a blow up! He said I'm going to burn in hell forever."

Janek laughed. "Burning in hell doesn't sound promising. Eternity is a long time."

Evan pulled a whiskey flask from his jacket pocket and took a swig from it. "I'm not worried. Want a drink?"

"I didn't dig the grave for the reverend, but he had a lot of other work for me," Janek said. He took the flask from Evan's outstretched hand.

"Aye, was the pay fair?"

"I don't know. I've never been paid for work like that before."

"Niklas claims the church council controls the purse strings, but I think he's just cheap. He would've been digging that grave himself if he didn't have more important things to do."

"What do you mean?" Janek said as he passed the flask back to Evan.

"He has a crush on Lise. He thinks no one knows, but it's obvious. If she's there, he's completely focused on her and what she's doing. Digging that grave would've taken time he could've been spending with her."

Evan passed the flask back to Janek. "Don't get me wrong, the reverend is a good man. It's just that I find it entertaining to watch any man fawn all over a woman who ignores his advances."

They talked and drank whiskey for hours. Something watched them. The bond they were forming pleased the watcher.

Chapter 5

On Monday morning, Janek and Lise met in the boarding house parlor. She read his diploma and letter of recommendation.

"Mr. Doyle was taken by you and your work," she said, handing him back his letter of recommendation. "I'm not a bit surprised."

She tried not to stare at him. His physical beauty coupled with his gentle and educated way of speaking was intoxicating, but the attraction she was developing for him wasn't sexual. It was something she couldn't explain. Her heart yearned for Christer, but that feeling faded when she was near Janek.

"Why did you leave Oregon? It seems you had every opportunity there."

Janek had not formed a credible allegory, which to him represented an acceptable lie. He had to suppress his pensive avoidance and melancholy behavior, which served to encourage intrusiveness. He feigned cheerfulness. "I needed a new start. Mr. Doyle suggested San Francisco."

Lise nodded, but looked unconvinced.

"I know nothing about you," Janek said, steering the topic away from his life.

She saw through his charade. "I promise not to pry into your life any further."

Janek mentally sighed.

"My parents emigrated from Denmark over forty years ago," Lise said. "I was born and raised in Richmond, Virginia. They had just died when I met Christer. We married a few years later. Christer believed we could have a better life in the West with all the land to be had for free. We had nothing

32

keeping us in Richmond, so, thirteen years ago, we left Virginia bound for Los Angeles and ended up here. He died two years ago. He was a wonderful man, and I miss him terribly."

"I'm sorry. No one should be alone."

"I have been lonely, but your arrival in Ferndale has begun to mend my spirit."

"What do you mean?"

Lise wondered what had encouraged that vagary.

Janek was looking at her, but not in an expectant manner. He looked apprehensive.

"Do you hear that?" Lise stood up. Her eyes widened a little as she cocked her head and listened. She took several small steps, stopped, and then walked to the kitchen. Janek followed her. The kitchen was deserted. The other boarders were gone for the day. There was no sound except crackling embers in the firebox.

Lise walked onto the back porch then into the backyard. Janek trailed behind her.

"There's no one here except you and me," Janek said. He grabbed Lise's arm and turned her around to face him. "What did you hear?"

"I thought I heard murmuring."

Janek thought this was an intimation of what had happened to him in the church. He looked around the yard, and then back to Lise. The last thing he wanted to do was arouse unfounded fear by mentioning his experience in the church.

They contemplated one another for a few seconds before Janek followed Lise back into the house.

Three weeks later, Janek was still staying at Lise's boarding house. He had taken on more accounting work and was meeting with Lucas Dodd, the owner of the general mercantile store, at the kitchen table when Evan appeared at the kitchen door.

"Good morning. I don't mean to interrupt, but I've letters for Janek," Evan said.

"Good morning," Janek said.

"I'm surprised to see you, Evan," Lucas said. "I thought you'd be gone by now."

Evan went to the stove and poured a cup of coffee. "The schooner's coming to pick me up on Monday morning. I'm planning on spending this weekend drunk and unruly. Would the two of you care to join me?"

"You know I will," Lucas said.

Lucas Dodd was twenty-six and single. He inherited the general store and the apartment above it after his father died. With no surviving family, his life revolved around the store and a few friends. He worked hard all week and spent his Saturday nights drinking and playing poker at the Palace Saloon. He was sandy-haired and tall with a slim build and had the innocent face of a boy. While he had an even temperament, if provoked, he revealed the heart of a lion. Lucas was one of the few men in Ferndale whom Evan liked and trusted.

"I'll be on the porch," Evan said.

"There's no need. We're done," Lucas said. He stood up, gathered his papers from the table, shoved them into his satchel, and said, "I'll see you both tonight."

"You said you had letters for me?" Janek said when Lucas had gone.

Evan handed him two envelopes. "One of them is from Eureka, and the other is from Salem. I hope it's good news."

Janek opened the letter from Eureka.

"This letter is from an accounting firm. They want me to interview for a position. I'm not looking for something permanent."

Evan set his coffee cup on the table. "Aye, well I think you should go anyway. I'll be there for a few days before we start our lumber runs up and down the coast. I can show you around."

"I'm supposed to make enough money to move on to San Francisco. I'll be wasting someone's time if I go for the interview. It's not ethical."

"To hell with that, you have to look after yourself! I don't understand

34

how a smart guy like you found himself near penniless. Do you think you got robbed?"

"I wish I knew."

Evan's voice took on a serious tone. "You know, sometimes things happen for a reason. Maybe losing your money was fate. I know you're running away from what happened to your family, but maybe you've run far enough."

Janek's heart quickened and he felt his chest tighten. "I told you about my family?"

"Aye, the day we went to the church. You don't remember?"

Janek rubbed his chest without thinking. He didn't understand why he couldn't remember telling Evan something so important.

"I won't breathe a word to anyone," Evan said. "I know you've been carrying this burden with you all along. Some days it seems worse than others."

"Do you think I'm going crazy?"

"I wouldn't be here if I thought you were a lunatic. In fact, I'd like to see you stay for a while."

Janek exhaled a soft laugh of relief. "I appreciate your honesty and discretion. This is not your problem, therefore, there's no need for you to keep secrets for me."

"I'm your friend, that's all. I have to get back to the house. I'll see you tonight at the Palace."

Janek went to his room and opened the letter from Salem. It was from the law office handling the probate on his father's will. The letter read:

September 12, 1872

Bright and Wilson
10 Duval Street
Salem, Oregon

Janek Walesa
PO 377
Ferndale, California

Dear Mr. Walesa,

We have received your request for probate concerning your father, Aron Walesa and mother, Freya Walesa's last will and testament. This office will be happy to represent you at the hearing that is scheduled for October 15, 1872. At the time of the settlement, we will act as your agent for the sale of the property in Albany, Oregon.

Enclosed, you will find the documents authorizing us to act in your behalf. Please sign and return them without delay. You will receive notification of the outcome of the probate hearing. If all is in order, the property will be put up for sale in accordance with the terms stated in the enclosed documents.

Regards,
Patrick Bright, Attorney at Law

Janek tossed the documents to the floor and ran his hands through his blond hair. He needed to rid himself of his constant companions: guilt, grief, shame, and loneliness. He was inundated by a state of mind foreign to his nature. It was like a malignant tumor, and he had no idea how to cure it.

There was no one he could talk to apart from Evan. The church was the only place he could hide from his constant companions. Despite his unsettling experience in the church, he decided to spend the afternoon sitting in the pew in front of the pulpit.

He walked to the church and entered the courtyard. When he touched the knob on the vestibule door, he heard murmuring. He took three steps backward and scowled at the door. The murmuring amplified into the voices of a thousand lost souls begging for a human life.

Janek rubbed his face to clear the imploration from his mind. The murmuring stopped. He contemplated the door and thought, I *am* going *crazy*.

He went back to the boarding house.

Chapter 6

The Palace Saloon was crowded every Saturday night. Guthrie Sullivan stood behind the bar wiping beer glasses.

Rules and self-righteousness didn't sit well with Guthrie, but these days he didn't fight it much. At sixty-two, he was stocky and strong, but his lined face told the story of the harsh adult life he had chosen to live. He grew up in Yorktown, Virginia in the shadow of old world traditions, strict paternal rules, and Methodist dogma. He joined the army in 1830, much to his proper English mother's dismay.

Guthrie left the army in 1848 and settled in San Diego, where he met a Mexican woman named Liliana. She became his companion and traveled with him when he tried his hand at gold mining. He was successful and managed to keep his fortune out of the hands of thieves.

Liliana became pregnant and died giving birth to Guthrie's only child on January 1, 1850, in Sacramento, California. The child was a girl, and he named her Abigail. He wrote his mother to tell her he had a new daughter, and to ask for advice on the matter of babies. His mother wrote back, instructing him to have the infant baptized within the Methodist community and find either a nanny or a wife.

When she was three months old, Guthrie moved to Ferndale, California with his baby daughter. He hoped the young community would be more forgiving of a half-Mexican child than those in Sacramento. He built a modest house and found a nanny for Abigail. Guthrie was one of the first businessmen in Ferndale. Twenty-two years later, he was an old man whose life had stalled.

Abigail Sullivan walked behind the bar and poured two glasses of beer. She worked at the Palace on the weekends, and when Guthrie needed extra help. "Daddy, will you take these beers to those men at the end of the bar?"

Guthrie dropped the bar towel and delivered the beers.

In a back room, Evan and Lucas sat at a poker table with Matt O'Neill and Josef Paullo, two men with whom they had grown up and attended school. Like Evan, Matt was from an Irish Catholic family. Josef's family was a blend of maternal Danish and paternal Portuguese Catholic. They were tall strapping men; each worked their respective family dairy farm alongside their parents and many siblings.

The men were struggling to keep a straight face. This was obviously Janek's first poker game. If Evan didn't do something, Janek was going to lose his shirt.

"Janek, let's go get a couple of tequila shots."

"If you leave the table, you're out of the game," Matt said. "We aren't sitting around here waiting for you to come back. I know you, Evan. You'll get drunk and forget about poker."

Evan *was* drunk. If he didn't get Janek away from the table, he would be too drunk to do it later. He motioned for Janek to follow him. They shouldered their way through the crowd to the bar. Abigail knew Evan well. She brought two beers and set them on the bar in front of him without looking at Janek.

"Abby, have you met Janek Walesa?"

Abigail regarded all strangers in the saloon with suspicion, but she would be cordial for Evan's sake. The person standing beside Evan made her forget about suspicion. He was beautiful.

Evan said, "Janek, this is Abigail Sullivan."

"You're Guthrie Sullivan's daughter. Evan has mentioned you. I'm pleased to meet you."

"I'm pleased to meet you, too," Abigail said, hoping she wasn't staring or worse, blushing.

"Abby, can you bring us a couple of shots?"

She forced her eyes to shift from Janek's face to Evan's face. "Do you want whiskey?"

"Janek prefers tequila," Evan interjected.

When Abigail was out of ear shot Evan said, "She's pretty and petite with all that long dark hair. Her mom was Mexican. Most of the women in town shun her because of that, including my mother. If I married somebody it would be her. I love a woman with mystique."

"She's very attractive. However, I believe you would marry any woman your mother disapproved of."

Guthrie brought the shots. He ignored Janek and said to Evan, "Me and Abby are taking the schooner to Eureka on Monday. Are you sure you can bring us back on Wednesday?"

"Aye, we're scheduled to bring the mail back that day."

Guthrie eyed Janek then walked away.

"Are you going to Eureka?" Evan said. "I still think you should go to the interview."

Janek thought about his metaphoric tumor. He wondered if he could find a metaphoric elixir in Eureka. After a moment, he agreed to go.

Abigail returned with a bottle of tequila and set it on the bar.

"This should hold you boys for a while. That boatload of prospectors who came into town today will keep me busy all night. We need a hotel in town. A lot of these men had to pay for beds on porches and in barns. It's going to get worse when they build the new port on the Salt River."

Evan filled the shot glasses.

"That explains why Lise is offering beds on her boarding house porches for ten cents a night," Janek said. "Did you know about the new port?"

"Aye, they're going to start construction in a week or so. It's for sea-going vessels. The schooners will continue to use the docks on the Eel River."

Janek considered what Abigail said in regard to needing a hotel in town. It sounded as if Ferndale was on the brink of becoming an important port of call.

"Janek, what are you doing? Get to drinking, man!"

39

"I'm sorry. I was thinking."

"Well, if you're thinking about those two women hanging on the bar over there, forget it. You don't want to wake up with something crawling on you that you can't get rid of. Now, that little thing sitting at the table in the back, she's new in town. Maybe you should introduce yourself."

"No. You go if you want."

"Nope, not me, I tend to my personal business out of town. I don't want some local woman thinking I'm beholden to her just because I spent time with her. I made that mistake once and I won't do it again."

Janek supposed if he had stayed in Salem, Sarah Williams would have expected a marriage proposal after they had sex the night of his graduation party. He was grateful for his absolution from the responsibility of marriage.

It was past midnight when Evan said, "I'm gonna go take a piss. If I don't return in a few minutes, you may want to look for me."

Evan made it to the back door but was unable to walk to the outhouse, so he did his business where he stood. As he buttoned the last button on his trousers, the leaves at his feet fluttered like baby birds preparing to fly. A cold vortex formed among the leaves, rising upward and spiraling around Evan's body, pulling him closer and closer to the center of its life force. With each rapid rotation it whispered, "Janek is vulnerable and weak. You must take care of him and keep him near."

II

The Commencement of Repression

Chapter 7

September 1872

The schooner arrived in Eureka on Monday afternoon. The harbor pulsed with life; its heartbeat to the ebb and flow of Humboldt Bay's sacrificial offerings and weary travelers.

Janek was walking through a hive of people disembarking from a nearby clipper ship when Niklas found him and led him to the hotel.

As they entered the hotel lobby, Niklas said, "Since Evan has to stand duty on the schooner tonight, would you like to join me and my friend for dinner? The hotel restaurant has decent food and good service. I'm sure my friend won't mind."

Niklas' friend was a seventy-two-year-old reverend named Otto Young. He and Niklas grew up in Carlisle, Pennsylvania generations apart. Reverend Young was a fascinating man who spoke of his travels as a missionary and his search for spiritual guidance in the cathedrals of Europe.

Niklas and Reverend Young declined Janek's invitation to join him for after-dinner drinks, so he sat in the hotel bar alone and drank tequila. He considered returning to Salem to face his demons in his own environment. *At least people there will remember my family, and I can talk about them. On the other hand, people will expect me to behave in accordance with social mores during the bereavement period.* That prospect, above all, kept him from going home.

Janek awoke the next morning with a nauseating headache, which he blamed on the tequila. He pulled himself out of bed and got dressed.

His health deteriorated during the two-hour interview at the accounting firm. When the interview concluded, he went back to the hotel and fell into a feverish sleep. It was almost evening when the banging on his door woke him up.

"Janek, are you in there?" Evan said from the other side of the door. "I'm off duty. Open up!"

Janek dragged himself out of bed, shuffled to the door, and opened it.

"You look terrible! What's wrong?"

"I'm not sure. I have a headache and my stomach is queasy." Janek sat on the edge of the bed to ward off the dizziness.

"Do you want me to find Abby? She probably has something to make you feel better."

"I just need sleep. I know you were looking forward to showing me around tonight, but I don't feel well enough."

"We can do that another time. I promised I'd look after you."

"Who did you promise?"

Evan's forehead wrinkled in thought as he tried to remember whom he had promised.

Janek got back in bed. "Never mind, it's not important."

Evan's forehead relaxed. "Aye, well I'm going to find Abby."

As he got to the bottom of the stairs, he saw her entering the hotel lobby. She was returning from shopping, carrying bundles of fabric and a bag of sewing notions.

"Give me all that, and I'll take it to your room. Can you look in on Janek? He's sick."

"Of course. What room is he in?"

"220."

Abigail shifted her load onto Evan. She went to Janek's room and knocked on the door. "It's Abby. Evan said you're sick. May I come in?"

44

Janek sat up in bed in an attempt to look less pathetic. "Come in."

Abigail entered the room and lit the gas lamp on the bedside table.

"Evan is behaving like a fussy old woman. I'm fine," he said.

"I'll make that decision," she replied. She placed the palm of her hand on his forehead. "You have a fever. Do you feel nauseated?"

"Please, don't make a fuss."

"It's not a fuss. Answer me."

"Yes, and I'm dizzy when I stand up."

"I'm going down the street to the druggist," she said. "When I get back, I'll make you a cup of tea."

"I'm fine. Please don't…"

She was gone. Janek slid beneath the sheet and closed his eyes.

Abigail encountered Evan in the lobby.

"He has a fever and with his other symptoms, I can't tell if it's a serious ailment so I'm going to the druggist. There's no need for you to stay. I'll tend to him."

"If you're shooing me away, I won't be back."

"I'm aware," Abigail said. She knew he would get too drunk to return to the hotel. Some woman would have him in her bed by the end of the night.

Abigail returned from the druggist and went to the kitchen to make tea. She put the capsules with the medicine in her pocket and climbed the stairs to Janek's room. When she entered his room, she saw he was shivering within the confines of a feverish sleep.

Janek's dream was a continuous loop. Liv's sweet voice was ominous with dire potent: *go home if you want to get well.* But he didn't know where home was, let alone how to get there.

Abigail set the cup of tea on the bedside table and sat on the edge of the bed. His beautiful face, ruddy from fever, glistened with sweat. She gently stroked his sweltering forehead.

"Janek, wake up."

Amidst his dream, he sighed.

As she stroked his forehead, Abigail perceived his physical flawlessness. It distracted her to the point that she forgot why she was touching his face. If he had not awakened, her hypnotic revelation would have continued without end.

Janek didn't recognize her at first. He blinked his eyes and said, "Abby?"

She snatched her hand from his forehead.

"I was trying to wake you so I could give you a dose of medicine for your fever."

He struggled to sit up. The smell of the tea made him gag.

"I can't drink that," he said and nodded his head toward the cup.

He offered the palm of his hand. She dropped two pills into his open palm and watched as he swallowed them dry. He slid beneath the sheet and closed his eyes. Although she wished it, there was no valid reason for her to stay there after he fell asleep. She turned off the gas lamp and quietly left his room.

At eight o'clock the next morning, Abigail sent a messenger to Reverend Young's house to fetch Niklas. She needed help with Janek, as Evan was preparing to get the schooner underway. It took Guthrie, Niklas, and Abigail to get Janek's coat and boots on, pack his bag, check him out of the hotel, and help him into a carriage.

When they arrived at the dock, Evan and Niklas dragged him on board the schooner and put him in the captain's cabin. Abigail stayed with him during the trip home. The schooner rocked and swayed. Janek threw up until there was nothing left in his stomach.

They arrived at the mouth of the Eel River late in the day. When the schooner docked, Evan sent a deckhand to tell Lise they had returned. They used the waiting mail wagon to take Janek to the boarding house. Lise met them at the gate. She was shocked by his condition. Niklas and Evan helped him to his room and into bed.

Abigail was reluctant to leave her patient, but she was obligated to go home with her father. The Sullivans gathered their belongings from the mail wagon and walked home.

"Daddy, it was kind of you to help Janek even though you don't like him."

"I like him fine, Abby."

"No you don't! You blatantly ignore him."

"What difference does it make? He's just passing through. In a month or so he'll be gone and that'll be that. Are you sweet on him?"

"Don't try to change the subject."

"If you promise not to keep nagging me I'll tell you. I get this feeling he's brought something with him that's gonna change things around here, and I'm not sure if I like that. It's something I can't quite put my finger on. I'm not ignoring him. I'm sizing him up."

Abigail shared her father's suspicious nature, but she didn't sense anything dishonest about Janek, but she had to admit, they weren't well acquainted.

"Are you saying he's a criminal?"

"I don't reckon it's anything like that. I told you, it's something I can't quite identify. Can we stop talking about this?"

"No."

"I'm just saying there are times when we meet people who'll have a lasting impact on our lives. I think Janek Walesa may be one of them people. It's nothin' more so don't go getting all in a dither."

"Daddy, I still don't understand what you're trying to say, but I'll take your word that it's nothing to worry about. You know I love you."

Guthrie patted her on the back and said, "I love you, too. Now, let's get on home. It looks like it's gonna rain."

Chapter 8

Liv told Janek to board a train bound for Salem, Oregon. When he arrived at the train station it was deserted. A thick layer of dust covered the rotting wood floor. Janek's boots stirred the dust as he walked to the crumbling ticket counter. The dim brown light seeping through the tarnished windows was suddenly extinguished. He was plunged into darkness.

Liv said, "Run, Janek! For the love of God, run now!"

His orientation was skewed in the black train station, but he turned and ran anyway. The unseen monster that dwelled within the darkness panted and scraped the floor as it pursued him. It exhaled putrid breath on the back of his neck. He was shoved to the floor with violent force. Somewhere in the darkness, a bleating voice said, "The train stopped running the day you were born! You can never go home!"

Janek sat up in bed with a start. He got up and washed his face and hands in the basin on the washstand. The mirror over the washstand reflected a healthy face. His blue eyes were bright. Whatever had been ailing him was gone. The nightmare he awakened from was the remaining residue, and it left behind an innuendo. He had to make a decision: *stay in Ferndale or go to San Francisco.*

He was surprised to see Niklas and Evan sitting at the table when he entered the kitchen. Their presence early in the morning gave him the impression he was being guarded.

Lise dropped the pot she was washing in the sink and frowned at Janek. "Are you sure you should be out of bed? How do you feel?"

"I feel fine," Janek said. "I apologize for being a burden in Eureka. Thank you for your care."

Evan dismissed it. "Abby was your nurse."

Janek sat at the table, poured a cup of coffee, and filled his plate with eggs and toast. As he picked up his fork, two new boarders appeared in the kitchen.

Lise made the introductions. "This is Emily and Stephen Hartmann."

Stephen Hartmann and his wife were tall, and they painted a somewhat imposing picture standing side by side. They sat at the table and helped themselves to breakfast. Stephen was a brunette with graying hair at his temples and in his mustache, which he stroked on occasion, as he explained his participation in building a new creamery. He talked on and on while his wife looked bored.

Emily Hartmann was attractive with abundant auburn hair and eyes to match. Her forty-five-year-old husband was eleven years her senior. He often neglected her in favor of his many business ventures; therefore, Emily sought attention elsewhere. She insinuated her intentions by wearing her necklines low and sweeping her skirts high. Many men had been lured to her bed by the enticing manner of her behavior and appearance.

Emily poured herself a cup of coffee, and then appraised the faces gathered around the table. When her eyes fell on Janek, she favored him with a lascivious stare. She licked her lips, and the corners of her mouth rose to form a vague smirk.

Evan interrupted Stephen's monologue. "Mr. Hartmann, your stories have been fascinating. Unfortunately, I have a schooner to catch. See you all in a month."

Much to Janek's relief, he now had an excuse to escape Emily Hartmann's promiscuous sneer. He walked outside with Evan. "I'll be here when you get back."

Evan smiled and slapped him on the shoulder. "I didn't think you'd sneak off to San Francisco without letting me know."

"I've been thinking about what you said before we went to Eureka.

Maybe I have run far enough. I need to decide. I can't go on like this."

"A man has to have peace of mind no matter how he finds it," Evan said.

Janek hated to see Evan leave.

Janek walked to city hall to investigate the plans for the creamery and the new port on the Salt River. City hall was a small two-story building that housed the sheriff's office, the jail, and the political comings and goings of Ferndale. He saw a clerk's window to his right as he entered. Janek described what he wanted, and the clerk brought him two large leather-bound books.

"Are you one of them investors?" the clerk said. "We get quite a few coming in asking to see public records."

Janek shook his head. The truth was he didn't know what he was doing or the motivation behind it. He took the books to a small table in a corner of the room to study the content.

He read that a man named J.B. Kinyon was driving the enterprise for the new port. Stephen Hartmann was one of several investors backing the new creamery. Local farmers and other investors from Sacramento were pledging funds. As he read on, an item caught his attention. There was a spacious lot for sale on Main Street. The seller was Guthrie Sullivan.

He left city hall and stopped for lunch at the Gingerbread Café. Stephen Hartmann entered the café before Janek ordered his meal. He asked Stephen to join him.

"I appreciate your hospitality, Mr. Walesa," Stephen said when he was seated.

While they waited to be served, Stephen leaned back in his chair and began his well-rehearsed rhetoric concerning his business ventures. He described The Brothers, Inc., the corporation he and his partners had formed, and their investment endeavors in Humboldt County and Northern California. Following a lengthy dissertation on his quest for wealth, he asked Janek what he did for a living.

"I'm an accountant."

Stephen leaned forward in his chair. "Do you have experience in corporate accounting?"

"Yes. I worked for a corporate accounting firm in Salem, Oregon for two years."

"Are you degreed?"

"In fact, I have an advanced degree."

"You don't say? What are you doing in this one-horse town?"

Janek thought, *what am I doing in this town?* He said, "I provide accounting services for some of the local businesses."

"We could use a local man to manage our accounting needs at the creamery. If you have proof of your degree and a letter of recommendation from that accounting firm in Salem, I could arrange an interview with The Brothers. Would you be interested?"

Janek was uncertain if he wanted to work for this self-absorbed and avaricious man. *However,* he considered, *perhaps this opportunity will move me out of the mire I find myself stuck in...* He agreed to the interview with reluctance and hopefulness all the same.

"Good. I'll be in touch," Stephen said.

Janek left the café and went to Clara's Boutique. The shopkeeper assisted him with his purchase. Then, he walked to the Sullivan house.

Abigail was sweeping leaves from the front porch when he walked up the cobblestone path to her house. The sight of him brought joy to her heart. She dropped the broom and hurried to meet him.

"Good day, Abby. I want to thank you for your care in Eureka. This is for you."

He held a small box wrapped in pink flowered paper in the palm of his hand. Her eyes fell upon it, and she recalled his open palm awaiting the medicine for his fever. Her eyes moved to his boots, then slid up his body. She beheld the physical flawlessness she saw when he was sick. All the breath left her lungs. Transcending her experiences, she saw an obscurity...an elegance. Elegance lived in the books she read, not in real life; yet, here it was standing in front of her. Everything about him was elegant from his dress and grooming, to the way he pronounced his words. She was spellbound.

"Abby?"

She blinked and breathed. Janek took her hand and wrapped it around the box. His gentle hands were enchanting, and they persuaded her to take the gift. She regarded his resplendent face. His hands dropped to his side, and the spell was broken.

She opened the gift and lifted a delicate tortoise shell hair comb from the box as if it were gossamer. "It's beautiful!"

"My mother always said that a job well done should be rewarded."

"Thank you! I'm glad you're feeling well."

"Please tell Mr. Sullivan I appreciate his help. I must be going. I hope we meet again soon."

Abigail watched Janek's tall figure recede. She recalled her father's words, *"He's brought something with him that's gonna change things..."* She knew the change had begun.

Chapter 9

The First Congregational Church of Ferndale stood silent, draped in the tree-cast shadows of late afternoon. No one was around, but the church was not empty. A soul suffering from an unrequited human life lurked among the pews and in the dark corners of the church. It was only a shadow of what it had once been.

Its life force took shape thousands of years before at a time when few humans walked the earth. Innumerable souls waited for their promised pre-destination as mankind reproduced in abundance. Each soul elated when their seed was conceived and planted within its mother's womb.

The years passed and many disparate souls were dispossessed of their consummated destiny. They existed in a state of undesirable despondency that enfeebled their life force, making their seed less seductive and harder to descry.

Some lost their life force altogether, as they no longer remembered why they existed, and imploded like a star under the weight of its own mass. Some strayed from their karma; settling in desperation for a lower order life form.

Others drifted, which left them destitute of the characteristics and emotions needed to sustain a human life. The shadowy life force lurking in the church was one of those souls. And it was delusional.

It believed within its vaporous heart that the characteristics and emotions needed to sustain a human life persisted. This soul imagined it possessed a superior form of love, and a stalwart ability to protect a fragile human body. It learned mankind's vulnerabilities, and the effortless art of exploitation.

It learned it had the power to take what it lusted for: the body and soul of a transcendent human being. The arrival of that soul would, at long last, set it free. Janek Walesa was that soul.

After leaving Abigail's house, Janek went to the First Congregational Church. With Evan gone, he had no one to talk to. He hoped that Niklas would be able to help him sort out his confusion.

He was confident when he woke that morning that he had defined a good place to begin by educating himself on development in and around Ferndale. As the day waned, he found himself in a state of emotional confusion because he did things for reasons he couldn't discern. The worst assumption was accepting Stephen Hartmann's invitation to an interview, and believing the opportunity would impel him in the right direction.

He felt like a castaway on a deserted island who would die from loneliness long before he had a chance to starve to death. He needed his mother's advice and comfort; yet his mother's death was the source of his loneliness and confusion. The irony couldn't have been crueler.

To his chagrin, Niklas wasn't in the church. Janek would have to peruse the day's events on his own. The last time he was at the church, he heard murmuring when he reached to open the vestibule door. The recollection of that incident made him feel uneasy. Nonetheless, he sat on the first pew in front of the pulpit and focused on the crucifix on the wall. He was afraid to let his eyes roam for reasons he couldn't define.

"Mother, are you here?"

The sound of enormous wings threshed in the nebulous rafters. He was tempted to search for the source of the sound, but he kept his eyes on the cross.

"Mother, answer me!"

A down draft whooshed through the church as Anguish dived from its hidden perch among the rafters. He threw his arms over his head and ducked. It ensnared him in its talons, and its cruel beak crippled his ability to think.

"Mother, answer me!"

Anguish was devouring the memory of why he had come to the church. "Mother!"

Freya's voice resonated. "I'm here, son."

Anguish released him and returned to the dark rafters. Janek waited until his breathing slowed to normal before he said, "Why didn't you answer me?"

"I'm here now."

"Can't you understand what my grief does to me?"

"I understand it frightens you, and you have no defense against it."

Anguish had succeeded in damaging the memory of why he had come to the church. He groped his mind to retrieve what was forgotten.

"You're crippled and confused son. You'll have no defense from your grief unless you heal."

"I don't know how to heal."

"You must stay here. If you leave this place you will die of a broken heart."

"Why?"

"They must care for you."

"They?"

"Those around you."

"I haven't told them what happened to our family."

"Why not?"

"They won't understand how I feel."

"They don't need to understand. They need to love and protect you."

"I won't ask people I hardly know to do that."

"There's no need to ask."

All in one moment, Janek sensed his mother had gone, and his sobs for her resounded in the church. The darkness enveloped his mind in its celestial arms. It ingested his cognition and suffocated his memories. When his sobbing abated, he saw a harrowing shadow within the darkness.

Janek sat in a rocking chair on the porch drinking tequila. The parlor windows behind him shimmered with pale yellow candlelight. Drizzle blurred the hedges beyond the fence and suppressed the sounds of the windless night. He relinquished the feeling of isolation nights like this induced. There was something more pressing.

He had decided to stay in Ferndale.

The frightening experience he'd had in the church was placing doubt on his decision. Something or someone other than his mother was in the church. The strange darkness soothed his anguish, but there was something horrifying within that darkness.

If I leave Ferndale because of what happened in the church, I'll continue to run from grief and fear the rest of my life. The solution seemed simple. *Avoid the church.*

But he knew that was a lie. It wasn't that simple.

The latch on the gate clicked open, and the hinges whined. Lise and Niklas walked through the gate. They were returning from Sunday dinner at Lise's boarding house on Little River Street.

He set his tequila bottle on the floor beside his chair.

"I have dinner for you," Lise said to Janek. "It's cold so..."

"Thank you, Lise. Do you and Niklas have a moment to talk with me?" *Before I lose my nerve and take the next stagecoach to San Francisco. If I tell someone, it will validate my decision and I'll have to stay.*

Niklas and Lise raised their eyebrows at one another.

"I've decided to stay in Ferndale."

Lise touched her chest and sighed. Her dead husband, Christer, had come to her in a dream and told her that Janek would stay. She was terrified he was wrong.

Janek glanced at Lise before he said, "I have an interview for an accounting position with the new creamery."

"I doubt the idea of working for the creamery has inspired you to give up your quest for San Francisco," Niklas said with mild amusement.

Janek wasn't sure if he *had* given up his quest. "I was at city hall a few days ago looking over public records. I noticed Guthrie Sullivan has a lot for sale on Main Street. Do you know anything about it?"

"It's been for sale for twenty years, and it's overpriced," Niklas explained. "I think the old man doesn't really want to let go of it. The original Palace Saloon was built on that site, but it burned to the ground four months later."

"Why didn't he rebuild there?"

"Guthrie doesn't discuss his personal decisions with anyone except maybe his daughter. He used to own several parcels of land on Main Street."

"I had no idea he was a man of means."

"He was successful at gold mining back in '49. Are you interested in buying that lot?"

"I don't know."

"If you're interested, you'd better brush up on your power of persuasion. Guthrie's obstinate, to put it mildly."

Lise said, "I'm going to retire early tonight. Janek, your dinner will be in the kitchen if you want it. Good night."

"Are you feeling all right, Lise?" Niklas asked as she opened the front door.

She didn't look at him when she said, "I'm fine."

Niklas stared through the parlor windows for a few seconds, trying to decide if he should follow her inside. He preserved his dignity and bid Janek good night. On the sidewalk, he stopped and looked back at the porch. Janek was gone.

Niklas suspected there was something between Janek and Lise, and Lise had confirmed it. She wasn't shy in regard to voicing her opinion. Tonight, she seemed distracted as if she was keeping a secret. Her lack of reaction to Janek's decision to settle in Ferndale led Niklas to believe she was privy to that decision.

He walked home to the vicarage next door to the church. He got the bottle of whiskey hidden in his desk drawer, and then sat on an old tree stump in the backyard. The cemetery seemed to watch him from the steep hillside behind his house. The full moon illuminated the tombstones and cast sharp shadows through the trees.

He swigged whiskey and focused on his jealousy. Lise would *not* acknowledge his amorous advances, yet she looked at Janek Walesa as if he were a divine being. She shielded her feelings for Niklas behind claims of mourning her dead husband. He was certain it was an excuse to avoid a romantic relationship with him.

A passing cloud eclipsed the moon, smearing the sharp shadows in the cemetery. A breeze sighed and rustled the trees; their leaves murmured an antiphony. Niklas listened to the peaceful exchange. The latch on the cemetery gate disengaged with a resounding clank. Niklas set his bottle of whiskey on the ground and looked in the direction of the gate.

Something vaporous brushed his cheek. Murmuring words said, "Look past your jealousy and you will see."

Niklas was neither alarmed nor afraid.

"Love is many things," the breeze moaned.

A tear escaped the corner of Niklas' eye. He didn't expect this, but he realized he should have.

Chapter 10

October 1872

The first day of October dawned cold and rainy. The heavy leaden sky intruded on Ferndale. Despite the weather, Janek tried to be optimistic. His interview with Stephen Hartmann and his associates was scheduled for one o'clock in the afternoon. That afforded time to look at an office space for rent next door to Lucas Dodd's general store.

When Janek arrived at the office space, he stopped to look through the wide front window. A bell jingled when the landlord opened the door. The space was modest, but decent furniture was included in the month-to-month lease. And a smaller room in the back of the office contained a large floor safe. Janek signed a lease agreement and paid the first month's rent.

He crossed the street to the Gingerbread Café. While he was eating, he happened to look through the café window as Lise walked by on the footway. He sensed hesitancy on her part when he announced his decision to stay in Ferndale. The notion that she might be unhappy with his news was upsetting. Their friendship must have been a delusion. He couldn't let his dilemma over Lise distress him this afternoon. It was time for his interview.

Stephen Hartmann's office was in a house adjacent to Main Street. The Brothers, Inc., and six local farmers Janek didn't recognize, read his credentials and references and asked him questions. Thirty minutes later, he was offered the job. Janek counter offered their proposal.

"Instead of employing me, I propose that I take the creamery as my client."

While the men whispered and conferred among themselves, Janek wondered if Evan's father was among the farmers. The whispering hushed. Stephen said, "We agree to your proposal. We'll draw up the contract while everyone is here to sign it. Can you start first thing in the morning?"

Stephen handed Janek a pamphlet without waiting for an answer. "Read this. It contains ownership and financial information about the creamery." He turned to the man seated at the roll top desk, "Mr. Dodson, draw up the contract while Mr. Walesa familiarizes himself with our monetary intentions."

Mr. Dodson opened a drawer and extracted two sheets of paper, which he laid on the desktop. The fountain pen scratched across the paper as he wrote the contract.

The scratching pen combined with the watchful eyes of men he didn't know caused Janek immense emotional discomfort.

When the interview concluded, he went home to calm his frayed nerves. He sat on the settee in the silent parlor and closed his eyes.

Emily Hartmann, her arms laden with packages from a shopping spree on Main Street, swept through the front door, disturbing the silence. She saw Janek, dropped her purchases on the floor in the entryway, and swept into the parlor.

"Mr. Walesa?"

Janek used expedient tactics to avoid Emily from the day they first met at the boarding house kitchen table. There was no escape route today. He sighed and opened his eyes.

Emily's auburn eyes flamed, and she smirked. "I apologize if I woke you."

Janek rubbed his tense forehead and looked at the floor.

She sat beside him and reached to touch his cheek.

He jerked his head from her encroaching hand.

She slid closer. "You're a quiet man, but I suppose you don't need to talk. You're ravishing and arousing without saying a word." She brushed Janek's left thigh with her fingertips.

"Mrs. Hartmann, please don't do that."

"Why not? We're alone."

Janek looked at her and saw unadulterated lust in her eyes. He had no idea what to say to make her leave him alone.

"I'm offering myself to you, Janek." She took his hand and pressed it to her breasts.

He yanked his hand from her grasp and stood up. "Stop it, Mrs. Hartmann! What you're suggesting is inappropriate."

Emily wasn't used to this type of response. One touch in the proper place and men became clay in her hand to form as she wished. Something was different about Janek Walesa. That difference was a mystery to be discovered and conquered. The battle was worth any and all collateral damage for he was the most beautiful man she had ever beheld.

Janek started for the parlor door.

"Will you help me carry my packages to my room?" Emily said, hoping to delay his exit. "Isn't that what a gentleman would do for a lady?"

You're no lady, Janek thought. He left the parlor. Lise was standing in the entryway. He glanced at her before he opened the front door and walked out of the house.

Emily walked from the parlor into the entryway. "He is magnificent!" she said and stared at the door as if a spark of his physical energy lingered. "Is he married?"

Lise frowned and narrowed her eyes. "No, but you are."

"What are you insinuating, Mrs. Anders?"

"Nothing, Mrs. Hartmann."

Emily scowled at Lise.

Janek moved his accounting business into his office on Friday, October 11, 1872. The bell jingled when he opened the door. As he walked in, for an instant, he imagined his father was sitting in the leather chair behind his desk.

"This is what you wanted, Father. Six years at the university so I would have the prerogative to control my own life and achieve gentility. I suppose this is the beginning of what's to come."

He dropped the satchel he was carrying in the chair. An unsettling feeling of fate clung to him, which sustained the doubts he tried to ban from his mind.

This office, the contract with the creamery, and the small business agreements couldn't be the culmination of the hard work he put into his studies and his job with Doyle and Stromberg in Salem. This was nothing like the career he envisioned. *Why did I choose to stay in Ferndale when San Francisco must hold the key to true success and possible modest wealth?*

The door opened with a jingle, and a man from the print shop entered the office. "Your sign is up, Mr. Walesa."

Janek followed the man outside and looked at the sign that hung from the cantilevered support over the footway. The lettering read, *Janek Walesa, Acct.* He handed the man a dollar to pay for the sign and labor.

Lucas Dodd walked out of his general store next door. He eyed the sign and said to Janek, "Does this mean you've decided to stay in Ferndale?"

"I suppose it does."

Janek's decision made Lucas feel like a partisan in the birth of an emotional allegiance yet to be named. He thought about his father Elijah—dying from a lung ailment, burning alive with fever, and wracked with an unceasing cough that made his throat so sore that he spoke in a whisper.

Elijah Dodd reached for his seventeen-year-old son who sat beside him on the bed and said, "You'll be...alone...soon. Promise me...you'll find... something...in this world...you can...be a part of.... Not just...a wife...and children. Wives die. Children leave."

Terrified to face the world alone, Lucas had promised. *Perhaps, now I'll be able to keep that promise.*

"Congratulations, Janek. You're saddled with poker nights at the Palace indefinitely."

"Perhaps I'll learn to play well."

"We should make a run to Eureka with Evan. I heard you were sick on your first trip."

A brief smile brushed Janek's lips. "I'm sure Evan will see to it."

Two ladies entered the general store, so Lucas cut off the conversation to tend to his customers.

Inside the office, Janek emptied the contents of the satchel onto the desk. Pencils rolled across the surface and fell on the floor. A draft from the open door caused the papers on his desk to flutter like moths. He looked up. Abigail was standing in the doorway. He didn't remember hearing the bell jingle.

"I saw you through the window and noticed the sign hanging over the footway. This must be your accounting office, which means you've decided to stay in Ferndale!"

"Abby, it's nice to see you," he said, stepping from behind his desk. "Yes, I'm staying."

"I'm glad things are working out for you."

Janek said, "Thank you," but it was only a polite reflex that held no joy.

She looked around the small office, and then at Janek.

"Where were you living before you came here?"

His instinct was to recoil from the question, but he remembered his vow to suppress pensive avoidance and melancholy behavior. "Oregon."

"Evan told me you were going to San Francisco to start a new life."

"I was."

"San Francisco sounds interesting and exciting. Why did you choose Ferndale instead?"

He winced at a sudden throbbing in his temples.

"What's wrong?" Abigail said.

"I'm fine."

He massaged his temple, unmindful of the action.

"That's not true," she said, studying his face.

He realized what he was doing and dropped his hand from his temple.

She saw an odd coupling of grief and grace emanating from his bewitching blue eyes. "You've lost someone."

The familiar sensation of losing mental focus brushed him with its fingertips. If he didn't do something, the darkness would prevail, and his ability to control or remember what he wanted to say would be lost. He struggled to maintain a calm façade, but Abigail's intense scrutiny was making it difficult.

There was something else in his eyes that transfixed and bound her. She saw his desolation. It penetrated her heart and settled in an empty space she thought would remain vacant forever.

"You came here as a misplaced soul and found something powerful enough to make you stay. What?"

He was losing the battle to maintain his faculties. The darkness was swallowing everything he recollected. With great effort, he reached for the edges of his mind and heard Abigail say, "You did find something, and it's scaring you."

His reply edged on inaudible. "I think it's in the church."

"What's in the church?"

"Abby, I…"

The edges of his mind were dragged into the darkness. From somewhere in the distance, his mother was whispering his name. Warm hands stroked his face and loud words he didn't understand echoed in the darkness.

"Janek, answer me!"

The darkness retreated.

"Janek?"

He looked at her.

Abigail sighed with relief and said, "You scared the life out of me!"

With some confusion, he realized she witnessed the darkness consuming his thoughts.

"Your face went blank, and you weren't responding. If you had not come around when you did, I was going to get Lucas."

"I'm sorry I scared you."

"There's no need for an apology. What happened?"

"I can't talk about it."

At that moment, she understood that he was hiding something terrible and terrifying. "Maybe I can help if you talk to me."

"No!"

"But …"

"Abby, let it go. Please! Promise me!"

She nodded, but didn't promise.

Chapter 11

Lise lifted her wedding dress from the cedar chest in her bedroom. The smooth peach-colored taffeta was cool to the touch. She draped it across her bed then removed the crinoline from the chest. A fading photograph of Christer floated from the crinoline to the floor. With an unsteady hand, she retrieved the photograph and studied his handsome face. What did his face look like after lying in his coffin for two years? She shook her head to clear the visualization and placed the photograph in a basket of fresh flowers on her dressing table.

She donned the crinoline and tied it at her waist. Then, she stepped into the wedding dress and fastened it up the back the best she could. She studied her reflection in the dressing table mirror. Her life was on the brink of change. What was to come was her destiny, and it was inescapable. Christer's spiritual voice warned her to practice prudent actions, but he didn't explain the nature of those actions. His ambiguous counsel was confusing.

With the basket of flowers in her arms, she began her journey to the inevitable. She walked downstairs and through the front door into the chilly October air. Unpredictable gusts of wind twisted her skirts around her legs. The sun disappeared and reappeared as cumulus clouds sailed across the sky.

A gray tabby cat examined her with suspicion from its perch atop a fence post. It jumped to the footway and followed her.

When Lise reached the cemetery gate, a sighing zephyr traded places with the wind. She crossed the church courtyard and climbed the steps to the cemetery. Christer lay in his grave near a towering Douglas fir tree on the southern edge of the cemetery hill. The stone marker was engraved with the words:

Christer Baltasar Anders
Beloved Husband and Friend
Born May 12, 1835
Died July 31, 1870
With the Angels

Lise kneeled in front of the tombstone. She removed the flowers from the basket, arranged them on the grave, and placed the photograph of Christer on the flowers.

Pieces of memories from the day he died chipped from her broken heart: the knock at the door, the sorrowful faces of the men who brought the news, shock, stinging tears, and wretchedness. *We are very sorry, Mrs. Anders. Your husband was found lying dead in the road near his horse.* Christer had been on his way home from Mendocino. The cause of death was unknown.

She covered her face with her hands and wept.

The cat watched from a branch on the Douglas fir tree.

Janek was recording account receivables information for the creamery when Lucas entered the office with a combination of worry and amusement on his face.

"Mrs. Russo told me she saw Lise walk past her house wearing a wedding dress."

"What?" Janek said. He rose and stepped from behind his desk.

"I'm just telling you what I heard. Maybe you'd better go look for her."

"I think I know where she is."

Janek pushed past Lucas, yanked the office door open, and ran to the cemetery.

Lise had stopped weeping, but was now talking to her deceased husband.

"Christer, you are the love of my life and my best friend. People assured me my broken heart would mend as the days passed, but it hasn't. Soothe my aching heart and show me how to move on."

The zephyr soughed through the trees and Christer's spiritual voice sighed, "Reach for him."

"Does he know?" Lise asked.

"No, but he will."

"What is our destination?"

"I don't know, but walk the road with caution. There are signs of darkness along the way," Christer's voice warned.

"Darkness?"

"I can't shelter you, Lise. He must do it. Don't despair, and know I love you."

The breeze fondled the photograph of Christer. It swirled near the ground; then it was swept aloft the treetops. The sighing zephyr died, and he was gone.

Lise sobbed.

Janek took the steep steps two at a time and ran through the cemetery. He reached Christer Anders' grave and sat in the grass beside Lise.

Between gasping sobs she said, "Christer has set me free. Now, I'm alone just as you are."

"What do you mean?"

Lise buried her face in Janek's chest. "I know your family is lying dead in Albany, Oregon. Christer said that's the reason you're here."

He wrapped her in his arms and rested his chin on the top of her head. They both cried until the sun sank below the rim of the Pacific Ocean. Janek helped Lise to her feet and they walked out of the cemetery. The gray tabby cat jumped from its branch and followed them.

Janek was sitting on the porch when Lise came home from Sunday morning service at the First Congregational Church of Ferndale. He lie awake the night before, trying to make sense of the absurd events he had experienced. He had become convinced Lise could help him sort through the confusion.

"Lise, I need to understand what happened yesterday."

She sat in the rocking chair beside him. "Do you mean you need to understand why I did what I did?"

"Yes, that's part of it. Donning your wedding dress and walking to the cemetery isn't an everyday occurrence. It's…"

"Crazy?"

"Does this have something to do with me?"

"Yes."

"How did you know my family was gone? Did Evan tell you?"

"I told you it was Christer. I wasn't aware Evan knew."

Janek got up and paced the porch. He ran his hands through his hair, tousling the tidy blond waves. "You were talking to your dead husband like he was really there. That scares me."

"You know Christer was there. That's not what scares you at all. What is it?"

"Something is happening to us that we can't control. I don't think you had a choice about what you did yesterday. I think something compelled you and Christer even though he's dead."

Lise inhaled a sharp breath.

"I've been having episodes of some kind of darkness," Janek said. "It seems to happen when I'm feeling dismayed over my family. At first, I thought I was losing mental focus or daydreaming, but now I recognize when it's coming. It robs me of my ability to remember or control my thoughts. There's something unclear and frightening in that darkness."

He tried to suppress his growing agitation.

"The last time I was in the church the darkness came for me after I was attacked by something I didn't understand and couldn't fight off. I called out for my mother, and when she answered, the attack stopped. I know the two things are connected. I think whatever is looming in the darkness means to do me harm, whether it's real or imagined. If it's a figment of my imagination, does that mean I might hurt myself? Or someone else?"

She hesitated, unsure of what to say. If she acted under the influence of compulsion, there was nothing she could do to change that. His harrowing confession sounded unbelievable, but she knew it was the truth. Her journey to the unforetold would be by his side, and what Christer presumed to be distant signs of darkness along the way was much closer than she realized.

Janek's agitation bordered on hysteria, and he moved closer and pulled Lise up and out of the rocking chair by her shoulders. "Help me understand! I've been struggling to keep my sanity for the past two months. I feel like I'm losing the battle!"

Terror stained his eyes as he anticipated her reply.

"Please, Lise."

"Regardless of your mental state, I don't think you're capable of hurting anyone."

He relaxed his grip on her shoulders.

"After you told Niklas and me that you had decided to stay in Ferndale, I didn't speak to you for a week because I was terrified you would change your mind. Compelled or not, Christer has freed me from my grief so that I may be here for you, just as you were there for me in the cemetery."

His hands slid from her shoulders.

"Whatever this is has only just begun," he said. "I told Abby I thought it was in the church."

"You talked to Abby about this?"

"She witnessed one of my darkness episodes. She saw my grief and asked me about it before the darkness came."

"She knows?"

"No. I wouldn't talk about it. I made her promise to leave it alone."

Lise sighed. "She may not keep that promise. I know this is all very frightening, but Christer told me not to despair, and I believe him."

Her last words calmed him. Their conversation had done nothing to further his understanding of the darkness, but he was relieved to find the friendship he had with Lise was real, and she believed, whether it was his insanity or something malevolent, the darkness was real.

Chapter 12

Lise invited Chad Winston, a thirty-eight-year-old hotel owner from Mendocino, and business associate of the Anders, to Ferndale to meet Janek. Lise settled Chad into a room at the boarding house. The men spent the afternoon discussing their perspective endeavors.

Chad was a fountain of knowledge on hotel establishment and management. He owned hotels in Eureka, Weaverville, Sacramento, and Mendocino. Janek's budding interest in building a hotel in Ferndale had withered. Chad resuscitated it.

"I started out near penniless," Chad said. "I built my first hotel in Mendocino on a wing and a prayer. Enthusiasm and promises go a long way until it comes time to pay the bills, but I managed. I was lucky. I had trusted friends and associates."

Janek knew Chad wasn't just lucky. According to Lise, he was smart and loyal and optimistic.

"Guthrie Sullivan owns a parcel of land on Main Street that's large enough to hold a structure the size of a hotel," Janek said.

"I know him," Chad said. "I didn't take him for a land owner."

"The lot isn't priced to sell, and even if it was, I have nothing to back up my interest."

"If you have the desire to pursue your interest—that's back up enough, but I can't council you on personal aspiration."

Janek understood and decided there was no harm in asking Guthrie for information.

"Let me know if you do pursue the hotel business. I'm happy to offer support and guidance."

"I appreciate that. We're playing poker at the Palace tonight. Care to join us?"

"Poker is one of my many vices," Chad said, laughing.

Lucas, Janek, and Chad entered the saloon at eight o'clock. Guthrie was standing at the end of the bar talking to one of his cronies. He acknowledged Chad with a nod.

"I'll join the game in a few minutes," Janek said. "I'm going to talk with Guthrie."

"He's not going to like it if you start questioning him about his land or, for that matter, anything else," Lucas said.

"I'll take my chances."

Lucas shrugged. "It's your hide."

Chad said, "Don't push him too hard."

Janek nodded. Chad and Lucas walked to the poker room.

The crony Guthrie was talking with got up from his bar stool and walked through the back door to the outhouse. Janek sat in his place.

"Mr. Sullivan, may I speak to you?"

"About what?"

"About the parcel of land you own on Main Street."

"It ain't for sale."

"It is for sale. I saw the notice at city hall."

"It ain't for sale to you."

"Hear me out."

"Nope."

"Why not?"

"Because you're nothin' but a tenderfoot who's got my daughter thinking he's the sun and the moon!"

"What? This has nothing to do with Abby."

"You gave her a gift. It ain't proper for a man who ain't related to give a woman a gift."

Janek mentally sighed. He was doomed from the start because Guthrie was old-fashioned.

"I ain't talking to you. I'd hoped you'd leave town."

Janek's reticent temper flared. "You will talk to me! Do you want to spend what's left of your life rotting behind this bar?"

Guthrie clenched his jaw and said, "You don't know nothin' about me, boy!"

"Old man, I want to know why you're hanging on to that land like you have something buried there! I will find out. Life is going to go on with or without you."

Guthrie went to fetch his shotgun from beneath the bar then thought better of it. Janek walked to the poker room. Guthrie let him go. If he threw him out of the saloon, their argument would become public knowledge, and that was something he couldn't abide.

Laughing children carrying pumpkins traipsed through the streets on their way to the first pumpkin carving contest held at the Halloween festival. Small groups of people, toting baskets of food, drifted toward the fairgrounds on the northern edge of town. Their voices carried through Guthrie's open bedroom window.

He was trying to take his daily nap, but he was unable to sleep. Janek's angry words taunted him: *Life is going to go on with or without you.*

Maybe Janek had a point, he thought. The years of his life were dwindling with his reasons for keeping that parcel of land on Main Street. The land was a status symbol, which would make no difference when he was rotting in the ground. Abigail would inherit the land when he died, and she would sell it to Janek without a second thought.

Guthrie went downstairs to his study and poured a generous glass of whiskey. Abigail had gone to the festival to help Lise with the bake sale booth. He was alone with his doubts.

He drank his whiskey and said, "I didn't give the boy a chance to say what he was gonna say, but I ain't sure if I can believe a word he says. He's up to something he ain't letting on about, but he ain't done nothin' wrong. In fact, he's working hard to establish himself a business, unlike those no counts who hang around the saloon all day."

Guthrie refilled his whiskey glass. His mind lingered on the argument. Despite Janek's harsh words, he didn't believe the boy had meant to be hateful. He recalled telling his daughter that Janek Walesa was one of them people who would have a lasting impact on their lives.

His instinct told him that impact, whatever it was, had begun, and his visceral response was to protect Abigail. Until he was able to put a finger on signs of what was to come, there was nothing he could do but keep a close eye on the boy.

Janek was certain he had only succeeded in making Guthrie mad. Niklas and Lucas had warned him about Guthrie's reaction. In the future, he would heed well-given advice.

He finished his work for the day, gathered the papers on his desk, and put them in the safe in the back room. As he was locking the safe, the bell over the door jingled. A loud thump followed, and then he heard, "Well, I'll be damned! You do have an office."

Janek emerged from the back room. Evan was sitting in the chair behind his desk. He jumped up, pumped Janek's hand, and slapped him on the back.

"I heard you were staying, and you got yourself a real business going!"

"When did you get back?"

"Last night. My mom cooked enough dinner to feed an army. She thinks I'm starving when I come home. Then, I had to listen to my father's stories about the new creamery and how many calves were born while I was gone."

"How long are you going to be home?"

"I'm not sure. The schooner's going to dry dock for repairs. What did I miss besides Lise parading around in her wedding dress?"

Janek didn't know where to begin. The business deals and strange experiences amassed to form a paradox he couldn't explain.

"Listen, my little sisters are at the festival. I'm going to spend a few hours with them before I take them home. Do you want to come along?" Evan asked.

"I don't care for festivals. The crowds make me uncomfortable. I'm sure your sisters would prefer to have you to themselves."

Evan's sisters had his green eyes and dark hair and, unlike his father, they loved him heart and soul.

"Suit yourself. I'll be back in town around seven o'clock. We have some drinking and catching up to do." He rose from Janek's chair, slapped his friend on the back, and left.

Janek locked the office door and went home. He spent the rest of the afternoon sitting on the porch, listening to the laughter of passing children and thinking about the Halloweens he had spent with his sister.

If Liv were here, she would be at the festival helping the children carve their pumpkins. She would insist Janek help, and they would argue because he would refuse. Their arguments were short-lived. He had found it impossible to stay mad at Liv.

The sounds of the festival drifting on the breeze made him feel isolated from happiness and hope. He went inside the house and ate dinner alone.

Evan arrived at the boarding house at seven o'clock as promised. He and Janek walked to the Palace. They sat at a table in the back of the crowded saloon. At first, conversation was impossible as people came to the table to welcome Evan back. Abigail was one of those people.

"Evan, how dare you come home and not stop to say hello to me!"

"I didn't realize you were working. It's Thursday."

"It's Halloween. Daddy needed help."

Janek had not seen Abigail since the day she stopped by his office and he confessed his fear of something in the church. He didn't want her to mention the incident in front of Evan. He was relieved when she lingered a moment to look him in the eye and smile.

"What was that about? Is something going on between the two of you?" Evan said after Abigail went back to the bar.

"No. No. I had a falling out with Guthrie a few days ago. I think she was letting me know she wasn't mad. Don't worry. I'm still a Ferndale virgin."

Evan laughed. "That reminds me of what happened in Portland. I was keeping time with a little thing I met in a saloon. I swear she was as pretty as a Christmas present. Well, we ended up in a hotel room. Some guy kicks in the door and starts swinging a board at me. I was scared to death! I was able to grab my pants and get out of there with my head still on. I'm running through this hotel butt naked. Have you tried putting on pants while you're running? It can't be done."

Evan talked on and on about what he did while he was gone. Janek had forgotten how carefree he felt around Evan, and he was thankful to have him back.

When Evan ran out of stories, he asked Janek about his decision to stay in Ferndale. Janek explained what he had done at city hall. He described how he won the contract with the creamery. He relayed his conversation with Chad Winston. Janek kept to business. The last thing he wanted to talk about was the darkness.

Niklas and Lise walked to the boarding house from the Halloween festival under the starlit skies of a new moon. He had not questioned her regarding her conduct the Saturday she wore her wedding dress to the cemetery. Though the gossip had quieted, the spectacle continued to badger him.

"Will you explain your odd behavior the day you went to the cemetery?" he said. "I've spent the past three weeks making excuses for you so the whole town won't think you're crazy. I deserve to know the truth."

"I'm sorry I put you in that position, but we decided it was the only way to say goodbye."

"Who's we?"

"Christer and I. The time had come for us to let go of one another. We came up with a plan together."

His expression turned to disbelief. "Lise, do you know how you sound?"

"Don't act surprised. You've had a recent spiritual encounter."

He didn't like the way the conversation was going. The spirit Lise was referring to was neither the Father nor the Son nor the Holy Ghost. He tried to deny what he experienced that night in his backyard, but the words disintegrated in his mouth.

"Lise, I know things have been strange as of late, but this is…"

"The truth you asked for."

Chapter 13

November 1872

A building contractor working on the new port project needed an accountant to keep track of material and payroll expenses. Janek was in the parlor reviewing the proposed client agreement when he heard banging on the front door. He went to the door and opened it. Evan was standing on the porch holding a bundle of clothes. A steamer trunk sat beside him.

"Evan, what are you doing?"

"I'm running away from home. Why the hell else would I be standing here with everything I own?"

Lise hurried into the entryway, wiping her hands on her apron. "Evan? What in the world?"

"He's running away from home," Janek said to Lise in the most serious tone of voice he could muster. He fetched the trunk off the porch and put it in the entryway.

"What happened?" Lise asked as she led Evan to the kitchen.

Evan piled his clothes on the table. "Me and my old man got in to a fight for the last time. I got a job working at the port until the schooner is out of dry dock. When I told my father, he started yelling at me because I won't be helping him out on the farm. I'm not putting up with that anymore. I'm twenty-six—I should've left a long time ago. Lise, do you have a room for rent?"

"Yes, but are you sure this is what you want?"

"This has been coming for a long time. My father has never approved of me. He was yelling about how I come home drunk all the time, and how I have no sense of responsibility. I told him I got that job on the schooner just to get away from him. The only reason I kept coming home was because of my mom and little sisters. Otherwise, I'd be living in Eureka."

Lise gathered the clothes from the table. "Janek, take the trunk up to the room at the end of the hallway on the second floor. I'll be there in a minute to tidy up."

She turned to Evan. "Is there something else I can get you? I hate to see you so distressed."

"Nah, I just need to let off some steam. Thanks for letting me stay. I'll follow the rules of the boarding house like a good boy. No drinking or women in my room. I'm going out on the porch. When Janek gets done will you ask him to come out?"

A few minutes later, Janek joined Evan on the porch. A flask of whiskey was in an empty rocking chair.

"That's for you. I need mine to myself tonight," Evan said, pointing at the flask.

Janek sat in the rocking chair. Rain drops pattered like tiny feet on the roof and interrupted the quiet night. They sat in silence for a few minutes before Evan continued his tirade.

"I wanted to punch him in the face and break his nose. I don't understand why he treats me so bad. I feel sorry for my mom; she's had to put up with him all these years. She was crying and begging me not to leave. I told her she could come to town and see me as often as she wanted. I'm never going back there as long as he's alive."

Evan realized his last sentence may have been harsh, considering Janek's father was dead. His shame served to extinguish his immediate anger.

"I don't understand your relationship with your father," Janek said. "But I'm here if you need me."

Evan took a swig off his flask. "That's good enough for me. Listen, I've been thinking about what you said the other night about building a hotel here in town. I wouldn't mind being a part of that if you'd have me. I've got connections. There's a banker in Eureka who owes me a favor or two. I can help you get funding."

Janek was astounded at Evan's capriciousness. It was a trait Janek wished he possessed.

"Are you serious?"

"Hell, yes. Lise's boarding houses are always full because there's nowhere else to stay in town. Frankly, I was surprised she had a room for me. With the increase in travelers through Ferndale, her boarding houses will stay full despite a hotel in town."

"That parcel of land Guthrie owns on Main Street would be the perfect location, but it would take a miracle to get the old man to sell it to me. When I broached the subject, he was insolent. That's why we argued."

Evan considered his flask for a moment, then said, "Why not ask him to partner up with you? That way, he wouldn't have to sell his precious property."

"Guthrie hates me. After the argument we had, he probably despises me."

"Guthrie hates everyone, or at least he pretends like he does. Don't let that stop you. He's got good business sense."

"You have some good ideas, Evan. I appreciate the encouragement. Unfortunately, the biggest obstacle I have right now is lack of money. You said you could help me get funding, but I would have to borrow the entire amount, and I can't afford the monthly payments. What's more, I don't have the knowledge to build or run a hotel."

"You said you met Lise's friend Chad Winston, and he offered to help."

"Yes, but I..."

"Listen, if you sit around waiting for everything to fall into place, you'll never get what you want. I'm not wasting another minute waiting for people or situations to meet my expectations. Tonight was a perfect example."

"I'm sorry about your father," Janek said. "Is there any chance the two of you can patch things up?"

Evan shook his head and took another long swig from his flask. "My father and I are through. It's not what I want, but that's the way it's going to be."

A registered letter was delivered to Janek on the morning of November 4th. He held the letter in his sweating hand and stared at it. If this was what he thought it was, his father's estate was settled. He read it in his room.

October 22, 1872

Law Offices of Bright and Wilson
10 Duval Street
Salem, Oregon

Janek Walesa
PO 377
Ferndale, California

Dear Mr. Walesa,

Enclosed you will find the documents representing the settlement of your father and mother's estate and execution of their last will and testament. A bank draft has been included in the amount of twenty-nine-thousand-five-hundred-thirty-two dollars. Our fee has been deducted from the payment.

Further, there has been an offer to purchase your property located in Albany, Oregon. The proposed contract has also been enclosed. If you find it satisfactory, please sign and return the contract to our offices. A bank draft in the amount of the sale price will be sent to you within three weeks.

Regards,
Patrick Bright, Attorney at Law

Janek was stunned at the amount of the settlement. The farm seemed to produce a modest living at best. He unfolded the settlement papers and read them. To his astonishment, a good sum of the money came from his mother. His grandfather died in 1870, leaving everything he owned to his only child, Freya.

He opened the sales contract on the farm. The buyer was his former employer, Thomas Doyle. The farm's soil and water supply was tainted with cholera. It would be years before the land was suitable for planting. No one was going to buy the farm unless they had the foresight to wait it out. Janek believed Thomas Doyle's offer came from a place of compassion rather than premeditation.

A single sheet of paper was left in the envelope. It was a personal note from Patrick. He wrote that he was engaged to be married, and he had been told to convey good wishes from their mutual friends in Salem. Patrick went on to say that he hoped they would meet again. The note sparked pangs of remorse, causing Janek to wonder how he could have left his home, and the people he had known his whole life. No matter the decisions he had made in Ferndale, he couldn't help but wonder: *Is it too late to return to Salem?*

Sudden pain rumbled through his head. The rumbling pain intensified into thunderous pounding, which erupted into blinding white heat. The darkness was approaching.

Janek had an urgent need to get to the church where his family could protect him. He managed to fling his bedroom door open and run down the hall. The stairs were a white blur. His boot missed the first riser and he fell. When he hit the floor at the bottom of the stairs, renewed pain shot through his head, and he screamed.

Lise and Evan ran to the entryway from separate directions. No one was there. Evan banged open the front door, ran across the porch and through the gate. Lise was right behind.

Janek ran to the church. In the vestibule, he fell and threw up. He struggled to his feet and stumbled inside. The combined murmurs of Liv's sweet voice and Freya's gentle voice filled the church with an angelic hymn. Liv was a dim figure within the blinding whiteness. She stood in the aisle with open arms, ready to embrace her brother. When he reached for her, he was shoved to the floor. His chin hit the edge of a pew. Blood dripped from the gash onto his vest and shirt.

He smelled putrefied hate mixed with fragrant adoration. The shadow was there. Its red fury exploded, provoking Janek to issue a primordial scream.

Niklas was at home and heard the scream. He ran to the church and collided with Lise in the courtyard. She grabbed Niklas by the hand and dragged him with her. Evan bolted through the vestibule. He came to a sudden stop, which caused Niklas and Lise to stumble.

Janek was in front of the pulpit. He was curled in the fetal position with his knees and face touching the floor. Lise dropped to his side and stroked his sweat matted hair. He stirred and pushed himself into a kneeling position. His face and hands were smeared with blood.

"What the hell happened?" Evan said to Janek.

Janek didn't answer. He tried to stand, but couldn't. He tried to crawl, but couldn't. The blinding white heat flashed through his head, and he covered his eyes with the palms of his hands. Evan and Niklas pulled Janek to his feet and dragged him outside.

Before Lise stepped into the vestibule, she heard rustling among the dark rafters. She looked up. A gentle down draft brushed her face and she shivered.

In the courtyard, Janek came around and was able to stand on his own.

"This is what you avoided telling me on Halloween night," said Evan. "I knew you were hiding something. What the hell is this?"

Janek glanced at Lise.

"Lise, do you know what he's talking about?" Niklas said.

She nodded in shame.

Janek glanced back at Lise, then looked at Evan and said, "I've been having episodes where I'm consumed by darkness when I think about my family or second guess my reasons for being in Ferndale. There's something horrible within that darkness. When the darkness retreated, it left behind a force that appeared as a shadow, and then it attacked me. I can't tell if that force is a monster or if it's insanity—my insanity."

Lise looked at Niklas and Evan, and then back at Janek. "Is this the thing that attacked you the last time?"

"I'm not sure."

"Where is your family?" Niklas said.

"They're dead and buried in Albany, Oregon. That's why I came to Ferndale, to escape the horror of their death."

Evan twisted the vestibule door knob.

"Don't!" Janek said.

"I'm going in there to kill that thing!" Evan pushed the door open.

"We don't know what that *thing* is or if it even exists! Please, Evan, don't!"

Niklas shifted his eyes between Janek and Evan, watching their standoff. He felt he should say something a reverend would say, such as: *If there's something evil in my church I haven't sensed it, or, if it's spiritual, God will have an answer*—but he remained mute.

Evan studied Janek's pleading eyes before he said, "I'll leave it alone for now, but if that thing goes after you again, I'm killing it!"

Chapter 14

It was poker night at the Palace. Evan and Janek were playing with Lucas Dodd, Matt O'Neill, and Josef Paullo, when a group of workers from the port came into the saloon. Evan went to get a round of beers from the bar between hands. He recognized the workers. They were a sleazy bunch of scumbags who enjoyed causing an uproar. He returned to the poker table without the beers.

"We've got trouble, boys. There's some shithole low downs from the port hanging at the bar. They're already drunk. I think we should keep an eye on them."

All the men walked out front. Janek and Lucas sat at a table near the back door. Matt and Josef stationed themselves by the front door. Evan went to the bar to get the beers he had gone to fetch in the first place. Abigail was working, and if one of those bastards even looked at her wrong, he was going to kill them. Guthrie caught Evan's attention and gave him a nod.

Evan sat beside Lucas. An hour went by, then two, and nothing happened. It looked like the night was going to pass without incident until one of the workers tapped Evan on the shoulder.

"I know ya. Ya're workin' on the dock construction. Ya're pretty full of yarself ain't ya?"

Evan had participated in plenty of bar brawls, but none in the Palace. He preferred to make a fool of himself out of town. He stood up and tucked his ponytail into the neck of his shirt.

Lucas stood up. He and Evan had been in a lot of bar brawls together in

Eureka. There was an unspoken code between them: when Evan tucked in his ponytail, Lucas knew he meant business.

The worker pointed at Janek. "Who's ya milk toast friend? I bet ya he cried when he cut his chin. Whatta ya say I prove it?"

Before Evan or Lucas could make a move, the worker punched Janek in the jaw. The blow propelled his head against the wall, and knocked him out of his chair. The wound on his chin ripped open. Blood streamed from a new gash on the side of his head.

"You son of a bitch!" Evan grabbed the worker by the hair and slammed his face into the table.

Lucas pulled an old Green River knife from its sheath in his boot. Janek scrambled to his feet. The other scumbags were coming at them fast. Josef and Matt ran toward the back of the saloon. Lucas saw Abigail running right behind them.

"Get her out of here, Matt!" Lucas said, pointing at Abigail.

Matt turned and bear hugged her. She kicked and argued that she needed to help Janek. Matt put his mouth to her ear and said, "You're gonna make things worse. I'm taking you outside. Get yourself home and I mean it!"

The melee was in full swing.

The troublemaker who attacked Janek swung at him again. Janek punched him in the stomach. When the man doubled over, Janek kneed him in the mouth. The man spat bloody teeth into his hand. He spat the blood that pooled in his mouth at Janek, and then ran out the back door.

Evan pulled a switchblade from his pocket. Someone hit him in the face with a chair. The switchblade flew from his hand as he felt the familiar crunch of his nose breaking. He used the chair to pummel a man who rushed him with a broken beer bottle.

A worker shoved Lucas to the floor. Lucas lost his grip on his knife and it skittered into a corner. The worker continually kicked him in the ribs. Josef kicked the man who was kicking Lucas in the groin and cussed at him in Portuguese. The worker looked surprised and stopped kicking. He covered his crotch with his hands and bent over in pain. Another man hit Josef in the back of the head with a chair. Lucas rolled over and jerked that man's feet out from under him. The man hit his head on a table as he went down.

Matt threw one of the degenerates against the wall and held a .36 caliber Remington revolver to the side of the man's neck. The pinned man sliced Matt's left cheek with a pocket knife. Matt fired. Blood spurted from the bullet hole in the man's carotid artery and drenched Matt's face and shirt. The slob raised his hands to his neck. His eyes bulged with terror, and then he collapsed.

Two men came at Evan. One held a loaded Springfield Rifle-Musket aimed at Evan's torso. The other raised his hand and threw a butcher knife. Evan skittered to his right and ducked his head. He felt the knife slice the air as it sailed past his head. The blade stuck in the wall. When Evan shifted his body, the scumbag who was holding the rifle tried to adjust his aim. Evan ran straight at the man with the rifle and tackled him. The rifle flew from the man's hands as he and Evan fell to the floor. Evan managed to stay in control. He sat on the man's stomach and slammed his head against the floor until he passed out.

Someone slipped an arm around Janek's neck from behind and choked him. He felt the tip of a knife separate the skin between his ribs and plunge through the cartilage. Then he was shoved into the wall. There was an abrupt shotgun blast. The man who had stabbed Janek did a funny jig in the air and flew backwards.

Guthrie stood in the middle of the saloon; a smoking .12 gauge shotgun was in his hands. The blast sent scalawags scattering, and those who were able ran from the saloon.

Evan and Lucas got to their feet. Matt brushed at his bleeding check. Josef had a man's neck gripped in his beefy arm. He kneed the man in the face and threw him to the floor. Janek struggled to catch his breath and slid the knife out from between his ribs.

Guthrie looked at Evan, Matt, Josef, Lucas, and Janek. They all had bleeding wounds.

Abigail didn't go home as Matt had ordered. She went to Sheriff Dell

Tate's office to tell him there was a brawl at the Palace. The sheriff strode into the saloon, followed by Abigail.

He surveyed the damage and the remaining men. The man Guthrie shot lay dead in a heap on the floor behind Janek. There were several unconscious derelicts scattered around the saloon. The sheriff kneeled and examined the man with the gaping shotgun wound to his torso.

"What happened here, Guthrie?" the sheriff said as he stood up.

Guthrie walked behind the bar and stowed his shotgun on a shelf out of sight before he said, "I can't recollect. There was a lot of filth in here tonight. It clouded my vision."

Sheriff Tate scanned the guilty looking group of men who stood near the back of the saloon. His eyes came to rest on Matt and he said, "That cut on your cheek can't be the reason you're soaked in blood. Whose blood is it?"

Matt nodded toward the bloodied mess of a man lying on the floor in front of him. The man stared at the ceiling with glazed fixed eyes.

The sheriff sighed. Assault was a distant acquaintance in Ferndale. Murder was a complete stranger. Now, they were staring him right in the face. He removed his hat, wiped his forehead with a handkerchief, and put his hat back on. He fiddled with the brim until the hat sat just right on his head. Everyone left standing watched him with expectation.

Sheriff Tate inhaled, held his breath, and then exhaled. "I'll send the coroner to fetch the bodies. I'll get Doc Mason to check on the others. I'd advise you boys to get home. I'll try to make this a case of self-defense, but I can't promise it'll stick. Matt, you'll want to let your brothers and folks know what went on here tonight so they don't hear it from someone else first."

Matt nodded.

Lucas fetched his knife from a corner of the saloon and left through the back door with Matt and Josef.

Abigail stood beside Guthrie behind the bar. She watched Janek help Evan look for his switchblade. She felt guilty about bringing the sheriff to the Palace. Her father and Matt O'Neill could be arrested for murder. She should have listened to Matt and gone home.

Guthrie saw her grab her handbag from a shelf under the bar. "You ain't leaving without me," he said. "I don't want you on the streets at night with that scum on the loose."

Evan found his switchblade. He and Janek walked to the front door. Guthrie stopped Janek. He pointed at the blood on Janek's shirt and said, "That ain't too bad, but you better get Lise to take a look."

Janek looked at his wound.

Guthrie continued, "If you're feeling up to it tomorrow, come by my house and we'll talk about that piece of land I own on Main Street."

Janek looked at Abigail. She shrugged. He nodded at Guthrie.

Evan and Janek went back to the boarding house. To their relief, Lise was asleep. They snuck to their rooms like naughty children avoiding parental questioning. They knew it was a temporary respite.

Lise gasped and carried on when she saw them at breakfast. Janek's face was swollen and bruised around a three-inch laceration on his temple. The existing gash on his chin fissured, traveling the length of his jaw bone halfway to his ear. Blood seeped from the stab wound between his ribs. Evan had two blackened eyes. His broken nose was scraped and swollen.

"Evan, your behavior doesn't surprise me at all, but I didn't expect this out of you, Janek. What in the world happened?"

Evan recounted the brawl between bites of biscuits and gravy. He left nothing to the imagination, including the man Matt shot to death, and the moment Guthrie shot and killed the scumbag. "You should've seen Guthrie when the sheriff arrived. He was composed and..."

"Guthrie probably saved my life, and I have no idea why," Janek said. "I was under the impression he hated me. What's even more puzzling is he's willing to discuss his parcel of land on Main Street. He asked me to come by his house today so we could talk about it."

"Don't praise the old man for saving you. He'll deny he fired that shotgun," Evan said.

"What's your interest in Guthrie's parcel of land?" Lise said. "I remember that you asked Niklas about it a few weeks ago."

Janek wasn't ready to discuss his plans with Lise so he condensed his answer. "I'm curious."

"I doubt that's the real reason, but I won't pry…for now," Lise said.

Janek arrived at the Sullivan house late in the afternoon. Abigail answered his knock on the door. She was wearing a dark green dress with a full light green flounced underskirt. The collar and cuffs were frilly white lace. Her long dark hair was twisted into a loose bun secured with the tortoise shell comb Janek had given her.

"Good afternoon, Abby. You look lovely."

"Thank you for the kind words. On the other hand, you look awful! Does your face hurt? It looks like it does."

"I'm fine."

"Daddy is expecting you. Please come in."

He followed Abigail to the study. Guthrie laid the book he was reading on the desk when they entered the room. "Janek, sit there," he said, motioning to a wing backed chair. "Abby, I want you to stay."

She sat in a chair beside Janek.

Guthrie said, "I guess you're wondering why I've decided to talk with you after all. I can't say I know myself, except I thought it over and supposed you might have something worth saying. You better get started before I change my mind."

"I'm interested in building a hotel on the parcel of land you own on Main Street. I came into an inheritance recently; therefore, I have the initial funds to begin such a venture. I was hoping we might form a partnership; your land and my money."

Guthrie snorted. "What makes you think you're qualified to build and run a hotel?"

"I'm gathering a lot of good information from one of Lise's business associates, Chad Winston. We've met face to face and are now corresponding. He has promised to stop and see me next week on his way home to Mendocino.

He's bringing some hotel trade books and other related materials."

"I know him. He comes in the saloon every time he's in town; likes to sit at the bar and talk. You got an expert holding your hand. What else you got?"

Janek leaned forward. "You know I'm a corporate accountant. I don't think I need to explain my capabilities when it comes to handling finances."

"You said you had the initial funds. Where do you plan on getting the rest?"

"There's a banker in Eureka who may be willing to do business with me."

"You think a banker who doesn't know you is gonna agree to lend you money? That has the smell of Evan all over it, which probably ain't bad. Abby, speak up if you got something to add."

She said, "Do you plan on building a bar and restaurant in the hotel?"

That was something Janek had not considered. In fact, there had to be *a lot* of things he had not considered. He wondered if he was in way over his head.

"I suppose we should."

"If you do, maybe Daddy and I could take ownership. The customers would be different from those at the Palace, but the premise would be the same."

"Why don't you and your father discuss that privately?"

Guthrie said, "Son, if you can come up with a solid business proposal, I'll consider a partnership. Abby, do you agree to look over a proposal?"

"Yes."

Janek rose from his chair. "Thank you for your time. I'll have a proposal ready within two weeks. I'm curious. Niklas told me the Palace was originally built at that location, but that it burned down a few months later. Why didn't you rebuild there?"

Guthrie rubbed his chin. "At the time I considered it a bad omen. After a while, the land became a status symbol. Could be I was waiting for this to come along and I didn't know it."

Abigail walked Janek to the door. "I didn't expect Daddy to consider this business venture so easily. He tends to be skeptical and pessimistic. Have the two of you talked about this before?"

"Not about the hotel, but I did ask him about his land a few weeks ago."

"That's why you argued wasn't it? You tried to force him into talking to you and he got angry."

"Yes."

"So Daddy has had time to think about this?"

"I don't know. It seems like everything has been expedited since I arrived in Ferndale. Suddenly, I'm at the point of building a hotel. It's like something is pushing me."

"What does that have to do with Daddy?"

"Nothing I guess."

Abigail hoped his confusion had nothing to do with what he thought was in the church.

She spent the remainder of the day contemplating what had occurred in Janek's office a month ago, and what had occurred that afternoon. At ten o'clock that evening, she went upstairs and went to bed.

The moon was setting when she woke to the sound of dogs barking. She got up and looked through the window. Moonlight filtered through the trees, casting odd shadows in the backyard. The barking ceased. She closed the curtains and opened her nightstand drawer. Rosary beads lay nestled on a piece of silk in the drawer. The prayer beads were the only item she possessed that had belonged to her mother.

Abigail sat on the edge of the bed, fingering the rosary beads and thinking of Janek. His beauty, elegance, and intelligence were seductive and foreign, as if he was an erotic prince from a utopian land. She was powerless to do anything but want him in every way.

She lay back on the bed and tried to envision his dream hotel. Within her vision, she saw herself following him on a path through a dim redwood forest. Guthrie walked beside her. Dark shadows moved through the forest in unison with Janek's every step. The path ended and they stood at the edge of a misty garden nestled among the redwood trees.

The garden dissolved. Abigail was standing behind an exquisite well-polished L-shaped saloon bar. The hem of her dress fell above her knees and the fabric was strange to the touch. Her high-heeled shoes hurt her feet. The bar patrons were speaking English, but it sounded infused with another language. Their grooming and dress was odd or inappropriate.

Small round tables flanked by black leather chairs filled the floor space beyond the bar. The pale warm glow from petite lamps left shadows on the faces of those who sat at the tables.

A large painting, illuminated by a strange looking cylinder, hung on the far wall. The artist had painted wide vertical rolling swaths of yellow, orange, red, and green across the canvas over and over. Some of the colors ran together at the edges of the swaths. The effect was mesmerizing.

Something soft brushed her forearm. A gray tabby cat weaved like a serpent through the glasses and bottles on top of the bar. His tail flicked and waved as he walked. She reached for the cat. He barked and bit her hand.

Abigail woke with a start. The dream would stay buried in her subconscious for a long time.

Chapter 15

With The Brothers, Inc. out of town, Emily Hartmann was responsible for the daily transaction receipts. She arrived at Janek's office early in the evening with the receipts for that day. The bell jingled as she walked through the door.

Emily was wearing a new dress. The crimson skirt was layered in black and white lace and flounces. It boasted a high bustle in the back and a full petticoat underneath. The skirt rustled when she crossed the room.

Janek, who was engaged in conversation with Chad Winston, stood as she approached his desk. She was his client; therefore, he had to be polite and professional, regardless of her behavior.

"Good evening, Mrs. Hartmann. Let me take that for you," Janek said and reached for the Gladstone bag in her arms.

She handed him the bag. "I'll return on Friday to go over the accounting entries from today's business."

"Yes, until then. Have a nice evening."

Emily lifted her skirts and swept toward Chad. "Whom may I ask is your handsome friend?"

Janek sighed. He had tried to avoid the protocol of mandatory introductions by cuing her to leave. "Emily Hartmann, this is Chad Winston."

Chad appreciated everything about Emily's appearance from her dress to her stature. He straightened his six-foot-three frame into a standing position. He was dressed like a dandy, sporting a new black silk suit and vest complete with ruby cuff links. The ruby ring he wore on the middle finger of his right hand flashed when he took Emily's hand.

"It's a pleasure to meet a lovely woman like yourself, Mrs. Hartmann."

Janek resisted the urge to roll his eyes. Chad was either a flirt or a good actor. It made no difference to Janek as long as he didn't have to engage in conversation with her. But there was no respite. Emily noticed the injuries he sustained on his face and swept her skirts in his direction.

"Whatever happened to your face?"

"I tripped in church and fell."

"I haven't seen you in church. Are you referring to the First Congregational Church? Reverend Arnold's church? I would love to see you at services. There are too many old fogies and not enough young men like you. I believe that gash on your jaw is going to leave a scar," Emily said as she reached to touch Janek's face.

"Mrs. Hartmann, it's near candle-lighting. I would be more than happy to accompany you home if you don't have an escort," said Chad.

"Thank you, Mr. Winston. Shall we go? Janek take care of your gorgeous face."

The bell jingled when Chad and Emily left the office. Janek plopped into his chair. *Thank God Chad stopped that woman from touching my face.* He was certain he would have slapped her hand, which of course, would have been an insult. A shallow flirtatious woman like that would go back to her husband, claiming she had been assaulted. She was trouble waiting to happen.

Chad returned to Janek's office at seven o'clock. Evan arrived a few minutes later.

"Guthrie told me about the fight at the Palace," Chad said with amusement as he noted Evan's blackened eyes and swollen nose. "I hope you look better than the ruffian who did that to you."

"My first fight at the Palace, and I get my nose broken."

"I'm sorry I missed that," Chad said with a chuckle.

"Can we get started?" Janek said. His temples were throbbing. He prayed it was a normal headache.

Earlier in the day, Chad and Janek had sketched designs for the hotel. An architect would have to draw out official blueprints, but in the meantime, the sketches would suffice. The business proposal was outlined. They were ready to fill in the details.

Janek laid the sketches and the outline on his desk.

Evan flipped through the sketches. "I'm not good with this kind of thing. I couldn't design and build an outhouse." He picked up the outline and read it. "I can do this."

"Good," Chad said. "I suggest we add a section to the business proposal that identifies possible obstacles, and solutions to those obstacles."

"This isn't an obstacle, but I think we need to tell Lise what we're doing, and we need to tell her tomorrow," Evan said.

Janek's headache was worsening and dulling his ability to think. He nodded in response to Evan's suggestion.

Chad saw stress in Janek's eyes. "Are you up to this?"

"I'm fine. Add your obstacles section to the document."

Evan handed the outline to Chad and said, "Maybe my father will have more respect for me when this is done."

Janek wanted to tell Evan to forget his father's opinion, but he would sound like a hypocrite.

They worked on the business proposal until midnight. When Chad and Evan had gone, Janek locked the hotel documents in the safe. He turned off the gas lamps and sat in his chair. The throbbing in his temples was horrible, and his stab wound ached.

He thought of Evan's discord with his father. *Would Evan grieve when his father died?* Janek felt guilty conceiving William O'Malley's death. On the other hand, Evan's desire to prove himself to his father appeared to have everything to do with his motivation to be a part of their business venture.

What is my motivation? Janek thought.

His father's immediate reply startled him. "Have faith in what you're doing, son. This is your destiny."

"What is my destiny?"

"Close your eyes and I will show you."

Janek laid his aching head on the desk and closed his eyes. The darkness washed over him and this time, it caressed his wounds and embraced his soul with whispered words of love and devotion. He saw himself walking with his father on a path through a dim redwood forest. The path vanished and they were walking across an expanse of well-manicured lawn. People were sitting in the grass. Some were strangers, others were not. Niklas, Abigail, and Evan were there.

The garden faded away. Janek perceived that the shadow was in the darkness. He felt it touch his mind with passionate lust.

He tried to retreat from its hideous groping, but his thoughts were pounded to a pulp. He could no longer fight his insanity.

The next morning, Chad Winston stopped by Janek's office before catching the stagecoach to Mendocino. Janek was asleep in his chair. He awoke to the jingling bell as the door opened.

"Apparently, you didn't go home last night," Chad said.

"Are you leaving?"

"Yes."

Janek dragged out of his chair. His neck was stiff and his ribs hurt. At least the headache he had last night was gone.

"I owe you a great deal of thanks. My vision of building a hotel wouldn't have been possible without your guidance and knowledge. I'm in your debt," Janek said.

"It's been my pleasure. I think California is big enough for two hotel moguls."

"Just the fact that you kept Emily Hartmann from mauling me puts me in your debt," Janek said as he smoothed his wrinkled jacket.

Chad laughed. "You might as well know, a woman like Emily Hartmann is exactly my type: beautiful and married. No obligations. It's for the best that she only has eyes for you. That woman is trouble. Well, I'd better get going.

Keep in touch and let me know how things are progressing. If you need anything, drop me a line."

Janek walked to the boarding house. He went to bed and slept the rest of the day. A pounding on his bedroom door woke him up at eight o'clock that evening.

"Go away!"

"We're supposed to talk to Lise!"

"Give me a minute!"

Janek dragged himself out of bed and went to the parlor dressed in his rumpled suit. His blond hair was in disarray. Lise and Evan watched as he attempted to tidy his hair by running his hands through it.

"Are you up to this?" Evan said.

Janek stopped combing his hair with his fingers.

Evan gave him a sideways glance, then said to Lise, "We're putting together a business proposal to construct a hotel on Main Street."

"Ferndale is now the terminus for stagecoach runs to all points with daily runs to Eureka," Janek said. "The new port on the Salt River will become a port of call for sea-going vessels, not just schooners like the port on the Eel River. Ferndale is evolving into a busy transportation center, and there is a market for a hotel."

Lise narrowed her eyes. "So this is what you and Chad have been up to. I was under the impression he was sending accounting business your way."

"I wasn't trying to deceive you."

She regarded the bruises and cuts on Janek's face, his wrinkled suit, and tousled hair. Dark circles insinuated themselves under his bewitching eyes. The culmination of all he had been through, and what lay ahead, was beginning to wear him down. The last thing on earth he was capable of was deception.

"You know that's not what I meant."

Janek ran his fingers through his hair and sighed. Evan gave him another sideways glance.

"Please continue," Lise said.

Anxiety pressed hard on Janek's chest. He walked to the parlor window, parted the curtain, and looked through the window as if he was expecting to see spies lurking. The curtain dropped from his hand and he turned from the window.

"The money I inherited from my parents' estate will finance a good portion of the venture, but I can't devote all of my assets. We're still looking for investors."

"What's your interest in this Evan?" Lise said.

"I've some money saved up."

"I thought you were saving your money to buy a schooner."

"I've changed my mind."

Janek rubbed at the anxiety on his chest without thinking and said, "We're preparing a business proposal. Guthrie has agreed to consider the use of his property on Main Street as the site for the hotel, if he feels the proposal is sound. We need to have everything in order before we can move forward."

"But you can't move forward until you find other investors?" Lise said.

"No, we can't."

Lise crossed the room to where Janek was standing. She placed her hand on top of the hand rubbing his chest and held it still. Blue eyes regarded one another. Her words were quiet and breathy. "I go with you, remember?"

He nodded.

"Evan too," she said in a louder voice.

"Yes."

"I'm going to sell my boarding houses and invest in your hotel."

"Lise, are you sure?" Evan said.

"Yes, I'm sure." She went to his side. "We both know our journey is with Janek." She looked into his bright green eyes. "If someone had suggested that I would be business partners with Evan O'Malley, I would have laughed at them, but not now. I'm proud to be your partner."

Evan thought of his father and decided to leave it alone. His place was with people who saw the good in him.

98

Chapter 16

On Wednesday night, November 20, 1872, Evan and Janek sat in the back room of the Palace Saloon and discussed their plans. Evan made good on his claims that he had connections. The banker who owed him a favor had arranged to extend the partnership a line of credit. An architect, with whom Evan often drank and caroused, agreed to draw up the hotel blueprints. Janek had to travel to Eureka to sign the bank papers and meet with the architect.

"I've booked passage on a steamer ship that's running building supplies for the new port. We leave tomorrow afternoon and won't be returning until Sunday. I'm going with you. I'd like you to meet a couple of ladies who are at the Blind Pig Pub every Friday night. I figured you might be up to having some fun after all the work you've done on the hotel."

Janek didn't know how to tell Evan he was afraid to go to Eureka. His fears would make him look like a weakling. After staring at the foam floating on top of his beer for several minutes he said, "I can't go."

He swallowed the rest of his beer and ordered another one. His death was a certainty if he left Ferndale. His mother had warned him—*If you leave this place you will die of a broken heart*. It was a paranoid delusion conjured by a crazy man who couldn't discern reality from a figment. The same man who had somehow convinced his new friends to change the course of their lives and embark on building a hotel. He couldn't accomplish what he needed to do without going to Eureka. His reticence made him feel selfish and ashamed.

"Guthrie, can we get a couple of shots," Evan said.

Guthrie brought two shot glasses and a bottle of tequila. "Looks like you might need more than a couple."

They sat at the table drinking in silence, avoiding what needed to be said.

"A few nights ago, I dreamed I was walking behind a dark figure up a path in a dim redwood forest," Evan said. "It was guiding me to its object of affection. I knew it had something to do with you. The path came to a sudden end and I was standing in a clearing of mowed grass."

Janek was horrified. He knew their archetypical dreams were not a coincidence. His persecutory shadow had made itself known to Evan on purpose. The words he uttered to Lise weeks ago rang in his ears: *Something is happening to us that we can't control. This has only just begun.*

"Evan, don't …"

"It's about what's in the church isn't it? Why didn't you tell me?"

Janek jumped from his chair, hurtling it backward across the floor. "You know damn well I've been scared to death I'm losing my mind! I've been grappling with what's happening, which gets more and more bizarre with each day that passes. I can't protect any of us from whatever this is. I can't stop it from coming!"

"Wait a minute. You're misunderstanding me."

"No I'm not! You're accusing me of manipulation and dishonesty!"

"That's absolutely not true!" Evan said. He stood to face Janek. "I believe you when you say you can't go to Eureka."

Janek grabbed Evan by his jacket lapels and slammed him against the wall. He shook Evan and said, "I don't give a damn what you believe! I've been here just three months. Everything is moving too fast and gotten too strange. I'm going back to Oregon even if I die trying!"

Janek let go of Evan and bolted from the saloon.

Evan started after Janek, but Guthrie called after him, "Let him go, son. None of us can change what's gonna happen."

The two men regarded one another, and then Evan walked out the back door. *I'll be damned before I let Janek face this alone.* He knew where Janek was headed. He began running.

Janek stood outside the church and stared at the long windows. He felt miserable about his altercation with Evan. The bright waning gibbous moon shone from its realm in the sky. A freezing wind wrapped around every living thing and extracted warmth, exchanging it for bone-chilling cold. The strong wind rocked the church bell back and forth. It emitted a low bong every few seconds, reminding him of a haunted harbor bell tolling for a doomed ship.

The eerie sound reverberated through his pounding head. The pain was merciless. He wondered if death was an acceptable recourse. *At least I would be reunited with my family.* The struggles of the past months would come to an end. The horrors hounding him would have no prey to chase through the darkness. He would have peace at last.

He pushed open the gate and followed the path to the courtyard. The dead watched from their dismal graves. He thought of his father telling him to have faith in what he was doing and this was his destiny. But his father was a ghost. *How can I live on the reassurances of a ghost?*

He entered the vestibule, hoping that Freya or Liv could tell him how to save himself from the incubus that was punishing him for his treasonous promise to return to Oregon. On the other hand, he was afraid to go inside the church. He closed his eyes and rubbed his temples. Suicide was his only choice.

He stepped into the courtyard and looked up at the looming cemetery hill. He didn't own a gun or a weapon of any sort. He hatched a plan to walk through the woods on the hill behind the cemetery, find an unprotected spot to sit, and, he hoped, freeze to death before morning.

He climbed the steep steps. When he reached the tenth step, he was shoved backward. The skin on the palms of his hands abraded and his trousers ripped as he skidded across the cobblestones. He came to an abrupt halt before he slammed into the church wall. At that moment, planted on the cold cobblestones, Janek knew he was no longer in control of his life. His choices were becoming intertwined with the desires of another entity. Possession was an inaccurate description. It was more like repression.

The freezing wind twisted into small tight spirals that blew the leaves in the courtyard from their path like cyclones. A breathless voice said, "I have waited for you for a millennium. Our time has come."

The shadowed unrequited soul from within the darkness was there.

Janek closed his eyes and dropped his head into his skinned hands. The horrid sound of its voice was more than he could stand.

"Do you know who I am?"

Janek clenched his jaw and pressed his hands hard against his forehead.

"I am jealousy and compassion. If we were one, I would be joy and happiness. I love you more than anyone who will ever desire you. Each of us is weak, but together we can be strong."

Tears wet Janek's cheeks. *This thing believes I am weak because I grieve for my family, and that grief confuses me.* He had no response to give.

The soul took advantage of his sorrow and loneliness. It claimed to love him, but it hurt him each time he invoked its anger. He was certain he was in hell.

"My energy has waned with each passing year. Now, I can draw strength from the anticipation of our life as one."

Janek lifted his head from his hands. "I don't understand!"

"You do understand!"

"No I don't!"

"I have watched you since the day you were conceived within your mother's womb. I will continue to watch you and keep you near me until I am strong."

"I'm not yours to keep!"

"You belong to me."

Janek tried to stand, but he was shoved to the ground. He screamed into the wind. "You don't exist!"

"My existence is different from yours, but I am real."

"You are my insanity and nothing more!"

"You know you are not insane."

"You are not real!"

"You cannot deny my existence. You will feel my constant presence."

The tornadic wind vanished, leaving a cold silence in its place. The pounding in Janek's head worsened as if to remind him of the shadow's parting words. He leaned against the outer wall of the church and pulled his knees up to his chest. He rested his forehead on his knees. A gentle hand touched his shoulder.

"I'm not insane, Evan. It's worse."

"I know."

"I'm a prisoner. How do I go on from here?"

"I don't know, but you will."

Janek raised his head and looked at Evan. "I brought this on us. It has stalked me all my life, but I didn't know. If I had known, I wouldn't have come to this town. What have I done?"

Evan sat beside Janek. "You haven't done anything. You aren't going to start beating yourself up do you hear me?"

"Yes, but ..."

"We'll do what we have to do."

Janek shook his head. "I won't do this. I'm only twenty-five years old. I'm supposed to be building a future. I'm supposed to be whoring around with you whenever and wherever I like. How am I going to live a full life if I'm trapped here with that monster? Help me put an end to this. Help me kill myself!"

"It's not going to let me and you know it."

"Please, for God's sake you have to try! What's the worst that can happen?"

Evan was silent for a moment. This was so terrible and so out of his control that he was unsure what to do.

"Did you think about killing yourself before it talked to you tonight?" he asked.

"Yes, but my idea was weak."

"Did it know your intentions?"

Janek glanced at the stone steps. "It must have."

"It's watching us right now isn't it?"

"Yes, and it's trying to keep me under control by mentally and physically hurting me."

Evan recognized the reason Janek couldn't go to Eureka. That monster had sickened him for leaving Ferndale in September. He shuddered to think of the agony Janek would suffer if he made another attempt to leave.

"I'll go to Eureka and take care of things. It's freezing out here. Let's go home."

Lise was in the second floor hallway when they climbed the stairs. She saw they looked tense and unhappy.

"Both of you turn around. There's something wrong, and I want to know what it is," she said steering them downstairs.

Evan tried to deflect her by saying, "I'm leaving for Eureka early in the morning."

Lise ignored him and continued to nudge them downstairs and into the kitchen. She shut the door that separated the kitchen from the hall.

"What happened tonight?" Lise asked. "Don't say it was nothing because I won't believe you."

Evan and Janek avoided looking at Lise.

Lise studied them. "Well?"

"It spoke to me," Janek whispered.

Lise's skin crawled and goose bumps formed on her arms and the back of her neck. "What…spoke…to you?"

"The shadow from the darkness I thought was in my mind. It's manipulating us, and if I don't do what it wants, it's going to make my suffering worse."

Lise was silent for a long time. She shifted her gaze between Janek and Evan. Finally, she gathered the courage to ask, "What does it want?"

Janek's answer was near inaudible. "It wants to be one with me so it can live a human life. It wants my body and my soul."

"It wants to possess you? Do you realize what you're saying?"

"Not possess me, join with me."

Lise sat at the table to steady her trembling body. This is what she and Janek had wondered about weeks ago. All the strange things that had occurred were because of the desires of this shadow. "Can we stop it?"

"I don't know how," Janek said with pain and panic in his voice. "It's a hideous enigma and I don't understand it. I have to get this thing away from you and Evan. I have to leave Ferndale." His stomach cramped, and he ran onto the back porch and threw up.

"That thing has made him a prisoner," Evan said.

Lise bit her lower lip to stave off threatening tears and nodded. "How much time do we have before it tries to take him?"

"I wish I knew."

III

The Prelude

Chapter 17

August 1873

Niklas looked at his reflection in the small mirror in his modest bedroom. His sweating and shaking hands made it difficult to button his shirt. He kept looking at the small velvet-covered box on the dresser below the mirror. Inside the box on a cloud of cotton lay the diamond engagement ring he purchased on his last trip to Eureka. The ring was for Lise.

As he dressed, he recalled the events of the past nine months. Last November he had witnessed an incident in the church courtyard that frightened him and confirmed his dread that something was at work in Ferndale that had nothing to do with the God he cherished.

He had gone to the church to check on the gas lamps inside. A soft rustling noise drew his attention to the back of the church. Beyond the open back door, Niklas saw Janek suffering at the hands of an unseen force. Like a coward, he hid in the vestibule and did nothing to help. To this day, he regretted his lack of bravery and compassion.

That was not the only thing he regretted. Last January Lise sold her boarding house on Little River Street to Stephen and Emily Hartmann. On February 10, 1873, Janek, Evan, Lise and the Sullivans formed a corporation that gave them the legal rights to construct the hotel. After that, Niklas watched Lise slip more and more into the world Janek Walesa was constructing. No matter the consequences, he had no intention of letting her go into that world without him.

Niklas succeeded in getting his shirt buttoned. He put on his jacket and tucked the velvet-covered box into his pocket. A rented carriage waited on the street. A picnic basket and a blanket were on the floorboard. He had invited Lise to join him for a picnic lunch in Lowery Park, which was outside of town. They had picnicked there in the past; therefore, he hoped Lise wouldn't be suspicious of his intentions.

Before getting into the carriage, Niklas took a deep breath to calm his nerves. The late morning sun was warm. The sky was a deep shade of baby blue and cloudless; a rare event in Ferndale. He noticed the gray tabby cat lounging on the footway near the carriage's passenger running board. Sometime back, the cat had decided to make Niklas his new friend, often sitting with him on the front porch or perusing the church for mice. The cat stood and stretched his back. He trotted to Niklas, meowed, and brushed against Niklas' leg.

"I hope that's your way of telling me good luck," he said to the cat. "Lord only knows I need it."

Lise was waiting on the porch when the carriage drew up to the boarding house. Niklas jumped from the driver's seat. She met him at the gate. As he helped her into the carriage, he said, "You look lovely this morning. I don't believe I've seen the dress you're wearing. Is it new?"

The dress *was* new. She had ordered it from a Sacramento-based mail order magazine, and it was delivered a month later. The dress was the latest conservative style, with an overskirt draped to an apron front. A full flounced underskirt and full petticoats flared the bottom of the skirt. The overskirt was pulled up at the sides to reveal the underskirt. The dark blue material was infused with delicate baby blue pinstripes. The garment made her feel pretty.

"Since when are you interested in my wardrobe?" Lise said with a soft laugh as she settled into her seat.

Niklas shrugged. His mouth was dry. If he attempted conversation, he would choke on his tongue.

They rode to the park enfolded in their familiar companionship. Lise tried not to keep glancing at Niklas. He seemed nervous and fidgeted with something in his jacket pocket. As they arrived at Lowery Park, it dawned on her what this late morning date was about. He was going to ask for her hand in marriage. The idea made her giddy and terrified at the same time.

Niklas stopped the carriage near an old elm tree. He tethered the horse to the tree, and then helped Lise from her seat. They fetched the wicker basket and spread the picnic out under the elm. Niklas managed to regain his voice. They ate and laughed and talked about the latest gossip and happenings in town. Then, Niklas took the small velvet covered box from his pocket, which reminded Lise of her theory on why they were in the park.

"Lise, I have something for you. I mean I have something to ask you," Niklas said. His sweating palms and shaking hands returned. "I feel we have something more than just friendship. I...well...I love you and would you marry me?"

Her face warmed as she blushed. She looked at the box in his trembling hand. *Do I love him?* she pondered. *Yes. Is it a passionate love? No. Am I prepared to be a reverend's wife? Indeed, not.* A much larger question remained.

"Niklas I do love you, but we need to talk about this," Lise said as she tried to deter her words from sounding dishonest.

"Lise, first and foremost, I'm in love with you. I know..."

"No, you don't understand..."

"Let me finish. I do understand. I know in our society a wife follows the whims and callings of her husband. I'm willing to follow you wherever our future may take us. I need you in my life," he said.

A tear formed in the corner of her eye. She knew if she agreed to marry him, she would be responsible for his destiny. It would be unfair and cruel to drag him down a path she knew would destroy his faith. The tear escaped and coursed its way down her cheek followed by another and another.

"Do you have any idea what you're saying? Things have been quiet lately, but it's just the lull before the storm. Do you *really* understand?"

Niklas answered by opening the velvet-covered box and revealing the diamond ring. He offered it to her like a sacrificial lamb laying its neck on the slaughter stone.

"I can't be a reverend's wife. I can't greet parishioners at the church door or organize charitable events," Lise said between sniffles. "I plan on selling my other boarding house this winter. I'm through with that part of my life. I'm on another path, but I can't tell where it's going."

"Then we go together."

"My journey is with Janek."

"I'm aware."

"But you can't possibly want to take that journey if he's leading. There are signs of darkness along the way. Not just his consuming episodes of darkness, but something much bigger and more terrifying."

His outstretched hand dropped to his lap. "I have to look past my jealousy and understand love's many facets."

"You truly mean it, don't you?"

"I truly mean it."

Lise searched his face. His expression was devoid of any thought but her and that moment in time.

"Christer told me Janek was my destiny." She looked at the box Niklas held in his hand.

He watched in silence as she worked through a dilemma he couldn't understand. She looked into his eyes. Dry tears stained her cheeks.

He took the ring from its box and held it between the thumb and forefinger of his right hand. With courage and confidence, he said, "I want to be a part of your destiny if you have room for me in your heart. Lise Anders, will you marry me?"

Her laughter resembled a sigh of relief. "I'll marry you, Reverend Niklas Arnold, if you swear to me we are of one mind."

"I swear."

Niklas took her left hand and slid the ring onto her third finger. The fabric of their first kiss was made of tenderness and the eventuality of corporeal love.

Janek was in his office trying to organize the piles of paperwork on his desk. He had not anticipated the endless stream of legalities and contracts that came with constructing a hotel. The day to day work of his accounting business was challenge enough, but the hotel business was overwhelming. To make matters worse, today was the first anniversary of his family's death. His mind wandered between the stacks of papers and his family. After a while he said, "To hell with this!" and pushed his chair back from the desk.

He stood up and ran his hands through his well-kept blond hair and massaged his temples. Another headache was threatening like a gathering thunderhead. He was plagued with them. Many times the headaches were accompanied by nausea and jagged bolts of white light in his peripheral vision, which forced him to lie down in a quiet dark place until they passed.

His decision to go home and rest coincided with Emily Hartmann sweeping into his office. She aroused in him a feeling of helplessness, which he despised.

For months, Emily had been playing a game of proximate intimacy, making up reasons for her appearance more or less any place he went. If he was at the hotel construction site, she happened to be on Main Street shopping. When he was at the boarding house, she would breeze in with various excuses up her sleeve to speak with Lise. The last thing he felt like doing today was dealing with Emily.

"Here are the transaction receipts from last week. I'm late bringing them to you because Stephen has me planning a company party and I don't have time to do everything. He's out of town until Friday. I swear I think he has a mistress," Emily said as she dropped a Gladstone bag on the desk.

Janek continued to rub his temples and said nothing.

"Do you have a headache? Sit down and I'll rub your shoulders and neck."

She walked around the desk with a swish and attempted to hook her hands around the back of his neck.

He shrank from her reach. "Please, Mrs. Hartmann, don't do that. I'm fine."

She moved closer and stroked the side of his face with the back of one hand, while the other hand wandered over his chest. "Why do you resist? I won't bite. Don't you find me attractive?"

"I fail to see what that has to do with my headache."

Emily giggled and wrapped her arms around his neck. She whispered in his ear, "Let me make you feel better." Her tongue brushed Janek's earlobe. "You know I would love to share your bed."

He threw her arms off his neck and stepped back, hitting the credenza.

"The grapevine says you haven't tried courting a woman since you arrived in Ferndale a year ago. Why is that? You obviously don't prefer boys."

He clenched his teeth and clutched his hands on the credenza to avoid slapping her face and shoving her across the room.

"Mrs. Hartmann, your behavior is inappropriate. You're a married woman and my client."

She traced the scar on his chin with the tip of her finger. "You've seen for yourself that Stephen neither notices nor cares what I do."

He removed her finger. "*I care* what you do when it involves me. I'm sure there are many men who would be happy to accommodate your wishes."

"That may be true, but *you* are the only man I wish for." She touched her lips to his ear and with breathless words said, "I can see your perfection. You are magnificent in every sense of the word." Her finger traveled back to the scar on his chin. "Apparently you have no interest in any of the women in Ferndale so why not satisfy yourself with me?"

The bell jingled and Abigail entered the office unnoticed. "Leave him alone!"

A look of surprise crossed Emily's face, but she was undaunted. She turned and stepped toward Abigail. "Well, well. It's the bastard half-breed Mexican girl. Don't tell me you're sweet on him."

"He doesn't belong to you!"

"Is that so? I suppose you imagine he belongs to you."

"No, I don't. He…" Abigail saw that Janek was scrutinizing her with his bewitching blue eyes. *No wonder Emily Hartmann is obsessed with him. I feel the same way.*

114

"Did he reject your advances?" Emily said with a smirk. "Are you jealous?"

Abigail's brown eyes flared. She did what Janek had avoided; she slapped Emily across the face. "Don't talk to me like that! Don't call me a bastard and don't assume I behave like a whore!"

Red finger-shaped welts formed on Emily's left cheek. She glowered at Abigail and put a hand to her stinging cheek.

"You harlot! I'll see to it that you're punished for this!"

Emily favored Janek with a sneer and swept from the office, banging the door shut. The bell jingled.

Janek sat in his chair. "Why did you do that?"

"She insulted me!"

"I didn't realize you talked like that."

"I don't talk like that. It just spilled out because I was so angry."

"She's going to cause trouble, but at least you got her out of here. What brings you by?"

"Evan's schooner just arrived at the dock. They brought the glassware and linens for the hotel. A runner is waiting for instructions on what to do with it all."

"Naturally," Janek said with disgust. "Every last thing seems to get done in an accelerated manner. It pushes and pushes."

Abigail knew very well what was pushing at *all* of them. Last November, after his encounter with the shadow in the church courtyard, Janek agreed to let Lise tell Guthrie, Niklas, and Abigail what happened. Janek had referred to the shadow as Erebus after the Greek primordial god of deep darkness and shadows.

All six people, including Evan, had met at the Sullivan house where their conversation wouldn't be overheard. Janek stared through the kitchen window into the backyard while Lise described his abominable encounter with Erebus. He couldn't stand hearing the words, but the thought of having to say those words himself was worse.

He walked into the backyard before Lise finished what sounded like an implausible story. No one was shocked when the tale was told. In fact, Niklas looked as if he had prior knowledge of the incident.

When Abigail went outside to look for Janek, he was gone. His decision to abscond revealed the extent of his torment more than words could portray. It also revealed that he didn't see her as a safe haven where, no matter the circumstances, he had respite. Lise and Evan were his sentinels.

During the past nine months, her relationship with him changed as their friendship evolved, and their lives became intertwined. She tried to accept their platonic relationship, but that acceptance was insurmountable. Now, as Abigail surveyed his paper-littered desk and credenza she thought how it was unlike him to be untidy and unorganized. *He's falling apart,* she concluded.

She said, "I'll have the things for the hotel sent to my house. There's plenty of storage room in the basement."

He closed his eyes and massaged his temples with his fingertips.

"You should go see Doc Mason and get something for your headaches."

"I have and he prescribed laudanum. It helps, but I can't stay focused. I'm struggling as it is to keep my wits about me. That monster hasn't spoken to me for almost nine months, but I can feel its presence all the time."

His hands dropped from his temples to the desktop. He opened his eyes, but he didn't look at her. "It's made time move faster. The hotel should have taken two years to build, but it's almost done. I'm afraid of what's going to happen to us when it gets its way."

"I'm not afraid."

"You should be. My mother died a year ago today. Sometimes I wonder if it killed my family to get to me."

"What makes you say that?"

He put his elbows on the desk and massaged his forehead with his fingertips. His headache was worsening and confusing his thoughts. "I don't know."

"Is it still in the church?"

"Yes."

"Do you think it would leave you alone if you avoided the church?"

The answer to her naïve question made no difference because he was no longer afraid to go inside the church. It was the one place he could find peace and take solace from his dead family's spiritual comforts. Avoidance was not an option.

He stopped rubbing his forehead. "I need to go home. Thank you for taking care of the delivery."

She fought off an intense desire to enfold him in her arms. Between Emily Hartmann's seduction attempt and his tormented pain, she knew that he would recoil from her like an abused animal. She hated Emily Hartmann.

He walked Abigail to the door and then locked the office. He decided to go to the church instead of going home. As he walked through the small yard that led to the church's front stoop, a carriage stopped in front of the church residence house. Janek watched Niklas disembark then walk to the passenger side to help Lise. Her smile was radiant as she stepped from the carriage. Janek saw she was wearing a fashionable new dress. The effect was genteel.

He inhaled a deep breath and exhaled in a controlled manner so he could focus and pull himself together. With his wits gathered, he went to greet them. "Good afternoon. Have you been at Lowery Park?"

"Yes," Lise said. "It's a lovely day for a picnic."

His eyes fell on her ring. Lise knew he wouldn't ask about it out of politeness. She whispered in Niklas' ear, and he nodded.

"I've asked Lise to marry me, and she has accepted."

Despite his pounding headache, Janek felt a sudden rush of happiness and hope. Life was going on as it should, regardless of the shadow's ominous threats and cruel repression. As he offered his hand to Niklas in congratulations, the cat bounded across the side yard. Janek excused himself and went inside the church. The cat followed.

Janek ignored Abigail's suggestion to avoid the church, which led her to believe there was something there that was strong enough to eclipse his fear of Erebus. If that was true, she wanted to find it.

As the afternoon waned and candle-lighting waited, Abigail stood on the front stoop of The First Congressional Church of Ferndale and gathered the fortitude needed to cross the threshold. She was not a congregant and was unfamiliar with the interior of the church. The Sullivans were members of the United Methodist Church.

She opened the door but before she stepped inside, she looked around as if she was a heretic plotting to murder the congregation. She shut the door and waited for her eyes to adjust to the gloom. The long windows, which gleamed and flashed at Janek as he walked up the aisle for the first time, scowled and dared her to do the same. Goose bumps bloomed on her arms.

The large cross behind the pulpit beckoned and reinforced the windows' dare. She loitered in the aisle and stopped to take a hymn book from its rack on a pew. Curious, she opened the book and held it up to catch what little light defused through the windows. The words were difficult to read in the duskiness.

A whisper floated from the pews: *Who are you?*

Her eyes darted from the page in alarm to search the pews within the gloom. *Am I expected to answer?* The fear she denied to Janek lay heavy in her stomach and tightened around her throat.

The sound of enormous wings threshed in the nebulous rafters overhead. A down draft whooshed through the church. She ducked as if a hawk had sailed from the rafters to ensnare its talons in her hair.

She exchanged her fear with her love for Janek. If he could face enigmas, then she could face them too. With her eyes on the cross, she continued up the aisle. Murmuring exhaled from the pews. Abigail stayed the course until she reached the pulpit. The gloom in the church was transitioning to blackness that concealed what or who had bid her to say her name. Her eyes shifted to the last bit of gloom that remained in the windows.

The front door flew open and the doorknob slammed against the wall. The open door framed a large dark form. The form moved up the aisle. Her resolve to remember why she was in the church and that she should remain brave evaporated. She screamed and threw the hymn book at the form.

A voice said, "What?" A light flared in the form's hand, chasing the blackness from the aisle.

"Abby?"

She breathed a loud sigh of relief, "Niklas."

He walked between a row of pews to the gas lamps mounted on the right side wall and lit them. Then he walked up the aisle and set the lantern in his hand on a pew.

"What are you doing here?"

"I thought churches were open to anyone who wishes to pray," she said, defending her presence.

Niklas gave her a doubtful look. "The doors of the Methodist church are open as well. And that doesn't explain why you're here alone in the dark."

There was no point in lying. Perhaps he could help her find what she was seeking. "Are you frightened of…I mean…frightened to be alone in the church?"

"Abby, we all know Janek thinks his tormentor is in this church, but it hasn't made its presence known to me when he's absent."

"I'm not looking for his tormentor. I'm looking for the reason he keeps coming here alone."

"He won't tell you so you came to find out yourself?"

She nodded and looked into his light brown eyes. "I suggested, perhaps, if he avoided the church, Erebus might leave him alone. He acted as if I had said nothing at all."

"You can't help him."

"And you can?"

Niklas grabbed the lantern and walked to the left side of the church. She followed him as he lit each gas lamp.

"Please…you know why he keeps coming back…don't you?"

He lit the last lamp and set the lantern on a pew with a sigh. "I've seen that thing attack him and the aftermath. That's the only reason I know why he returns to this church, and even then, he has circumvented the subject. Lise and Evan know more about his grief than you or I."

Tears welled in her eyes.

"You know his family is dead, and he hasn't found a way to accept that," Niklas said. "Do you understand?"

She shook her head and the tears spilled.

He pulled a handkerchief from his coat pocket and handed it to her.

"I'm speaking to you as a reverend. It's obvious why you're here. He leaves you with more questions than answers, and he doesn't come to you when he needs comforting."

She nodded and wiped her eyes with the handkerchief.

"So you came here seeking some of those answers."

"Yes."

"He's trapped in his own hell, yet he's trying to live a normal life. Be his friend and don't expect anything more in return."

"I can't."

Niklas thought of his love for Lise, and the years he spent waiting for her to reciprocate that love. He knew better than to give Abigail that advice when he was incapable of doing the same. He looked at her tear-stained cheeks and the misery in her eyes.

"You're right Abby. We all have our crosses to bear."

Chapter 18

October 1873

On Wednesday, October 1, 1873, an endless stream of wagons delivered goods to the back service doors of the hotel. Chad Winston inspected the deliveries and shouted orders. His grooming was, as always, impeccable. His brown silk suit and creamy linen shirt were tailor-made. Narrow ankle boots made from kidskin were polished to perfection. Today, the ruby ring he often wore on his right hand was replaced by a dazzling topaz.

Chad had arrived two days before with a crew of workers who specialized in appointing hotels. The hotel hummed with activity as furniture was placed in the lobby, curtains and pictures were hung, and beds and dressers were carried up the grand staircase to the guest rooms.

Lucas and Matt traversed the service hall. The hall ran the length of the back wall between the bar on the far north end and the banquet room on the far south end. The downstairs areas were accessible from the service hall, as was the staff staircase to the second and third floors.

Because of his size, cocksure personality, and skill with a pistol, Matt sometimes worked security jobs in Eureka on special events. Evan used those qualifications to lure Matt from dairy farming and hired him as the head of hotel security. He ensured what was brought into the hotel stayed there.

Janek paced the first floor, releasing nervous energy as he inspected the progress. He passed the grand staircase and the registration desk on his way to the bar. In keeping with the popular medieval Gothic revival theme, twisting vines and fleur-de-lis were carved in the pointed arch of the entryway to the bar. Inside, a massive L-shaped bar was to his right. The imposing twenty-foot-long back bar was empty. When the bar opened for business, glassware and liquor bottles would reflect in the mirrors behind the glass shelves. In front of the bar, there was open floor space for tables and chairs.

Wooden boxes filled with glassware and linens covered the floor space. Abigail was unpacking each box, trying to determine what belonged in the bar and what belonged in the hotel. Mary Kellen, the woman who oversaw Lise's former boarding house on Little River Street, was head of housekeeping. She knelt beside Abigail as they unpacked the boxes and instructed the maids where to take the items.

Abigail glanced at Janek. For a change, her mind was on her task and not on him.

He left the bar and traversed the lobby. Beveled glass panels inlayed on the mahogany double front doors glowed red and yellow in the weak sunlight. From the street, the doors opened into a lobby dressed in elegant furniture, lamps, and ornamental pieces. Parquet floors polished to a high shine were adorned with Oriental rugs. The bottom half of the walls were decorated in raised paneling, and the top half was painted in rich brick red. The long windows were covered with wooden shutters flanked by heavy, red velvet, fringed draperies. An elaborate cut glass gas chandelier hung from the center of the high ceiling.

A man who worked for Chad approached Janek. "Mr. Walesa, Mrs. Anders sent me to tell you that your suite has been prepared. Mr. O'Malley's suite is ready as well."

Janek walked to the registration desk, which was across the lobby from the front doors. The desk was made of mahogany and topped with a long green marble counter that ran between the walls, enclosing the registration area. Behind the desk on the far wall, a worker was installing a large cabinet outfitted with pigeon holes, shelves, and locked storage.

To the right of the registration desk, a wide grand staircase flowed like a lazy river to the first floor landing. An elegant stained-glass window overlooked a baroque sideboard and the landing. From there, the staircase diverged to the left and right in a continuum to the second and third floors.

Janek took the staircase to the rectangular second floor. The guest rooms lined the outside walls and raised dark paneling covered the inside walls. The hallway ran in a continuous path between the guest rooms and the interior walls. Wall-to-wall brown carpet patterned in beige roses and blue irises covered the floors in the hallway and the guest rooms.

After looking through each room, Janek went to the hotel office to fetch Evan. They climbed the staircase to the third floor where the resident suites were located. Lise greeted them in the hallway.

"Niklas brought your things from the boarding house. I was feeling useless with all the activity, so I unpacked for both of you. Come see your new place!" Lise said. She motioned to the doors marked 302 and 304.

They walked through suite 302. The bedroom was furnished with a carved and gilt-incised mahogany poster bedroom set. The heavy armoire, dresser, and four-poster bed commanded most of the attention in the room. Multi-colored horizontal striped wallpaper covered the walls. Floor to ceiling windows flanked the bed and hid beneath navy blue velvet draperies. A separate sitting room branched off to the left of the main bedroom area and a private dressing room branched off to the right.

"Holy shit!" Evan said.

Lise frowned at Evan's expletive.

"I'm sorry, Lise. Which one is mine?"

"Yours is 304. The suites are identical. I'll let you boys settle in."

Evan slapped Janek on the back. "When we have everything up and running, I'm bringing a little party to our new domain in the world."

Their new domain opened for business on October 26, 1873 as the Ferndale Hotel.

One week later, on Sunday, November 2 at five o'clock in the evening, Lise and Niklas were married in the First Congregational Church of Ferndale.

Lucas and Janek served as ushers. Abigail was bridesmaid, much to the disapproval of many of the guests. Guthrie sat in the back of the church grumbling under his breath because Abigail had forced him to attend. The Hartmanns were in attendance, and Emily watched Janek during the entire ceremony. The gray tabby cat crouched unseen beneath the front pew and took advantage of its superior view. Niklas' friend from Eureka, the Reverend Otto Young, conducted the ceremony.

The reception was held in the banquet room in the Ferndale Hotel. The guest services manager and his team prepared everything. Festoons of evergreens and ribbons hung in scallops on the walls. A profusion of white and gold garnishments glittered in the flickering candlelight. Round tables draped in white linen tablecloths were set for dinner. Food piled in bone china serving dishes waited on long sideboards. The wedding cake, flanked by the bride and groom's cake, towered from a lace-draped table adjacent to the wedding party's dinner table.

The corner of the room designated as the location from which Mrs. Arnold would receive her guests was ornamented in traditional extravagance. As the guests arrived, Lucas and Janek escorted them to the receiving area. Etiquette dictated that guests address the bride first, unless they were only acquainted with the groom, in which case they congratulated the groom and were then introduced to the bride. The bride was never congratulated, as it was implied that the honor was conferred upon her in marrying the groom.

The wedding party and Reverend Young were served dinner while the guests filled their plates from the buffet. After dinner and the wedding cake ceremony, the Arnolds waltzed to the first dance of the evening. Guests floated in pairs to the dance floor. Waiters served champagne and drinks. Laughter and music pranced and promenaded among the guests.

The gaiety in the room gave Janek an interlude from the terrors of the past and the dark promises of the future. He didn't dwell on his dead family or Erebus. For a short while, he felt normal. He wanted to enjoy being with his friends as he did when optimism was a part of his life.

He was inspired enough to cross the room and ask Lise to dance. "You look beautiful tonight," Janek said as he placed his hand on her small waist. "Actually, you always look beautiful."

They beheld one another in a mirror image of enchanting blue eyes. Lise glided with Janek through the steps of their waltz. They were wrapped in the arms of an intimacy they would consummate only through friendship. It was their oneness.

"Thank you," Lise said, smiling. "Thank you for rescuing me from a lifetime of grief."

Janek stopped dancing and hugged her with all of his heart and soul. "You have given me everything you have to offer, albeit I was nothing more than a complete stranger. Your generosity and faith has kept me from falling into total despair. These are the darkest days of my life, and you remain my loyal friend."

They realized, with embarrassment, the music had stopped. Their embrace unfolded.

As they walked off the dance floor, Lise said, "Maybe this time next year, I'll be dancing at your wedding. You know Abby is in love with you. She would be mortified if she knew I was letting on, but she'll never have the nerve to tell you."

"I know. I can see it in her eyes."

"Well?"

"I can't...I can't have a relationship. You know that and you know why."

"I'm sorry. I didn't mean..."

"Please don't."

Lise looked into his divine face and made an aphonic promise to let it go.

He offered his arm, and she took it with her delicate hands. Niklas watched them cross the room. His jealousy smoldered until Lise removed her hands from Janek's arm. Niklas marked his territory by putting his arm around her shoulders.

"Your suite is ready. You may go up whenever you like," Janek said. "Please excuse me."

Niklas watched Janek leave the room, and his jealousy reignited. Lise belonged to Janek Walesa, and though Lise was his wife, Niklas was powerless to break that bond. He took her hand and led her to the dance floor.

The Arnolds retired to the honeymoon suite at ten o'clock, ending the wedding reception. Some guests went home while others wandered into the hotel bar. Evan, Lucas, Matt, Guthrie, and Chad were sitting at the bar drinking whiskey when Janek arrived. Abigail and Paulina Slaski, a school friend who lived in Mendocino, chatted and drank champagne at a table. The Hartmanns and the men who comprised The Brothers, Inc. sat at another table. Janek sat beside Evan at the bar.

"You know I've never gotten drunk with Guthrie. He's usually on the other side of the bar, giving me dirty looks all night," Evan said.

Guthrie gave Evan the evil eye and continued drinking his whiskey.

"Shall we sit with Abby and her friend? You were dancing with that girl all night. Don't you think it's rude to ignore her?" Janek said to Evan.

"She's a nice girl, and I'm pretty damn drunk. I'll make a fool of myself. I prefer to be a drunken mess around whores."

"You're right. You're one uncouth bastard when you drink too much," Janek said. He rose from his seat.

Evan slid off his bar stool. "I'm coming."

Janek greeted Abigail and introduced himself to her friend.

"Please sit down," Abigail said. He had paid little attention to her all night. She felt snubbed despite knowing he had not done it on purpose.

Evan flopped into a chair. "I warned Janek. I'm not good company right now. If I say anything offensive, feel free to knock me in the mouth."

Paulina blushed and looked at her hands. She whispered to Abigail, "He's drunk, but he's so cute. I was afraid he had brushed me off!"

Abigail knew Evan *had* brushed Paulina off. If Janek had not come to their table, Evan would still be at the bar.

"Janek, I was telling Paulina your father was from Poland. Her parents are also from Poland," Abigail said.

"Polish people are great!" Evan said in a loud drunken voice. "My friend is Polish!"

Janek elbowed Evan in the side. Paulina giggled. Abigail sighed and rolled her eyes. When she did that, she saw the scowl on Emily's face. If looks could kill, Abigail would have been dead where she sat. Emily leaned in toward her husband and whispered. He shook his head. She appeared to pout. Abigail knew trouble was preparing to make an entrance.

Stephen walked to Abigail's table and said, "Janek, may I have a word with you in private?"

"It's late, and we've all had too much to drink. Can't this wait?"

"Mrs. Hartmann says it can't wait. I think you have an idea of what this is about. I doubt you want to discuss it in front of your friends."

Janek glanced at Evan. Guthrie and Matt and Lucas sauntered to the table.

"If you want to air your dirty laundry in public that's your prerogative, but I'm not discussing anything with you tonight. Perhaps you should go home and talk with Mrs. Hartmann further just to make sure she has her facts straight."

Evan jumped up and said, "Your wife's nothing but..."

Guthrie grabbed his shirt collar. "Shut up, boy. Let Janek handle this."

Stephen ignored Evan and gave Janek a doubtful look. "All right, not tonight, out of respect for the Arnold's wedding. We need to discuss the creamery accounting contract anyway. I'll be in touch."

Everyone seated at the table with The Brothers, Inc. rose and began leaving. Emily gave Janek a piercing look. Stephen grabbed her hand and led her out of the bar.

Chad wandered to the table. "You have real trouble, Janek. That Hartmann woman is on the war path. I'm sure Stephen knows how she behaves, but it's a matter of honor now."

"She's a damn slut," Evan said, swaying on his feet.

"I'd keep that opinion to myself for the time being," Chad said.

Janek left the bar without a word and climbed the grand staircase to his suite. He was exasperated. Emily Hartmann would pursue him until she got what she wanted, just like the hounding shadow. For a moment, he felt self-pity. He wondered what he had done to bring so much perversion on himself.

Janek drove Lise and Niklas to the port on the Eel River the following afternoon. They were taking the schooner to Eureka, and from there, they would catch a steamer ship bound for Sausalito. Evan was going to Eureka to tend to some business he opted to keep from the Arnolds.

When Lise and Niklas were on board the schooner out of earshot, Evan said to Janek, "While I'm gone, Hartmann's probably going to confront you with his wife's filthy lies. It's best I won't be around to beat his face to a pulp."

"He's going to try and ruin me."

"I know. Just watch your back."

"There's something more powerful than Stephen watching my back."

"Aye, just be careful. Listen, I'm bringing a little party back from Eureka. Be ready for booze and women. I swear I don't know how you've gone this long without…"

"I understand."

"One more thing, I'm changing my schedule on the schooner. The captain said I can start working part-time on short runs. That way, I'll be gone for a few days instead of a month. I can do my job managing the hotel and hold onto my sailing days a little longer."

Janek said nothing. He was dependent on Evan, but it would be a mistake to manacle him to a desk. Life on the schooner would be ripped from Evan the day their choices evaporated into the compulsion of another being. Janek could feel that day stalking them like a hungry Minotaur.

"You have one of those headaches don't you?"

"Yes."

Someone yelled from the deck of the schooner, "Evan, you comin' or not?"

"I have to go. I'll be back with some headache relief!"

Janek experienced abandonment as the schooner got underway. The affairs of the hotel would keep him engaged and, with luck, preoccupied until his friends returned. He climbed into the wagon borrowed from Lucas and turned the horse toward town. As he traveled the deserted road, he tried to organize his thoughts around what needed to be done that day. He didn't see the thugs hiding in the woods beside the road.

Two thugs jumped into the back of the wagon. Two others grabbed the horse's bridle and brought it to a stop. A man in the wagon rushed Janek from behind and held a knife to his throat while the other jumped into the seat.

"We got a message from a man who says ya been toyin' with his wife," the thug in the seat said. He held the sharp tip of his knife to Janek's cheek. "He says if ya don't admit to what ya done, we can cut yar pretty boy face into a thousand pieces. Ain't no woman gonna want ya after that."

Dead silence followed. Janek's throbbing headache ignited into blinding white heat. His body shuddered with nausea. The cold knife blade at his throat pressed harder against his windpipe.

"Did ya hear me, smart ass pretty boy? We're gonna cut ya up like a spring pig."

The thug's breath smelled of rotting teeth. Janek's stomach churned, and he vomited on the man holding the knife to his cheek.

The man jumped back in disgust. "What the hell kinda trick is that?"

Janek's blinding headache imprisoned him in agony and confusion. He tried in vain to remember what he had done to provoke Erebus' rage. Hands shoved him sideways. Cold metal pricked his check and pressed against his throat. He couldn't remember the source of those sensations.

"I asked ya a question, pretty boy. What the hell kinda trick is that?"

Janek wiped his mouth with the back of his hand.

"Chuck, cut him!" the thug in the seat said to the one holding the knife to Janek's throat.

As Chuck raised the knife to Janek's face, Janek passed out and fell face first from the wagon onto the dusty road. For a moment, the thugs in the wagon were stunned. The man holding the horse's bridle ran to Janek and rolled him onto his back. He kicked Janek in the ribs and said, "Wake up, ya fucker!"

The two thugs in the wagon jumped to the ground and dragged Janek to a sitting position. They slapped his face.

"Wake up, ya shit hole! Ya ain't gettin' out of this by pretendin' to be sick. A little puke ain't scarin' us off! We're still gonna kill ya!"

Janek couldn't see the men surrounding him let alone speak. If he didn't do something, he was going to die in the dirt like an animal.

But Erebus had no intention of letting Janek die. A frigid wind roared through the trees and over the road with tempestuous force and created a blinding dust storm.

"No one is allowed to touch my love in that manner! Hell will inflict torment upon your souls! You will regret what you have done!"

The rush of words resonated like the drumbeat of deafening thunder. The thugs ran into the woods. The horse whinnied in terror and galloped from the heinous noise.

Erebus' words and the wind evaporated. Janek managed to get to his feet. He took one step and passed out.

When the horse and wagon came back to the general store without Janek, Lucas drove it to the hotel to fetch Matt and Chad.

He found Matt by the back service doors. "Something's wrong! I lent the wagon to Janek so he could take Lise and Niklas to the port. My horse and wagon came back empty. There's puke on the floorboard and the seat. Where the hell is Chad?"

"Slow down!" Matt said. "Chad's in his room packing. He's leaving for Mendocino in a couple of hours."

"Get him and meet me at the front door! Make sure Chad's armed!"

Lucas ran to the wagon and drove it around to the front of the hotel. Matt and Chad ran through the front doors. Chad tucked an old army revolver into the arm holster under his jacket. Lucas whipped the horse into a run down Main Street and toward the port.

They found Janek lying in the road unconscious. The boot prints and vomit and dirt troughs that surrounded his body gave the appearance of a struggle that didn't occur.

Matt walked into the woods.

Lucas put a hand to Janek's chest and said, "He's breathing. Let's get him in the wagon."

Chad and Lucas lifted Janek into the wagon.

"Come look, boys. I found some trash," Matt said. He stood at the edge of the woods.

They followed Matt through the woods to a gully filled with rocks and trickling water. A thug lay in the gully maimed with a broken leg.

"Get away!" the thug said as they approached.

Chad pulled the army revolver from its holster and held it to the thug's forehead. His topaz ring winked golden light when he cocked the revolver. "Did you attack the man who was in that wagon?"

"That shit hole layin' on the road out ther' is crazy. He's possessed by the devil."

"Answer my question," Chad said between clinched teeth.

"Not me! It wer' Chuck and Dirk. I jus' held the horse."

"Who sent you?"

"I ain't never been so scared in my life. The wind started blowin' and that crazy man started talkin'. The sound made my blood curdle. I think Chuck shot hisself in the face. He's over ther'."

"Answer my question or I'll shoot *you* in the face. Who sent you?"

"Jus' shoot me! I ain't never gonna get over the sound of the devil. I ain't never!"

Chad pulled the trigger. They decided to leave the body to rot in the gully. Matt didn't want to be implicated in another murder. He figured Sheriff Tate wouldn't be as lenient this time.

When they returned to the road, Janek was waiting for them.

"Are you alright?" Matt asked.

Janek nodded.

"Did that dead trash heap down there attack you?"

"Yes."

"Did Hartmann send them?" Chad said.

"Yes."

"He was ranting and raving about hearing the devil."

"I'm sure he did hear the devil," Janek said in a dead tone.

Chapter 19

November 1873

Evan bounded through the hotel's double front doors accompanied by two young ladies. He registered them into a suite on the third floor and had a bell hop carry their luggage to the room. When the ladies were settled, Evan went to find Janek.

He was in the hotel office with Guthrie. They were reviewing the terms of a contract to begin construction on a restaurant attached to the bar.

"How was your trip?" Janek said.

"Better than usual; I got my business taken care of and I brought back a treat."

"Your mother's looking for you," Guthrie said without looking up from the contract.

"Did she say what she wanted?"

"Nope. Just that she'd be back around three. You better keep them treats stashed until she leaves."

Evan slapped Guthrie on the back. "Thanks. You're a ton of help."

"You do that again, son, and I'll kill ya."

Evan shrugged and turned to Janek. "Did Hartmann come by?"

"No. I sent a certified letter informing him that I was closing my office on Main Street, and that all business would be conducted here. He hasn't responded."

Janek thought about what happened on the way home from the port. He had asked Lucas and Matt to keep the incident quiet. He wanted to keep it from Evan as long as possible.

"Guthrie, are you working at the Palace tonight?" Evan asked.

"Yep. So is Abby if that's what you're really asking."

"Who's working the hotel bar?"

"That poker buddy of yours, Josef Paullo. Abby hired him part-time."

"I'd better find my mother. Janek, meet me in my suite at six o'clock. We're having dinner there." Evan bounded out the door.

Guthrie stood and stretched his back. "I appreciate you boys having enough respect for my daughter to keep her from seeing what you're up to. I reckon her feelings would be hurt. The contract looks fine to me. I'm heading home for a nap."

Guthrie left Janek alone to ponder Abigail's feelings. He decided to dispense with the thought. They weren't betrothed.

At six o'clock, Janek was groomed and standing at Evan's door. The last woman he had sex with was Sarah Williams on the night of his graduation party. He couldn't believe he was nervous about tonight, but so much had happened since then. It felt like a lifetime ago in an altogether different life.

He knocked on the door.

A smiling young woman with big brown eyes opened the door. "You must be Janek! I'm Cassy! Come in."

Janek gave Cassy a vague smile. Evan and another woman greeted him.

"This is Kate," Evan said, pointing to the other woman.

Kate was a petite redhead with a sweet face. Her eyes roamed over Janek's upper body then came to rest on his face. Tall stature, broad chest, blond hair, blue eyes—he was magnificent.

Dinner was in the sitting room. Janek waited for Kate and Cassy to be seated before he sat at the table. Evan popped the cork on a bottle of wine and poured wine into long stem glasses before taking his seat.

The thought of engaging in polite small talk at dinner made Janek feel nauseated, but the feeling passed. He swallowed his wine in one gulp then reached for the bottle.

"Are you feeling nervous tonight, sugar?" Cassy asked after Janek refilled his wine glass.

Janek looked at her, but said nothing.

"Don't be. Kate and I are really a lot of fun, aren't we, Evan?"

"You bet," Evan said. "The girls know how to play poker. I thought we'd get us a game going after dinner."

Kate also noticed Janek's rate of wine consumption. It was obvious he wasn't going to start a conversation, and she didn't know what to say to this beautiful shy man.

"Janek, tell us a little bit about yourself," Cassy said, noting Kate was tongue tied.

He looked at his plate. *What am I supposed to say? Should I start with the story of my dead family and how I ran like a coward all the way to California? Maybe recount the delusional dark soul that will, in time, turn me into some being that I can't even imagine? What about the tale of Emily Hartmann and the trouble she has caused?* After a long pause, he realized Cassy and Kate were looking at him with anticipation. Evan seemed more interested in his food and whiskey shots than Janek's impending reply.

"I'm sure Evan has told you something about me."

Cassy said, "He told us you're from Oregon, you have an advanced degree in accounting, and you own the primary share of this hotel except for the land."

Janek sighed with relief. Evan had stuck to the superficial facts.

Kate and Cassy filled the conversational void Janek had created. Evan took up part of the void when he realized his friend couldn't and wouldn't talk much until he got drunk. After several more glasses of wine and a few tequila shots, Janek did unwind and relax.

After dinner, a bellhop arrived to remove the dishes and outfit the table for poker. Evan dealt the cards.

"Janek, this is seven-card stud. The loser of each hand has to take off a piece of clothing. Are you in?"

"I'm in."

Janek grabbed the tequila bottle from the table and started to pour a shot for Kate. Her hand hovered over the mouth of the shot glass. She managed to make eye contact as she reached for the bottle. Her tongue traced the lip of the bottle, and then she slid the bottle's neck into her mouth. She slid the bottle from her mouth, sipped the tequila, handed it back to him, and said, "We share."

Kate had succeeded in getting his full attention. Janek leaned over and kissed her hard on the mouth. Her jaded preconceived notions about lust and desire had all been lies. Arousal's luminescent desire ignited her passion. She reached for him, but he let their kiss die. Their eyes met.

Deep within his blue eyes she sensed his unspoken resonating mind. His mere presence made her feel ashamed of who she was and how she lived her life. She was incapable of meeting the standards he would expect when courting a woman. For the first time in her life, she realized her choices had ruined her chance to have a man as exquisite as Janek Walesa. No matter whom she yearned for, wistful longing would break her heart in the long run.

As the night wore on, the poker game became tiresome. By nine o'clock, Cassy and Evan had lost their clothing. They were in Evan's bed making unashamed erotic noise.

Kate opened another bottle of tequila and sat beside Janek on the floor. "Why are you laying down here, handsome?"

His inhibitions had disappeared with his clothes. He was so drunk that he had no idea why he was laying on the floor.

Kate straddled his hips with her naked thighs. She kissed his neck. Her tongue traced down his chest to his waist, then it licked the head of his cock. Her lips encircled his rising hard-on, and she took it in her mouth a little at a time until she felt it touch the back of her throat.

Janek pushed her off and managed to stand without swaying. He took her hand and led her to his suite. He lay back on his bed. She slid her naked body on top of him. He held her face in his hands and realized he was starving for human touch and affection.

She gazed down at his angelic face and said, "You don't know how beautiful you are, do you?"

Her question penetrated his tequila-fogged mind and caught him by surprise.

"You're a pure and gentle soul," she said, quickening her avidity to understand what lay in his psyche. "Has no one desired you so much that they can't live without you?"

He placed a finger on her lips and shook his head.

She squeezed and stroked his erection. Janek's moans were loud and wet. Her touch was his whole world—a place where self-control didn't exist. Kate cried out as she felt his exhilaration build. She wouldn't let him have an orgasm without experiencing the rapture herself. She rolled off him and onto her back. He rolled on top of her and got to his knees.

In her eyes, he was an angel hovering over her body, bending to kiss her lips. His tongue searched for hers, and she gave it willingly. Her kiss fulfilled Janek's lust for human affection.

He spread her legs apart with his knees, lowered his hips and thrust his cock inside her. He fucked her hard and fast. The euphoria she felt was overwhelming. Their orgasms exploded simultaneously, and she screamed his name.

IV

The Passing

Chapter 20

November 1873

J anek was in the lobby speaking with some of his guests when Stephen came into the hotel. Matt intercepted him before he could approach Janek.

"Can I do something for you, Mr. Hartmann?" Matt said, trying to control his temper.

"I need to see Janek. Tell him I'm here. I'll wait in his office."

Janek saw Stephen. He nodded at Matt and excused himself from his guests.

When they entered the office, Janek said, "Matt, I would appreciate it if you stayed."

Stephen said, "The contract between you and The Brothers, Inc. has expired. We won't need your services in the future."

The contract with the creamery had not expired, but Janek had no intention of arguing the point. He had anticipated this and had packed up Stephen's belongings. He went into the back office and retrieved from the safe a Gladstone bag filled with accounting records.

Janek handed the bag to Stephen and said, "You owe me two weeks salary. I expect payment now."

Stephen snickered. "You owe me for what you've done to my wife. This hotel is doing well, but I can change that. I would hate to have to waste my time ruining your reputation. However, in lieu of that, I would accept a public apology to Mrs. Hartmann."

"Your wife is not the one who has been fouled, and you know it."

"She said you've been speaking to her and touching her inappropriately since we arrived in town."

"None of that happened."

Stephen took a step toward Janek. "Are you saying my wife is a liar?"

Matt took a step toward Stephen. "Take your things and go, Mr. Hartmann."

"I'm not through with you, Walesa. Mark my words; you *will* make this right."

Matt and Janek escorted Stephen from the hotel.

"He's not gonna give up until he gets satisfaction," Matt said. "Maybe I should rough him up. His bad manners are getting old."

"I don't think that's..."

There was a sudden loud commotion outside on the street.

"You son of a bitch, I'll kill you!"

Janek and Matt ran through the hotel front doors.

Stephen was lying face down in the muddy street.

"Get up, you bastard, and face me!"

Stephen pushed himself out of the mud and stood to face Evan. Janek and Matt reached the perimeter of the surrounding crowd.

Abigail, who heard the noise from inside the bar, ran out of the hotel.

Evan grabbed the front of Stephen's mud-slicked vest and jerked him in close to his face. "You thought I wouldn't find out what you did because you knew Janek wouldn't tell me!"

Stephen shoved Evan. "Don't touch me, you dirty drunken Mick!"

Janek and Matt shouldered their way through the crowd. Janek caught Evan by the arm and yelled, "Stop it!"

Evan jerked his arm from Janek's hand. "Like hell I will! Why didn't you tell me this bastard tried to have you killed? I overheard Sheriff Tate talking to Doc Mason. Some lowlife tried to off himself yesterday. When they brought him in to see Doc, the scum ranted about seeing and hearing the devil on the road to the port. He asked to see the sheriff and confessed what he was doing there. Hartmann hired him and three other lowlifes to kill you!"

Evan lunged at Stephen and jabbed him in the stomach, then left hooked him in the jaw. Stephen doubled over and staggered sideways. Evan repeatedly pummeled him in the face, dogging Stephen as he stumbled.

Janek and Matt attempted to restrain Evan, but he was crazy with rage and hard to handle.

Abigail pushed her way through the crowd and managed to get close enough to elicit Evan's attention. "Stop it! If you kill him they'll hang you!"

Evan stopped struggling and looked at her.

"We kept Janek's assault from you for this very reason. You can't lose your head."

Evan shrugged Janek and Matt off. He gave Abigail a sideways glance, then pointed at Stephen. "You're going to pay, Hartmann. That slut wife of yours is going to pay too. You haven't seen the last of this dirty Mick."

Evan spit in the muddy street and looked at Abigail. "Are you happy now?"

She nodded.

Evan gave Stephen a vicious look, and then headed toward the Palace.

Stephen panted. Blood smeared his face. He pulled his bag out of the mud and tried to gather his dignity.

Abigail saw Janek walking down Main Street in the opposite direction of the hotel. She caught up with him. "Where are you going?"

Janek stopped and looked at her. "I'm going to the church."

Abigail's eyes filled with tears.

"I'm sorry, Abby. I can't give you what you want. You and I might have had a chance if…" Janek wiped the tears from her eyes. He pulled her into his arms and kissed her with strength and passion. Then, he turned and walked to the church.

It was there, waiting for him. At last it was ready to leave its vaporous world and join the human being it worshipped. But something had gone wrong over the past year as it prepared for this day. Its energy had turned to ferocity.

Its love had evolved into selfishness. The joy and happiness it had promised was forgotten, replaced by a lust for sadistic control. It gained unexpected pleasure from the constant perverse pain it inflicted on Janek. The perversion eased its jealousy and made it feel powerful. It felt strong enough to take everything he desired.

For all that the brash volatile soul believed in its own strengths, it had underestimated Janek's tenacity. It had not tested the exertion it would need to find the doorway to his inner self. It believed a soul devoid of direction and happiness was also devoid of determination and fortitude. Worst of all, it had not considered the delicate nature of the physical being, that Janek's body may not be able to withstand the torment of the joining.

Janek stood on the church front stoop. The sun was setting. A gentle breeze absconded through the trees, rustling the leaves. He shuddered.

"Father, please be here."

He opened the door and stepped into hell.

It was freezing in the church. He exhaled gossamer puffs of frost. The gas lamps burned and flickered, casting presaged illusionary flames on the walls. Unexpected trepidation caused him to linger at the threshold. He faltered before sitting in the first pew facing the pulpit.

"Father, are you here? Liv? Mother?"

Silence.

"Please, answer me!"

A reticent divinatory damnation answered and sudden dread paralyzed his immediate instinct to flee from the heinous soul he knew was in the church.

"They are not here, Janek."

He cringed at the abhorrent sound of his name.

"Father, answer me! I know you're here!"

"They have never been here. It has always been me."

Janek winced, but he stood his ground and said, "You're a liar!"

"I tried to provide you with the solace you needed from your family. If you found them here, I knew you would stay."

"You used my grief and my weaknesses to entice me?"

"I gave you comfort."

"You trapped me!"

"We are both trapped."

"You can't keep me a prisoner any longer. I need to be free to choose my own path and fulfill my own desires."

"Like you did with that whore? She experienced your transcendence. I will not allow that ever again."

"You will not allow it? You have no right to tell me what I can and cannot do!"

"You are my possession. Therefore, I have the right."

Janek stood up and looked at the cross on the wall behind the pulpit. *Is this thing so strong that God cannot stop it? Does God even know it exists?* he wondered.

"I killed the holy men who tried to take you from me through baptism."

Erebus' statement was so appalling that he couldn't help but wonder if it was true. His parents never talked about his baptismal rite. *Were they so afraid of what had happened that they couldn't speak of it? No! It is trying to vex me with delusions.*

He stepped into the aisle. The front door seemed distant and out of reach. *Leave the church through the vestibule,* he thought. *Take one small step backward; then turn around and run.*

"Why do you think you can escape me?"

"I don't know who you are!"

"I have told you who I am."

Janek took a step backward. "You've told me nothing."

"I am heaven's forgotten creation, an unrequited soul who has never been given a human life. I have yearned for your perfection, for your arrival. You are the soul I should have been—untarnished and virtuous. We were predestined to mate. You are my long lost love."

"We are not lovers! I loathe you!"

"That will change when you feel my spiritual being intertwine with yours. You know this is our time. Tonight, we will copulate."

"I won't let you!"

"You have not been strong enough to stop me thus far. As I destroy your desires, I will heal mine."

Janek sensed revolting spiritual tentacles twisting and slithering toward his soul and when they reached it, he would go insane. He screamed at his psyche; *For the love of God, run!* White heat burst into flames inside his head and blinded him. It knocked the wind out of him, and he gasped to breathe.

Abominable shrieking permeated the church and made his ears bleed. He tried to cover them with his hands, but something wrapped around his wrists and yanked his hands from his ears.

"Give yourself to me!"

A demoniac roar coalesced the shrieking.

He turned to run to the vestibule, but fell and gashed his forehead on a pew. Blood flowed from the deep wound into his eyes and down his face.

The spiritual tentacles were getting closer, dragging with them the rancid smell of Erebus' putrid lust. Janek's sanity was evanescing. There were few precious minutes left. He reached for the back of the pew and struggled to his feet. Without hesitation, he ran toward a destination he could not see. Something intercepted him and slapped his face so hard that he fell to his knees.

He was shoved onto his back. Anguish plummeted from its perch among the dark rafters, falling fast and then soaring low. Its razor sharp talons lacerated his chest and stomach, ripping his vest and shirt and the skin beneath to ribbons. Pain hurled him into the flames of hell, and he battled to stay conscious. He threw his arms up to shove anguish away, but his hands struck only vaporous rage. He pushed backward along the floor with the heels of his boots, rolled onto his stomach, and got to his knees.

His arms were kicked out from under him. His face was slammed into the floor. Anguish circled around and plunged its talons into his back, shredding it from shoulders to waist. The pain was excruciating. He screamed and fought to hold on to consciousness.

Anguish flew to the rafters, supplanted by a demoniac roaring leviathan that crushed his body to the floor, snapping his ribs and incinerating his lungs. He couldn't move under the weight of its barbaric and ravenous desire. The blinding incandescent inferno in his head flashed as he suffocated. Pressure detonated in his chest and erupted into searing agony. He knew dying would be painful, but he had not expected this horrendous suffering. His tears dropped to the floor one after another in a steady stream.

The annihilating leviathan suddenly stopped crushing him. Janek panted and with herculean effort stood up. He couldn't rationalize what was happening, let alone understand how to escape the hell of his conflagrant mutilation.

Anguish hurtled downward. Its powerful open talons seized Janek and threw him high up against a wall. His head struck a gas lamp. He ricocheted off the wall and plunged to the floor. He broke his left leg and arm on impact. The gas lamp exploded and shot flames upward and outward.

The groping spiritual tentacles snaked up his legs. Some twisted around his thighs and slithered over his crotch while others reached to stroke his chest and touch his face. His broken limbs made it impossible for him to escape their probing putrid lust.

Erebus and its minions renewed their assault. Blinded and mutilated, Janek had one last lucid moment before his sanity vanished. He knew he was dying by crucifixion, and he begged his father to come for him.

Chapter 21

Abigail ran into the Palace, sobbing and screaming unintelligible words. Sweat and tears drenched her face. She ran behind the bar, grabbed Guthrie by the hand, and dragged him into the street. Evan ran after them. The air outside was heavy with the smell of burning wood. He looked skyward. Orange light flamed within the smoke that rushed and swirled above the treetops.

"It's the church. Janek is in there!"

Abigail ran toward the church. Evan and Guthrie ran after her.

The volunteer fire department was trying to control the fire. Flames shot from the windows and licked the wood siding off the outer walls. Hot embers blew in every direction, catching the surrounding grass and trees on fire. A burning Douglas fir tree fell onto the roof of the church residence house. There was a loud whoosh as the house caught fire. A wide stream of fire burst through the church roof and climbed the steeple.

When Evan arrived, the shock of seeing the fire and feeling its heat caused him to hesitate, but Abigail kept running toward the church, screaming Janek's name. Guthrie reached her before she got to the walk leading to the church's front stoop. He tackled her, and they both fell with a grunt.

Evan jerked Guthrie and Abigail to their feet and dragged them across the street before they caught fire from the blowing embers. Evan clenched Abigail's upper arm with his hand. She tried to break free.

Guthrie said, "You can't help him if he's in there. Do you think he'd want you to die trying?"

Abigail kept screaming for Janek.

Evan grabbed her shoulders and shook her. "Did you hear what your father said? Answer me!"

"Yes, I heard, and I don't care!"

"Listen to me, Abby! If Janek's dead, that thing that's been pursuing him can't hurt him anymore. Didn't you see what it was doing to him, to us?"

Abigail cried harder.

Guthrie hugged her to him. "She ain't gonna try to run. Go help them put out the fires."

When Evan reached the fire brigade, he saw Lucas and Matt throwing ineffectual buckets of water on the flames. The church was reduced to a skeleton that mocked life before its bones crumbled to dust. From above, he heard fracturing and snapping. He looked up to see the steeple bend sideways. It plummeted to the ground like a missile, the bell inside clanged as it fell. It exploded on impact, flinging chunks of burning wood like cannonball-sized shrapnel.

Someone said, "The roof's getting ready to go!"

The firefighters backed away. Evan prayed to a God he no longer believed in, that his friend wasn't in the church. The roof fell in with a roaring crash and detonated a fusillade of flames, sparks, and debris. Then, the rest of church succumbed to its final destruction and collapsed to the ground.

As the dark of night was banished by the dawn, a group of exhausted firefighters surveyed the incinerated remains in the light of the rising sun. Smoke rose from the smoldering rubble like wraiths portending death. Evan wiped his grimy face with his grimier sleeve. Abigail and Guthrie stood behind him, their clothes drenched in ash-caked sweat. The realization that Janek had to have died in the fire clung to them like the remnants of a bad dream.

The gloom blanketing the churchyard was disturbed by the arrival of a carriage. Niklas and Lise disembarked. The driver removed their luggage from the top of the carriage then moved on. Niklas scanned the devastated church and residence house. A surviving hymn book lay at his feet. He picked it up and flipped through the singed pages as if they held answers to the cause of the fire.

"This is my fault," Lise said.

Niklas tossed the hymn book to the ground.

"No it's not. This is a part of our destiny. I won't deny this hurts, but as long as we're together, we can get past it. Let's go talk to Evan. I see him standing over there."

As Lise and Niklas approached Evan, they saw exhaustion on his face and deep furrowed lines on his brow. Fear overcame Lise. Abigail, Guthrie, Lucas, and Matt were among the small crowd of people who stood in the churchyard. Janek was absent. She prayed he had gone home.

"Evan…where's Janek?" she asked, terrified of his answer.

Abigail began to cry.

Evan didn't think his voice would cooperate and say the words. He swallowed hard. "He was in the church when the fire started last night. No one has seen him since."

Lise buried her face in Niklas' chest and sobbed. He wrapped her in his arms and stroked her hair.

"Are you sure he was in the church?" Niklas said, looking toward the smoking rubble.

"No, but he's missing. Abby was the last person to see him. Right before sunset, he told her he was going to the church. The fire broke out less than an hour later."

An unexpected sound rose from the cemetery. The gray tabby cat was sitting on top of a mausoleum. He lamented a loud and drawn out meow.

"I'll get him," Evan said. "He's probably as shaken up as the rest of us."

He climbed the steps to the cemetery and reached to pick up the waiting cat. The cat hopped to his feet and ran further into the cemetery. When he saw Evan wasn't following, the cat stopped and meowed. A cold shiver ran up Evan's spine. He ran wildly toward Christer Anders' gravesite.

Janek was lying on the ground beside the grave. His broken arm was flung in a bent and twisted position behind his back. His snapped tibia had punctured his leg, leaving horrible tatters of skin and tendons in its aftermath. The few threads of what was left of his clothing were stuck to the dried blood covering his body.

Evan dropped to his knees. He said in a whisper, "Oh Jesus. What did it do to you?"

He touched Janek's hands. They were ice cold. He tried in vain to hear the rhythm of a heartbeat or the gentle sigh of breathing.

Fury propelled him to his feet. He punched the air with fisted hands.

"Show yourself, you piece of shit!"

Silence.

"Come on, you son of a bitch!"

Evan's demands were answered by Lise screaming, "What's wrong?"

He saw Niklas and Abigail first. Lise, Lucas, Matt, and Guthrie followed. All six people stopped short and gasped. Abigail screamed, "JANEK!" and started to drop beside him.

Evan grabbed her by the wrist and jerked her back. "Don't touch him! I'm taking him to the hotel."

Niklas took off his coat and held it out to Evan. "Matt and I will help you. Wrap this around him as tight as you can before you move him. You'll hurt him more if you aren't careful."

Evan took the coat. They wrapped it around Janek, and then they helped Evan lift his friend into his arms. Matt ran ahead to ensure the hotel service door was unlocked. Then he ran to fetch Doc Mason and Sheriff Tate.

Lise looked upon Christer's grave. She wondered if he had anything to do with Janek's rescue from the church fire.

Amidst the staring townspeople, as if in a reverse funeral procession, Abigail, Guthrie, Niklas, Lise, and Lucas followed Evan as he carried Janek through the streets of Ferndale.

When they reached the hotel, Evan laid Janek on his bed in suite 302. Lise lit the gas lamps and closed the drapes. Matt arrived a few minutes later, followed by Doc Mason.

"He's still alive," Doc Mason said as he removed the stethoscope earpieces from his ears. "I can barely make out his pulse and heartbeat. He's lost a tremendous amount of blood. I've never seen anyone beaten and filleted like this in all my years as a doctor. It's almost...unbelievable."

"I want you to fix him," Evan said.

"It will be a miracle if he lives through the day."

Sheriff Tate knocked on the suite door and let himself in. He went to Janek's bedside and stared at him for a minute before he said, "Is he dead, Doc?"

"No, but he won't survive much longer."

"It looks like someone tried to beat him to death, but those horrible lacerations on his chest look like he was mauled by an animal. The word around town is he died in the church fire. He isn't burned. Who's gonna tell me what really happened?"

Guthrie said, "I reckon you should ask Stephen Hartmann. That lowlife tried to have him killed a few weeks ago."

"That's hearsay. I can't arrest a man on the word of a raving suicidal criminal."

"It ain't hearsay. You didn't bother to follow up on that lout's confession did you, Dell?"

"Guthrie, I…"

"You got a good look at that boy. He wasn't just beat up. He was shredded. You got someone else in mind who might have a reason to do that?"

Sheriff Tate looked at everyone in the room. No one moved or said a word. "You might have a point. I'm sure most of you are tired after the night you've had. I want each of you to come by my office sometime tomorrow so I can take your statements."

The sheriff turned to leave then thought better of it. "By the way, Lucas and Matt, I suspect you know what Guthrie's referring to. The bodies of some known thugs were found in the woods off the road to the port. It looks like they shot themselves in the face. We can talk about that when I see you."

Lucas and Matt didn't respond.

"One more thing, I'm really sorry about Janek. He's a good man."

The minute the sheriff left, Evan said, "Get started, Doc. He needs a lot of attention."

The doctor sighed and said, "He's going to lose more blood if I set his broken arm and leg, and it's going to hurt something awful because I have no chloroform or ether. Let's leave him in peace."

Horror crossed Abigail's face, "Are you saying he's going to die no matter what you do?"

This wasn't the first time Doc Mason had to tell friends and loved ones it was futile to do anything but let his patient die in peace. He thought he had made it clear that Janek was dying. He didn't want to have to repeat it. Evan O'Malley's fury was daunting.

"Answer my daughter's question," Guthrie said.

Doc Mason's eyes darted around the room before moving back to look Abigail in the eye. "Yes, that's what I'm saying."

Evan's face turned red with rage. "Do what a doctor's supposed to do and fix him!"

"You aren't listening…"

"Do it!"

Doc Mason saw no point in continuing the argument. "All right, I need some things from my office." He scribbled out a list and handed it to Lucas. "Go fetch these items from Mrs. Mason. She's in the office."

Evan said, "He'll need morphine."

"Morphine is a precious commodity. If he comes around, I'll bring it to him."

"Get it!"

Lucas handed the list to the doctor. Doc Mason wrote morphine on it and handed it back.

"We'll need clean towels and sheets. Let's get the blood washed off him so I can better assess his injuries."

"I'll get them," Abigail said, fighting off hysteria. She was afraid Janek would die while she was gone, but she couldn't stay there and do nothing.

Lise saw Abigail's emotional battle as her own hysteria wrapped its hands around her throat. She took Abigail's hand and said, "I'll go with you. Now look at me." She forced Abigail to look at her by putting a finger under her chin. "We will not allow hysteria to become a distraction. Agreed?"

Abigail bit her bottom lip and nodded.

They began the grueling task of patching together Janek's ruined body.

Guthrie went into the sitting room. He wasn't leaving until his daughter was ready to go home. Matt didn't know what to do so he followed Guthrie. Lise and Evan helped Doc Mason wash the blood from Janek's body. Lucas and Abigail made round trips to the kitchen to refill the basins with water from the pump.

On their fifth trip to the kitchen, Lucas gave up his effort to appear stalwart. "You and Evan know what happened to him don't you?"

Abigail avoided looking at him. She knew if she spoke, the remains of her hysteria would coil around her and squeeze her to death.

"I heard Evan cussing and screaming at something in the cemetery when he found Janek. I could tell by the look on your faces you weren't that surprised to find Janek there; you were more surprised by the condition of his body. Matt and I have been friends with Evan since we were little kids. He's been over protective of Janek while shutting us out of whatever this is."

She managed a mute look at him.

"I've seen a change in you too. You're in love with Janek."

It was a brazen thing for him to say, but it was a truth she couldn't deny. She looked away and wiped at her eyes.

When Abigail and Lucas returned to the suite with clean water, Doc Mason asked everyone to come to Janek's bedside so he could issue a warning about setting Janek's broken bones.

"He's going to scream and try to pull away from me. We can't let him. It will make things worse and take longer. If any of you have the guts to pin him down while I do this, I'll need your help. The same goes for when I have to stitch up his forehead and his leg."

Matt was at his best when physical strength was required. This was something he could do to help. He gave the doctor a nod.

Niklas followed suit.

Doc Mason caught Evan staring at him with disapproval. "Yes, I'll give him morphine, if he can swallow it."

"Maybe we should leave him in peace like Doc Mason said," Lise said to Evan. "I don't think any of us are prepared for this. Can you in all honesty witness his unbearable pain while he's being restrained?"

"When I was in the army, I seen and heard the screams of men whose broken bones were set without anesthesia or morphine. It ain't something I want to see or hear again," Guthrie said. "You ain't never gonna be prepared, Lise."

Abigail put a hand to her mouth to suppress a hysterical outcry; her pact with Lise forgotten, she fled to the sitting room.

"If he survives and his bones aren't set, he'll be a crippled freak," Evan said. "Can you carry that around for the rest of your life, Lise, knowing we didn't do all we could for him? Do you think I want to watch this anymore than Abby?"

"You best make up your mind right now, son. I'm gonna go sit with Abby."

Lise shook her head in response to Evan's lingering question.

Evan gave Doc Mason a nod.

Janek couldn't swallow the morphine, and he didn't scream or struggle. It was as if he no longer occupied his body.

Three grueling hours later, the doctor announced he had done all he could. "I guess it's in God's hands now," he said as he packed up his medical bag.

"Do you think God let this happen, and now he's going to make amends by saving his life?" Niklas said with disgust.

"Reverend, I don't know what to think. I'm leaving. I'll return in a few hours to check on him."

When Doc Mason was gone, Evan said, "Everyone get some rest. I'm going to do the same. None of us will be any good to him if we're exhausted. Lise, will you stay?"

"Of course, but I want to know what this has to do with Stephen Hartmann."

"Hartmann's slutty wife accused Janek of molesting her. Four thugs jumped Janek on the road to the port the day you and Niklas left for your honeymoon. They had a message from Hartmann. Lucas, Matt, and Chad found Janek in the road passed out. They also found one of the thugs injured and begging to be shot. Chad obliged him."

"And Hartmann threatened him yesterday afternoon when he came in to pull the creamery contract," Matt said.

"Stephen Hartmann didn't do this to Janek, and you know it," Lise said.

"Does it matter?" Evan said. "He's guilty as hell of trying to kill him. He'll go after Janek again."

Lise swallowed hard and chased away her tears. "Let Stephen hang. I don't care. But we have to face what really happened. That monster tried to join with Janek last night. It tore him apart because he fought it."

Evan ran a hand across his mouth and exhaled. "Yes."

Abigail slept in the chair beside Janek's bed. Niklas and Lise slept in suite 308. Lise had sold her remaining boarding house two days before Niklas and she married. They were left homeless when the church residence house burned to the ground. Evan was in the sitting room in Janek's suite with Matt and Lucas. They had bathed and slept. Tonight, they were keeping vigil, drinking whiskey and talking.

"Matt and I need to know what's really happening," Lucas said to Evan. "We got the feeling Lise was talking about ghosts this morning, but that's not it is it?"

Evan looked at their anxious faces. He hesitated for a moment, and then said, "It's not ghosts. It's insanity. At least that's what Janek thought at first. He thought he was going insane."

"I'm not following."

Evan paced the sitting room. He was thoughtful for a long time before he stopped and said, "Do you believe in God, Lucas?"

"Yes."

"You believe in him even if you can't see him, right?"

"Yes."

"You can feel his presence, his power, right?"

"Sometimes."

"Do you think there are unseen forces out there powerful enough to punch a hole into our world?"

Lucas looked uncomfortable. "I know the answer to my question isn't going to be something I want to hear so get on with it."

Evan took a long swallow of whiskey. "Janek calls it Erebus, for a Greek god of darkness and shadow. I guess you learn that kind of thing in college. It's been pursuing him since he was a baby. It wants to be part of his body and soul. It's imprisoned and persecuted him. Erebus made itself known to me, but I don't know what it is."

"Does Janek know what it is?"

"I don't know."

"Those thugs were carrying on about hearing and seeing the devil," Matt said. "Do you think they were right?"

"Listen to what I'm saying! Our friend is dying because something we can't explain or control hungers for him. It'll stop at nothing to have what it wants. I'm afraid it'll pull us to the edge of eternity if that's how long it takes to join with Janek."

"I'm sorry, Evan," Matt said. "This is hard for us to get our minds around."

Lucas shot his whiskey and set the glass on the table beside his chair. It was his turn to pace the room. "I wouldn't have asked you the question if I had no intention of believing your answer. I've known you my whole life, Evan. You don't make up stories. You're not scaring me off this easily. I'm staying to help look after him."

"Same here," Matt said.

"You're both as stubborn as I am. You have to know that you may be on the outside right now, but…if it changes its mind and wants you…"

"We're trapped," Lucas said. "We've been forewarned."

Abigail's soft sweet voice floated into the sitting room. "I won't leave you."

The men abandoned their whiskey and went to Janek's bedside. She put a finger to her lips to keep them quiet. Janek stirred and whimpered like a newborn kitten.

She wetted a washcloth in the basin on the nightstand, and then wiped the sweat from his lacerated, bruised, and swollen face. He hushed. She motioned for them to follow her into the sitting room.

In the dim light, Abigail saw the change in their demeanor.

"You told them," she said to Evan.

"They have a right to know. They're his friends, too."

"Lucas tried to ask me about it this morning, but I couldn't..." She covered her lips with her fingertips. It didn't matter. Keeping Janek alive was the only thing that mattered.

"He's running a fever," she said. "We have to get him to take the pills Doc Mason gave me for fever. And he's dehydrated. He'll die if we don't get him to drink some water. Evan, I want you to try to rouse him. I know he's going to be in a lot of pain if he wakes up, but this has to be done."

Evan looked doubtful, but he agreed.

Abigail poured a glass of water from the pitcher beside the basin on the nightstand. "Call his name and pat his hand, and when he responds, even in the slightest way, hold up his head."

Evan took Janek's right hand in his. "Janek, wake up. Abby says you need to drink some water. Try to wake up."

He patted Janek's hand and repeated those words for five minutes before Janek stirred and moaned. Abigail managed to get the pills down Janek's throat before he screamed in pain. Evan let go of his hand and jumped to his feet.

She stroked Janek's hair and said, "It's all right. It's all right."

"If he wakes up we're giving him morphine. I'm not going to let him suffer. He's suffered enough. I should've been there for him. I should've helped him die in the cemetery. He'd be better off dead."

Evan's hysterical words led him to do something he had avoided his entire adult life: he cried in the presence of another person.

Abigail pulled Evan into her arms. "You've loved and protected him from the first day he came to us. You've been his friend, the brother he never had. You've helped him in every way a man can help another."

"I failed Janek, and I failed my father."

"Your father can't accept you for who he *thinks* you are. He hasn't bothered to look beyond the obvious to see the wonderful man you've become."

Evan took a deep breath, stopped his weeping, and wiped his face with his hands. "I need a drink."

She looked into his green eyes. They were clouded with fear and doubt. "You didn't fail anyone. He needs you and you're here. That's all you can do for now."

"Abby, we don't know who or what he's going to be when he wakes up. His lack of response when Doc set his broken bones was unnatural. I have to think of a way to get us out of this nightmare."

"It isn't going to let you. It's cruel and vengeful. It will only hurt him more and punish the both of you."

Evan knew what he was risking, but he had to try.

Chapter 22

Abigail and Lise battled Janek's raging fever. Doc Mason came to the suite several times a day to check on his patient. Some of Janek's wounds festered, oozing blood and puss onto his bandages and bed sheets. Fever racked his body with cold chills and hot flashes. His unconscious mind was rampant with delirium.

In his incoherent world, Erebus imprisoned him in St. Mary's Episcopal Church in Albany, Oregon. It raped and demoralized him in its perpetual attempt to join their souls. Terror and agony transmuted into grotesque living creatures that played a continual game of hide and seek, which kept Janek confused and afraid. Anguish brandished its talons each time he tried to find a way to escape the church.

Something unexpected was there, too. A temptress, with auburn hair and eyes to match, prowled the nave and sanctuary, the sacristy and robing rooms, and the pews. Her minions, perversion and lust, followed her down the center aisle like bridesmaids in a wedding procession.

"I can smell you, Janek!" she said, her voice resounding in the quiet church. "I can smell your semen and your blood."

He recognized her voice.

"I'm going to lick the blood from your ruined body."

Janek couldn't sort out what horrified him more: Erebus or the temptress.

"Why do you resist? Don't you find me attractive?"

He felt perversion and lust coming closer and closer. He didn't know where to hide or which way to run.

"I know what you're thinking, but your body is too broken to run from me. I'll suck the semen from your cock before I eat it. Wouldn't you like that?"

Abrupt shrieking drowned out the temptress' voice.

"You will not touch him in that manner!"

Janek realized he was standing between rows of pews. He looked toward the front of the church. There seemed to be no impediment between where he stood and the front doors. He ran between the pews, and then turned to run up the aisle. The demoniac roaring leviathan tackled him from behind and fell on top of him as he hit the floor. His spine snapped before his bones pulverized.

His family was not there to greet him as he passed through the veil between life and death. He was confused by his new surroundings. Continuous towering walls of hedges suggested that he was in a maze, and within that maze, a chimera of his own making roamed the pathways. It hissed and roared and cawed from somewhere in the dark of the maze, hidden amid sharp corners, serpentine turns, and spiral twists. If he couldn't find a way out, the chimera would tear his soul from his dead body.

He ran through the maze until the towering walls disappeared, replaced by the darkness where the shadow and its terrors resided. He heard scratching and scrabbling in the distance. Footsteps retreated. A woman laughed and said, "You have no power here." It was his mother's laugh.

Something wet touched his face. His mind recoiled in fear.

"You're safe," an unfamiliar voice said.

"I'm dead."

"You aren't dead. Open your eyes."

"My eyes are open."

"No, they aren't."

"Liv, is that you?"

"No, it's Lise."

The wetness touched his face. He thought he would go crazy if it touched him one more time.

A dim glow illuminated the darkness then flared into a brilliant white light. The light brought pain, and he was thrown into a convulsed sea, writhing with thundering waves of agony.

"It's hurting me!"

"I know it hurts, but you have to stay in the light. Fight for your life!"

The darkness was coming, and he was too exhausted to stop it.

"Look at me, Janek!"

Within the light, he saw a blond-haired, blue-eyed woman, bending to wipe his forehead with a washcloth. Water droplets from the washcloth dripped on his cheek and rolled down his neck.

"Have you come to help me?"

"Yes."

"Where am I?"

"You're in your bed."

"In the farmhouse?"

"No, in your suite."

Warm liquid touched his lips and slid down his throat. His helplessness was overwhelming. The pain ebbed and the darkness engulfed him, but this time it was the sweet shelter of sleep.

Two more wretched days passed before Janek's fever broke. During that time, he existed in a two-dimensional world of misery and morphine-induced sleep. At ten o'clock at night on November 20, six days after the church fire, and one year to the day after the shadow had first spoken to him, Janek awoke from his sleep. He felt foggy, but able to think. The scourge of his wounds greeted him. He pushed the affliction to the back of his mind so he could understand what had happened.

He recognized that he was in his suite, lying in bed. The sheet beneath him was soaked with sweat. The top sheet felt damp and heavy on his skin. His left arm and leg were propped up on pillows and immobilized in plaster casts. Both limbs seemed to be the primary source of relentless throbbing.

Burning and stinging radiated from his chest and stomach and back.

With his right hand, he jerked the sheet from his chest and saw the ragged lacerations. He was mutilated. A cry of distress escaped his mouth, and his broken ribs wailed in protest. The cry brought Evan, Lise, and Niklas running from the sitting room to his bedside.

Evan sat on the edge of the bed and searched his friend's eyes. "Is it you, Janek? Just you?"

"I think so. I don't feel...different inside."

"You've been through hell. Maybe you can't tell yet."

"Take the sheet off. I need to see what it did to me."

Niklas looked at Lise. She and Abby were Janek's caretakers, and although Lise saw Janek naked every day for the past six days, the idea was vexing. It was petty jealousy after everything they had been through together.

Evan removed the sheet. Janek lifted his head and surveyed his body. His right leg was covered in huge black bruises and long scratches, but it was in one piece. To his relief, his manhood was also intact. His eyes returned to the inflamed lacerations on his chest and abdomen. The scars were going to be horrible. He recalled Kate erotically kissing his chest as he lay on the floor in Evan's suite. He wondered if any woman would want to kiss his chest after this.

"What about my back, Evan? Did it rip up my back?"

"Yes."

Battling his pain and discovering his disfigurement was draining the tiny bit of stamina he possessed. Janek let his head fall back against the pillow.

Evan replaced the sheet and said, "Do you remember what happened?"

"Yes, up to a point."

"He needs to rest," Lise said.

"I don't want to rest just yet."

Evan's need to know whether or not Erebus had joined with Janek had to be satisfied. "Up to *what* point?"

"I don't remember everything that happened or *how* it happened, but I remember the agony and the deafening noise. I remember thinking I was dying by crucifixion, but I don't know if that was before or after I was thrown against the wall."

The color drained from Evan's face, but he continued. "Do you remember Doc Mason setting your broken bones?"

"No."

"I don't understand how you endured pain like that, unconscious or not. In fact, I don't understand how you survived at all."

Lise and Niklas made eye contact. It dawned on them, at the same moment, what Evan was trying to prove.

"The church burned to the ground," Evan said. "We thought you were inside; that you died in the fire."

"The church burned?"

"Yes. We found you next to Christer Anders' grave."

"I don't remember any of that."

"You stopped it from getting what it wanted, didn't you?"

Janek winced. His ribs felt like they were on fire. "I didn't stop it. It became enraged because I wouldn't go to it willingly. It was overwhelmingly strong, but I don't think it expected to expend so much energy fighting me. It expected me to be weaker."

"You mean it failed because it wore itself out fighting you?"

"Yes."

"The church is gone, but Erebus is still here isn't it?"

"Yes. And it's watching us."

Chapter 23

December 1873

Two weeks later, Evan and Guthrie confessed to Janek that they had implicated Stephen Hartmann in both attacks. Janek didn't challenge their motive. If Erebus didn't kill him, Stephen Hartmann would.

Doc Mason, accompanied by his wife Harriet, who was also his nurse, arrived to care for his patient. He checked Janek's vital signs and removed the stitches from his forehead. Mrs. Mason softened the plaster cast on his arm with water while Doc Mason cut it apart with plaster shears. Janek stared at his shriveled forearm.

"You'll get the strength back in that arm in a few months," Doc Mason said as he wiped off the plaster shears. "I'll remove the cast from your leg in two weeks. You owe a huge debt of gratitude to Evan for insisting I set your broken bones. Otherwise, you'd be crippled just like he feared. I honestly believed that you were going to die. I'm still scratching my head over how you survived something so utterly devastating. Your internal organs should have been damaged beyond repair judging by your external injuries."

That was when Janek began to suspect that Erebus had something to do with his recovery. *How* was a mystery. *Why* was obvious. He was alive so that monster, when it was strong enough, could make another attempt at slaughtering his life.

Later in the afternoon, Sheriff Tate came to take Janek's statement about the assaults. When the sheriff entered the suite, he saw Janek sitting up in bed with the gray tabby cat sleeping at his feet. Niklas had brought the cat to the hotel after the fire.

"You look a lot better. How are you feeling?" Sheriff Tate asked.

The loose shirt Janek wore irritated the healing lacerations on his back and chest. If he breathed or moved the wrong way, his ribs screamed. The skin under the cast on his leg itched. He was weak and disoriented. What's more, he had a headache, the same kind he was tormented with before the attack in the church. Still, he responded that he was feeling better.

The sheriff pulled a notepad and pencil from his jacket pocket and said, "Let's get down to business. What makes you believe Stephen Hartmann wants you dead?"

"His wife accused me of inappropriate behavior. I denied it and refused to give in to his demands for a public apology, so he threatened me."

"Did you make inappropriate advances toward Mrs. Hartmann?"

"No."

"What did Mr. Hartmann say?"

"He said, in front of Matt O'Neill, that he wasn't through with me, and he'd see to it I made things right."

Sheriff Tate paused, scribbled notes on his pad, and then continued. "Tell me about the attack on the road to the port."

"Three or four men jumped my wagon and held knives to my throat and face. They said they had a message from Stephen Hartmann. If I didn't agree to publicly apologize to Mrs. Hartmann, they were going to kill me."

"Did you tell the men threatening you that you would apologize?"

"No."

"What happened after you refused to do what they asked?"

"I don't know. I passed out."

"You didn't see or hear anything else?"

"No."

Sheriff Tate scribbled more notes. Janek knew the next question would be related to the attack in the church. He couldn't talk about what happened that night: it was indescribable and unbelievable. Evan and Guthrie had advised him to say enough to make it look like Stephen orchestrated his murder and nothing more.

"What happened the night you went to the church?"

Janek hesitated. He'd heard Erebus shrieking and the leviathan roaring. Terror churned in his stomach. He lost focus and rubbed his face with his hands.

"Let me make this easier on you. Did you recognize your attackers?"

"No."

"Did they speak to you?"

"Yes. He said I wasn't strong enough to stop him."

"Are you telling me *one* man did this to you?"

"No! I have no idea if there was one or more." Janek's voice rose to a hysterical pitch. "I'm telling you I almost lost my life in that church, and my assailant was vicious and cruel!"

Sheriff Tate returned his notepad and pencil to his pocket. He leaned forward. "Janek, if I arrest Stephen Hartmann can you honestly tell me I have the right man?"

"Yes."

The sheriff rose to leave. "By the way, you mentioned Matt O'Neill. He and Lucas Dodd have been cleared in the deaths of those thugs. I filed the case under unsolved."

The next morning, Stephen Hartmann was arrested for attempted murder. He was arraigned in the tiny courtroom at Ferndale City Hall, and then sent to the Humboldt County Jail in Eureka to await his trial. Not long after, Emily appeared on the deserted street in front of the hotel. A steady freezing rain soaked her hair and clothes. Mud caked her shoes and the hem of her dress. Her auburn eyes glared at the hotel's third-floor windows.

"Janek Walesa, you dirty bastard! I know you're up there, and I know you can hear me! I know you and your worthless friends did this to Stephen!

You and that dirty Mick and that half-breed Mexican whore! You're nothing but an ignorant Pollock. Do you hear me?"

Curious faces peered from the hotel windows. Lucas stepped out of his general store onto the footway to see what the commotion was about. In suite 302, Janek, Guthrie, and Evan heard Emily loud and clear.

"I'm gonna go down there and shut that woman up for good," Guthrie said. "She can call the two of you all the names she wants, but she ain't talking that way about my daughter."

"No," Janek said. "Let her go on. She's making a fool of herself."

Guthrie looked at Evan. "I reckon you agree with that?"

Evan shrugged.

Emily continued her tirade. "Come on, you coward, answer me! Oh, I forgot. You're incapable of answering me because you're a crippled freak confined to your bed. I'll wager your cock won't get hard now! No one would want your filthy Pollock babies anyway."

Sheriff Tate walked through the muddy street to stop Emily's ranting. "Mrs. Hartmann, I know you're upset, but you must stop this. Besides, you're gonna catch your death out here in this rain. Let me take you home."

"I'm not through with you, Janek, do you hear me? You're going to answer to me, you bastard! I will get what I want!"

"Stop it, Mrs. Hartmann! Are you gonna go home quietly or do I have to drag you kicking and screaming?"

She was desperate to get Janek's attention. Her ego had been damaged each time he rejected her advances, and it wouldn't heal until she consummated her sexual desire for him.

"Mrs. Hartmann?"

Emily knew her behavior was ridiculous. There was no value in continuing to make a scene. "I would appreciate it if you walked me home, Sheriff Tate."

Guthrie watched her through the window. "Looks like Dell's taking her home. I reckon we oughta get back to what we were doing. Janek, are you gonna sign them contracts or are you gonna just stare at them?"

"I can't sign them. I don't understand what they say."

"What are you talking about? We drew those up ourselves," Evan said.

Janek tossed the contracts onto the coverlet. "Something's wrong. I can't concentrate. I…" He closed his eyes and rubbed his temples. His headache was incessant; it beat at his brain and confused his thoughts.

"Finish what you were going to say," Evan said, trying to hide his apprehension.

Janek opened his eyes and whispered, "I'm faded."

Evan bit his lower lip. A part of him didn't want to hear anymore. He made a weak attempt at rationality. "You're just worn out."

"You know that's not it."

"It took a piece of you, didn't it, boy?" Guthrie said.

"Yes."

"After it was done with you, it went to lick its wounds, and to its surprise, it found a small ragged piece of your soul stuck on its claw. That monster made a bad mistake. Ain't that right?"

Janek nodded.

"How did you know that, Guthrie?" Evan said.

"Your guilt and anger is blocking your view, son. Hold on to them emotions because you're gonna need them, but don't let them blur your vision."

Evan walked to a window. He stared at the place in the street from which Emily had delivered her hateful denunciation.

"There's something else," Janek said. "Emily is going to touch me, and when she does everything is going to change."

The church council and several congregation members met at a parishioner's home to discuss rebuilding The First Congressional Church of Ferndale and the residence house. Niklas and Lise stood in the crowded parlor and said little as the council debated the church's future.

"We need to rebuild, but the funds in the church treasury are low," a pompous cigar smoking council member said. His statement evoked murmuring in the room. "Does anyone have an idea on how we can raise additional funds?"

A man who stood in the back of the parlor said, "Henry, some of us think if we dig deep in our pockets, we can come up with enough money. Word is Mrs. Arnold sold her boarding house a month ago and made a pretty penny on it. We figure she may have the deepest pockets here."

Niklas went to the front of the room. "Hold on one minute. What my wife does with her money is none of your business. Mrs. Arnold and I don't want the church rebuilt…"

Everyone in the room inhaled a shocked gasp. Henry, the pompous council member stepped forward. "Reverend, what are you talking about? This is your church and your congregation. You have a duty to participate in the rebuilding of the church and the residence house."

Lise said, "You didn't let Reverend Arnold finish what he was saying. We don't want the church rebuilt on its original site."

"Mrs. Arnold, pull in your horns," the man from the back of the room said. "You aren't in charge here and neither is the reverend. The council makes the decisions."

"Don't speak to my wife that way, Sam. You heard what she said. We don't support rebuilding the church where it used to be."

There was an outburst of raucous arguments.

"Let me finish!" Niklas shouted.

The clamorous arguing was reduced to a few whispers.

"Thank you. Mrs. Arnold and I want the council to consider using the land the church owns on Beacon Road. There's enough acreage there to construct a church and a residence house."

"Why, pray tell, would we do that?" Henry said. "Beacon Road is on the outskirts of town. That's not a convenient location for our parishioners who have trouble getting around."

"Several of the congregation members have expressed doubts about rebuilding where the fire occurred," Niklas said. "They see the fire as a bad omen."

"Is that so?" Henry said with an air of authority. "I've heard no such thing. In fact, some of us are of the opinion that Janek Walesa is responsible for the fire. If he had not been lusting after another man's wife, the church would still be there."

Niklas was losing his temper, which he knew was a mistake. The people in the parlor listened to him deliver sermons week after week. They believed it was their duty to obey his consecrated words. He had to convince them to obey what he said to them today.

His tone became serious and he raised his voice to the volume he used when preaching. "We aren't here to discuss the alleged behavior of Janek Walesa. I doubt everyone in this room is as pious as he or she would like us to believe."

"He's your friend, Reverend," Agnes Johansen called out from the front of the room. "I think we *should* talk about him."

"Mrs. Johansen, you know nothing about him!"

"I know enough!" she said, defiantly. "My neighbor, Mrs. Russo, and I have both overheard women talk about him in a lustful manner! He's using the devil's trickery to beguile them. And that nice Mrs. Hartmann; her husband is sitting in jail, wrongly accused of trying to murder Janek Walesa. Everyone knows his behavior toward her was inappropriate!"

Niklas couldn't believe the topic of discussion had turned to Janek. He was the last person on earth who would beguile a woman on purpose.

It took every ounce of self-control Lise had to keep from stomping to the front of the room and slapping Agnes Johansen in the face until her head lolled on a broken neck.

"Agnes, have you seen him or spoken to him?" Lise said in an insolent tone.

Agnes turned and glared at her in response.

"I have," Harriet, Doc Mason's wife, said. She arose from her seat beside Mrs. Johansen.

"Mrs. Mason, we don't…"

"Shut your mouth, Henry! Sit down!" Harriet said. Henry sat down like a naughty child forced to wear a dunce cap in front of his classmates. "Albert and I have been caring for Mr. Walesa. He's handsome and polite and shy. He talks like a book."

She turned on Mrs. Johansen. "Agnes, you might fool a lot of people, but you don't fool me. You're bitter because your husband left you, and... because you know a man like Janek Walesa would never look your way."

Harriet fetched her handbag from her chair and said, "Reverend Arnold, Doc Mason and I will contribute money toward rebuilding the church. Please call on us Saturday morning. Good day."

Agnes Johansen avoided eye contact as she marched from the parlor with her head held high. She slammed the front door as she left the house.

Henry continued in his pompous demeanor, "Reverend, can we resume?"

"Yes. Mrs. Arnold and I contend that a garden should be installed where the church stood. Perhaps a memorial garden since it will be located next to the cemetery."

"A garden?" Sam said. "Why would we agree to that?"

"He will need it someday."

"Who's he?" Henry said.

"God, of course; we *are* here to serve Him."

Lise struggled to maintain a straight face.

"God told you He wants a garden? I think you're making this up, Reverend. You must have some other motive," Henry said.

Niklas ignored him. "There will be benches and cobblestone pathways winding in and around flowerbeds. The garden will be a place where a man can set aside his troubles and bask in its serenity."

Sam walked to the front of the room. He jabbed his index finger into Niklas' chest. "We aren't building a garden, Reverend."

Niklas' vow to stay calm evaporated. He shoved Sam against a wall and pinned him there with a hand to Sam's throat. "You will build that garden! If you don't, God will see you burn in hell. Do you want to burn in hell? A simple yes or no will do!"

"No."

Niklas dropped his hand and stepped back. He looked at the silent council and congregation members and said his last words as a reverend. "Good day."

Everything Lise had feared for Niklas the day he asked for her hand in marriage was coming to pass. She was uncertain if the path they were on was destroying his faith, or if it was the congregation members who sat in the parlor. Perhaps it was both.

She slipped her hand into his on their walk back to the hotel.

"You've lost your congregation, and it's my fault."

"No it's not."

"It is. I knew this would happen if you walked the path with Janek."

"You warned me, and I followed you anyway because I love you."

"But…"

He stopped, put his hand beneath her chin, and tilted her beautiful face up to look into his light brown eyes.

"I began to lose my faith over a year ago, Lise. I knew the events that occurred after Janek arrived in Ferndale were not guided by the hand of God. God has turned his back on a man who doesn't deserve the scorn I heard today."

"Those people aren't going to build that garden."

"They will. That monster will compel them if they don't."

"You asked them to build the garden we saw in our dreams."

"Yes."

"What will we really find in that garden?"

"I don't know, but we'll find out together."

V

The Turning Away

Chapter 24

January 1874

The holiday season came and went with little notice among the eight people whose lives had changed after Janek's attack. They were conjoined by Janek Walesa's fate, forming a strange fellowship. They lived in a world that transcended the limits of thought and existence, a world that should not have been real.

Lucas and Matt volunteered to live in that world with little time to absorb the landscape.

For Lucas, that world was acceptable because as inconceivable and obscene as it was, he felt that at last, he was living a legitimate life. Apart from his friends, he was alone: a man who would live and die and no one would notice. In their new world, he had influence and a place where he was wanted and belonged. And, just as important, he fulfilled the promise he made to his dying father.

Matt found something rational he could hang on to: a woman. His subconscious lied to his psyche and convinced him there was a chance for a normal life. On New Year's Day, he became engaged to Augusta Newhall, a young woman who lived in Eureka. Though he had a new fiancé, he was unable to abandon the world where he and his friends walked the road to perdition.

Abigail and Lise continued to worry and fuss over Janek, often times more than necessary, but he didn't mind. He still needed care. He was diminished in every sense of the word. What was broken or lost seemed irretrievable, and his search for a way to restore even the smallest piece of self left him adrift and exhausted.

Lucas suggested painting as an undemanding way of expressing the things Janek had lost. He was in his sitting room painting when Abigail knocked at his suite door. She had a letter for Janek from the Humboldt County Courts.

"Abby?"

"Yes, it's me," she said and entered the suite.

The letter slipped from her hand when she saw Janek seated in front of an easel holding a huge canvas. Vertical wide and rolling swaths of yellow, orange, red, and green flowed across the canvas. Some of the colors ran together at the edges of the swaths. It was the painting from a forgotten dream.

"What are you doing? Did you paint this?"

"Is it that bad?"

"When did you start painting?"

Janek labored to stand. He detested using the cane propped against the easel, but his left leg was stiff and painful, and he couldn't take the stairs or walk any distance without the cane.

"Lucas thought painting might help some of my…my issues. I thought it was a good idea. He ordered the painting supplies, and they arrived yesterday."

Why did you choose those colors and that style?"

"I don't know. Maybe it brightens up the part of me that's faded."

Abigail drew in a sharp breath. "I saw this painting in a dream. How could I have forgotten? The L-shaped bar and the gray tabby cat. I saw all of it in a dream I had the night you came to talk to Daddy about his lot on Main Street."

"Are you saying you modeled the bar after something you saw in a dream?"

"I must have done it subconsciously."

"And the cat?"

"I didn't make the connection until now."

Apprehension wrapped its cold arms around Janek. He tried to shake it off.

"Are you saying the bar and the cat have a connection?"

"Other than appearing in my dream together, I don't think there is a connection. But there was something else." Every detail of her dream came flooding back.

"Abby?"

She concentrated on characterizing her mental images. "I was standing behind the bar. My dress and shoes were inappropriate. The dress exposed my legs from the knee down and my shoes exposed my ankles. The customers were also dressed inappropriately. Everything about them was odd: the fabric of their clothes, their hairstyles, and the way they spoke."

In addition to his physical and metaphysical disabilities, Janek had concentration and memory problems. He wasn't sure if he understood what she was trying to convey.

"Are you saying you saw the future?"

"No more than your premonition about Emily Hartmann."

"You don't believe my premonition?"

"Yes…no…I mean, my dream has nothing to do with your premonition…does it?"

He couldn't comprehend the importance of her dream in relation to his premonition. There was a connection, but it was in a part of his mind he had difficulty accessing. The events that would culminate from that connection would be out of their control by the time they occurred. In fact, none of them knew it was already too late.

An apology was all he had to offer and that cut her to the quick. When his painting dried, she would hang it on the wall she saw in her dream. It would remind her of what he had lost. What they all had lost.

"Is that for me?" Janek said, pointing to the letter on the floor.

"Oh, yes. This was delivered this afternoon."

"Please read it to me."

She retrieved the letter and opened it. "You have been summoned to the Humboldt County Courthouse to testify at the trial of Stephen George Hartmann on January 26, 1874, at ten o'clock in the morning. Failure to appear will lead to your arrest for interfering with due process of the law..."

"How could I have forgotten this would happen?"

Janek grabbed his cane and limped to the door.

"Where are you going?" Abigail asked as she followed him.

"I need to find Evan."

"I'll find him."

"No!"

They descended the last step on the staircase just as Evan walked through the hotel doors. The panic he saw in Janek's eyes was unmistakable.

"What's wrong?"

"I've been summoned to testify at Hartmann's trial! They want me there on Monday! I can't go!"

Abigail handed the summons to Evan. He read it then handed it back. "The presiding judge is the Honorable Roy Cumberland. Old Roy and I go way back. Let's go to the office and I'll fill you in."

In the office, Evan explained that Judge Cumberland had a little problem with opium and women. He tended to talk in excess about both vices when he was drinking. Evan spent many nights at the Blind Pig Pub in Eureka listening to Roy's stories and watching the judge grope anything in bloomers.

"I can promise he'll accept your written testimony from Sheriff Tate. I'll ask Doc Mason to write a letter confirming you're too weak to travel. I'll take care of everything. Lucas and I are going to Eureka in the morning. We'll be gone all weekend."

The rush of relief Janek experienced was waylaid by anxiety. With Evan gone, he was vulnerable. Although Stephen Hartmann was in jail, he still had friends in Ferndale, not to mention his crazy wife. She scared him more than the thugs Stephen hired to kill him. He rubbed his face with his hands.

"Niklas will stay close while Evan's gone," Abigail said in an attempt to calm his obvious fear.

He dropped his hands from his face.

Evan laughed. "You forget. Abby knows how to deal with Emily."

Janek laughed and it startled him. He had forgotten the sound of his own laughter.

"It's five o'clock," Abigail said. "I have to open the bar."

Evan slapped Janek on the back, which caused him to stumble. "It's been too long since you and I bent an elbow. Come on."

They walked with her to the bar. She stopped under the pointed arched entryway. "Let me show you where I'm going to hang your painting."

"What painting?" Evan said.

"Abby thinks the painting I'm working on should be hung in the bar. She said she dreamed about it."

Evan wasn't surprised. Their lives were an endless stream of interconnected strangeness.

She pointed at a wall shared by the new restaurant and the bar. "There."

"I wouldn't dare argue with your dreamed of decorating sense," Evan said, and smiled. "Can you set us up with whiskey? I'm going to show Janek around the restaurant before we crack open the bottle."

They surveyed the restaurant construction for twenty minutes. Janek was exhausted by the time they returned to the bar and sat at a table. Evan poured whiskey into shot glasses and slid one to Janek.

"I miss our poker games at the Palace," Janek said after he shot the whiskey. He started to say, *When my concentration improves, I'll be able to play*, but it felt like a lie.

Lightning bolt pain lambasted his left leg from his thigh to his ankle, which reminded him of the reason he didn't go to the Palace. Walking or sitting the wrong way caused a variety of crippling leg pain. He couldn't fathom going to the Palace as a pathetic diminished man. Another bolt beleaguered his leg, and he winced.

Evan watched Janek's silent torment. It reinforced the reason he had just returned from the port. He waited until Janek's pain appeared under control before he poured more whiskey. They threw back the shots. Evan refilled the glasses and said, "I quit my job on the schooner."

"Why?"

"It seemed like the right time."

"The schooner gave you the freedom to get out of town."

"The captain gave me free passage anytime to anywhere."

"You didn't answer me. Why did you quit sailing?"

Evan leaned back in his chair. "The truth is I'm afraid I won't be here when your prediction about Emily Hartmann changes things."

"That thought has crossed my mind many times, but I don't want you to sacrifice another minute of your life for me."

"We're friends."

"I owe you everything, Evan."

"You owe me nothing. This fellowship we've formed is important to all of us. No one should suffer alone without a chance for hope."

Janek didn't know what to say.

Evan glanced at Abigail and leaned forward. "Listen, I can bring Kate back with me on Monday. I know she'd love to see you."

"It's not safe for her to be with me. Besides, one look at my scars, and she'll run for the hills."

Chapter 25

February 1874

E van was having lunch with his mother and little sisters at the Gingerbread Café when Sheriff Tate interrupted and asked to speak with him in private.

"Before I tell you why I came here, promise you'll stay calm. I won't tolerate a public outburst in front of the folks in here. Do you understand?"

Evan nodded.

"Stephen Hartmann was found guilty of attempted murder. He's gonna spend the next twenty years in San Quentin State Prison. I suspect there'll be trouble once word of his sentence gets around. Do you get my drift?"

"I get your drift."

"I'm warning you; keep your eyes open and your head clear. If you need me, you know where to find me."

Evan tried to sort out what the news would stir up other than revenge. *Was Janek's premonition about Emily classified as revenge?* He didn't think it was, and Janek had no explanation for *what* would change. He considered their archetypical dream about a path through a redwood forest and shuddered. *When will we be forced to begin our fateful journey on that path?* Evan was certain it was on the horizon or hovering above them like the noonday sun.

He walked back to the table. "Mom, I have to go."

Claire O'Malley arose from her seat. "Is everything all right?"

"It's nothing I can't handle."

"Is it Janek? You said he was feeling better…"

"Mom…"

She watched as he circled the table, kissed Margaret, and then Ellen and Eliza on the forehead.

"You girls be good for Mom. Remember I love you."

Margaret asked, "Where are you going?"

They waited for his answer, but he had none; nothing sensible or plausible. He went to his mother and took her thin upper arms in his hands. Their bright green eyes met. She loved him with a fierceness matched only by his father's hatred. He tried to determine when his father's indifference toward him turned to hatred. *Was it after his three younger brothers died years apart at age two?*

He swept a lock of dark hair from her forehead and said, "I love you. I'm sorry for everything I did that hurt you. Do something for me. Promise you'll tell Father I wasn't a failure in the end."

The thought of losing her son was so hideous it was beyond comprehension. "What do you mean in the end? I don't understand! Talk to me, please, Evan!"

"I don't want you involved. Now, promise me you'll tell Father what I said."

"I promise."

Eliza, whose temperament matched her brother's, bounced from her chair and wrapped her arms around Evan's waist. She tilted her head so she could see his face and said, "I love you!"

Margaret repeated her question with fear in her voice. "Evan, where are you going?"

He had stalled long enough to think of an ill-conceived answer. "I need to stay with my friend Janek. He can't take care of himself, and there are things that need all of my attention. It's for the best."

Margaret and Ellen joined Eliza, and the three sisters hugged their beloved big brother.

Claire O'Malley knew he was lying to shield them from something horrible. She said, "I love you, Evan."

He smiled at his mother, and pulled away from his sisters. Then he turned his back on his family and left the café. His heart shattered into fine slivers of glass that cut so badly he couldn't cry.

He walked to the Palace Saloon. Guthrie was behind the bar talking with his cronies who preferred to drink their lunch instead of eat it.

Evan interrupted their conversation. "Guthrie, can you close up and come to the hotel with me? There's something important we need to talk about."

"I got customers, can't this wait?"

"The boy looks flustered, Guthrie. You best go with him," one of the cronies said. "I reckon we can finish our lunch later."

"Is Abby at home?"

"Yep," Guthrie said as he locked up the saloon.

They collected Abigail then walked to the general store to tell Lucas to meet them in the hotel lobby. With Lucas and Matt gathered, they went to the Arnolds' suite where they had privacy. Evan repeated what Sheriff Tate said to him in the café. Then, they went to the hotel office to find Janek.

He was sitting at the desk recording entries in an accounting ledger. The depth of concentration on his face made it apparent he was struggling with comprehension. He looked up when they came through the door.

"Six years of college gone to hell," Janek said to no one in particular. He slammed the ledger shut. "What do you want? I'm not up to an inquisition today."

"We came to tell you about Stephen Hartmann," Evan said. "They found him guilty of attempted murder. He's going to rot in San Quentin for twenty years."

Janek blinked his eyes as if a bright light shined on them. With shaking hands, he gripped the arms of his chair and labored to stand. His eyes opened wide to chase off whatever had caused them to blink. Lise saw that his beautiful blue eyes had turned gray overnight.

"I'm going to the druggist for more laudanum."

"Did you hear what I said about Hartmann?" Evan asked, forcefully. "When Emily gets back from Eureka, she's going to cause trouble!"

"I heard you."

Lise reached for Janek's hand. "Your faded feeling is worse, isn't it?"

He recoiled. "Please don't touch me. Yes, I suppose the faded feeling is worse."

She said, "You don't seem concerned about Stephen's sentence or impending trouble. Something more important is on your mind."

"I thought this wasn't going to be an inquisition."

"Please talk to us," Abigail said.

Janek sighed. "I can hear it all the time. Sometimes it sounds like a maniacal lunatic, slobbering over the piece of my soul it possesses. Other times, I can hear its discontent with what I've become. Not that it's sorry for what it's done to me. It's afraid I'll die before it can take the rest of my soul and join with my body. And it…"

He told himself to stop talking before it inflicted something else upon him for betraying its thoughts. *Tell them. It's horrifying.*

"It's made my skin insufferable. Erebus doesn't want anyone to touch me. It's saving its diminished strength for actions deserving its attention. I can't and won't endure the agony of contact with my skin."

Without looking at them, he grabbed his cane and walked to the door.

"I don't think it's safe for you to be alone," Evan said.

Niklas said, "Why don't I get the laudanum for you?"

"No. I need to get out. I need to see the sun and feel the wind on my face. I need to hear the sound of my boots as I walk. I need to do it before it's too late."

They watched him leave; he wore his pain like a shackled spirit. A few weeks ago, his fears were centered on the situation with the Hartmanns. The possessive shadow shifted the focus of Janek's fears back on to itself.

Evan was ashamed that he didn't see the change. "We're losing him and I don't know what to do to save him."

184

After Janek purchased laudanum from the druggist, he went to the cemetery. The walk was long and painful, but he felt compelled to stand where the church had been. Erebus had claimed to be masquerading as the celestial voices of his dead family. He wanted with all his heart for that to be untrue. Although the church was gone, he thought perhaps they were there waiting for him.

The small grassy yard that surrounded the church was incinerated. Soot stained the mausoleums. Those were the only remaining signs of the fire. Mounds of cobblestones and bags of cement crowded what used to be the courtyard. Rakes, shovels, and picks were piled by a wheelbarrow.

Janek made his way around the mounds and sat on the stone steps that led to the cemetery. A thin layer of gray clouds spread across the sky. The wind he longed to feel on his face ruffled his blond hair and stung his gray eyes.

"It told me you were never here. Please tell me it lied."

He paused and waited for an answer. There was none, so he continued.

"I don't know what happened to my life, why everything went so wrong. I worked hard at the university. I had friends. I thought I had a future. When you died, the course of my life changed. It took advantage of my grief and doubt. If it killed you to get to me, I'm sorry. I didn't know."

The gray clouds thickened and obliterated the sun. Light rain drops mingled with his tears. He wiped his eyes and resumed his lonesome monologue.

"I don't have much time left in this world, at least not in the world as it is now. I hope I die soon. I dreamed of dying. Death was a desolate place. I don't want to be alone, but I can't go on like this. I've lost control of my life, and there's too much pain. Please be there to greet me when I pass through the veil."

The rain was falling harder. Janek struggled to stand. He looked around at the place where his life was plundered.

"Father, I'm sorry I was weak. I fought it, but I wasn't strong enough. Until now, I didn't know there was a thin line between a man's soul and its destruction."

As Janek walked from the courtyard, he heard his family speaking. He stopped to listen. Freya and Liv's voices faded as Aron's voice rose. "I know of no man who has endured what you have and still had the courage to push on. Your strengths are what attracted it to you. Can't you see that? If hope is gone, it's not because you let it go. It's because it disintegrated in your hand. We'll be there when you pass through the veil. We love you. And... Erebus lied."

The clouds covering the starless sky had changed into evening's black gown when Janek arrived at the hotel. He went in through the back service door and labored to climb the staff stairs. He slammed the suite door shut, and in a fit of anger, threw the cane at a wall.

He went to the dressing room and stripped off his clothes. His inflamed skin felt like tiny glass shards were embedded in every cell. A housekeeper filled the bathtub every night at seven o'clock. If he soaked in warm water, the inflammation abated a little.

He submerged his body in the water and laid his head against the rim. He reached for the tequila bottle on the dressing table beside the tub and guzzled the golden liquid until he was light-headed.

His thoughts turned to suicide. If he closed his eyes and fell asleep perhaps he would drown. That was wishful thinking. Consuming an entire bottle of tequila and laudanum was realistic. The last time he contemplated suicide was the night Erebus came to him in the church courtyard. Erebus stopped him then, and it would stop him tonight if he tried to slip through a back door out of life.

When he stepped from the bathtub, the floor mirror taunted him with his reflection. He was reminded of the fairy tale *Snow White* and the Evil Queen who asked her magic mirror, "Who is the fairest in the land?"

His mirror told him he was a disfigured freak with the eyes of a stranger. A laceration ran from his right side hairline across his forehead to the top of his left temple, where it intersected with the gash that began at his chin and lined his jawbone. There was a hideous mass of thick irregular scar tissue where his broken tibia had punctured his lower left leg. Highways of thin white scars ran the length of his right leg. The red raised scars on his chest and stomach and back were a constant reminder of mutilation and agony.

He flung the tequila bottle at the mirror, shattering the glass.

The sitting room door creaked open. The cat wiggled through the crack between the two doors. He padded across the suite and jumped onto the dressing table. Janek stroked the cat's back.

He took the bottle of laudanum from the inside pocket of his coat and walked to the bed without bothering to dry off or dress. His clothes tortured his skin. Lying between the sheets and blankets on his bed was worse, so he slept naked on top of the blankets.

He gulped the laudanum and sat on the edge of the bed. His mind lost focus and wandered as he tried to remember the faces of his family. He was as faded as their faces. His head fell forward until his chin touched his sternum.

Emily watched through the open sitting room door. She left Eureka before Stephen's trial ended, claiming she was ill. Stephen's fate was inconsequential. Her obsession with Janek had grown to rival Erebus. The fantasy of his sweat-slicked skin sliding over her body as they made love, his tongue savoring her breasts, and his promised love consumed her life. Tonight, his diminished strength and drugged condition made him easy prey.

She pictured her hands cupping his cheeks and lifting his face so she could kiss his lips. The horrible scars coursing his back heightened her desire. He was naked before her eyes, and he was the most beautiful man she had ever beheld.

He lay back on the bed. The laudanum obliterated the pounding in his head. Sleep engulfed his exhausted soul and worn out body.

Emily stepped from the sitting room, wearing only satin bloomers. Her dress and corset and stockings lay in a pile on the floor. She locked the suite door. Then, she crossed the bedroom to the dressing room and fetched the bottle of tequila from the glass littered floor. Charged with desire and lust, her clit pulsed like a beating heart.

She went to Janek's bedside and stared at his exquisite face and body. Restraint battled with masturbation lest she explode before he touched her. She sat in the chair beside his bed and drank tequila. She wondered what he was dreaming of and conjured her own dreams. An hour passed. Her orgasm threatened.

The cat watched her from the dressing room doorway.

She stripped off her satin bloomers and slid onto the bed beside Janek. His breath was soft and shallow. His body was warm. She kissed his ruined chest for a moment then moved to kiss the place where his scars ended near his waist. His angelic sleeping face held no sign of awakening. Laudanum and tequila were making it difficult to arouse him in the gentle romantic fashion she envisioned.

She crawled between his legs and sucked his sleeping cock into her mouth. Her tongue licked his manhood, enticing it to awaken. Her orgasm was eminent. Her moans were lewd and erotic.

Janek awoke disconcerted and in terrible pain. Emily's presence in his bed confused him. Then he understood. Her molestation was caustic to his skin. He cried out and sat up. Emily let go of him and sat up as well. He slapped her face so hard that she fell on the floor.

He ran to the dressing room amidst a fog of laudanum and tequila. His spinning head and stiff left leg caused him to lose his balance and stumble when he grabbed his clothes from the floor. He shrugged into his shirt and pulled on his pants and boots. Lightning-charged pain seared his left leg when he ran toward the suite door.

Emily intercepted him.

"Stay with me, Janek. I can make you forget everything you've been through. I'll pleasure you however you wish."

He shoved her.

A frigid vortex formed at her bare feet and rose and spiraled tighter and tighter around her naked body. With each rapid rotation, the vortex sucked her in closer to the center of Erebus' being until she was paralyzed. She wasn't afraid.

A thick shuddering sound emanated from the walls. The vortex's rapid rotation slowed as it absorbed the shuddering, little by little, until it was gone. As the rotation accelerated, a barrage of vibrating thunder erupted from the vortex, spewing forth Erebus' jealous rage.

"You have touched my love in a manner that is forbidden!"

Emily sneered at Erebus' compulsion.

"I have watched you lust for him! I am taking him with me to a place you will never exist! Before this night has ended, you will turn to dust!"

Janek knew his premonition had come to pass. The change was beginning. He felt it in his body. He heard it in Erebus' crazed jealous threats. A strange warped sensation passed through him and with growing horror, he realized what was happening.

He ran from the suite and tried to take the stairs, but he stumbled and fell to the second floor landing. His ribs and left leg screamed in pain as he fought to stand.

The staircase swayed. It took every ounce of strength he had to stay on his feet. He reached for the banister as the staircase rippled and whipped back and forth like a frenzied dragon. Terror pilfered his rationality, and he screamed for Evan.

Evan was in the bar drinking with Lucas, Matt, and Guthrie. Abigail was working. The liquor bottles on the shelves behind her rattled. The bar swayed then stopped. A bottle fell to the floor and shattered. The bar was silent for a moment, and then the patrons returned to their drinks and conversation. Earthquake tremors were common in California. No one gave the event a second thought—no one, except Evan.

In that brief moment of silence, he heard Janek calling his name. The swaying was no earthquake tremor. He ran across the lobby to the staircase. Janek's frantic screaming was louder. Evan ran up the staircase two steps at a time. When he reached Janek, he saw Niklas and Lise descending the stairs from the third floor.

Janek's cries for Evan turned to panicked shrieking. "It's turning us away! Get them out of here! They're all going to die if we don't get them out!"

"What are you saying? Who's going to die? Oh shit! The change! It's happening isn't it?"

"For God's sake get everyone out! Do it now!"

"Take Janek to the banquet room and stay with him," Evan said to

Niklas and Lise.

Evan ran back to the bar and grabbed Matt and Lucas by the arm. "Listen to me! Sound the fire alarms, evacuate the hotel and secure the outside doors. Then get out of the hotel as fast as you can or go to the banquet room if you're staying with us. You have a matter of minutes! Hurry!"

Evan turned around to tell Guthrie and Abigail what was happening, but they were gone. He climbed the staircase to the third floor and Janek's suite.

Emily was curled up in a corner of the dressing room. She was wearing Janek's frock coat and holding the tequila bottle.

"The demon said I was going to die. I don't care. I can't be happy without him. Why didn't he want me, Evan? Why?"

For a fleeting second, he felt sorry for her. She had decreed her own death sentence.

As he turned to leave, he saw the cat perched on Janek's bed grooming himself as if nothing had happened. Evan picked up the cat and left Emily alone with her fate. He ran to the banquet room.

"Everyone is out of the hotel," Lucas said as Evan entered the room. "Matt went with them."

Janek was sitting on the floor rocking back and forth like a child. Evan sat beside him and was reminded of the first time Erebus spoke to Janek in the church courtyard. The cat jumped from his arms and edged closer to Janek.

"Talk to us," Evan said.

Janek stopped rocking. He didn't think he could speak. Even if he could speak, his thoughts were a useless jumble of confusion.

Guthrie squatted and looked Janek in the eye. "Focus on what needs to be said, son."

Janek focused on Guthrie's brown eyes. Abigail had brown eyes. Lucas had brown eyes. He couldn't remember what color his eyes were before the fading began.

Guthrie's gruff voice cut off Janek's wandering thoughts. "Niklas said you told Evan it's turning us away. What did you mean?"

Janek's body trembled. Abigail sat beside him and stroked his hair. Comfort was a feeling he had forgotten. It eased his tremors and quieted his confusion. When he spoke, his words were dry and edged on inaudible.

"It's turning us away from the world and changing our perception of time. It took hundreds of years for it to become strong enough to…" Janek's thoughts wavered. He rubbed his forehead and bit his lower lip to keep his thoughts from disintegrating. "It waited thousands of years for me, and hundreds of years to become strong enough to come for me. It will be years before it will be strong, before I will be strong. Erebus is taking us with it as it moves forward in time. As we sit here, a generation has passed."

"That's why you wanted everyone evacuated," Niklas said. "Time was beginning to pass at a rapid rate inside the hotel. The guests and staff would've died from old age in less than an hour."

Guthrie drew Janek's attention. "Is Niklas right?"

"Yes."

"Keep focused," Guthrie said. "Emily Hartmann touched you didn't she?"

"Yes."

"When Erebus is through with her, time is gonna slow down."

"Yes." Janek's ability to concentrate was crumbling. "Guthrie, I can't…"

"I ain't gonna ask anything else."

They sat in the hushed banquet room awaiting their fate.

Lise watched Abigail stroke Janek's hair. She thought of the first morning they sat together at the kitchen table in her boarding house. He captivated her with his shy ways and polite mannerisms and bewitching eyes. He was transcendent. From that day, she followed where he led, and she had no regrets.

Janek resumed his childlike rocking. Each thought his mind tried to conjure was defeated by the horrible throbbing in his head. He collapsed into Abigail's arms.

How can you see into my eyes like open doors? Leading you down into my core where I've become so numb. Without a soul my spirit's sleeping somewhere cold. Until you find it there and lead it back home.
— Evanescence

VI

The Convocation

Chapter 26

December 4, 2016

The noise was deafening. The agony was terrible. Talons shredded his back, ripping the skin like rice paper. Every rib in his chest snapped when the leviathan crushed his body. His screams for mercy were stifled. A gas lamp exploded, shooting flames upward and outward, catching everything on fire. He choked on acrid smoke as the fire rushed closer to his ruined body.

Bryan sat up in bed trembling and drenched in sweat. He wiped a hand across his face. *Where in the hell did that dream come from?* The violence and terror were worse than anything he had ever experienced, real or imagined. Something like that couldn't have come from his inner conscious. He didn't have it in him.

The clock on the nightstand glowed 4:13 a.m. Bryan went into the bathroom and brushed his teeth then stared at his reflection in the mirror. *What kind of man could survive that kind of agony?* he wondered.

He switched off the bathroom light. A mental image of a cemetery presented itself and refused to leave when he got back in bed. The image shifted. He was standing on a cemetery hill overlooking a small town. He scanned the vista and saw what appeared to be the Pacific Ocean. Judging from the architecture, the presence of horses and carriages and wagons, and the absence of cars, the time period was Victorian nineteenth century.

No matter the effort, Bryan's cognizance couldn't leave the cemetery.

When the alarm sounded at 6:30 a.m., his mind remained in the 1800s on a hill somewhere in the United States.

His wife, Natalie, woke and went into the bathroom to shower. The Townsends were on their honeymoon at a bed and breakfast in Mendocino, California. The next stop on their Highway 1 road trip north was Florence, Oregon.

"Get your shower honey," Natalie said. She came out of the bathroom, drying her hair with a towel. "We need to hit the road right after breakfast."

Bryan showered, ate breakfast, packed, and loaded the car like a robot programmed to go through the motions. He drove north on Highway 1. Natalie dozed. Something compelled him to turn onto north Highway 101.

He drove across the Ferndale town line three hours after leaving Mendocino.

Natalie stirred, opened her eyes, and yawned. "Where are we?"

"Ferndale."

"California?"

"Yes."

When Bryan parked the car on Main Street in front of the Ferndale Hotel, she raised her eyebrows and said, "Why are we stopping here?"

He opened the car door and got out. "We're checking in."

"What?" Natalie got out of the car and walked to the trunk where Bryan was removing their luggage. "What are you doing? We're supposed to be in Florence, Oregon tonight. We can't stop here!"

"Nat, it's fine," he said. He set a suitcase on the sidewalk. What he couldn't tell her was he could no longer concentrate on driving. The cemetery hill vehemently commanded his attention.

"It's not fine!" she said. She snatched up the suitcase and shoved it back into the truck.

"Stop it, Natalie!" He jerked the suitcase from the trunk and slammed the lid shut. "Call the B&B in Florence and cancel. We're staying here tonight. End of discussion."

"But we'll be charged for the room…"

Bryan wheeled the suitcases through the hotel's mahogany double doors.

"Bryan!"

She followed him through the doors and across the lobby to the registration desk. "Why are you doing this?" Natalie whispered before he could speak to the desk clerk.

"I *need* to do this."

The chilling dream repeated in his mind. He felt the agony and heard the noise. If he didn't check into the hotel, he would go crazy. He turned his back on his wife and checked into the hotel.

"You're in room 212 on the second floor," the desk clerk said. She handed Bryan the keycards. "You can take the staircase or the elevator, which is just past the staircase."

As they walked to the elevator, Natalie noticed the lobby's elegance and it doused her bewildered anger. Every appointment held some element of luminosity and patrician.

"Beautiful!" she said aloud.

"I'm glad you're impressed, Nat," Bryan said without looking at her.

It was a lie. Her opinion made no difference. The moment the clerk handed him the keycards, his mind was freed of its prison on the cemetery hill. The relief was unexplainable.

Bryan and Natalie descended the grand staircase early in the evening. They passed the registration desk and walked to the bar. Bryan paused to note the carvings on the pointed arched entryway.

They sat at the bar. The bartender greeted them. Bryan ordered beers. When the bartender brought the beers, she studied his face as long as she could without seeming obvious.

A man sitting beside Bryan reached across the bar to put money in the tip jar and spilled Bryan's beer. The man grabbed a wad of cocktails napkins from a stack on the bar, dropped them on the puddle of beer, and said, "Sorry."

"No problem."

The man thrust a hand toward Bryan. "I'm Alex Spelman."

"Bryan Townsend," Bryan said. He shook Alex's hand. He turned in his bar stool and touched Natalie's shoulder. "This is my wife, Natalie."

She smiled at Alex.

A man approached Alex and said, "A table opened up. Let's sit over there."

"This is Bryan and Natalie Townsend," Alex said to the man.

"David Channing," the man said.

Alex said to Bryan, "Will you and your wife join us?"

After they were seated at the table, David said, "What brings you to Ferndale?"

Natalie anticipated Bryan's reason for this detour.

"We're on our honeymoon, and we…I had an urge to visit Ferndale. And you?" Bryan asked.

She was robbed of an explanation.

"Alex and I are here to look at an old church. We're real estate brokers from Sacramento. A real estate agent from Ferndale contacted us. Alex thinks if we market it right, we can sell it to some millennial who wants to brag about having a vacation home."

"Not to mention my interest in old buildings," Alex said. "This hotel was built in 1873. It's hard to believe because it looks new, not renovated."

"It's a beautiful hotel," Natalie said.

Alex leaned forward. "I was reading about Ferndale on the drive up from Sacramento. This hotel has some folklore. A woman named Emily haunts the third floor. In 1874, her husband was convicted of attempted murder and sent to San Quentin State Prison. She came to the hotel to confront her husband's accusers. No one ever saw her again. Some say she was murdered. Others say that she was in love with the hotel owner. Her love for him was unrequited so she killed herself in his suite."

"Yeah, right," David said with a sarcastic laugh.

Alex ignored David and said, "Previous guests have claimed to hear shuddering walls and phantom voices murmuring in unison."

"I noticed the detailed carvings in the pointed arch over the entryway to the bar. They look medieval," Bryan said.

"I noticed that too," Alex said. "Medieval carvings and symbols were popular during the Victorian era. Nevertheless, it exudes a ghoulish feeling. Did you see the painting on the wall over there? It's mesmerizing the way the colors flow across the canvas."

"I saw it. He painted it."

David turned to look at the painting and said, "Who painted it?"

"The man Emily was in love with," Bryan said. "He owns this hotel."

"You mean he *owned* this hotel. The current owner couldn't have been alive in 1874. Besides, how do you know who the artist is?"

Bryan shrugged. "I'm going to take a closer look. Maybe, the artist signed it."

Alex joined Bryan. They studied the painting, but found no signature or date.

"This looks like the artist used watercolors, but the intensity of the hues indicates something more acrylic-based," Alex said.

Bryan didn't know Monet from Van Gogh, but the painting begged to be touched. He brushed his fingertips across the canvas and was overwhelmed by a feeling of desolation.

"The artist tried to recapture what was taken from him."

"How do you know?" Alex said.

"Touch the painting."

Alex brushed the canvas with his fingertips. "A wrong was committed against him that was never righted."

David interrupted them. "I'm going to get some sleep. Good to meet you, Bryan."

"I suppose we should do the same," Bryan said. "It was nice to meet you both."

"You were taken with that painting," Natalie said as they climbed the staircase. "What's the attraction?"

"I'm not sure."

While Bryan and Natalie slept, a beautiful blond man with haunting eyes stared through a window in suite 302. The irises in his eyes had faded to spectral white; their once gray color reduced to a halo. He held a letter written in 1874. It was found only last week on the floor beneath the registration desk, when the desk had been removed and replaced. A construction worker gave the letter to the desk clerk who gave it to Evan. Evan read Chad's neat writing to Janek.

January 15, 1874

Dear Janek,

I have only now received the news of your unfortunate attack. I am not surprised that Stephen Hartmann went to such extreme measures to get at you. My one wish was that I had been there to take care of him myself. Nonetheless, I am pleased to hear that you are recovering well, aside from the headaches that have plagued you for so long.

I have been in Europe over two months now and have had a wonderful trip thus far. I am in Paris at the time. It is an exciting city filled with music, art, and lovely ladies. You would enjoy this city and all it has to offer. I plan on visiting Italy next, perhaps Rome and Florence. This has truly been the vacation of a lifetime.

I will be returning home near the beginning of March. I look forward to seeing you again. Take care of yourself.

Best Regards,
Chad Winston

Janek remembered Chad. He could not, however, remember how they had gotten to this place in time. Evan recounted the story with patience each time Janek asked to hear it. Not that it mattered. The world in 2016 was as familiar to them as their world had been in 1874.

Over a century had passed, but their situation was unchanged. The fellowship they had forged remained strong. Erebus continued to repress Janek, and in doing so had succeeded in accidental subversion.

Erebus' strength had returned, but Janek's mind and body were weak. All the damage done to his body, and the resulting scars, remained. Touch was agony to his tortured skin. Lightning bolt pain crippled his stiff left leg. His horrendous headaches were relentless. Erebus confused his thoughts by stirring the truth with lies, making him unable to discern what was real and what was feigned. Janek didn't trust himself anymore.

The wound he sustained the night a piece of his soul was ripped from him in the church, festered. Drop by drop, his soul seeped from the wound, taking with it the essence of his humanity: emotion. He couldn't remember the feeling of mankind's visceral instincts. Fear and suffering was all he had left.

Hell was forgetting what it was like to be human.

Erebus promised to heal Janek by feeding him. The undefined promise was terrifying, but tonight he understood what Erebus meant. His lost soul would be forced upon his dead spirit.

When he was healed, Erebus would come for him with a renewed ferocity, but Janek held on to the idea that he may be able to beat Erebus if he was strong enough. He and Evan had talked about that possibility many times. They had all talked about it. They had promised to do what they had to do.

Chapter 27

Natalie and Bryan had a late breakfast in the hotel restaurant. While they ate, they thumbed through travel brochures boasting the Victorian Village of Ferndale's listing on the National Register of Historic Places.

"There might be a little something to do here. The beach is just a few miles away. We could stay another night," Bryan said.

"Now that we're here, we might as well make the best of it."

He kissed her on the lips. "Thanks, Nat."

They finished their coffee while they waited for the waiter to bring the check. Natalie noticed a blonde woman enter the restaurant. She crossed the restaurant and spoke to their waiter, then approached their table.

"Mr. and Mrs. Townsend, I'm Lise Arnold. I oversee guest services at the hotel. Breakfast is on the house as long as you're our guests."

Natalie said, "That's very nice."

"Because you changed your plans and decided to stay here instead of the bed and breakfast in Oregon, that's the least we can do to show our appreciation."

Natalie narrowed her eyes. "How do you know that?"

"I overheard you talking about it with your husband."

"We weren't talking about the bed and breakfast."

Bryan stood and offered his hand to Lise. "Thank you, Ms. Arnold." She studied his face with an intensity he found seductive. For a moment, his mind emptied of all thought but her wanton scrutiny.

Lise's blue eyes dropped to look at his offered hand, but she didn't take it. "Welcome to the Ferndale Hotel, Mr. Townsend. If you need anything, ask for me at the front desk."

"Wait." Natalie arose from her chair. "You didn't answer me. How did you know we had planned to stay at a bed and breakfast in Oregon?"

"I did answer you."

Natalie stared at Lise as she left the restaurant. She wasn't sure if what had taken place was an act of hospitality or something else. Lise Arnold's reaction to Bryan was more than the run of the mill *pleased to meet you*. It was as if some preordained event had occurred. Lise Arnold looked at Bryan with passion.

"Nat, are you listening to me? Let's reserve our room for another night."

"Did you get a strange feeling from that woman?"

"Stop it."

"You still haven't told me why we're here."

Bryan walked to the restaurant door and pushed it open. "Nat, are you coming?"

She sighed and nodded.

When they entered the lobby, a group of tourists, who were there to experience the North Coast hikes, were checking into the hotel. Lise and Niklas and Evan were standing near a window that looked out onto Main Street. They watched the Townsends get in line to reserve their room for another night.

Niklas adjusted the strap on the shoulder holster hidden beneath his jacket. He was head of hotel security; the job Matt O'Neill left vacant the night Erebus turned them away from 1874.

"He's one of them?" Niklas asked, eyeing Bryan.

"Yes," Lise said.

Evan said, "Does Janek know?"

Lise nodded. "He sensed them when they touched the painting. He was sure they, in turn, sensed him or at least his desolation. Janek knew something significant had occurred. Erebus is preparing to carry out its plan to feed him his lost soul."

"He's terrified of the feeding," Evan said.

"This feeding has to take place no matter..." Niklas shut his mouth. He was preaching to the choir.

"We need to figure out that nightmare's plan."

"Why?" Lise said.

"I don't like being caught off guard," Evan said.

"It's compelling us. I knew the Townsends intended on staying at a B&B in Oregon. I mentioned it, and the woman didn't like my answer when I tried to cover my mistake."

"I think some of us should be in the hotel bar tonight," Niklas said. "I'll keep an eye on the third floor. I'd get some of my security people to do it, but I don't think it's a good idea to engage outsiders."

"I agree," Evan said. "Who the hell knows what that nightmare would do to them? I don't want anyone to tell Janek. He doesn't need to be burdened with trying to understand what we're doing."

David Channing and Alex Spelman were scheduled to meet the real estate agent at the church at two thirty in the afternoon. David parked the car curbside on Berding Street.

"The address on the sign for the Ferndale Memorial Garden matches what we were given, but I don't see a church," David said.

Alex got out of the car.

David rolled down the car window. "Where are you going?"

Alex walked under a tall ivy-covered trellis and into the garden. Oak, weeping willow, and Douglas fir trees shaded the peaceful garden.

David got out of the car and walked around the block. Then, he walked through the garden and found Alex sitting on a bench facing several mausoleums set into the hillside of a cemetery.

"There's obviously no church, and the real estate agent is a no show. Let's go."

"Wait a few more minutes."

David sat on the bench, pulled a pack of cigarettes from his pocket, and lit one. "I'm calling the real estate agent. Do you have her number?"

Alex reached into his pocket for his phone then searched through the contacts.

"That's strange. I'm positive I stored her number in my phone, but I don't see it. Maybe it's in the email." He ran his fingers through his light brown hair and searched his emails. "I can't find the email either."

David dropped his cigarette on the cobblestones and ground it out with his shoe heel. "Let's go."

"You boys lost?"

David and Alex stood up and turned around. A man with a folded newspaper in his hand was looking at them, expectantly.

"I'm not sure," Alex said. "Do you know if there's an old church for sale?"

"You ain't being too specific."

"It's the First Congregational Church of Ferndale."

The man grunted and gave Alex a suspicious look.

"I'm Alex Spelman. This is my business partner, David Channing," Alex said. He reached out to shake the man's hand.

The man ignored the offered hand shake. "The name's Guthrie. You boys sure you got the name of the church right? The First Congregational Church of Ferndale used to sit right here. It burned down on November 14, 1873 and was never rebuilt. Instead, they saw fit to put in this garden."

Alex and David looked at one another and raised their eyebrows.

"Do you know a real estate agent named Mary Kellen?" David asked.

Mary Kellen was the head housekeeper at the hotel from 1873 to 1881. She died in 1890 and was buried on the cemetery hill. A woman and a church, both no longer existed but were used as a ploy to lure these men to Ferndale. Guthrie could see that now. *Erebus brought them here because of Janek.*

"Nope." Guthrie tucked the newspaper under his arm and walked away.

"What the fuck was that?" David said under his breath.

As they walked through the ivy-covered trellis and out of the garden,

Alex prophesied that he would be back, but not with David. He decided to stay in Ferndale another night.

Natalie and Bryan spent the day rummaging through the shops on Main Street. On the recommendation of one of the shop owners, Lucas Dodd, they ate dinner at a small café off the beaten path. When they returned to the hotel, the clerk at the registration desk stopped them.

"Mr. and Mrs. Townsend, I have a message for you. Mr. Alex Spelman has asked if you would meet him and his friend in the bar for drinks."

Natalie said, "Bryan, I would rather go to our room."

Bryan knew what she expected, but talking with Alex and touching the painting were more important. The sweeping swaths of green, yellow, orange, and red colors stayed in the forefront of his mind. He *had* to touch the painting another time.

He said, "I'm curious to find out how their church thing turned out."

Natalie exhaled a loud sigh, which Bryan ignored. They entered the crowded bar and found Alex and David sitting at a table near the painting.

"It's a great night to get drunk," David said as he waved the waitress over to the table. "We've had one hell of a strange day."

Alex explained the missing real estate agent and church. He recounted their encounter with Guthrie.

"I wonder if he was telling the truth," David said.

Alex swigged his beer then choked as the beer went down the wrong way. "Hey, there he is. That's Guthrie."

Everyone at the table turned to look. Guthrie was sitting at the end of the bar where it met the back wall. Beside him, a man with long dark hair pulled back into a ponytail was flirting with two young women. The man filled four shot glasses with whiskey and slid one in front of Guthrie.

"Do you need something?"

Everyone at the table realized they had been outright staring, and looked up to the waitress calling their attention.

"I'm Abigail Sullivan. My father and I own this bar. You were staring at him."

David's eyes roamed over Abigail's slim body before he said, "I apologize. My friend and I met your father today in the memorial garden next to the cemetery. We were surprised to see him in here."

Abigail gave him a doubtful look. "If you don't need anything, I…"

"Wait a minute. Do you know if there's a First Congressional Church of Ferndale?"

"My father already told you about the church."

"You knew who we were when you came over here?"

There was an outburst of loud laughter. The people at the table looked at the people sitting at the end of the bar. The two young women were laughing at something the dark-haired man had said. The dark-haired man was frowning at the people sitting at the table.

"Who's that guy staring at us?" David said.

"That's the hotel manager, Evan O'Malley," Abigail said with a smirk.

Alex had no interest in Evan. He said to Abigail, "What do you know about that painting?"

She forced herself not to look at the painting and said, "Nothing. Excuse me."

David watched Abigail's retreating figure. She was his type of woman: beautiful and feisty.

Alex and Bryan left the table to study the painting. They reached for it in unison and caressed the canvas with their fingertips.

Natalie was beginning to feel uneasy. "David, do you think what happened to you today has anything to do with their excessive interest in that painting?"

"No."

She chewed on her lower lip for a few seconds before saying, "Is Alex acting peculiar?"

David chuckled and swallowed the rest of the scotch in his glass.

"I'm serious," she said.

"If you're referring to this dreamy obsession crap, then the answer is yes." David pointed at Bryan and Alex. "Check it out. They've managed to attract a crowd."

Two other men were standing by the painting. They looked like art critics conferring over the creative intention of the artist. Natalie heard them use words such as color, hue, and expression.

"I guess that's my point," she said. "I've known Bryan for five years, and he has never expressed interest in or knowledge of art in this form. What's more, he's somewhat of an introvert. Look at him. He's animated and enthusiastic."

David waved at the waitress to bring him another scotch. "I don't know what you want me to say."

"It seems like that painting has a life of its own, like it's deliberately doing something to them."

David leaned in toward Natalie. "I'll agree that today has been strange, but I don't buy into conspiracy theories or the paranormal. Alex can get worked up over ghost stories, but he's a big boy who can take care of himself."

Bryan and Alex returned to the table accompanied by two men and a woman.

"I'm Justin Turner," one of the men said. "And this is my wife Ava. We're part of the hiking group that arrived this morning."

Ava gave David and Natalie a shy smile that didn't touch her eyes.

"Sean Ackerman," the other man said. "I'm in the area for a firefighters' convention. I'm a paramedic/firefighter for the Sacramento Fire Department."

Alex started to tell Sean that David and he were from Sacramento. The look on Natalie and Ava's faces dissolved his unspoken words.

The women were watching a man enter the bar through the service door in the back of the room. They appeared as if the man was seducing them from afar. Their lips were parted. Their eyes smoldered. Their breathing was fast and sharp.

He was the most beautiful man they had ever beheld.

His haunting eyes, their white irises haloed in gray, were filled with suffering and fear. He glanced behind him as a second man came in through the service door. Natalie recognized him as the shop owner whom Bryan and she had met earlier in the day. Lucas walked to the bar and whispered to the hotel manager. The hotel manager slid from his bar stool and went to the beautiful man's side.

The beautiful man stepped backward as if something had frightened him. His eyes came to rest on Bryan, Alex, Justin, and Sean. He stopped his backward motion. All four men stared at him, and their eyes met his. The beautiful man winced and raised a hand to his chest. The hotel manager moved in front of the beautiful man to shield him from the people in the bar. The beautiful man turned and disappeared through the service door.

Bryan and Alex sprinted toward the door with Justin and Sean at their heels. Lucas and Evan intercepted them. David stood up. A hush fell over the bar as the customers watched the men confront one another.

Lucas and Evan stepped in front of the door.

"I remember you," Bryan said to Lucas. "You own the general store on Main Street. Who was that man?"

"What man?"

"The man who was just here."

"I didn't see anyone."

"A man was standing here. He came through that door. Everyone at my table saw him."

The service door swung open. Niklas stepped into the bar. He closed the door and surveyed the scene.

Alex glanced at Niklas and then said to Lucas, "We don't want to cause trouble. We only want to know who that man was."

Lucas folded his arms across his chest. Niklas stepped toward Bryan, Justin, and Sean. Evan pressed his back against the door. A long silence ensued and finally, the four men mumbled apologizes and went back to their table.

Chapter 28

Janek innocently eluded Niklas' watch on the third floor and went to the bar. Lise went downstairs to the service hall with Niklas when they realized Janek was missing. They found him there, leaning against a wall, overwhelmed by the inferno in his chest and gasping for breath. Niklas left Lise with Janek and went to the bar.

Janek hugged himself and slid down the wall until he was sitting on the floor. He brought his knees to his chest then rested his folded arms on his knees. His head fell forward onto his arms. Lise sat beside him. She couldn't touch him; that would cause more pain and calling 911 wasn't an option. She waited for what was going to happen.

Minutes passed before she heard Janek draw in a deep breath. He coughed and tears from his watering eyes wet his forearms.

Lise whispered, "I'm here."

He raised his head and looked at her through tear-blurred eyes. The inferno in his chest was subsiding and with it, the hope that he was having a heart attack and dying.

When the pain subsided, he said, "I heard them, Lise. They were discussing me as if they know who I am. They don't know who I am."

Lise remained quiet so he could stay focused on his train of thought.

"I felt them touch the painting. It was an emotional feeling, not physical. Something naked and exposed, but I couldn't tell what it was. I had to see what they looked like, what they were doing."

Evan, Lucas, and Niklas rushed through the service door. Lise frowned, shook her head, and raised a finger to her lips as a warning for them to stop and be quiet.

"I'm not used to this strange spiritual voyeurism. It's different from what Erebus does to me." He wiped the wetness from his eyes. His thoughts dwindled, and he let out a long sigh.

"You were in pain. What was wrong?" Lise whispered.

Her question confused him, and he said, "Oh."

She tried again. "You were in pain. What was wrong?"

"Oh. My chest hurt."

Evan sat on the floor beside Janek. "Is that why you winced right before you left the bar, because your chest hurt?"

Janek's white eyes shifted to look at Evan. "When those men looked at me, pain exploded in my chest. It was the same feeling I had when, when…" The point he wanted to make was pertinent, but it eluded him.

"It was the same feeling as what?" Evan said. "Try to remember where you were going with this. It's important, isn't it?"

The service door opened, and Abigail stepped through the doorway. It was obvious the conversation between Evan and Janek had gone awry, as was the case with most conversations with Janek. She motioned for Niklas. They exchanged whispered words then Abigail went back into the bar.

"Was that Abby?" Janek said.

"Yes," Evan said.

"Why did she leave?"

"Guthrie closed the bar. She said she was going home," Niklas said.

Evan didn't revisit the topic of Janek's chest pain. It was a lost cause. He needed to take Janek to his suite. He didn't trust those men in the bar. They were desperate to find out who Janek was, and he wouldn't put it past them to skulk around in the hotel service areas.

"Let's go upstairs," Evan said to Janek.

"No. I want to stay a minute. Tell me what happened after Erebus turned us away from 1874."

Evan looked at Lise. She nodded, knowing this would be at least the two hundredth time he had recounted the event. Evan's green eyes met Janek's white eyes. Evan smiled and said, "Okay."

"I'm going back to my apartment," Lucas said. He saw no reason to hear the story for the two hundredth and first time. "Call me if something comes up."

Niklas gave Lucas a nod.

Evan began their story. "I don't know how long we sat in the banquet room waiting for our fate. Our watches had stopped. We weren't thirsty or hungry or tired or anything like that. After a while, I wanted to leave the room so I could figure out what was going on. Guthrie and Niklas wouldn't let me."

Janek sighed.

"We heard a sharp click and saw that the banquet room doors were ajar. Guthrie warned me again about leaving the room. Then the damnedest thing happened. The cat trotted to the doors and wiggled his way out and into the lobby. It was like he knew it was safe."

"Was I awake?" Janek said.

"No."

"Did I feel better then?"

Lise wiped a tear from her cheek. She remembered when Janek still felt well enough to sit in the hotel bar and drink, or walk to Lucas' store, or walk to the police station to visit his new acquaintance Lt. Jim Berggren.

But Janek's fall into decay had been swift and merciless.

Evan said, "Yes."

"What year was it?"

"2000. Of course, we didn't know that at first. I insisted that everyone wait in the banquet room until I checked things out, but Lucas refused to let me go alone. The shock we experienced when we walked out of the banquet room into the lobby was indescribable. The lobby was *so* bright, and the noise—the elevator, ringing phones, TVs, and the terrible growling outside on the street."

Janek rested his forehead on his folded arms.

"Janek?"

"Go on."

"We were scared shitless. Lucas said, 'We don't belong here and someone is going to notice,' but no one noticed. In fact, the front desk clerk called me by name and asked me about the guests checking into suite 306."

Evan knew Janek had lost track. He gave him a gentle nudge on the shoulder. "Come on. Let's go upstairs."

"No. Go on." Evan's voice chased away his fears.

Evan complied, "Lucas noticed how the women were dressed, and said we needed to find clothes for Lise and Abby. When we went outside, the noise was so much worse. The cars alone were...anyway, we ran to Lucas' store. It was still there and had evolved with the passage of time."

Without raising his head, Janek said, "Do you miss Matt?"

Evan looked at Niklas and Lise and said, "He's lost track. You guys might as well go upstairs."

Niklas shook his head. "We aren't leaving you alone until you're safe behind locked doors."

Evan nodded then said to Janek, "Yes, I miss Matt. He died in 1928. I visit his grave when I go to St. Paul's cemetery to visit my parents' graves."

"What happened to your sisters?"

Evan put a hand to his mouth and shut his eyes tight to ward off tears. When he was under control, he opened his eyes and said, "Margaret married Josef Paullo's youngest brother Martin. She died in 1880 giving birth to their third daughter. I don't know what happened to Eliza and Ellen."

"I'm sorry, Evan. My sister is dead too," Janek said. "Maybe I can go with you to the cemetery to visit Matt when I'm feeling better."

"Of course you can."

"I'm sorry that I've been so much trouble."

"Friends are never too much trouble. You know that."

"I would do the same for you."

"I know."

"I'm ready to go upstairs. Will you stay and talk to me so I won't hear Erebus' constant whispering in my head?"

"Sure."

When Evan and Janek entered suite 302, the cat woke from his slumber on the bed. He stretched and yawned, and then jumped to the floor to greet them. They walked into the living room.

"What does Erebus say to you?" Evan said as he poured tequila shots.

"It tells me it loves me."

"That's it?"

Janek shrugged and sat on the couch. "Most of the time it confuses me."

"Did it tell you anything about feeding your soul?"

"Maybe. When I consider things, I'm never sure if the thought I had was mine or if Erebus has told me."

"Do you have any idea how Erebus plans on carrying out this feeding?"

"Only that those men in the bar have something to do with it. You were watching them tonight, weren't you?"

"Yes. I didn't want anyone to talk to you about it because I didn't want to burden you. Obviously, I'm an idiot for thinking that bastard shadow wouldn't tell you."

The cat jumped into Janek's lap and nuzzled his chin.

"I wish Erebus would let me die."

"It isn't going to let you die."

"I'm not human anymore."

Evan reached for the tequila and poured two more shots. "We've talked about this. We have to let it get you stronger."

Janek took the shot glass from Evan's outstretched hand. He stared at it, and then set it on the coffee table. He stood up and the cat spilled from his lap and onto the floor. When he spoke, his words sounded angry, but they were born of fear. "If you were in this situation, what would you want?"

"I wouldn't want you to give up on me as long as I had breath in my body. There's still hope. As long as there's hope, you have a chance."

"I can't live and I can't die!" Janek shouted. "If I do get strong enough, it's going to come for me and..."

"Stop it! You can't fight if you've already surrendered. I won't let you give up!"

Janek left the living room and crossed the suite to the bathroom. He slammed the door behind him.

Evan threw his shot glass across the room, shattering it on the tile floor. Then he punched a hole in the wall with his fist.

VII

The Callow Knights

Chapter 29

December 5, 2016

Evan awoke with a stiff neck from sleeping in the chair in Janek's living room. How much sleep he got was open for debate. Back to back old movies showed on television, but Evan didn't notice. His thoughts wandered between the heinous shadow and Janek's deterioration.

As the hours passed, his frustration grew, but so did his determination. Somehow, he had to end this nightmare. He remembered Guthrie telling him to hold on to his guilt and anger because he was going to need those emotions. Guthrie reminded him every day to keep his vision clear. Last night, Evan's vision had cleared.

Erebus has to have a weakness that makes it vulnerable to destruction, Evan concluded. He knew he had to find that flaw and use it to obliterate Erebus. The task seemed as impossible as grabbing the wind and holding it in your hand.

He couldn't see Erebus, and he only felt its presence when Erebus allowed it. *Maybe, I don't have to be aware of its presence to find the weakness. Its life force is vaporous, but it has emotions. It's desperate and needy, but it's also perverted and powerful.*

Evan rubbed his stiff neck. Glass from the broken shot glass littered the floor. The gaping hole in the wall mouthed reminders of his exasperation last night.

The previous evening, Janek had stayed in the bathroom for what seemed like an eternity. Evan tried not to worry while he was in there. If Janek had gone into the bathroom with the intention of blowing his brains out, Erebus would have made it impossible for him to pull the trigger. Janek had gone to bed sometime after midnight. This morning, he was asleep, sprawled naked on top of the blankets. The cat slept at his feet. Evan wondered why Janek didn't cringe from the cat's touch.

After he cleaned up the broken glass in the living room, Evan went to his suite. He ordered breakfast and took a shower. At twelve thirty, his phone rang. It was Rob Copeland, the clerk at the registration desk. A guest wanted to speak to the hotel manager.

When Evan entered the lobby, Rob caught his eye and pointed to the bar's entryway. Bryan and Alex were peering at the painting through the darkness.

"I'm Evan O'Malley, the hotel manager. Did you ask to speak to me?"

Alex extended his hand to Evan. "I did. I'm Alex Spelman."

Evan ignored the offered hand shake.

This was the second time Alex's handshake had been rebuffed. He wouldn't offer it again.

"I'm Bryan Townsend. We saw you in the bar last night."

Bryan was tall and stocky. Evan thought he was at least forty years old. Alex was younger, but thin and shorter. Evan was sure he could take either man with one punch if they tried to start something.

"We frightened that man who came into the bar through the service door," Alex said. "We want to apologize to him."

They were using passive aggressive tactics to find out who and where Janek was, and there was no way in hell Evan was going to acknowledge that. He realized his hands were fisted. He forced himself to relax. "Is that all?"

He's evading us, Bryan thought.

"Can you tell us who painted that painting in the bar?" Alex asked. "It's a fascinating piece."

"Why is that important?"

"I told you. The painting is fascinating."

220

"I don't believe you."

"Why not? It's a simple question."

Evan narrowed his eyes; he frowned. "No it isn't."

"I had a strange dream last night," Alex said, making eye contact with Evan. "A man was sitting on a grave on the cemetery hill behind the memorial garden. He was crying and begging for help. His white eyes shone through the darkness that shrouded his face. I knew it was the artist. When I asked how I could help, he reached out for me. I saw his soul in his hand."

Evan clenched his jaws to keep from screaming.

"I had the same dream," Bryan said.

Evan struggled to regain his composure. He was an imbecile if he thought understanding Erebus' plan would prevent him from being blindsided. His fear and anger were blocking his vision.

"Please tell us who he is," Alex said.

The urge to protect Janek from these probing strangers overcame Evan. *They don't deserve to know Janek. They wouldn't see the man he is; they'd only see what's left.* However, Evan knew if he didn't tell them about Janek, Erebus would, and he didn't trust Erebus to tell the truth.

"What about the other men who were with you last night? Where are they?"

Bryan pointed at a couch in the lobby. "Justin and Sean are over there, waiting for us."

Evan looked at the other men. Their facial expression revealed they had also dreamed of Janek. He hated them for barging in on a struggle that was private among friends.

"I know you want to protect him from strangers, but they've come to help." It was Lise. She saw them standing in the shadows of the bar and went to Evan's side.

Evan killed his animosity and cleared his vision. He told Alex and Bryan to get their buddies and bring them to the bar.

Muffled voices from the restaurant haunted the bar. The blinds on the double glass doors to the restaurant were drawn. Darkness beset every corner.

Lise led the men to the painting.

Evan's voice trembled as he began to speak. He cleared his throat.

"This man is our friend, and we love him. He's like a brother to me. He took some terrible beatings, but he just kept coming, and now he can't take anymore. He's intelligent, loyal, and strong, but those qualities have been destroyed. This painting symbolizes the things he has lost; his longing to have a normal life again. His physical strength is dwindling. Fear and suffering are the only emotions he has left. His humanity is almost gone."

Evan's words exposed an open wound and poured salt into it. Lise tried to restrain her tears, but they broke free and soaked her cheeks.

Sean brushed the painting with his fingertips. "He was the man we saw last night. His white eyes were once blue. He's starving to death."

Justin asked, "How did this happen?"

As much as he wanted to tell them, Evan knew it would be a terrible mistake. They were being watched, and only Lucifer knew what Erebus would do to him and Lise if he told the truth.

"I can't tell you."

"Thank you, Evan. You've helped us understand. Will you tell us his name?" Alex requested.

Evan shook his head.

When the men had gone, Evan hugged Lise and held her as she sobbed. His tears dropped from his eyes and wet her hair.

Abigail was at home when she heard Evan's melancholy monologue in the bar. The group sensory they had developed was often a painful experience. She didn't want to hear the words, but she couldn't block them out of her mind. The raw description of Janek's predicament made her feel crazy. They knew how horrible his life had become, but hearing Evan describe it to strangers was hideous.

The phone rang. It was Janek. This was the fourth time in the past hour he had called to ask if she would come and stay with him. Each time, she assured him she would be there soon. She was ready to leave when the colloquy between Evan and the others commenced. Janek had to have heard the exchange. The phone rang as she was locking the front door.

When Abigail arrived at the hotel, she walked to the bar entrance. In a whisper she said, "Evan, Lise are you here?"

Lise and Evan emerged from the darkness. They looked drained. There was no need to ask if they were okay. Nothing was okay.

"What are we supposed to do now?" Abigail asked.

"As usual, we're relegated to waiting," Evan said, disgusted. "I'm going to check on Janek."

"I'm going up there now," Abigail said. "He wants me to stay with him. I don't think he should be left alone anymore."

Lise sighed and said, "It's sunny for a change so Niklas is taking me to Lowery Park. I need to get ready." At Lowery Park they could pretend, if only for a few hours, life was normal and the horrors they were living didn't exist.

"Maintenance is coming up to Janek's suite. I punched a hole in the wall in his living room last night," Evan said in shame. "Listen, I'm going to the Palace with Lucas. Call us if you need *anything*."

Lise put a hand on his cheek and smiled. "You look after everyone but yourself. Go have fun. The best thing you can give Janek right now is a less tense version of Evan O'Malley. Do you understand?"

He felt like he didn't deserve praise, and he avoided eye contact for fear she would see his lie when he said, "Thanks."

"Evan, please tell Daddy I want him to have dinner with me in Janek's suite at seven o'clock."

"Okay." He watched them get on the elevator. The doors closed, and he was alone.

Abigail heard the music in the hall. She fished the keycard out of her purse and unlocked the door. The rock music was deafening inside the suite. She recognized the music. It was *Led Zeppelin*. Robert Plant's mournful voice sang about a lady who was sure all that glittered was gold.

She lowered the volume and crossed the suite to the bathroom. Janek was soaking in the bathtub trying to relieve his inflamed skin. He asked her to turn up the music.

"Why does it have to be so loud?"

"It keeps me from feeling dead."

He looked like he was dying. His skin was pale, and he was thin. What little gray remained in his tired eyes yesterday was gone. He constantly massaged his temples and forehead with shaking hands.

"Can I get you anything?"

He shook his head.

"Okay. I'll be in the living room."

Robert Plant's melodious voice sang the lady was buying her stairway to heaven. She raised the volume, and sat on the couch. This particular album enchanted her and Janek the first time they heard it.

Music was an oddity for them when they landed in the year 2000. It came from everywhere and in all forms. It was hard for them to grasp the concept of digital music. She thought about the moment they left the banquet room after Evan and Lucas returned. She and Lise changed into men's clothes because Lucas insisted, and he was right. The people in the year 2000 were tolerant and open-minded, but a full-blown Victorian outfit would have turned heads.

She laid her head against the couch cushion and let the music envelop her. It represented something familiar and soothing like a lullaby. There was nothing to concentrate on because the music took one wherever one wanted to go. She wondered where the music took Janek.

The album ended, and the room was silent. Someone sat on the couch. She raised her head. It was Janek. He was naked. A bottle of painkillers lay in his open palm.

"I don't know how many I'm supposed to take."

She took the bottle and shook two into his unsteady hand. "Have you been taking these without knowing the dosage?"

"No."

Abigail believed him, and that scared her. *His mental capacity must have decayed at an alarming rate in only a few hours.* She wondered how he had been able to play the *Led Zeppelin* album without help.

"When was the last time you took these?"

"Last night."

"Did you know how many you were supposed to take then?"

"Yes."

"I better hold on to these for you. Do you have more?"

"I don't know."

Janek swallowed the pills without water. He was dizzy and nauseous and tired. Sleep beckoned. He dragged his exhausted body to his bed and stretched out on top of the blankets. The cat jumped onto the bed and nestled in by his feet.

Abigail checked on him a few minutes later. He was sleeping, existing in a world without torment and confusion.

She whispered, "I promise I'll take care of you. I'll be here when you wake up. I love you."

Chapter 30

Natalie and David stopped Evan on the sidewalk in front of the hotel. "Mr. O'Malley, I'm Natalie Townsend and this is David…"

"I know who you are."

Natalie didn't like Evan's tone. He looked at her like she was trash. She endured it because she needed to find Bryan.

"We're looking for my husband Bryan and David's friend Alex. Have you seen them?"

"Yes."

"Do you know where they are?"

Evan had a perverse urge to tell them that Bryan and Alex were with Erebus making plans to save a dying man. He swallowed the urge and said, "No." Then he walked toward the Palace.

"I think he was being rude to us on purpose," Natalie said.

David dialed Alex's cellphone number. The call connected, but it was directed straight to Alex's voice mail. David had left one message. He hung up without leaving another. Natalie experienced the same thing when she tried to call Bryan.

"I'm going inside to look for Bryan," Natalie said. "Will you join me?"

"Sure, but I have a feeling they don't want to be found."

Evan sat beside Lucas at the bar. The Palace was crowded with football fans, tourists, and Guthrie's cronies. Like Dodd's General Mercantile store, the Palace

Saloon had evolved with the passage of time. The men who hung out at the saloon all day in 1874 were long dead, replaced by a sixth generation of cronies.

"We need to talk," Evan said to Lucas.

Sometimes, Lucas didn't hear or feel what the rest of them did as a group. He chose to stay with the fellowship, and Erebus allowed it, but he was often left out of the group sensory. He lowered his voice and said, "I heard you talking to them in the bar this morning."

Evan breathed a sigh of relief. He wasn't going to have to repeat it.

Guthrie brought a bottle of whiskey and three shot glasses. He said to Lucas, "Pour out three, son. I reckon I could use one myself."

Lucas poured. They shot the whiskey.

"Heard anything?" Guthrie asked.

Evan said, "Townsend and Spelman are missing in action. Townsend's wife and Spelman's friend were looking for them this afternoon."

"Is someone with Janek?" Lucas asked.

"Abby is. That reminds me. Guthrie, she wants you at Janek's suite at seven for dinner."

"Maybe it ain't a good idea for her to be alone with Janek. Those men might try busting into the suite or hurt her if she walks out."

"I don't think they'll go to that extreme. They didn't seem physically aggressive."

"Hey, check it out," Lucas said to Evan. He nodded his head toward the saloon entrance. "The girls we were hanging out with last night just came in."

"You boys keep me informed, and don't let them women distract you too much."

Evan wanted to tell Guthrie that Lise had given him permission to have fun, but it would sound juvenile; although acting juvenile for one afternoon would be a relief. He watched the girls walk to the bar and order beers. Jessie, the woman he intended on getting in bed, saw him and waved. He nodded. She picked up her beer and joined him. Her friend Amy followed.

"Well, if it isn't the sexy Irishman I met last night," Jessie said. "I didn't expect to see you slumming it in here."

"The Palace is more my speed."

"You boys might want to go shoot some pool *right now*." Lucas and Evan looked at Guthrie. Guthrie tilted his head toward the front door. Bryan, Alex, Justin, and Sean were entering the Palace.

Evan took Jessie's hand and led her to the pool room in the back of the saloon. Lucas tried to do the same with Amy.

She pulled her hand from his grasp. "Slow down. Let's watch some of the game first."

"There's a TV in the pool room," Lucas said. He grabbed the whiskey bottle and left her standing alone at the bar.

"Okay," she relented. "I'm coming."

"This sucks," Evan whispered to Lucas while Jessie and Amy chose pool cues. "I'm going to see what those guys are doing."

Evan went to the door and listened. The men were sitting at a table close enough for Evan to hear them discussing the painting's artist, and commiserating over his predicament. Lucas joined Evan.

"They're talking about Janek," Evan said. "Can you hear them?"

Lucas nodded, and then motioned for Evan to leave the doorway. The women were watching them eavesdrop.

Evan went to Jessie, put his arms around her, and kissed her on the mouth. He pressed his crotch against her hips and said, "I'm sorry I made you wait."

Jessie reciprocated. *He's probably great in bed*, she thought.

They played pool and drank whiskey for several hours. At four o'clock, they heard an angry voice say, "What are you doing?" It was Natalie Townsend.

"Jessie, you and Amy play this game. Lucas and I have something to attend to. Don't argue with me or ask me why," Evan said.

Jessie ran her fingers through his hair, "Don't worry, I'll be a good girl," she assured him.

Evan patted her on the butt and waved Lucas toward the door. They slipped into the bar area within earshot, but out of sight of Bryan and the others.

Natalie sounded close to tears. "Bryan, where have you been all day?"

"I'm sorry. I thought I told you I was going to hang out with Alex."

"We're on our honeymoon! People don't hang out with the guys on their honeymoon!"

The other men were staring at Natalie like she was an intruder. She felt compelled to take her husband and get as far from Ferndale as possible. The look on Bryan's face told her it wasn't going to be easy. He was involved in something secretive. It all had to do with that damn painting.

"Nat, please," Bryan said. "Sit down and have a beer. There's no need to get upset."

David pulled up a chair and sat at the table. "Alex, I uncovered some interesting things about our missing church. I couldn't locate a living Mary Kellen in this area. There were several listed when I Googled her name, but they're all dead. One of them died in 1890. She was the first head of housekeeping at the Ferndale Hotel. The First Congregational Church of Ferndale burned to the ground, along with the residence house, in 1873 just like Guthrie said. A man named Janek Walesa was almost beaten to death in the church the same night. They think his attack was directly related to the cause of the fire. This same Janek Walesa, along with his partners, owned the Ferndale Hotel at that time. He's still listed as the hotel's owner, which doesn't make sense."

David had a captive audience, not only Alex, but also everyone seated at the table. "Now get a load of this picture. This was taken around 1880. Can you tell what it is?"

Alex took the picture from David. It was a snapshot of the hotel bar area. The painting hung in the background. Alex remembered Bryan saying the artist was the original hotel owner. David had bashed Bryan's theory by citing the original owner couldn't still be alive.

Alex handed the snapshot to Bryan. The two men exchanged knowing glances. The man Evan described to them had to be Janek Walesa. David was in danger of saying something that shouldn't be said.

Alex aggravated David on purpose by asking, "So what's your point?"

"What do you mean?" David asked. "We were lured here so someone could scam us. What's your problem?"

"I don't have one."

"Like hell you don't! I'm going back to Sacramento this afternoon. Are you coming?" David asked.

"No."

Ava Turner, Justin's wife, approached the table. She had taken the morning hike with the tour group and returned at one o'clock. "I'm sorry to interrupt," Ava said, avoiding eye contact. "Justin, I've been searching for you for hours. Why didn't you answer your phone?"

"I'm sorry, babe. I wanted to have a couple of beers."

Ava chose not to embarrass Justin in front of strangers. She gave him a weak smile. "We should go back to the hotel."

Justin got up and walked around the table to his wife. "Sure, babe. Alex, Bryan, Sean, I'll see you later."

Bryan decided he should leave with Natalie. Much to her dismay, he also promised he would see the guys later. Sean leaned back in his chair and drank his beer.

David said, "Alex, are you going to tell me what's going on?"

Alex didn't answer so David turned to Sean. "You're obviously a part of this clandestine operation. Are you going to give me a hint?"

"If you call having a few drinks and dinner later on tonight clandestine, then you found us out," Sean said. He threw a twenty-dollar bill on the table. "I'm out of here. See you tonight at seven, Alex."

"Tell me what's going on," David said to Alex.

"I'm warning you, David, leave it alone."

"If I don't, what are you going to do about it?"

Alex chuckled. "*I* won't do anything about it."

David left the saloon.

Evan and Lucas returned their attention to Amy and Jessie. After a few more games of pool, and a lot more beer, Evan asked Jessie to have dinner with him in his suite.

"How can I resist you?" Jessie said. She ran her fingers down the length of his ponytail.

The relief Evan felt when he closed the suite door behind him was overwhelming. Like Lise, he needed to escape the horror of what was happening to them and to Janek. He took Jessie in his arms and kissed her neck and face passionately. She was a beautiful blonde with green eyes, and for the first time in his life, Evan felt an honest attraction to a woman.

She unbuttoned his shirt and kissed his strong chest. He put a finger under her chin and tilted her head so she could look into his eyes. He wanted to kiss her lips for as long as possible. His hips undulated as he rubbed his erection against her firm belly.

Jessie unbuttoned his jeans and shoved them down with one hand while the other hand stroked his hard-on. He stopped kissing her and pulled off his jeans. Panting, she stripped off her clothes. She lay on his bed. He slipped over her and kissed her lips.

"I think you're going to drive me crazy," Jessie whispered as she wrapped her naked thighs around his waist.

Evan's green eyes flashed when he smiled. "I promise I will."

He savored her lips, her neck, and her small firm breasts. She tasted as beautiful as she looked. His tongue traced her nipples and left a trail of wet desire from her breasts to her belly button. Jessie groaned and let her legs fall from his back.

His tongue continued its journey down her body to her clit. She pushed the heels of her feet against the mattress and her knees dropped open. Evan's tongue moved to the lips of her slick pussy. His tongue darted inside her while his fingers moved to fondle her clit. She moaned and spread her legs further apart.

He sat up. His hands ran over her belly and up to her breasts. He forced her to roll over onto her stomach. She pushed her tight ass upward to touch his muscled stomach as he crawled over her. He straddled her waist and swept her long blonde hair away from her neck.

Evan's hard dick brushed her lower back as he kissed her neck. He was driving her crazy just as she knew he would. His sexual being was so virile that she was on the brink of an orgasm without his touch between her legs. She gasped and breathed, "Oh my god, Evan."

He felt her hips undulate beneath him as she rubbed her clit against the bedspread. Her moans were loud and unceasing. His erection followed her rippling movements and slid between her tight ass cheeks as he moved his body off her.

She got to her knees and begged him to fuck her.

Evan grabbed Jessie's hips and pulled them backward to meet his erection. His dick searched for and found the beating heart of her pussy. She felt glorious. He rocked his hips slowly, savoring her soft wetness, and scintillating them in a shower of orgasmic sparks.

Amy wrapped her arms around Lucas' neck and kissed him. Her hand wandered to his crotch and squeezed. She brushed her lips against his ear and said, "Evan doesn't have to be the only one who gets laid tonight."

Lucas' sexual being was awkward and shy. He'd had plenty of whores in Eureka, but women you paid for sex didn't require you to perform or romance them. He wasn't sure if his heart was into making the effort to make love while Janek was dying. It's not that he was judging Evan; sex was easy for Evan no matter the circumstances.

I must be an idiot, he thought. *This woman is doing everything she can to get my body to pay attention, and I'm hesitating.* The bottom line was that he didn't want to have to talk to her about his life. His decision to stay with Janek and Evan was in part a decision to step into their lives and out of his.

He knew that both Janek and Evan would tell him to get laid. Lucas knew for a fact that Janek didn't chit-chat with whores or any other woman he took to bed. It wasn't in his nature. Lucas offered his hand to Amy, and this time she reciprocated.

Chapter 31

Guthrie used his keycard to access Janek's suite. Abigail was anxiously waiting near the door.

"Daddy, will you talk to Janek? I'm trying to convince him to eat with us. He hasn't eaten all day, and he's taking painkillers."

"He ain't going to listen to me."

"Yes he will. Please, Daddy."

Guthrie grunted. "Where is he?"

"In the bathroom."

"I ain't going in there. You get him to come out here."

"That's the problem. He won't come out, and the door is locked. I think he's feeling a lot worse today."

Guthrie grumbled, "Men shouldn't be in the bathroom together," and then shuffled to the bathroom and banged on the closed door. "Janek, it's Guthrie. Open this door."

Silence.

"Did you hear me, son? Open up."

More silence.

"I'm gonna go get Niklas, and he's gonna kick this door in. Do you understand me?"

Abigail said, "I'm not sure he's…" She swallowed hard. "I'm not sure he's awake or even alive. I can't hear any sound on the other side of the door."

"Janek, if you're alive, make some noise so Abby can hear you."

The lock popped, and the doorknob turned. The door opened a crack. "Guthrie?"

"Yep, it's me. Come on out, son. Abby wants you to eat, and you're gonna eat."

"Abby said I have to get dressed, but I don't know how."

"Oh lord," Guthrie said. "Does he have to eat at the table?"

"Yes, Daddy, otherwise, one of us is going to have to sit in there with him and make sure he eats. I want him to have some normalcy."

Guthrie pushed the door open wider and stepped into the bathroom. Janek was standing on the other side of the door naked. Clothes lay scattered on the floor. His comb lay on the floor beside the sink.

"What's wrong, son?"

Janek sat on the edge of the bathtub and rubbed his temples. "My clothes don't make sense."

Guthrie went into the huge walk-in closet. He rummaged in the drawers until he found what he wanted. He came out holding a pair of boxer shorts, jeans, and a white t-shirt. Guthrie handed the clothes to Janek.

"Put these on. I'll talk you through it."

Janek examined the clothes in his hand. He dropped the jeans on the floor.

Guthrie shuffled back to the closet and came out with flannel pajama bottoms. "Put the boxer shorts on first."

Janek didn't move.

Guthrie took the boxer shorts from Janek and held them up in front of him. "Put this leg in that hole and that leg in the other hole."

Janek's hands trembled so intensely that it took him ten minutes to dress himself. Guthrie retrieved the comb from the floor and gave it to Janek. He managed to comb his hair with no help.

"You have to eat because Abby says so. Come on now."

Abigail was sitting at the table in the living room. Janek stared at the table. She said, "Sit down and try to eat something."

Janek sat at the table. He forgot what he was supposed to be doing. Guthrie saw his confusion.

"What's wrong, son?"

Janek looked at Guthrie then at Abigail. His white eyes were clouded with bewilderment. "What is this?"

"It's dinner," Abigail said, gently. "You need to eat. Can you do that?"

"I don't know." Janek propped his left elbow on the table and raised a shaking hand to his forehead. He rubbed his head and stared at his plate.

Abigail started to ask Janek if he needed help, but Guthrie motioned for her to be quiet. Before dinner she'd said that she wanted to give Janek some normalcy. Cutting his meat and feeding him like a baby wasn't normal for a twenty-seven-year-old man.

Fifteen long minutes passed, and Janek still had not eaten. He went to the couch and lay down. A sighing breeze blew in circles over and around everything in the room. The stereo came to life. *Led Zeppelin* poured from the speakers. *The Battle of Evermore* began, and the breeze died.

Abigail had a terrifying epiphany: Janek had told her that the music kept him from feeling dead. *The death of his soul is imminent,* she realized, horrified. The loud music was stimulating him enough to survive until Erebus could begin the feeding. Erebus was playing the music.

Guthrie went to lower the volume.

Abigail stopped him. "No! The music is filling up enough of his empty spirit to keep him alive. When the music stops, he will at least be able to function. Please, Daddy, be patient!"

Guthrie had every intention of being patient. If what Abigail surmised was true, Janek was already dead.

Alex, Bryan, Justin, and Sean dined in the hotel restaurant and talked about their favorite subject: the artist of the painting and his plight. Natalie and Ava had finished their meal and were tired of the small talk they'd attempted over dinner. The men hoped the women would become bored and leave. There were plans to be made that didn't include Natalie or Ava.

"Who wants to join me for a drink in the bar?" Sean said as he dropped his napkin onto his plate.

The men thought a drink was a great idea. Natalie and Ava followed their husbands into the bar. The men sat at a table near the painting. Ava sighed. Natalie rolled her eyes.

Natalie said to Ava, "Let's go to the bar. David Channing is there."

They sat on the barstools, flanking David.

"How are you doing tonight, ladies? Don't tell me you're bored with The Knights."

"Why did you call them that?" Natalie asked.

"They seem to be on some sort of crusade."

"I'm going to cut my own throat if I have to hear them talk about that damn painting another minute," Ava said. "Thankfully, we're leaving first thing in the morning, and that will be the end of it."

"I wouldn't be so sure about that if I were you," David said.

"What do you mean?"

David deflected Ava's question. "I'm disappointed that cute little bartender isn't working tonight. It's probably for the best. I don't think she's really what she seems to be on the surface."

"Cut the crap, David, and answer Ava's question. Why did you say you weren't so sure about that?" Natalie demanded.

David drained his glass of scotch. "Did you tell Ava what's going on?"

"I don't know anything!"

David let out a condescending laugh. "You can't be that dense. Think about what you know: The church that burned down in 1873, the picture that was painted before 1880, and the dead real estate agent, not to mention the original hotel owner who is still listed as the current owner. If that's not the makings of a ghost story, I don't know what is."

"But you said that you don't buy into the paranormal," Natalie said. "I was the one who was suspicious in the first place, and you made fun of me."

"Yeah, well something changed my mind. Would you ladies care to join me outside while I smoke?" David looked over his shoulder at Alex.

Natalie pasted a smirk on her face. "I wouldn't miss it for the world."

When they reached the sidewalk in front of the restaurant doors, David pulled a pack of cigarettes from his jacket pocket. He lit a cigarette and inhaled a long drag. The night was cold and damp. A misty rain formed blurred auras around the streetlights.

"There's a new moon tonight," David said, looking skyward. "I always thought the absence of moonlight was eerier than a full moon."

Ava gave her upper arms a brisk rub and said, "Come on, David. It's cold out here. Say what's on your mind."

"Ladies, I made a startling discovery earlier this evening. Do you remember I said the original hotel owner, Janek Walesa, had business partners?"

Natalie and Ava nodded.

"Well, the city hall records list the names of those partners. It reads like a who's who of people we have personally met: Evan O'Malley, Lise Anders Arnold, Guthrie Sullivan, and Abigail Sullivan. What's more, the reverend who presided over the church before it burned down was Niklas Arnold. He married Lise Anders in November 1873. Guthrie and his daughter, Abigail, owned, and still own, the Palace Saloon. They live in a house just a few blocks from here."

Natalie and Ava gaped at David. What he was saying was impossible.

"I tried to find death certificates on those people, and there were none. The general store owner, Lucas Dodd, apparently never died either. Now the question is what happened to Janek Walesa?"

"Are you saying those people are over one hundred and seventy years old?" Natalie declared.

"Guthrie Sullivan is two-hundred-six-years-old. He was born in 1810."

"That can't be! Someone in this town would have noticed they weren't aging!"

David shrugged. "Apparently, no one *has* noticed."

"Maybe we should call the cops," Ava said.

"What are you going to tell them—that your husband is spending too much time hanging out with the guys? How about telling them that you suspect, the hotel manager, was born in 1846?"

"David, are you sure you aren't mistaken? Maybe you're jerking us around because you and Alex got scammed, and now you're pissed off," Natalie said.

"I'm getting Justin, and we're leaving right now," Ava said. She pushed the hotel door open and disappeared into the lobby.

David threw his cigarette butt on the sidewalk and crushed it with the heel of his shoe. "He's going to be gone when she gets there."

Natalie went inside the hotel. She hurried to the pointed arch entryway and entered the bar. The Knights were gone.

At 8:30 P.M., room service came and removed the dinner dishes from Janek's suite. Abigail was in the shower. Guthrie was watching television. The music had stopped, but Janek wasn't any more alert than when it began. His open eyes were focused on a place where pounding headaches and painful skin didn't exist.

He was a fourteen-year-old boy living on the farm in the Willamette Valley. Lush green farmland, rolling hills, and mountain ranges enveloped him in their arms. He felt the warm sun on his face and back as he helped his father hang doors on their new barn.

In the dooryard, a litter of puppies born that spring frolicked after the chickens and geese. Cats prowled for mice and rats. The smell of baking bread drifted through the open kitchen window. His mother was preparing lunch. In this place, life was hard, but it was good. Janek was happy to be there. It was where he belonged.

"Hold the door higher so I can get the hinges on," Aron said to Janek.

The muscles in Janek's adolescent arms and shoulders flexed and tightened as he raised the door. Aron nailed the hinges to the outer wall of the barn.

"Let go of the door." Aron stepped back and surveyed their work. "It looks good. What do you think?"

Janek swung the door back and forth. "It's not wobbly and it's straight. I think we're done."

"Aron, Janek, come in for lunch," Freya called from the front porch. "Don't forget to wash up."

"Go wash up, son, while I put the tools away."

Janek walked to the backyard. He pumped water from the well, washed his face and hands, and then dried them on the towel his mother kept near the pump. He stepped onto the back porch. As he reached to open the back door, the sun disappeared behind a cloud. The bright daylight faded to gray.

He opened the screen door and went into the kitchen. The table was set for lunch. His mother and sister were not there.

"Mother, where are you? Liv? Answer me!" Janek ran through the empty house, calling their names. Panic cramped his stomach.

He ran onto the front porch. The puppies, cats, chickens, and geese had vanished from the dooryard. Janek screamed for his father. There was no answer. Dark clouds obliterated the sun. Cold wind beat his face and stung his eyes. A thousand lost souls begged for a human life. Erebus was there.

"No! No! Leave them alone! I'll go to you, just don't take them away from me!"

He ran toward the barn then stopped short. He was standing on an expanse of lawn in a dim, misty garden surrounded by towering redwood trees. The murmuring souls realized he had not come for them, and they fell silent.

The cold wind ruffled his blond hair and scurried through the redwoods. A familiar voice rode on the wind.

"You stupid Pollock, what are you looking for? You know they're dead," Emily Hartmann's voice cackled. "In a few hours, you will be dead too. That imbecile shadow that's been haunting you waited too long. You're dead, Janek! You're dead!"

Janek blinked and rubbed his eyes. He struggled to sit up. The cramping in his stomach was real. He gagged then wretched. Guthrie jumped from his chair and grabbed the small wastebasket by the table. He shoved it under Janek's chin.

Janek wretched and dry heaved. After a few minutes, his stomach settled down. He leaned back and wiped sweat from his face with his hand.

"Are you okay?" Guthrie inquired.

Janek nodded. He stood up and pulled off his t-shirt. It was hurting his skin. He began to take off his pajama bottoms.

"Leave those on," Guthrie said. "You ain't sitting around naked in front of Abby."

"She's seen me."

"Let me rephrase that. You ain't sitting around naked in front of me, and I ain't leaving."

Janek walked to the back of the room and fetched a bottle of tequila from the bookshelf. He went back to the couch and sat down. The cat bounded into the living room and jumped into his lap.

"Where's Abby?" Janek asked as he removed the cap from the bottle.

"She's taking a shower."

Janek drank from the bottle. His stomach didn't protest so he drank more. "I need my pills."

"I ain't got 'em."

"Abby has them."

Guthrie sighed and shuffled to the bathroom. Janek was a wreck, and there wasn't a damn thing he could do about it. *If the boy wants to wash down the whole bottle of painkillers with tequila, so be it. The maggot shadow will force him to puke anyway.*

Abigail came out of the bathroom dressed in pajamas and a robe. Her long dark hair was wrapped in a towel. "What's wrong, Daddy?"

"Janek wants his pills."

She took the pill bottle from the pocket in her robe and handed it to Guthrie. "Give him two."

"He's drinking tequila. I don't want you to stop him," Guthrie said. "I wouldn't let him take off his clothes, but other than that, let him be. Do you hear me?"

"Yes, Daddy."

Guthrie returned to the living room and gave Janek two pills. Then he sat in his chair and resumed watching television with one eye and Janek with the other.

Natalie tried to rationalize what she was seeing in the bar. Rain poured from the ceiling above the painting. Green, yellow, orange, and red paint streaked the canvas and dripped onto the floor. The effect was horrifying. The painting appeared to be weeping. What the artist had tried to convey was being annihilated.

Ava approached Natalie; her cheeks were stained with black mascara. "They're gone," she sobbed. "The bartender and the waitress claim they never saw them. The desk clerk didn't see anything either."

"Do you see the rain?" Natalie asked. Her eyes remained fixed on the painting.

Ava nodded and wiped her eyes with her fingertips.

Natalie walked to the painting. Water sprayed her face as she reached to touch the rain. It soaked her hand and the cuff of her sleeve. She looked around. No one in the bar was paying attention to the rain because they couldn't see it.

David walked into the bar. "What the hell? Is it raining in here?"

"This is your fault, you bastard!" Natalie said. "You set us up by asking us to walk outside! You knew they wanted to get away from us, so you helped them! Where are they?"

"That's not true! The notion that they would be gone hit me like a bolt out of the blue. I have no idea where they are."

Natalie gave him a vicious look.

"This is unbelievable," David said. "I get the feeling things are coming to an end."

Green, yellow, orange, and red paint amalgamated to a filthy brown and imbrued the wall below the painting. The showcase light popped and shorted out. The waterlogged canvas sagged.

Natalie knew if she witnessed the painting fall to the floor she would lose her mind.

Ava ran from the bar. Natalie and David ran after her. Ava stopped at the foot of the grand staircase and rifled through the contents of her purse.

"I'm calling the cops! Don't try to talk me out of it!" Ava said. She pulled her phone from her purse. Before she could dial 911, a tall man approached them with an aggressive stride.

"Is there a problem here?" he asked.

"Who are you?" David demanded.

"I'm head of hotel security. The night desk clerk called to tell me Mrs. Townsend and Mrs. Turner appeared to be frightened. Are you harassing these women?"

"I didn't catch your name."

Niklas narrowed his eyes. "I'm Niklas Arnold, and you're David Channing."

This man is the reverend himself, David thought. *Praise the Lord!*

Niklas favored David with a sneer. He knew David was ferreting information about their fellowship and the hotel. Niklas wanted an excuse to kill him.

"He isn't harassing us," Natalie said.

Niklas frowned at her.

"I met your wife yesterday morning," she said.

Niklas said nothing.

Natalie couldn't stop thinking about David's claim that this man was born over one hundred and seventy years ago. It was impossible to comprehend. *Only monsters live that long,* she thought.

Ava outright stared at Niklas for the same reason, however, her motivation to find her husband outweighed his intimidation. "Have you seen our husbands tonight? Justin Turner and Bryan Townsend? They were with two other men, Sean Ackerman and Alex Spelman."

Niklas let out a nasty laugh. "I saw them in the bar earlier tonight. They left before the rain began falling."

"Did you see the rain in the bar, Mr. Arnold?" Ava asked.

"I didn't, but you did."

He's screwing with us, David thought. *He knows what's going on. Let's see what he does when I ask him about his past.* "Someone told me you were once a reverend, Mr. Arnold."

"You're a liar. Nobody told you that. You found that out all on your own didn't you?" Niklas stepped closer to David. "I used to be the presiding reverend over the church you and your friend came here to see. I believe you know the story of what happened to it."

David didn't expect a confession and was unnerved by Niklas' boldness.

Niklas looked at each person as he said, "You think you know something that will stupefy the masses, but you don't know shit. You're naïve paltry bystanders. Mrs. Turner, please feel free to call the police or perhaps the FBI. They won't believe a word you say."

Niklas turned and walked toward the grand staircase.

"Jesus," David said under his breath. "What the fuck was that?"

"I'm calling his bluff," Ava tried to dial 911, but couldn't get a signal. She threw her phone in her purse. "I'm walking to the police station."

"Hold on, Ava," David said. "What are you going to tell them? Justin isn't technically missing. No crime has been committed. Think about it before you go spouting off to the police."

"Shut up, David! Ava doesn't need your permission to go to the cops. Do you think we trust your judgment just because that man claims to be Niklas Arnold?"

"There's no need to be hostile. I'm on your side."

"Then what's your problem with calling the cops?" Ava insisted.

"In this case, a paranormal investigator might be more effective. I know, Natalie, don't remind me of my self-proclaimed skepticism of the paranormal."

"If you don't want the cops involved, then what do you suggest we do?" Natalie asked.

"Let's go back to the Palace Saloon," Ava suggested.

Neither David nor Natalie thought The Knights would be there.

"The Palace is just down the street. It's worth a try. Please?" Ava insisted, "I don't want to go alone."

"Sure, we'll go with you," David said. *We should probably stick together,* he thought.

Chapter 32

At 3:00 a.m., Janek's dreamless sleep changed as his soul embarked on its final journey toward death. The darkness in which Erebus existed invaded Janek's vacuous body and began to suffocate the last of his humanity. White-hot heat exploded in his head and chest. His involuntary screams echoed throughout the third floor.

In suite 304, Evan was jerked awake by Janek's agonizing screams. He scrambled from his bed and threw on his jeans.

Jessie awoke and said, "What is that noise?"

"Go back to sleep, Jessie. I'll be back as soon as I can."

Evan ran from the suite, slamming the door behind him. He banged on the door of suite 302. Guthrie unlocked the door and let him in.

"What the hell is going on?" Evan asked. "Where's Janek?"

"He's on the bed."

Evan pushed past Guthrie. Janek lay in the fetal position. His screams softened to moans. Tears trickled from his closed eyes and wet his pillow. The cat licked and pawed at his chest.

Abigail was frenetic. She shouted hysterical accusations at Evan, "You said Erebus wouldn't let him die, but he *is* dying! You were wrong! You should have done something! Why didn't you do something?"

Her accusatory words devoured his guilty conscious. Like a drowning man, gripping the last lifesaving ring aboard a sinking ship, he had clung to the conviction that Erebus could keep Janek alive. He should have realized Erebus' sudden move to lure those men to Ferndale was a sign that Janek's condition had slipped from its control. He had no defense, and what was worse, he couldn't assure Abigail that Janek was going to survive the feeding, let alone live long enough for it to begin.

When the Arnolds came into the suite, Abigail ran to Lise in tears. She grabbed Lise by the hand and dragged her to Janek's bed side. "He's dying! I can't get him to respond to anything I say! His soul is completely gone!"

Lise's heart and acumen threatened to explode into a million pieces, but unlike Abigail, she was able to keep them intact through sheer grit. She sat on the bed beside Janek. If she could see into his haunted white eyes, perhaps they would reveal if any part of him still existed. But his eyes were closed, his spirit hidden from her view.

Guthrie called Lucas.

Lucas answered on the first ring. He sounded wide awake when he said, "I'll be right there," before Guthrie had a chance to speak.

"Janek, can you hear me?" Evan asked. He was trying not to shout or sound as scared as he felt inside. "You have to hold on to your life. There has to be something inside of you that's strong enough to survive, a part of you that Erebus can't get to. For God's sake, Janek, we said we were going to beat this. You can't give up!"

Evan saw no sign that Janek could hear his pleas. Erebus had miscalculated the length of time Janek would be able to hang on to life. Rage rushed at him like a barbarian, but he fought it off. *Keep your vision clear and focused,* he told himself.

He realized touch was the only way to stimulate Janek's senses. He shooed the cat from the bed and grabbed Janek by the shoulders. He pulled his body into his arms. The searing torment of touch reached Janek's primeval instinct and he screamed. Sweat dripped from every pore in his body. Rage returned to attack Evan and this time, he let it beat him.

"You waited too long, you son of a bitch! He's dying and when he does, you'll be shit out of luck!"

Erebus' answer was immediate. "I did not wait too long. He is at the brink of death, but I have the power to pull him back."

"You perverse bastard, why are you doing this to him?"

"He believed he had a chance to overthrow me. I have merely demonstrated how much stronger I have become. Pain and misery are excellent tools for keeping the human spirit in bondage."

"You're the one in bondage! Without Janek, you have nothing!" Evan said. He jumped to his feet and punched a fist in the air. "I hate and despise you for what you've done to my friend—for what you've done to all of us!"

"I hate and despise you as well! I would have turned you to dust with the Hartmann slut if you had not been necessary to him."

"Necessary? His soul is necessary! You've let it drain away until there's nothing left."

Erebus' laugh rolled like thunder. "Do you think his soul has emptied like water running down a drain in to the sewer? It has merely escaped."

"Escaped to where?"

"Here. It is here all around us."

"Then give it back to him!"

"That is something I cannot do. Only another human being can."

Lise scooted in closer to Janek like a mother protecting a helpless infant, before she said, "Let us do it."

"That is not allowed. You serve another purpose."

"Stop playing games!" Evan screamed.

"This is not a game! The task will be done by those whom I have chosen; human beings who are not tainted by the past. They will gather Janek's soul and feed it to him."

"He isn't responsive," Lise said, keeping her eyes on Janek. "How is he going to understand what's happening?"

"He doesn't need to understand."

The more Erebus spoke the angrier Evan became. It was playing with them, forcing them to beg for information. He could no longer stand its superior attitude and its lack of sympathy for what it had taken from Janek.

"Stop referring to him like he's a child who has no say in his own destiny! You have no concept of life. How dare you presume to control his life?"

Erebus hated Evan not only because he was confrontational, but because he was right. The feeding should have commenced days ago. Erebus failed to notice Janek's accelerated decay. It was blinded by its own conceit, admiring its new strength like a man flexing his muscles in a mirror. Regardless, Erebus had the upper hand. "I will presume whatever I wish. You will do as I say."

Guthrie whispered to Evan, "Don't say nothin' else, son. You're antagonizing it."

"They have already gathered," Erebus said. "By dawn, they will know what needs to be done to save him. You will take him to them. Some of you will go with Janek, and some will stay behind as watchers."

"Take him where?" Evan asked.

"You would do well to take Guthrie's advice and shut up."

Evan opened his mouth, and Niklas took several aggressive steps toward him. Evan shut his mouth.

"You will take him to his garden where he can be nurtured and fed."

Niklas' face paled. The garden was intended to be a place where Janek could begin to heal and find his way to freedom. *Why didn't I see the garden would be misused?* he lamented. He had been blinded by Erebus' deception.

"I warn you, the feeding will not be painless, and he may beg for it to stop," Erebus said. "You will not interfere. When the last piece of his soul is left for the feeding, the piece that I possess, we will become one."

"Do you really believe you'll live a life of harmony with someone who hates you?" Evan said, ignoring Niklas' threat and Guthrie's advice.

"He does not hate me! You have made him unable to feel the love he has for me."

They were stunned by Erebus' last remark.

When had it deluded itself into believing that? Evan wondered.

"Stay with him and ready him for his destiny. Do not think you will be able to do otherwise."

Lise said, "What if he dies before..."

"Abigail knows how to keep him alive."

Abigail realized hysteria had caused her to forget the music. She shoved hysteria away.

"What if we let him die?" Evan said in defiance.

"Do not question me any further!"

"Fuck you!"

Evan's face was slapped so hard that the others in the room heard his jaw pop.

Guthrie said, "Clear out your anger, boy."

Evan rubbed his jaw.

Lucas entered the suite during the confrontation with Erebus. He stood by the suite door with his Green River knife in his hand. The action of pulling his knife from the sheath in his boot was ludicrous. Weapons were of no use against this enemy.

"We can't let that monster have its way with Janek," Niklas said.

They looked at one another with fear and uncertainty. Their fellowship looked as drained of energy as Janek's body.

Evan returned his attention to Janek. He existed nowhere yet everywhere. The remains of his life force balanced on the edge of eternity. One push and he would die. *What would happen to his scattered soul then?* he wondered.

Guthrie eyed Evan. "I know what you're thinking, son. You're wondering what's gonna happen if Janek dies without his soul, or worse, dies joined with that monster."

"He'll go to purgatory," Lucas whispered. "When I was a little boy I asked my father where monsters went when they died. When he finally stopped denying there were monsters, he admitted they went to purgatory with the tainted souls and the soulless."

"Oh Jesus," Evan said. "Time is running out. Niklas is right. We have to figure out a way to get that piece of shit to let go of Janek."

Abigail played the *Led Zeppelin* album. She doubted it would do any good, but hoped it would buy them more time.

VIII

The Garden at the Edge of Eternity

Chapter 33

December 6, 2016

Natalie, David, and Ava failed at their attempt to find The Knights. Their final search was in Ferndale Memorial Garden. They saw no one.

But The Knights *had* gone to the memorial garden. They passed under the ivy-covered trellis and walked the winding pathways to a shadowed redwood forest. Through the forest the path led to another garden, a garden built by Niklas' faith and Janek's unbound soul. In this garden, time and destiny were meaningless. Serenity whispered promises of peace and love on the winds of eternity. This was the garden for which Niklas had sacrificed his congregation and his church.

The redwood forest surrounded the garden. The towering trees blocked out the sun and shrouded the expanse of a well-manicured lawn in gray light. There were no benches for sitting because if one lingered too long, they would be lost to eternity.

One by one, the men stepped into the garden. The fragrance of the ethereal human soul pollinated the air. The men were overcome with emotion because they recognized the scent.

As they crossed the lawn, they heard the voices of a thousand lost souls begging for a human life. The fragile qualities of the human soul surrounded them in the fringes of the gray light and misted the air with every emotion bestowed to mankind.

The Knights sat in the dewy grass. The begging souls quieted as they realized the men had not come for them. The presence of Janek's soul became apparent. The delicate fragments swirled in the garden like snowflakes in the wind.

"I can feel his fear," Bryan said.

They all felt his fear. The echoes of his desolation reverberated on the winds of eternity. If they didn't help him, he would cease to exist forever.

"His loss is far beyond what we imagined. How can a man come to this?"

Bryan's question bewildered them, and they sat in silence as they searched for the answer.

How can a man lose the essence of his life yet still live?

Religion teaches that the soul lives after the body dies. A body that lives after the soul dies is so wretched that it's only fit to become a zombie or a creature.

But his soul wasn't dead; it was displaced. Were the two things equivalent?

The answers to those unobservable questions weren't forthcoming so they concentrated on the visible. The swirling pieces of Janek's soul shined with luminous energy from within and emanated his transcendence. His perfection was bewitching and intoxicating. The Knights found it difficult to break the enchantment.

"His soul is so pure. I don't think we're capable of gathering it," Justin said.

Alex said, "Janek is dying. Let's get started. Close your eyes. Sense the part of him that's also a part of you. We all love. We all hate. It's the essence of humanity."

The Knights closed their eyes. The intimacy of human emotion comforted them, and they knew they were capable of capturing it in their consciousness. Each man reached for the qualities that he believed made him extraordinary, but without the ordinary they were not fulfilled. They attempted to gather every fragment. As Janek's soul filled their consciousness, they felt strong and powerful. Their task was within their grasp.

They opened their eyes. Snowflakes persisted in the wind. What had they missed? The Knights contemplated the resplendent flakes and understood that they were Janek's intrinsic self. His concept of right versus wrong, his perception of beauty, all the things that made a man different from another.

Alex said, "With our guidance, he will have the ability to gather his innate soul himself."

This infuriated Erebus. Janek couldn't be trusted to gather the remaining pieces of his soul. He had to be force fed to ensure nothing was left to chance. The piece of Janek's soul that Erebus possessed could not be overlooked.

It tried to compel the men, but Erebus had no power in Janek's garden. It decided that might be for the best. It would be free to focus on the moment of the joining. The men would make certain Erebus' precious shred of soul was returned because that piece was hope, and when Janek ingested hope, it would be infused with Erebus' soul.

⤛⤜

Evan was in the living room pouring whiskey shots when his phone rang. *Who the hell is calling me at four o'clock in the morning?* It was the front desk clerk. The police were in the lobby, and they wanted to speak to the manager.

Evan threw his phone at the wall. "Someone called the cops," he said to Niklas and Lucas. "Niklas, I want you to come with me."

"You can't go like that," Niklas said. "You're wearing nothing but jeans."

Evan went into Janek's closet and put on a shirt. He and Niklas left the suite and took the elevator to the lobby. A Ferndale police officer was waiting for them at the front desk.

"Evan, we've had a complaint that I'm obliged to follow up on."

"What's the problem, Jim? It's been quiet."

Lt. Jim Berggren looked uncomfortable. "Some woman came into the station ranting and raving about her missing husband, melting paintings, and one-hundred-seventy-year-old people. Frankly, I couldn't follow a word of what she was saying."

"Was that woman Ava Turner?"

"You know I can't tell you that."

"Mrs. Turner was beside herself earlier tonight," Niklas said. "Apparently, she was unhappy because her husband chose to spend time with the guys. At first, I was under the impression that one of our guests was harassing her, but that wasn't the case."

"Who did you think was harassing her?" Jim said.

"A man named David Channing. He was with Mrs. Turner and another woman, Natalie Townsend. Mrs. Townsend said he wasn't harassing them."

"David Channing was at the station with the complainant. He was asking questions about Janek."

"What did you tell him?" Evan asked.

"Nothing."

"Did you tell him you knew Janek?"

"Nope. Anyway, if you're sure you have nothing to tell me, I'm going back to the station."

Evan sighed. He was exhausted from stress. "I told you it's been quiet."

"Right, and as I said, I'm just following up. If you happen to see or hear anything you think I need to know, give me a call."

As Evan and Niklas walked back to the elevator, Evan said, "If Channing or those women get in the way, blow their brains out."

Niklas sneered and chuckled. "That was my plan."

When they returned to the suite, Abigail was pacing the living room. She was managing hysteria, but struggling with anxiety.

Evan poured a glass of whiskey and drank it in one swallow. He had to think hard about what Erebus had said. It had to have given away something, even the smallest clue that revealed a weakness. The music and the presence of the fellowship were derailing his thoughts. He needed to be some place quiet.

"I'm going to my room," Evan said. He retrieved his phone from the floor. "I'll be back soon. Come get me if anything changes."

Evan walked into his living room and looked at his phone. He had a text message from Jessie. She was in her room and would catch up with him later. *Fat chance*, Evan thought. At dawn, all hell was going to break loose.

He opened a bottle of whiskey and drank from it. He ran a hand across his lips between drinks from the bottle. Nervous energy discharged bolts of electricity through his body, catching everything it touched on fire. He couldn't sit down. He couldn't stand up. He fidgeted with the whiskey bottle. He paced. *What had Erebus said? Did it reveal anything I didn't already know? For that matter, what the hell do I know about that fucking nightmare?*

Evan went into the bathroom and turned on the shower. He needed to entomb himself in clarity. As he undressed, he considered the incredibly conceited façade Erebus presented when it spoke. It was sure it had total control. The truth was it *did* have total control. *Why?*

Hot water flowed from the showerhead and isolated Evan in the white noise of rushing water. *Clear your mind. Clear your vision.*

He dressed in a clean pair of jeans and a t-shirt. He pulled on a pair of socks and his boots. It occurred to him that Janek was wearing flannel pajama bottoms. He thought Janek would want to be dressed in appropriate attire when he met the men who would return his soul.

Evan's concern with Janek's dress was completely out of the ordinary, and it took him by surprise. He went back to the living room and his bottle of whiskey.

Erebus' conceit ate at him. He was reminded of what he was thinking of before he took a shower. *How had Erebus managed to dominate us?* The obvious answer was fear, but Evan was convinced that it had to be more than that. Its capacity to manipulate was astounding. He recalled the first time it had come to him. He was pissing outside behind the Palace. He had been falling down drunk, but he could remember the moment. It whispered lies. It told him Janek was weak and someone needed to look after him. It used the friendship Evan and Janek were forging to its advantage.

It did the same thing to Lise. She gave everything she had to give to Janek. Her physical attraction to him, as well as Abigail's, left an emotionally vulnerable soft spot that Erebus used to exploit them. Niklas' jealousy of Janek and Guthrie's love for his daughter served the same purpose.

Evan's agitation mounted. His mind wasn't clear enough. He was rehashing past events. He pushed his wet hair out of his face and took a long swallow of whiskey. He thought of the passing years, including how they'd arrived at where they were today, and how they'd remained loyal to one another. *Was it only because of our need to protect Janek?* That was part of it, but not all of it. The love and friendship they forged would have endured even if Erebus had never come into their lives.

But Erebus had come into their lives because Janek had come into their lives. Evan did not, for one moment, regret the day he met Janek. What he did regret was standing helpless while Erebus deprived Janek of a normal life—to marry and become a father. *Janek would have been a wonderful father.*

Evan thought of his father's disapproval and hatred. "You needed something from me that I couldn't give you!" Evan shouted at his dead father. "To this day, I still don't know what you wanted! Why the hell didn't you just come out and tell me instead of constantly ridiculing me? I wasn't a re-creation of you, and you couldn't stand that. Was that why? Did you hate me because you couldn't control me? You turned your back on your only living son! You never gave me a chance to show you that I was worth something!"

Evan sweated and panted under the weight of his anger. It revitalized him. It cleared his mind. He couldn't change what existed in the past, but he could change what was happening today. He refocused on Erebus' capacity to control. It was strong enough to convince four perfect strangers that they were divinely chosen to return a man's soul. Its power of persuasion had to be strong because it was incapable of performing the task itself.

Erebus told Lise the retrieval of Janek's soul had to be done by human beings. Its weakness had to have something to do with a shortcoming, something it had not been able to develop or learn. It depended on those who were closest to Janek to provide what it lacked. Its profound need for Evan, Abigail, Lise, Niklas, and Guthrie forced it to drag them with it through time. They were Erebus' minions, charged with furthering its agenda and protecting the human being it perversely loved. Their love for Janek was necessary as well. Necessary…

The suite door opened, and then slammed shut. Guthrie shuffled into the living room. Evan's anger hung heavy in the air. The boy was thinking about things hard enough to get himself worked up.

"Is Janek okay?"

"There ain't no change."

"Then why are you here?"

"I can leave if I'm interrupting."

"No, don't leave. Guthrie, I…"

"I'm listening, son."

Evan pushed his wet hair out of his sweaty face. He breathed deep and said, "I know what we need to do to end this. If I tell you, it has to stay between you and me until I say otherwise."

Guthrie nodded.

"It's going to be hard, but we can do it. There's one problem. If it's not done just at the right time it won't work."

"You're scared ain't you, son?"

"I can't be scared. *We* can't be scared. It uses fear against us. We can't let it use our emotions to control us anymore. You told me once that my anger and guilt were blocking my vision. You said to hang on to those emotions because I was going to need them. Well, you were right."

Guthrie waited in silence for Evan to continue.

"We have to do something it won't expect or understand. As the feeding begins and the time for the joining grows closer, Erebus will become more and more distracted."

"Surprise it when it ain't looking."

"Something like that." Evan wiped sweat from his forehead with the palm of his hand and pushed his hair out of his face. "I should've thought of this years ago, but honestly, I don't think the time was right until now. Before I tell you what we have to do, promise you won't try to talk me out of it."

"I know you've been trying to come up with a way to get rid of that nightmare since the night the church burned. I reckon you didn't come by this decision easy. I got a feeling that I ain't gonna like what you're about to say, but I got faith in you."

"I was thinking about my father just before you came in. Not once did he ever tell me he had faith in me."

Guthrie remembered Evan's father well. "Your father wasn't paying attention."

Evan was quiet for several minutes. Guthrie's comment about his father hurt him and helped him at the same time. *It doesn't matter anymore,* he thought. *All that matters now is fixing this mess.*

"There's something else. I can't figure out why Janek isn't in pain when the cat touches him. I've seen the cat sit in his lap and nuzzle his face. He was licking and pawing at him earlier tonight, and Janek never flinched."

"I've wondered that myself," Guthrie said.

"It bothers me because I'm the one who brought the cat with us. Do you think he's doing Erebus' work, spying or maybe even holding on to that piece of Janek's soul that Erebus ripped away from him?"

"I ain't never got a feeling like that from the cat. My guess is that he ain't significant to Erebus."

"That doesn't make sense. Janek's clothes hurt him. He can't stand lying between the sheets on his bed. I don't see how his clothes and sheets are insignificant."

"Since when do things make sense around here? Forget about the cat. It's distracting you."

"But what if the cat gets in the way of…"

"It ain't gonna get in the way. My gut tells me the cat is on our side. Stop complicating things. Now, are you gonna tell me what's on your mind or not? We ain't got much time left."

Evan admitted to himself that he was stalling. He dreaded saying the words aloud.

Lucas was sitting on an old settee at the end of Janek's bed. His omission from part of the group sensory fueled doubt, which, in turn, fueled fear. He was afraid for his life and afraid he would fail Janek.

Abigail and Niklas walked into the bedroom from the living room.

"Where's Daddy?" Abigail asked when she saw Lise sitting in the chair

Guthrie had occupied.

"He left the suite without a word. He's probably with Evan," Lise said.

Abigail sat beside Lucas on the settee. She took something from the pocket of her robe and fondled it.

"What are you holding, Abby?" Lucas asked.

"My mother's rosary beads."

"What are those for?"

Abigail looked surprised. "You don't know? They're for prayers and meditating on the events of the mysteries. My mother was Catholic."

"Oh." Lucas was confused, but a lesson in Catholicism was the last thing he wanted at the moment. "What else do you have that belonged to your mother?"

"Nothing. Not even a single memory. Didn't your mother die when you were very young?"

"Yes, when I was three years old," Lucas said. "I have a vague memory of her. My childhood home was filled with her things. My father never got over her death."

Sorrow veiled Abigail's eyes. "When I was a little girl, I'd pretend my mother was alive. I played 'wedding' as Daddy used to say and dressed up as a bride. Then I'd walk down the aisle and have the preacher join my parents in holy matrimony. I was sure if my parents were married, people wouldn't be mean to me."

"If your parents had married, you still would've suffered from racial prejudice."

"I guess," Abigail sighed. "Why didn't you ever marry?"

"I didn't want to."

"Why?"

"It didn't seem important," Lucas said. He remembered the promise he'd made to his dying father. "After everything that's happened, I don't think I'll ever marry."

Abigail fondled the rosary beads. "I wish I had married and had children. I have a feeling it's too late." She feared for who or what Janek would become when Erebus was through with him.

"Abby, I truly believe if all this hadn't happened, he would've returned your love."

"He told me that same thing just before he went to the church the night he was…the night the church burned." She bit her lip and looked at the rosary beads in her hands. "I want to go to the garden with him. I should change out of my pajamas and into some clothes." She got up and went into the bathroom.

"I'm going to the garden too," Niklas said to Lise.

Lise buried her face in Niklas' chest. He wrapped her in his strong arms and said, "I hope I haven't disappointed you. Your happiness has been the only thing I've cared about since the day I met you."

Lise raised her head and looked into his eyes. "I love you with all my heart. I doubt you'll ever be able to disappoint me."

"I was jealous of Janek. I thought you were in love with him. Your physical attraction to him was obvious. I saw the gleam in your eyes every time you looked at him. I was willing to take a back seat to him as long as I could be in your life."

"Niklas don't…"

"Please, let me finish. At first, I went along with everything you wanted when it came to Janek because it served my need to have you. I was selfish and cowardly. As time went by, I was able to see him for what he really was. He was our friend."

"I love Janek, but I'm not *in love* with him. I would do anything for him except hurt you. No matter what happens, I'll always be by your side."

Niklas cupped her face in his big hands. He kissed her and said, "I'll love you forever."

Lise sat on the bed. Abigail came out of the bathroom dressed in a pair of jeans and one of Janek's sweatshirts. She sat beside Lucas on the settee. All four people checked the clock on the wall.

It was 6:03 a.m.

Evan and Guthrie returned thirty minutes later. They went to Janek's bedside.

"How's he doing, Lise?" Evan asked.

"I can't tell. He hasn't moved or made a sound, but he's still breathing."

Evan stared at Janek for a few minutes, contemplating Erebus' plan and how little they knew about the feeding. Then, he asked everyone to go to the living room.

"Did you decide who's going to the garden?" Evan asked.

"Niklas and I are going," Abigail said. "So are you. Did you come up with an idea to stop Erebus from taking Janek? Isn't that why you went to your suite?"

Evan hated lying, but he had no other choice. "I'm sorry, Abby, I didn't. What about the rest of you?"

"I don't think we should help it," Abigail said. "If we don't help it, then he'll just die and it will be over."

"I don't think it's that simple," Evan said. "Erebus has compelled those men, and if we refuse to do anything, it will compel us too. I think that idea leaves too many things to chance."

"Oh really! You haven't come up with anything, so don't tell me my idea is shitty! You don't know if Erebus has enough strength to make us help and get Janek's soul back at the same time. It has to have a breaking point."

"Do you want Janek's soul to be trapped with Erebus until the end of time? Or maybe there is a purgatory and that's where he'll go. Didn't you listen to anything we said earlier?"

"You don't know if that's true!" Abigail said. "You're guessing; we're all just guessing!"

Niklas said, "Abby has a point. We don't know how this is going to play out. We may be able to see clearer once it begins."

"Or we may be dead, and Janek will be the only one of us that lives," Lise said.

Lucas realized he wasn't the only one who was confused and afraid. "Stop it! We haven't come this far to argue with one another. We're scared, and we're letting it get to us!"

"Evan, didn't you just tell me that nightmare is using our fear to control us? Now, get a grip or we ain't gonna have a chance in hell to win this fight," Guthrie growled at them.

"I'm sorry, Abby," Evan said. "I didn't mean to insinuate that your idea was stupid."

"I'm sorry, too. I expected you to do something the rest of us can't."

Niklas checked the time on his phone: 6:40 a.m.

Sunrise was expected at 7:25 a.m. They had forty-five minutes.

He unbuckled his shoulder holster and removed the semi-automatic Glock, then handed it to Lise. "Are you okay with standing watch?"

"Yes."

"Good. David Channing and the wives, Natalie Townsend and Ava Turner, have been snooping around. They went so far as to ask about Janek at the police station."

"I know, kill them if they get in the way," Lise said.

"Lucas and Guthrie are you okay with that?" Niklas asked.

"That's a stupid question now ain't it, son? I ain't armed, though. You reckon we have enough time for one of you boys to go fetch my shotgun from the Palace? It's under the bar."

"I'll get it," Lucas said. He knew a run to the Palace would relieve some of his tension.

Evan grabbed a bottle of whiskey from the bookshelf Janek used to store his liquor. His nerves were fried. He needed to drink—and drink a lot. The more he drank, the more fearless he became. It was the only way he was going to be able to reveal his plan.

Lise frowned. "Evan, don't you think you're drinking too much? We have to have our wits about us in less than an hour."

"Leave him alone, Lise," Guthrie said. "The boy needs to do things his way."

Lise shrugged. Evan could drink more than anyone she knew and still function. She laid the Glock on the coffee table, put on the shoulder holster, adjusted it to fit, and tucked the Glock into the holster. Then, she went back to Janek's bedside.

Abigail watched Evan. His hands shook as he put the whiskey bottle to his mouth. He kept rubbing the nape of his neck and pushing his hair out of his face. His hair fell around his shoulders and down his back. Abigail thought it was strange that he didn't have his hair in a ponytail as he always wore it.

Evan felt Abigail's stare. He went to talk to Janek.

"His breathing has changed," Lise said. "It's raspy, like he has fluid on his lungs."

"Like a death rattle," he said. He set his whiskey bottle on the nightstand.

"Yes."

"He's lost a lot of weight."

"He all but stopped eating weeks ago," Lise said.

Evan sat on the bed. Janek lay in the fetal position. He looked peaceful, as if he were asleep and not dying. The cat slept curled against his chest.

Evan said, "We're going to get through this, and, in the end, everything is going to be okay. I'll be here for you, I promise. If you can, you have to try to be strong. Fight this thing when it tries to take you. Whatever you do, don't be afraid."

Chapter 34

Natalie tossed and turned for three hours, and then abandoned trying to sleep. She needed coffee. Before going, she stopped at David's room and knocked on the door.

David looked exhausted and disheveled when he answered the door. "I didn't sleep at all. What about you?"

"None. I'm going to get some coffee. Care to join me?"

"Sure. I guess Bryan never showed up."

"No he didn't. I assume that means the others didn't come back either. Do you want to knock on Alex's door just in case he's there?"

"He's not there," David said. He stepped out and closed the door behind him.

"I thought I heard voices." It was Ava. "I've done nothing but watch the clock for the past three hours. If you're going for coffee, I'm going with you."

It was 7:02 a.m.

The front desk clerk, Rob Copeland, eyed them as they crossed the lobby and left the hotel. On the sidewalk, Lucas ran past them; he was carrying a gym bag. He flung open the hotel doors and ran through the lobby.

David ran after him. Lucas bounded up the staircase two steps at a time unaware he was being pursued. When they reached the third floor, David stopped near the elevator. He watched Lucas use a keycard to access suite 302.

David edged toward the door. He heard muffled voices inside the suite then a distinct noise. It was the sound of someone cocking a shotgun. Rock music was playing in the background. The deadbolt snapped shut. David scuttled down the staircase to the second floor landing. There, he gathered his composure, and then descended the staircase to the lobby. He went to the front desk.

"Is something wrong, Mr. Channing?" Rob said. "I saw you run up the stairs."

"I was trying to catch up with Lucas Dodd. He has something that belongs to me."

Rob stared at David.

"I'd like to stay another night, but I want to switch my room to one of the suites on the third floor."

"Some of the suites are residences, and the others are reserved through December 6th."

"Oh. What's today's date?"

Rob knew Janek, and he knew Janek was sick and confined to his suite. He sneered at David with suspicion. "It's December 6th."

"What are residence suites?"

"They're living quarters."

"Who lives in them?"

"I can't divulge that information."

David told Rob he'd changed his mind about staying another night.

Ava and Natalie were drinking coffee and eating donuts when David entered the restaurant. He sat at their table and waved at the waitress to bring a cup of coffee.

"Was that Lucas Dodd who ran past us outside?" Natalie asked.

"Yep, and I followed him."

"Ava and I have decided to lay low. We don't want to encounter that Niklas Arnold guy again. He's probably skulking around here watching us as it is."

"So where did Lucas go?" Ava asked. She nibbled on her donut.

"He went into suite 302. I did a little eavesdropping. Something is going on in there. I heard people talking and music playing. I think he's there."

"Who's there?"

"Janek Walesa. I think he lives there."

Ava exhaled a loud sigh. "So what? We aren't looking for him."

"We are looking for him," David said. *Is Ava that dense?* he wondered, and said, "I think Alex and your husbands are with him."

Natalie choked on her coffee. "Wait a minute! I remember Bryan said the artist of the painting was the current owner of the hotel. You corrected him and said that was impossible because the current owner couldn't have been alive in 1874. Well, he was, wasn't he?"

David smiled and snapped his fingers. "You got it! Janek Walesa painted that picture. He's our long suffering artist!"

"That's why we haven't seen him. He's sick or maybe even insane," Ava said.

Natalie recalled the man who made a brief appearance in the bar on Saturday night, and the reaction he induced in Bryan and the others. They had fallen all over themselves, trying to get a closer look. "Oh my God, that man couldn't be Janek Walesa! He was too young and gorgeous!"

David grinned. "You believe the man we saw in the bar was Janek. I believe that too. What were you expecting him to look like?"

"Not like that! He was absolutely beautiful! I guess I pictured some crazy zombie who looked like he just stepped out of the grave."

"That was him?" Ava said. Her eyes widened. "I agree with Natalie. He was breathtaking, but he seemed hurt and sad. I had an overwhelming urge to touch him and kiss him. Don't tell Justin I said that."

"What do you ladies say to a little field trip up to the third floor?"

"We can't just go up there and knock on the door of suite 302," Natalie said. "It's 7:15 in the morning."

"Why not? I bet you the guys are in that room."

"What would they be doing in there? Consoling the artist? Participating in some weird occult ritual?"

"That's possible. They've been acting brainwashed haven't they? Their interest quickly turned to obsession. Alex has ostracized me over this, and we've been friends for twenty years. I think they would do anything to help Janek Walesa."

Goose bumps bloomed on Ava's arms, and her stomach flip-flopped as she thought of the affair Justin had two years ago.

"I'm afraid to go up there. What if they're in that suite with women? Don't men usually stay out all night when they're with other women?" Ava asked.

"I don't think that's what they're doing," Natalie said.

A weak smile touched Ava's lips.

David signaled for the waitress to bring the check. "Do you ladies want anything else before I settle the bill?"

The women said 'no.'

"Are you ladies going upstairs with me?"

"I guess we have no choice," Ava said.

"Are you ready?"

The women said 'yes.'

⤜⤛ ⤜⤛

Lucas took the shotgun out of the gym bag and handed it to Guthrie. Guthrie inspected the chamber. "Did you bring extra shells?" he asked.

"They're in the bag," Lucas said. "I saw the first light of dawn approaching. Are we ready?"

"We're ready," Lise said.

Guthrie walked to a window and poked his head through the drapes. He looked down into the street where Emily Hartmann had stood screaming obscenities at Janek in 1873. He raised his head and looked toward the horizon. Sunrise had begun.

It was 7:25 a.m.

The music shut off.

A frigid vortex formed at the foot of Janek's bed, rising and spiraling tighter and tighter around the center of its being. A thick shuddering sound emanated from the walls. The vortex's rapid rotation slowed as it absorbed the shuddering little by little until it was gone.

Erebus was among them, and the feeding was about to commence. An unconscious sigh escaped Janek's lips. The cat awoke, stretched his front legs and yawned. He nuzzled Janek's face and mewled.

Erebus' command thundered in the suite. "Prepare to take him to his garden!"

Lise jumped from the chair. She removed the Glock from the holster and pulled the slide. Lucas unsheathed his Green River knife. They shoved their backs against the suite door.

Guthrie stood in the middle of the bedroom and positioned the .12 gauge shotgun barrel on his right shoulder.

The cat nestled against Janek's chest.

Niklas, Evan, and Abigail were unsure of what to do.

"DO AS I SAY!" Erebus said.

"How do we prepare him?" Niklas asked.

"You created his garden, holy man. You know what to do."

Niklas fought the urge to snatch Guthrie's shotgun and fire it until his contempt for Erebus disintegrated. "We have to lead him up the path to the garden."

Abigail remembered dreaming of the path through the redwood forest. She had walked that path with Janek and Guthrie. "How do we get him there?"

"Do it!"

Abigail saw Evan's face turn red with rage. She recognized that he was struggling to contain his anger, and his struggle was preventing him from beginning. She gathered a fortitude she didn't know existed within her and said, "Niklas, sit on the bed, on that side of Janek. Evan, sit at his feet, and I'll sit here."

Evan discovered he was holding his breath. He exhaled long and loud, which cleared the rage from his mind.

They sat on the bed and formed a triangle around Janek's body.

Niklas afforded a last glance at Lise.

"Take my hand," Abigail said, offering her left hand to Niklas and her right hand to Evan. They took her hands. "Evan, take Niklas' left hand. Good. Now, close your eyes and picture the path in the redwood forest that leads to the garden."

The buried memory of the path unearthed itself and appeared to them within the shadowed redwood forest. Redwood sorrel covered the forest floor. Its clover-like leaves were often obscured by the shaggy heads of sword fern thriving under the forest canopy. Mosses grew in the undercarriage and covered standing dead trees and rotting logs. Fog, condensed on tree leaves and needles, dripped to the forest floor. The sorrowful drops that fell upon the undergrowth were the only sound in the dark forest.

Niklas, Abigail, and Evan's consciousness entered the redwood forest. Their physical presence remained on the bed in a triangle around Janek.

"I'm on the path," Abigail said. "Look for me."

Niklas found himself standing on the path beside Abigail.

Evan couldn't see them. He labored to clear his vision.

Niklas said, "Abby and I can see you in front of us. Turn around."

Evan turned his head and apperceived he was in the lead on the path. He waited for them to catch up. "What do we do now?"

"We have to reach the only sense he has left," Niklas said. "Touch him."

They tightened their clasped hands into conjoined fists and pressed them with callous force on Janek's left upper arm, ankle, and outer thigh. Janek screamed and tried to curl his body tighter, but he was unable to move. Sweat drenched his body; drool ran from the corner of his mouth and wetted the pillow beneath his cheek. Tears seeped from his closed eyes. The cat raised his head in alarm, but remained against Janek's chest.

Lise flinched when Janek began screaming. Lucas rubbed her shoulder in a calming gesture. Guthrie restrained the impulse to look at the bed. He couldn't let what was happening to Abigail affect his emotions.

Evan, Niklas, and Abigail tightened their clasped hands until their knuckles were white. Their awareness was on the path. They had to lead what was left of Janek's consciousness to the path.

Janek stopped screaming. In the back of her mind, Abigail heard Lise. The inflection in Lise's voice led Abigail to believe Lise witnessed something she didn't expect to see, like angels on high or Jesus walking on water. "Did he just...die?"

Mercifully, Abigail was distracted by the presence of the cat on the path. He meowed with insistence, and then ran up the path, stopping once to ensure the humans were following. Janek was lying on the path ahead.

They released their clasped hands and fell to their knees in the soft spongy moss. His body was warm. Abigail didn't think he was dead, but she was certain they had a matter of minutes to get him to his garden.

"He's going to get through this," Evan said as he and Niklas slid their arms around Janek's chest.

"He has pierced the veil," a feminine voice said.

They stood up and turned to see a host of tenebrous spirits spilling across the path into either side of the forest.

The feminine spirit stood on the path alone—ahead of the others. "We are the revenants who walk this forest."

"Kate?" Evan said.

"Yes."

"What…why are you here?" His eyes darted across the host of spirits.

"Janek has pierced the veil between life and death. His soul is gone so he exists in the void between the two worlds where we cannot reach him and neither can you."

Niklas sat beside Janek in a protective gesture. His eyes roamed the path and the forest and the host of spirits.

Abigail said, "Evan, who is…"

"Shhh."

"We are the people who knew Janek in life and saw his transcendence. We are those who admired him, respected him, and loved him. We have come to warn you. There are those who roam this forest who want him to die. They will try to block your passage to the garden at the edge of eternity."

Kate was a sad reminder of the good times Evan had spent with Janek. She moved toward Evan. Her opaque hand touched his cheek. She said, "I'm sorry for all the things you and Janek have had to endure."

Tears stung the back of Evan's eyes, and he blinked until the pain dissipated. When he looked again, the host was gone. He knelt beside Niklas. Together, they slid their arms around Janek's chest and lifted him to a standing position on the path. They each took an arm and placed it around the back of their neck so Janek's body dangled between them like a rag doll.

The cat, desperate to nestle against Janek's chest, pawed at Janek's legs.

Erebus lost patience. *These inept humans were slow and clumsy and easy to distract.* It roared at them, "Get him to his garden now!"

Evan removed Janek's arm from his neck. Niklas lifted Janek into his arms, cradled him, and ran. Abigail and the frantic cat ran after Niklas.

Evan let them go. If he didn't release some of his rage, he would lose what little clear mind he possessed. "Shut the fuck up! If he dies, it's your fault!"

"If he dies, it is because you let him die!"

Erebus' abhorrence for Evan was so intense that it wanted to strike him dead at that moment, but without Evan's powerful and unconditional love for Janek they would be unable to get him to the garden. Unconditional love was a necessary emotion Erebus had not learned. It was forced to rely on the human being it loathed. When the joining was complete, Erebus delighted in the thought of killing Evan while the others were made to watch. It was going to torture him in ways not yet imagined until Evan could no longer beg for mercy.

The revenants moved through the forest as Evan, Niklas, and Abigail ran up the damp mossy path. They heard a woman laughing, and the path ahead darkened as a revenant impeded their way. The revenant's Cimmerian form changed to an auburn colored specter with auburn eyes. Niklas tried to thrust through the specter, but he was shoved back. He gripped Janek's body as he fell. Abigail helped Niklas move Janek from his arms onto the path.

The specter's hatred for Evan was evident in her sarcastic tone. "You stupid Mick, he's as good as dead! Those men in the garden can't help him now."

Evan ran at Emily Hartmann's specter and slammed his body against it. He bounced backward, but stayed on his feet. "Get out of the way, slut!"

Emily's laugh pierced the murky hushed forest. "I won't let you take him to that garden! He deserves to be dead!" she yelled.

"You bitch!" Abigail's anger bubbled to the surface, and she sobbed.

Niklas pulled her into his arms and whispered, "Don't let her manipulate you. Dry your tears."

Niklas said to Emily, "If those men can't help him, what difference does it make if we continue?"

Emily purposely teased Niklas. "Maybe I've lied. Maybe I haven't. You will never know."

Abigail wrenched from Niklas' arms and raised her hands in a threatening gesture.

"You are truly a dumb half-breed Mexican whore," Emily said with a smirk on her lips. "You can't hurt me."

Evan took a step toward Emily. Abigail grabbed his wrist and stopped him. "Go help Niklas pick up Janek. We'll leave the path and walk through the forest."

Evan gave Emily a loathsome look and jerked his wrist from Abigail's grip. They turned their backs on the specter and went to help Niklas. With Janek in Niklas' arms, and the cat in Abigail's arms, they stepped from the path. Emily's specter materialized and blocked their way.

Evan's unspoken plan was a terrible emotional burden and tension was fogging his ability to keep his mind clear. This abhorrent ghost was playing games with Janek's life, and the longer it took them to get him to the garden, the smaller Janek's chances of survival became. He glanced at Niklas who was side-stepping Emily.

"Why are you doing this? Do you hate him that much?" Evan asked Emily.

She laughed and slapped his face. He stumbled backward. "Shut up! I will do whatever I wish! That shadowed soul can't overpower me, and neither can you! It's watching us, and it's helpless."

The specter grew larger and surrounded them in an auburn haze, blinding their way. The haze emitted a smell that reminded Evan and Abigail of the acrid smoke-filled air the night the church burned.

From somewhere beyond in the forest, a muffled argument commenced. A dark nebula outlined the figure of a woman within the haze. The nebula absorbed the auburn haze like a planetary nebula absorbing ultraviolet radiation from a dying star. Emily Hartmann's specter vanished. The figure of the woman was clear, and she stood before them at the edge of the path.

Niklas looked at Janek's wan face. The resemblance was unmistakable. Freya Walesa's spirit drifted to Janek, regarded her beautiful son, and then evanesced. Evan, Abigail, and Niklas broke into a run.

The Knights heard the confrontation on the path between Janek's companions and the bitter revenant. Janek was too far away to hear them beckon to him, and, the distance Janek had yet to travel to reach the garden was unclear. They had to make a connection with his companions.

"We can hear what's happening on the path, so maybe, they can hear us," Justin said.

"Try calling Abigail's name," Alex said.

Justin said, "Abigail?"

She stopped running. The cat jumped from her arms and ran after Niklas. "Abigail?"

Her eyes strained to find a hint of human life in the redwood forest.

"Where are you, Abigail?

"I'm on the path to the garden. Who are you?"

"My name is Justin. I'm in the garden."

"You're one of the men who have come to help Janek."

"Yes. Where's Janek?"

"With Niklas."

"Are they near the garden?"

"I don't know."

"You must tell us when they arrive."

"I will," Abigail said, and she turned and ran.

The path came to a sudden end. Beyond the path, Niklas and Evan saw a clearing obscured by dim misty light. The cat ran past them, stopped and meowed, then trotted to the edge of the clearing.

Niklas walked to the edge of the clearing, but could go no further. He and Janek had reached their garden. Niklas tried to carry Janek into the garden, but he couldn't get in. That was as it should be. The garden had never been intended for Niklas. He laid Janek where the forest's spongy moss floor and the garden's grass intermingled.

The cat leaped through the garden's grass and disappeared. Abigail reached the end of the path and came to a sudden halt to avoid colliding with Evan. They walked to the edge of the garden.

"We've arrived," Niklas said. "I can't get in, but the cat can. He's run off. I don't know what we're supposed to do now."

Abigail kneeled and reached to stroke Janek's pallid cheek.

"You will not touch him!"

She jerked her hand away. Tears threatened, and she swallowed hard. All this was horrible enough without Erebus barking orders and spirits appearing on the path. It was petty, but she harbored a delusive jealousy of the revenant Evan called Kate.

Though they were unaware of the source, The Knights heard Erebus' thundering command. A gray tabby cat bounded toward them across the garden's expanse of lawn. The cat leaped into Bryan's lap, nuzzled Bryan's nose, and mewled.

"Where did you come from?" Bryan said. He ran his hand along the length of the cat's back to his tail. The cat answered with a long-drawn-out meow, and then jumped from Bryan's lap and ran back the way he came.

Sean said, "What was that about?"

"I think I know," Justin said. "Abigail?"

"Yes."

"We just had a visitor—a gray cat. Is Janek here?"

"Yes."

"Is he in the garden?"

"No. He's on the boundary. We can't get into the garden. He'll have to do it on his own somehow."

"He's not on his own," Justin said. "We'll help him."

Abigail exhaled a sigh of relief and said, "Thank you."

The Knights readied for their encounter with the man who needed salvation. Janek's archetypical essence existed within their consciousness, and his innate soul fell like snowflakes in the garden.

Niklas and Evan watched for signs of the revenants moving in the still redwood forest. Abigail sat beside Janek and gazed at his beautiful, reposed face as she watched him breathe. The cat returned to nestle against Janek's chest.

Chapter 35

"Call to him," Sean said to Alex.

Alex looked skyward as if he expected Janek to descend from the heavens as a shattered archangel. "Janek, can you hear us?"

Although Alex spoke in a soft tone, his voice thundered throughout suite 302. No one shrank from the booming noise.

Bryan said, "Janek, wake up and step into your garden. Your soul is here. We can restore it, but we must look into your eyes to see the place where your essence lived in order to understand how to help you."

There was a long reticent pause.

"Janek, try to enter your garden," Alex said.

"Is that you, Alex?" Evan said.

"Yes."

"He's breathing, but he might as well be dead. He was able to feel pain before we got him on the path, but now even that's gone."

Lise inhaled a gasp that caught in her throat. Lucas and Guthrie made eye contact as if to say, *What are we overlooking?*

There was another reticent pause.

Guthrie finally said, "We ain't sure if Janek's able to feel pain or not. Niklas has been carrying him, but not really hurting him. I think you gotta purposely inflict pain on him to get him to respond. "

Oh shit, Evan thought. Guthrie was right. They had to do *whatever* it took to get Erebus to commence the joining or his plan wouldn't work.

Abigail looked at Evan with watery brown eyes and bit her lip.

"We have to, Abby," Evan said. Misery quivered his lips and furrowed the lines on his forehead. He yearned to justify the method and the reason for torturing the man they loved. He looked at Guthrie's weathered face. It was evident that the burden of keeping their secret was weighing on him too.

Evan squatted, slipped his arms under Janek's shoulders, wrapped his arms around Janek's chest, and squeezed his arms tight. He pushed Janek into a sitting position.

"Niklas will you help?" Evan asked.

Niklas nodded and sat at Janek's feet.

Evan inhaled and squeezed with enough power to break some of the ribs on Janek's right side. Janek released a blood curdling scream, but he didn't move.

Abigail stood up and stepped back. She looked at Guthrie, but didn't ask the question on her lips: *Do we have to go to this extreme?*

Janek returned to his comatose state. Evan applied pressure to Janek's broken ribs with a forearm. Janek screamed. His hands raised a few inches off the ground then fell back.

Erebus watched. The human being it despised was doing the right thing without letting compassion get in his way. The joining was not lost. Erebus was joyful until another revenant dashed from the forest.

Evan was yanked from Janek and slammed backward into the trunk of a redwood tree. The air left his lungs, and he gasped as he hit the ground.

"I will not let him into the garden," the revenant said to Evan as he respired. "He left without saying farewell. Very ungallant of him after the night we shared."

Evan got to his feet and rubbed the back of his head. It was obvious the revenant was a woman who was from upper class society circa 1870. He had no idea who she was.

"Do not look at me with disrespect," the revenant said.

Evan had to admit she was a beautiful blonde, and he guessed she was someone Janek had fucked not long before he left Oregon. "I don't care what he did to you. Get the hell out of here!"

"I will not."

"Who are you?"

"I was Miss Sarah Williams when Janek Walesa knew me in 1872. My father was a senator, an influential man who believed men honored their obligations or suffered the consequences."

A Cimmerian form of a young woman moved to Janek's side. She waved her hand as if shooing a fly. "Go away, Sarah. Everyone in Salem knew of your lust for my brother. You are only embarrassing yourself further."

Sarah appeared insulted, but slid into the shadowed forest. The young woman bent to touch Janek's hair, and then she too, slipped into the dark forest.

Evan cussed under his breath about the revenant's interruption and hurried back to Janek. He wrapped his arms around Janek's chest and compressed the broken ribs. Janek shrieked. His hands grabbed at Evan's arms. Evan relaxed his grip. Janek's instinct registered the lingering pain, and he moaned for several seconds before he fell quiet.

It was working. His psyche was perceiving pain.

The Knights sensed this and Bryan said, "Janek, open your eyes."

There was no response.

Niklas saw the misery in Evan's eyes when he broke another of Janek's ribs. Janek bent his knees and dug his heels into the soft ground as he threw his torso forward. Evan's grip was severed. Janek rolled onto his left side and curled into the fetal position. His body quivered, and he moaned.

Abigail could no longer restrain the impulse to comfort Janek. She dropped to his side and reached to stroke his cheek. Evan lunged at her before she could touch Janek. "No Abby, he might…"

Evan lost his balance, and his left hand landed on Janek's ribcage. Janek shrieked. He rolled onto his back, crossed his arms over his eyes, and buffeted his legs like a man lambasting an unseen attacker. He kicked Niklas in the face and broke his nose.

Janek's immediate pain calmed. The muscles in his body relaxed. His arms slid from his face. His eyes opened. He stared unseeing at the forest's canopy.

The men in the garden sensed Janek's open eyes. They beckoned him to step into his garden, but Janek remained unresponsive.

"He doesn't understand what's happening," Abigail said. "He can't come to you! You have to come to him!"

"*He* has to come to *us*," Sean said.

"Does it matter? You're failing him!"

"Do not interfere!"

"Stop yelling at her, you fuck!" Evan said as he jumped to his feet.

"I will kill you, Evan O'Malley!"

"Go for it!"

"Shut up! There's someone outside," Lise hissed and jerked her head toward the suite door. She walked to the door and saw David Channing and Natalie Townsend through the peep hole. Natalie banged on the door. Lise positioned her hands on the Glock so that she was ready to shoot. Lucas slid his Green River knife under his belt at the small of his back to free his hands.

"Open this door!" Natalie said. "We hear screaming and my husband's voice. If you don't open up, we're calling the police!"

David said, "We know Janek Walesa lives here!"

The dead bolt disengaged. The door swung open. David and Natalie retreated a few feet. Lise stepped into the hallway; she was holding the Glock in front of her at arm's length. Lucas followed and then Guthrie. Guthrie slammed the door shut and pointed his shotgun at David's face.

Lise jammed the Glock's muzzle into Natalie's forehead. "Your husband isn't here. If you don't leave quietly, I'm going to blow your brains out."

Terrified, Natalie argued with Lise anyway. "You're lying. I heard his voice. Please, whatever it is you're doing, stop it and let him go."

"I warned you," Lise squeezed the trigger, but was distracted by the sense of movement to her left. Guthrie's shotgun blasted. Lise didn't flinch. She relaxed her finger on the trigger; shoved Natalie against the wall, and pressed the gun harder into Natalie's forehead.

The movement Lise sensed was Ava Turner sidling toward the stairs, and when Ava did that, Lucas grabbed David's arms, twisted them behind David's back and held his knife to David's throat. Guthrie fired his shotgun in Ava's direction and blasted a gaping hole in the wall behind her. Ava dropped to the floor in a dead faint.

Lucas slid the knife blade across David's throat, and said. "We aren't playing games. Get the hell out of here and keep your mouth shut. You go to the police, and your friend Alex is dead."

The blade left a shallow blood line across David's throat.

"I'd do what the boy says," Guthrie said in a low growl. "You ain't got no idea what you're dealing with. It ain't gonna be us that kills your friend or your husband. There's something out there that'll do away with all of us if you don't stop interfering."

"Just tell us if Alex and Bryan are in there with Janek," David said.

Lucas glanced at Guthrie as he released David and let his knife drop from David's throat. Guthrie punched David in the face and broke his nose.

"Did you hear what I said, boy? You're making things worse. Now, get yourself and these women out of here or Lise is gonna fire that gun into that woman's brain."

Blood dripped from David's broken nose.

Lise lowered the Glock, but kept it aimed at Natalie. Guthrie cocked his shotgun and aimed it at David. Lucas pushed the down call button on the elevator. Natalie went to Ava and patted her face until she came around. David helped Ava to her feet and steadied her as they got on the elevator.

The Knights were unaware of Janek's physical location in suite 302 at the Ferndale Hotel. They perceived Janek and his companions within the same microcosm and dimensional realm where they existed—in the garden at the edge of eternity. However, they were auditory audience to both worlds.

The confrontation that took place in Janek's physical location was disconcerting because the threat came from those The Knights viewed as outsiders. They were no closer to saving Janek than they had been when they walked into the garden. *What if the next interruption became fatal?* Alex wondered.

That fear pushed Alex to think in a different vein. Evan's attempt to get Janek to react to physical pressure worked to an extent, but Alex realized there was another physical aspect they were overlooking.

"Janek hasn't experienced human touch without pain in nearly one-hundred-fifty years. I wonder if he remembers there can be pleasure in that touch? Abigail, feel Janek's love. It's all around you. Give him one small piece, and he'll be able to find us."

Erebus' fierce jealousy ignited. "That is now allowed!"

Abigail closed her eyes and remembered the beautiful soul that lived in Janek's body. She lowered her head, brushed her lips across his, and whispered, "I love you."

"You are not allowed to touch him in that manner!"

Abigail ignored Erebus. She gazed at Janek's flawless face. *How many women had wanted to kiss his lips before his life was destroyed?* she wondered. She bent to kiss him and was jerked into mid-air to dangle from phantasmal gallows over the forest floor.

Evan screamed, "Fuck!" and ran to her.

Janek stirred and blinked his eyes.

Erebus released Abigail. She fell into Evan's arms.

"I think he's in the garden," Niklas said.

Janek *was* in his garden, but he was devoid of cognition and consciousness. The Knights saw him sitting in the grass.

Niklas, Abigail, and Evan's consciousness left the redwood forest. Their physical presence remained on the bed in a triangle around Janek. The cat stood and yawned and jumped into the chair.

Alex called Janek's name. Instinct forced Janek's eyes to shift toward the sound. His white eyes were opalescent and difficult to see through. The men extracted archetypical love from their consciousness. They guided it to the doors of the place where Janek's essence once resided. Love crossed the threshold and ensconced in his empty spiritual being.

Love's replenishment came with a price. Hot agony exploded in Janek's chest. He screamed like a man thrust into the fires of hell. He clawed at the blankets on the bed and kicked Evan in the stomach. Evan fell backward onto the floor.

Abigail and Niklas scrambled from the bed.

The pressure in Janek's chest increased. His animal instinct tried to escape the torment. He scuttled across the bed and fell onto the floor, face up. The pain eased. His white eyes stared at the ceiling.

"No!" Niklas said when Evan moved toward Janek. "Erebus warned us not to interfere."

The men in the garden were aware of love's successful return. Despite the pain it inflicted, they fed Janek the ethereal pieces of his soul with enthusiasm. Compassion entered the doorway to his essence like a cruel scourge. He got to his knees. His broken ribs ignited agony. He threw up, panted, and then tried to crawl from the excruciation.

He collapsed face first onto the floor. Evan ignored Niklas' warning and went to Janek. Janek's breathing was heavy and labored. He was sweating. Evan was sure the feeding itself was inflicting permanent physical harm on Janek.

The pieces of Janek's soul were filling his spirit faster and faster. The pain was unbearable. His consciousness returned, but his mind was in a state of confusion. He didn't understand where he was or what was happening. He struggled to his feet, and then ran with impetuous terror toward the suite door. Evan, Niklas, and Lucas tackled him, and they all fell to the floor.

Janek fought them under the delusion that they were aides to his crucifixion. Niklas straddled Janek's abdomen and pinned him to the floor. Before Lucas could get a grip on his sweaty flailing arms, Janek punched Niklas in the jaw. A fresh stream of blood ran from Niklas' broken nose. Janek tried to buck Niklas off his stomach. They looked like two men having sadistic sex. Evan sat behind Niklas on Janek's thighs, which was no easy feat because Janek was arching his back and digging his heels into the floor.

He screamed, "Get off me, you mother fuckers!" He tried furiously to pull his wrists from Lucas' grasp. "NOOOOOOO! Let me go!"

Niklas leaned forward and shoved Janek's shoulders into the floor to make it difficult for Janek to get enough leverage to pull away from Lucas. Janek whipped his head back and forth. He flattened his back against the floor and tried to bring his knees up to throw Evan off his thighs, and screamed,

"You fucking assholes are killing me!"

With great effort, Lise and Guthrie stayed focused on potential threats alive or dead. If there was someone in the hall, they wouldn't hear them for Janek's screaming. Abigail covered her mouth with her hands. Tears soaked her cheeks. She remembered Erebus' words: *"I warn you, the feeding will not be painless, and he may beg for it to stop. You will not interfere."*

Janek stopped struggling and panted. The men in the garden beckoned to him in unison. "We've given you all we can. Now, *you* must gather the intrinsic pieces of your soul."

Janek comprehended their words, but he was confused and fearful of continuing. He looked up and recognized Niklas' bloodied face.

Alex said, "If you don't gather your innateness, you don't know who you'll be when this is over."

Lucas said, "We'll stay with you and hold you down."

"See your innateness," Bryan said. "It's all around you, like snowflakes in the wind."

Janek saw nothing. He couldn't remember who he was because he had lost himself so long ago.

"Concentrate on something you remember," Bryan said. "Smell it, hear it, touch it, taste it, see it. Use all your senses. What were the things that made you who you are?"

Janek's eyes shifted. He saw Lise standing beside Guthrie with their backs against a door. The years had escaped his memory. He wondered how long it had been since he first met her. Did he know her when he was a child?

Lise saw that Janek's eyes had turned gray, and the doubt and bewilderment they held. He couldn't remember how she fit in his life. She managed a small smile and said, "You came to us after your family died. Your grief and despair and confusion were terrible burdens on your gentle soul. You were the most beautiful person I had ever met. You are my friend."

Janek remembered coming home after graduation and finding his family dead. The stench of human excrement; the sorrow in the Wilkersons' voices; the gritty dirt covering the graves; the taste of his salty tears; his eternal goodbye as he looked, for the last time, upon the place where he grew up.

His family had made him who he was. The Willamette Valley had made him who he was. Six years at Willamette University had made him who he was. When he believed what the Episcopal Church taught, he would have said God made him who he was.

He shifted his eyes. The snowflakes of his innate soul were everywhere. He looked at Niklas and said, "There's no need to restrain me."

Niklas dragged his exhausted body off Janek. Lucas let go of Janek's wrists. Evan leaned forward and said, "I'll be right here if you need me. You're going to be fine." He gave Janek an encouraging slap on the cheek then got to his feet.

The cat jumped from the chair and trotted across the room to Janek's side. He nuzzled Janek's chin and meowed. Janek concentrated on the snowflakes. The winds of eternity calmed, and the innocuous snowflakes showered upon his gray eyes, each one melting as it entered the door to his essence.

When the snowflakes were gone, Janek remained doubtful and apathetic. He sat up. The winds of eternity gusted and revealed one last swirling snowflake. Janek didn't trust what he was seeing, but the unconsumed snowflake had to be the reason for his apathy. He supposed he should make the effort to capture it.

As he reached for the snowflake, they heard the crescendo of an erotic moan. The sound was repulsive in its resemblance to sexual perversion. An analogy of a rapist preparing to defile its victim flashed in the thoughts of the fellowship. They shivered in unison. With horror, they realized Erebus was on the brink of its orgasmic joining.

"Come to me, my love. Feel my spirit as it intertwines with yours. Feel the ecstasy of our copulation," Erebus inveigled.

Janek panicked and scrambled to his feet, but he didn't know where he was or where to run to escape Erebus. He remembered Lise and Guthrie were standing with their backs against a door. He ran toward the door. "Let me out!"

"My love, you can't run. It's too late!" Erebus shrilled in the throes of its orgasm. The sound was deafening. Janek fell. His broken ribs caught fire. The explosion in his chest was worse than anything he had ever experienced.

Chapter 36

The explosion Janek thought he felt in his chest was a pistol discharging inside the suite. The noise was confusing, and muddled further by Erebus' chaotic words.

"This cannot happen! You cannot possess the strength to stop this! You cannot! I should have killed you a long time ago! I hate you! I hate you!"

Erebus' erection shriveled up like a boy whose mother caught him masturbating while wearing her underwear. Its disbelief that a human being had the power to interfere with the joining left it stunned. The precious shred of Janek's soul slipped from its grasp.

The winds of eternity died, and the snowflake melted, leaving hope to float in the air. The cat jumped and pawed at the freed shred of hope as if it were a butterfly.

Erebus had waited and prepared over millenniums for the arrival of a transcendent human being, and it was too late for another chance. "I deserve to have a human life! Why have you forced this upon me?"

Self-pity and despair were unfamiliar onuses that crushed the unrequited soul's essence. The core of its existence became denser and heavier. Erebus was exhausted. It tried, and failed, to summon its vortex to stop a mass from forming in its being.

If Janek surrendered himself and his soul he could free Erebus from the weight that was killing it. "Give yourself to me, my love! Do not let me die! Come to me!"

The fires of a million hells heated the mass within the unrequited soul and tortured its dying essence. "Janek, save me from this pain! He has forced this upon me!"

Janek couldn't make sense of Erebus' declaration of hate or its pleas for help.

"He has forced this upon me!" Erebus' once vaporous being collapsed and imploded like an invisible supernova.

Janek was physically sucked into a vacuum. His body stretched as he was dragged across the floor. The carpet burned his bare chest and stomach. He dug the heels of his hands and his knees into the floor to resist the suction, but it continued to force him toward an unknown destination. Someone called his name and fingers brushed his bare feet.

He experienced the sensation of being inside a deflating balloon. The suction stopped. Erebus had let go of him. Astounded, he lay on the floor and panted. *What in the hell?* He sat up, dumbfounded and dazed.

Abigail's scream snapped him out of it.

What he saw seemed so unreal, he disbelieved it for a moment. Evan was standing in the middle of the living room. His left hand was on his abdomen. Blood oozed and spurted between his splayed fingers. Blood soaked his jeans and showered on his boots and the tile floor. A 9mm pistol slipped from his blood-slicked right hand and hit the floor with a sickening thud.

Janek jumped to his feet and ran to Evan. "For the love of God, Evan! What have you done? What have you done?"

Evan felt no pain, yet. Internal bleeding pressurized his lungs, making him dizzy and short of breath. He felt his strength dissipate. It was an odd sensation, like water evaporating. It began in his face and traveled the length of his body. His knees unhinged and he collapsed. Janek was there, and Evan fell into his arms.

Lucas ran to help Janek support Evan's dead weight. They managed to sit on the floor and cradle Evan in Janek's lap.

Lise attempted to call 911. The phone slipped from her sweating, shaking hand. She snatched it from the floor and pressed the numbers.

Abigail grabbed towels from the bathroom, and then ran into the living room and dropped them beside Janek. "Compress his wound. We have to get the bleeding to slow down."

Janek pressed a towel on Evan's wound. Pain detonated in Evan's abdomen. He screamed in agony. The towel was immediately saturated in blood.

Guthrie watched in horror as Evan fought his pain. For the first time in his life, Guthrie was a prisoner of guilt and remorse. *How could I have let Evan talk me in to this?*

Evan coughed up blood. It trickled from the corner of his mouth and dripped onto Janek's chest. His voice was wet and raspy when he said, "Hope is all that's left. Reach for it."

"Evan…"

"Don't let me die for nothing."

Die for nothing? Janek had been Erebus' prisoner for so long that he couldn't wrap his mind around his freedom, let alone Evan dying in his lap.

The cat trotted into the living room with the delicate piece of hope in his mouth. Janek stared at hope as if it was poison, but he allowed the cat to stretch up and lick his gray eyes. Hope entered the doors to his essence. It felt like a stranger.

Evan coughed hard and choked on the blood in his throat. His flayed and burned skin, and torn muscle tissue around his gunshot wound ripped a little more. When he screamed, blood pooled in his mouth. He tried to spit it out. He was drowning. From somewhere overhead, he heard Abigail sobbing.

Lise sat beside Evan, and held his bloodied hand, and stroked his bloodied hair, and tried to smile at him when she said, "Everything will be okay. The ambulance is on the way."

Evan looked at Lise. His green eyes told her goodbye.

There was no regret or fear in his eyes. She thought of Christer dying alone on the road from Mendocino. Evan wouldn't die alone, but it held no consolation.

Janek noticed Lise had deliberately said *everything* instead of *you* will be okay. He swallowed the dread in his throat and reached for another towel. There was so much blood. He was covered in it. Evan was soaked in it.

Guthrie wrapped his arms around Abigail. Her sobs were terrible. He was afraid they would rip her apart. He, too, was afraid to say goodbye to Evan.

Niklas sat beside Lise. She struggled to stay dry-eyed for Evan's sake, so Niklas did the same. One hundred and fifty years ago, as a reverend, he would have been there to comfort the dying. This morning, he couldn't remember the things he would have done and said. He didn't know how to say goodbye.

The terrible sound of sirens rose and fell.

Lucas calmed his crying so he could speak. He managed to say, "Evan."

Evan looked at him. Lucas held his breath, bit his bottom lip, and managed a small smile.

Evan struggled to return the smile and whispered, "It's okay, Lucas."

Lucas lost self-control and sobbed. His lifelong friend was dying, and he couldn't do anything to stop it.

Agony and suffocation were tearing Evan apart. "I was strong," he whispered to Janek.

"I know."

"It couldn't complete the joining without me. I was necessary."

Janek's tears dripped on Evan's hair and face. Evan had sacrificed his life for him, for all of them.

"You're necessary to me," Janek said, memorizing Evan's face. "You're my friend and my brother. You have so much more life to live; so many things yet to do."

"Is Erebus gone?"

"Yes. I don't feel it anymore."

Evan knew he was losing consciousness. At least the horrible pain would stop.

Janek yearned to tighten his arms around Evan and never let go. "Thank you, Evan. Thank you for everything you've given me. I love you."

Evan's green eyes flashed when he smiled at Janek. The blue returning in Janek's eyes was the last color Evan would ever see. He said, "I didn't fail."

Evan died in Janek's arms. It was 9:18 a.m.

IX

The Farewell

Chapter 37

December 6, 2016

The Knights left the garden at the edge of eternity to their memories and traveled the path through the murky redwood forest. The revenants drifted through the dim light. Their opaque forms shadowed the forest. The cobwebs of Erebus' lingering influence dissolved as the men approached what used to be the courtyard of the First Congregational Church of Ferndale. As they walked through Ferndale Memorial Garden, they spoke of the lesson they learned from their successful task.

A human being's innate self was not to be taken for granted. It was delicate and mercurial—capable of evanescence to perish upon the winds of eternity.

When they arrived at the Ferndale Hotel, two cars from the Ferndale Police Department, an ambulance, and a fire truck were parked in front of the mahogany double doors with the inlayed beveled glass. Onlookers congested the sidewalks. The men shouldered their way through the crowd toward the hotel entrance. Lt. Jim Berggren stopped them. He was the cop who had spoken with Evan earlier that morning in the hotel lobby.

"You can't possibly think I'm gonna let you go inside the hotel," Jim said.

Justin threw a nervous glance at the hotel doors. "What happened?"

"The hotel has been evacuated."

"My wife was in there. Her name is Ava Turner. She wasn't involved was she?"

Jim remembered Ava Turner and her hysterical ranting. She had nothing to do with Evan's death.

"Go across the street. Your wife is somewhere among the crowd."

Justin couldn't ignore his guilt over leaving Ava alone all night. She was going to accuse him of being with another woman, and he had no believable alibi. There was a good chance his marriage was through.

The four men crossed the street and mingled with the gawking people on the sidewalk. Justin and Bryan searched the crowd for their wives. Alex saw David standing in the alcove of a store entrance. He walked over.

Alex observed David's bloody broken nose and the thin line of dried blood across his throat. "Who kicked your ass?" he asked.

David sneered at Alex. "The knight returns from The Crusades. Did you save Janek Walesa?"

"What?"

"You heard me."

"You tried to interfere, and they kicked your ass, didn't they?" Alex said, shocked, but not surprised.

"Interfere? That's what you call it? What the hell, Alex."

David paused, hoping Alex would confess his mission. When he wasn't forthcoming, David continued. "We thought you and the other guys were in suite 302. I went up there with Natalie Townsend and Ava Turner, and knocked on the door. Lise Arnold came out of the suite pointing a Glock. She jammed it against Natalie's forehead. Guthrie Sullivan fired his shotgun at Ava. Lucas Dodd cut my throat, and then Guthrie punched me in the face."

"Why did you think that I was in suite 302?"

"Because that's where Janek Walesa lives—your artist."

"Janek lives there?"

"You know him?"

"His friend, Evan O'Malley, told me about him."

David smirked. "Did O'Malley tell you he and Janek were born in the 1800s?"

"No."

"That doesn't surprise you?"

Alex shook his head.

"He's the reason we were brought to Ferndale isn't he?"

Alex nodded.

"Why?"

"He needed help. If Guthrie punched you in the face, and Lise held a gun to Natalie's head, it was for good reason. You could have ruined everything, David."

The hotel doors opened. David and Alex watched as paramedics wheeled out a gurney carrying a blanket-covered body. Sorrow stung Alex. He knew the dead person on that gurney was Evan. This was the unforeseen deprivation of renewing a life. The Knights gave Janek his life, and Evan was the sacrifice.

David saw the sorrow on Alex's face and decided to leave things alone. If Alex wanted to tell his tale, he would do it in his own time. He said, "Is it time to get the hell out of here?"

"Yeah," Alex said. "It's time."

The other Knights and the wives joined David and Alex on the sidewalk. They watched as the ambulance pulled away from the curb. Its siren was off. There was no need to hurry.

Sean pictured the scene inside the hotel: the bloodied and mutilated dead victim, the grief-stricken family and friends. As a paramedic firefighter, he was intimate with the setting. He murmured his condolences for Evan, and those who were inconsolable. *I'm sorry for all of you.*

In a few hours, Bryan and Natalie would be gone. They would spend the drive to their next destination discussing what he had done last night. He would tell her the truth and hope she believed his story. He needed to share this strange adventure, and the new burden it placed on his life.

Jessie Melrose heard the people of Ferndale whisper Evan's name. *How could the man I shared a bed with only a few hours ago, the man with the strongest sexual being I'd ever experienced be dead?* Jessie saw his bright green eyes looking at her with lustful passion. His carnal energy still throbbed between her legs. She cried as if she had lost a spouse.

Janek had refused to let the paramedics take Evan from his arms. He pulled Evan in closer to his chest and huddled over his body.

A paramedic, Chris Jackson, knelt beside Janek. Chris knew most of the people he helped, and in his experience, the deaths he encountered were age or heart related. A death like this was unusual in Ferndale. Evan's suicide and the condition of his body were unsettling.

"Janek, you have to let go of him. If there's a chance he can be revived it has to be done now."

Janek knew without a doubt his friend was dead. Once he let go, Evan was lost to him forever. He tightened his grip on Evan's body. The paramedic looked to the other people in the room for help.

Lucas said to Janek, "Evan is my friend too. You aren't the only one hurting. You aren't the only person who has lost him. I know you feel responsible, but you aren't. This was Evan's decision. You know, as well as I do, that none of us could've talked him out of it if we'd known."

Janek didn't raise his head when he let go of Evan's body. The paramedics moved Evan from his lap and began resuscitation efforts. The fellowship stood up and backed away.

Evan was pronounced dead five minutes later. Official time and date of death was 9:28 a.m., December 6, 2016.

When they draped Evan's body with a blanket, Abigail screamed his name, and then covered her mouth with a quivering hand. She could beg and scream and cry all she wanted, but he wasn't coming back. Lise went to Abigail. They cried in the arms of their wretched embrace.

Lt. Jim Berggren walked into the living room with two men in plain clothes. He knelt beside Evan and moved the blanket from his bloody face. Jim's lips moved in a silent goodbye. He and Evan had spent many nights drinking and playing poker at the Palace. Evan had a wild streak in him a mile long, but his heart was always in the right place.

Jim turned his attention to the grieving people in the room. He wondered why the seven of them were together in Janek's suite that early in the morning. These people had been friends since he could remember. They were an odd group whose loyalty was fierce. Evan's death had to be traumatizing.

"We need to leave the living room while forensics does its thing," Jim said.

What was left of the fellowship followed him into the bedroom.

"I need to ask a few questions, then you're free to go. Niklas, you and Janek look like you might need medical attention. There's another ambulance that's just arrived from Eureka. The paramedics are in the lobby."

"We're fine," Niklas said.

"Okay," Jim said. He walked to the open suite door, looked through it, and walked back to the bedroom. "I'd say that hole in the wall in the hallway is the result of a shotgun blast. That's funny, because no one reported hearing a shotgun go off in the hotel. It seems like someone would've heard that."

No one said a word.

"We're waiting on a ballistics expert from Eureka. When she gets here, she's gonna be all over that wall. Guthrie, I know you have a shotgun and I know it's here. Did you fire your shotgun in the direction of that wall or in this hotel?"

"I ain't telling you nothin, Jim. All I'm gonna say is that dead boy in there was the closest thing to a son I ever had. You got that?"

"Okay. Let's talk about Evan. Where did he get the gun? Was it his?"

No one said a word.

"None of you know whether or not Evan owned a gun? Janek, you have to know."

Janek said nothing.

"Did any of you see Evan shoot himself?"

No one said a word.

Jim removed his hat and ran a hand through his thinning brown hair. "Evan wasn't the type of guy who'd kill himself. Something went on in this suite that either drove him to it or he was murdered. Now, if you don't talk to me, the big guys from Sacramento are gonna come up here and rake you over the coals. That police report filed earlier this morning isn't gonna help matters. Do you get that?"

"We don't give a shit," Janek said. "We aren't talking about this to anyone."

Jim exhaled a loud sigh. "I figured this was how it would go. All of you go home. We're sealing off this suite and suite 304. Janek, we'll give you some time to clean up and pack your personals. I'll need to know where you're staying."

Janek was numb. He had endured pain and torture for years. His friends suffered every bit as much. Now Evan was dead. Evan told him once that as long as there was hope, there was a chance to change things. In the last minutes of Evan's life, he asked Janek to reach for hope. Now he didn't know if he could hold on to it.

Chapter 38

December 22, 2016

Janek dreamed that he and Evan were on the schooner headed for Portland. They were leaning against the rail on the top deck, watching the dark blue water rush by as they shared a bottle of whiskey. Evan's green eyes were bright with anticipation as he talked about what they were going to do when they got to Portland.

"The last time I was in Portland, I was keeping time with a little thing I met in a saloon. I swear she was as pretty as a Christmas present. Well, we ended up in a hotel room. Some guy kicks in the door and starts swinging a board at me. Have you ever tried putting your pants on when you're running from some pissed off guy? It can't be done."

Janek laughed and shook his head. "No, I've never had to do that."

"Well, then you've been missing out on all the fun, haven't you?"

Janek smiled. "I guess I have, but I'm sure you'll rectify that."

"You know I will!" Evan said and slapped Janek on the back.

Evan's good-natured slap caught Janek off guard, and he stumbled and fell to the deck. Evan offered his hand. Janek took it.

"I'll always be with you," Evan said as he helped Janek to his feet.

Janek heard a cannon blast. He turned to ask Evan why the crew was firing cannons, but Evan was gone.

Janek jerked awake. He was in the guest bedroom in the Sullivan house.

Though it had been two weeks, he couldn't adjust to being there. The cat woke from his slumber against Janek's chest. He yawned and stretched his front legs.

Janek took his time getting out of bed. The ribs Evan had broken were still painful. His skin no longer hurt, and his headaches were gone, but his physical damage remained.

His face was scared with healed lacerations across his forehead and along his jawbone. The mass of thick irregular scar tissue on his lower left leg, and the highways of thin white scars on his right leg, had not faded. The red raised scars on his chest and stomach and back continued to remind him of the mutilation and agony he had suffered.

And there was a residue of the damage caused by the explosions Erebus detonated in his chest. Every time he stood up, he was dizzy.

The cat walked to the edge of the bed and meowed. Janek lifted him into his arms and scratched the cat's neck. The cat had remained his loyal companion and became Janek's familiar. He had tolerated the cat's touch because they coexisted on the same spiritual level. They were both pure souls.

Janek put the cat on the bed and walked to the window. He parted the curtains and surveyed the gray cloudy sky. Today, they would bury Evan.

The big guys from Sacramento didn't come to Ferndale as Jim threatened. The local police took a week to rule Evan's death a suicide. The coroner took an additional week to confirm Evan had no next of kin before releasing Evan's body to Janek.

Yesterday, Jim allowed him to remove Evan's personal belongings from suite 304. Aside from the death of his family, it was the worst thing he had ever had to face in his life, and he did it alone.

Lise went with him to fetch the rest of his personal things from suite 302. That was a chore he couldn't face alone. Horror haunted his suite. While he packed, he tried not to look in the living room. He was afraid he would see Evan standing there covered in blood as it dripped from his annihilated abdomen.

Niklas and Lise moved into a rented house. The hotel's third floor was sealed. The suites were cleaned, and the wall in the hallway was repaired. The smell of desperation and death would dissipate with time. What took place there would not. Perhaps someday, they would have the fortitude to allow strangers to tread where they had once lived and died.

Evan's suicide would perpetuate the ghost story surrounding suite 302. Emily Hartmann would no longer haunt the hotel alone.

Janek couldn't adjust to living his life without pain and fear and repression. It was as if he'd been reborn an infant who had to learn how to walk and talk and reason. He wondered if he *did* learn how to live all over again if Erebus would become a distant memory? *Did Erebus truly die? Was its ethereal spirit destroyed by one gunshot?*

He couldn't remember the first few days of December. Abigail told him about their journey through the forest, and the men who went to his garden. Erebus lured them to Ferndale to do the work it was incapable of doing. Nevertheless, those men saved Janek's soul and his life. Janek was grateful to the strangers who were strong enough to stand up under the weight of a seemingly impossible task. He wanted to show his gratitude, but he would never have that opportunity.

Janek smelled coffee, which meant Abigail was awake early. She'd slept little since Evan's death. He was her champion in a world where people shunned those who were different. In Evan's eyes, she wasn't the bastard child of an unwed Mexican woman and the daughter of a saloon keeper. She was his friend—pure and simple. Janek knew she would stay busy all morning to elude the albatross of Evan's impending funeral.

He dressed in jeans and a sweatshirt, and then went downstairs to the kitchen. Abigail was washing dishes. He saw her run a knuckle across her wet left eye.

"Abby, may I get a cup of coffee?"

Her smile didn't reach her tired and strained brown eyes. "Help yourself. You know where everything is."

Janek got a cup from the overhead cabinet and poured his coffee. He sat at the table and watched Abigail.

She resumed washing dishes. When she finished, she dried each dish and put it away. Janek couldn't sit and watch her nervous attempt to drive the albatross from her mind. He got up and took the dishtowel from her hands.

"Abby, we're going to get through this together. Sit down."

She sat at the table. He poured a cup of coffee and put it on the table in front of her. She stared at the coffee cup. The tears she'd restrained thus far freed themselves and wet her cheeks.

"Come here," Janek said. He pulled her out of the chair by her shoulders and wrapped her in his arms. She laid her head against his chest and sobbed. She sobbed for Evan, for her unrequited love, for the horrors they had lived.

When she ran dry, she stepped from his embrace and looked into his bewitching blue eyes. She couldn't hide it anymore. Contrary to her old-fashioned beliefs, she said, "I'm in love with you."

Janek was taken off guard. She was waiting for his reply. He couldn't let her flounder in her confession. "Abby, I love you, but I…"

"You're not *in* love with me." She was asphyxiated by the words.

"That's not true. It's just that…I don't know who I am. I haven't known for a long time."

"I understand…you need time to adjust to being yourself again."

"It's more than that. I don't know what to give you. I'm afraid I'll hurt you."

"You *can* hurt me, but you won't. You're the most beautiful person I have ever met. It's not just the way you look. It's everything about you."

"I have scars…"

"That makes no difference. You're still flawless."

"Your perspective of me isn't real."

"You're wrong."

Janek was at a loss for words. He wanted to tell her that *she* was the beautiful person—an angel who gave up everything to care for him all those years. She fell in love with him when he was incapable of sharing and nurturing that kind of emotion with a woman. He was no more capable of loving her in the manner she deserved than he was in 1873. Erebus had released him, but he remained in bondage.

"I'm so sorry," she said, "It's selfish of me to expect something from you that you don't have to give."

"Abby, I don't feel…right."

She bit her lower lip and nodded, but her desire for him flamed bright and strong in her eyes. It was powerful enough to ignite a fire Janek had forgotten existed.

He pulled her back into his embrace. His kiss was hungry and feral. She responded with the same raging appetite. He lifted her into his arms, and she wrapped her legs around his waist. Repressed passion and forgotten lust summoned erotica, and they panted under its weight.

Janek laid her on the kitchen table. His hands swam through the flow of her long dark hair and ran beneath her sweatshirt to touch her warm breasts.

Abigail moaned. She tightened her legs around his back and slid her fingers through his blond hair, imprisoning his head in her hands. Whether this was real or a phantasm, she had no intention of letting him slip from her grasp. The touch of his divine hands on her breasts felt surreal. The scent of his magnificence was ambrosial.

His touch became rougher as he pinched her nipples and squeezed her breasts. One hand raced down her firm stomach to pull at the button on her jeans. Her moan was bestial, and she squirmed in lust on the table beneath him.

The wanton movement of her willing body, and her strong legs entrapping him aroused insanity in Janek's carnal mind. He prodded it with common sense. *Take her to your bed.* He stood up straight. Her unwilling legs unlocked and fell from his back. He took her by the hand and led her upstairs to his bedroom.

He stripped off her sweatshirt then grabbed her around the waist and pulled her to him. His kiss was animalistic, and she returned it with ferine energy. Her fingers savaged the button on his jeans and ripped down the zipper. She slipped her fingers around his hard cock. He groaned in brutish ecstasy, and his hands entangled in her hair.

She fell to her knees and pulled his jeans down. Janek stepped out of them then reached for her so she would stand and kiss his starving lips. She resisted his groping hands and sucked his hard-on into her wet mouth. For a fleeting moment, untamed rapture wrenched Janek's chest, and he thought he was going to pass out.

Abigail let his cock drop from her mouth when he urged her to stand up. She lay back on his bed. He straddled her waist, grasped her hands and pinned them to the pillow beneath her head. He kissed her forehead and her cheeks, and then he searched her face.

How many times had he looked at her without *seeing* her? Her skin was smooth and clean, free of blemishes or scars, but that wasn't what he was looking for. His eyes penetrated the doors to her essence. She was a vivid innocent soul.

Ardent adoration radiated from her essence and pierced the apathy cloaking Janek's blue eyes. Resonating light escaped his passionate eyes and blinded her.

He freed her hands and kissed her on the mouth as if she was a delicacy. Her arms encircled his back. She forced him to lower his chest onto her breasts. The raised red scars slid over her nipples, and the sensation of his past agonies aroused perverse ecstasy between her legs. She breathed his name.

His sweet kisses traced her neck to her breasts. She arched her back and thrust her hips into the cusp of his crotch. Janek unbuttoned her jeans and scooted backward, his eyes fixed on her bare skin, as he inched them off.

He crawled forward between her legs and tore her lace panties off in one smooth motion. She bent her knees and pushed her hips up. The crazed ecstasy between her legs met his waiting mouth. She spread her legs and rocked her hips as he kissed and licked her throbbing clit. Abigail's bridled salacious passion was shredding.

She touched the sides of his head to move his face out from between her legs. Her hands encircled his neck and forced him to kiss her lips to muffle the noise of her rapacious desire. He guided her hand to his hard-on. As she stroked it, he fought to keep from ejaculating in her hand.

His lips harnessed the cries in her mouth. She spread her legs and wrapped them around his waist. Abigail controlled her urge to cry out when he fondled her torrid wet vulva. His kisses kept her from screaming aloud when he stroked her convulsing clit and slid his finger inside her.

He unknowingly taunted and tantalized her fear that this was all an illusion. Then something she didn't expect or understand unleashed itself under the hallowed touch of Janek's hand, and its heat exploded deep inside her belly.

Her orgasm pulverized Janek's self-control. He slid his hot erection between the lips of her vulva and up inside her. She was warm and silky and tight, and he was driven to lasciviousness. He rocked his hips hard back and forth. His cock devoured her virginity until it exploded with gluttony. She felt his muscles flex then stiffen and heard him suppress the orgasmic howl in his throat.

He held his breath until he was sure he wouldn't announce his ecstasy to the world; then he gently collapsed on top of her. Abigail's warm unsteady breath fluttered on his cheek, and her heart pulsated beneath his heaving chest.

They lay together for time unknown. A door opened in the hall then slammed shut.

"Daddy's up. I'd better go downstairs," Abigail said in a breathy whisper.

Janek slid off her. She got out of bed and hurried to gather her clothes from the floor.

Janek didn't want to get out of bed for fear he would pass out, but he couldn't lay there while Abigail dressed in a panic. He got up and breathed slow and measured. The dizziness passed.

Abigail reached for the bedroom doorknob. He crossed the room and put a hand on her forearm. She looked at his face. It was exquisite despite the scars.

"Abby, I *do* love you. Please…"

She put a finger to his lips.

He removed her finger.

She opened the door, paused, and turned to look into his enchanting eyes. "I'll wait for you until eternity passes away if that's what it takes." She walked into the hall and closed the door behind her.

When Abigail entered the kitchen, Guthrie was sitting at the table reading the newspaper and drinking coffee. He laid the newspaper on the table and said, "Just toast this morning Abby."

She offered a small smile and said, "Okay, Daddy."

He had heard some of what went on upstairs. Janek had deflowered his daughter. Guthrie figured she deserved it. She had waited longer than any human being should have to wait to get laid because she wanted it to be with Janek.

Janek walked into the kitchen, poured a cup of coffee, and sat at the table. *The boy has guts*, Guthrie thought. Maybe he has no idea how fathers react to that kind of noise. He decided to give Janek the full treatment.

"I don't care if you think you're in love, but I ain't listening to that noise ever again. You got that, boy?"

Abigail was mortified, but she forced herself to stay on task and butter the toast. This was something her father was compelled to do. She couldn't interfere.

Guthrie saw extreme embarrassment on Janek's face. It had been so long since Janek was a person that his tendency to be taciturn and decorous slipped Guthrie's mind.

Janek looked Guthrie in the eye. If he didn't do it at this moment, it would be a long time before he would be able to do it. He said, "Yes, I understand. I'm very sorry."

"Damn right you are. I don't care what you've been through. This is my home and my daughter and don't you forget that."

Abigail set a plate of buttered toast on the table in front of Guthrie. She said, "The funeral is at St. Paul's cemetery at three o'clock. Janek and I are meeting Lucas, Lise, and Niklas at the funeral home beforehand. Do you want to go with us?"

"No. Watching them put Evan in the ground is gonna be bad enough. You ain't going there to look at him are you?"

"No, Daddy. We know Evan would hate that. We just want some time alone with him before the funeral."

"I hope Niklas ain't gonna be going on about the hereafter, and how Evan has gone to meet his maker. He'd hate that too," Guthrie growled.

Abigail sighed. "Niklas isn't going to say anything like that at the service."

Guthrie got up and stormed upstairs.

Chapter 39

Abigail drove Janek and Guthrie to the cemetery adjoined to St. Paul's Catholic Church. Rain clouds rolled in from the northwest. Thunder rumbled in the distance. Janek and Abigail got out of the car. Guthrie stayed in the back seat.

Abigail opened Guthrie's door and said, "Are you coming?"

Guthrie didn't answer.

"We're going to visit Matt's grave. We'll come back and get you."

Abigail led Janek to Matt's gravesite. Matt's wife and an infant son lay in graves beside his.

"I'm sorry I haven't visited you. I know you understand why," Janek said to Matt. "I'm glad you decided to stay behind and live a normal life. We lost Evan two weeks ago. Perhaps you already know. We're burying him today. If you see him, look after him for me, but don't ever let him know. I'll be back to visit you when I can."

They walked hand in hand back to the car.

Abigail opened Guthrie's door and gave him an expectant look. Guthrie grunted and got out of the car. He buttoned his coat and lagged behind Abigail and Janek as they walked to Evan's gravesite.

There were hundreds of people waiting for the service to begin. At the funeral home, Janek had talked to Evan alone and cried. He thought he was prepared for this, but he wasn't. The sight of all these people shivering in the cold made his throat constrict and his hands shake.

Lise and Lucas were standing apart from the crowd. Lise ran to Janek

305

and threw her arms around his chest. He hugged her close. Lucas looked at Janek with brown eyes that said *I hope we get through this.* They walked together through the crowd to the gravesite.

Niklas stood beside the casket. As a reverend, he had conducted hundreds of funeral services, but this was the first time he had to eulogize a loved one. Preparation for this moment was futile. Evan had denounced religion years ago. He tried to write his heartfelt thoughts, but the words seemed weak and sterile compared to his true feelings. At last, he realized Evan wouldn't want this day to be about pomp and circumstance. He would want it to be a party day filled with laughter and happiness. Niklas tried to take his cue from that. He motioned to the crowd and began the service.

He cleared his throat and spoke in his sermon-delivering voice. "Everyone here knows that Evan wouldn't want this day to be about grief and loss. He would tell us to think about the good times and hold on to those thoughts. We are here today to celebrate the life of Evan Francis O'Malley and acknowledge that he was a man worth knowing. Some of you loved Evan. Some of you just enjoyed having a drink with him at the Palace Saloon. No matter. We are all here for the same reason.

"Evan was my friend and I loved him. He was smart, uncomplicated, fiercely loyal, and capricious. He was quick-tempered and straightforward— traits that were often intimidating, but admirable. His ability to make the best of the worst situation was astounding. His passionate love for life and the ladies was well known. But Evan's capacity to give all he had to those he cared for was what made him extraordinary.

"I suppose I could go on and on about whom Evan was and what he contributed to our lives. Instead, I will leave us to ruminate on our private recollections of this man. There is one thing, however, we must all remember. Evan would not want us to forget him. I don't believe any of us ever will."

Niklas swept a hand across his eyes to wipe away his surreptitious tears.

The mourners stood silent.

Lucas noticed a young blonde woman standing aloof. He approached her. "Jessie. What are you doing here?"

"I hope I'm not intruding."

"Of course you aren't. I'm just surprised to see you."

Jessie's voice quivered. "I knew Evan only a few days, but I think he was the kind of man I could have loved my whole life. I didn't get the chance to find out, but I think I would've been right."

"I'm sorry."

It hurt Lucas to know she may have been the woman who would have offered Evan O'Malley true love. *It's a pity she didn't know Evan already had true love.*

"He didn't seem like the type to kill himself," Jessie said, trying to steady her voice.

"He wasn't the type."

"Then, why?"

"He was protecting someone."

"Who?"

"A friend."

Jessie didn't understand, but by the look on Lucas' face, it was best to let it go.

Lucas didn't ask about Amy because he didn't care. Today was a bad day for pretense. He couldn't imagine being with a woman who wasn't part of what had happened to them. It would be too hard.

He offered his hand to Jessie. "Come with me. I'd like you to meet someone."

A small smile dashed across her lips. She took his outstretched hand. She didn't see the point of meeting anyone because she was never coming back to Ferndale, but she let him have his way.

"Jessie Melrose, this is Janek Walesa."

Jessie was taken aback. The man who stood before her was the most beautiful man she had ever seen. Evan told her Janek was sick. She pictured a pasty weakling with watery eyes and a bad complexion. He had to be the friend Evan was protecting.

Jessie said, "I spent the last few days of Evan's life with him."

Janek stared at her. She was the last woman Evan held in his arms. She was beautiful, as were most of the women who'd shared his bed, but her green eyes said she was in love with Evan.

"He talked about you a lot. He said you'd been sick for a long time. I'm sorry."

Janek's indifference toward his recovery couldn't validate a response. The only thing that mattered was the loss of the man he would miss the rest of his life.

"Thank you for being with Evan and caring enough to come to his funeral. We're having a small gathering at the Sullivan house. Please join us. Excuse me."

Janek walked through the nearly deserted cemetery to the car. Abigail was leaning against the driver's side door. The wind blew her hair in circles around her face.

"Where's Guthrie?" he asked.

She nodded toward the gravesite.

Guthrie fondled the flowers sprayed across the top of Evan's casket. Then, he rested his forehead on the casket and wept.

They gathered on the Sullivan's front porch despite the storm thundering overhead. They needed to shed the years they'd spent ensconced in confinement and secrecy.

Niklas took a bottle of whiskey and seven shot glasses from the bag in his lap. He passed a glass and the bottle to Lise. Lise poured a shot and passed the bottle to Guthrie.

He poured whiskey into a big glass, and then walked to the end of the porch. Rain soaked the edges of the porch and the grass. He swallowed all the whiskey in his glass. It was time to admit his sin.

"I knew he was gonna do it," he said, staring at the wet grass. "I should've talked him out of it, but he made me promise not to. He reasoned that nightmare couldn't complete the joining if one of us was dead. I don't know how he came to that conclusion. The boy was scared, but that didn't stop him.

"When I was in the army, I seen men die horrible, and I killed plenty myself, but I ain't never felt so bad about anything in my life. I'm an old man who has lived long enough. I should've died that morning."

Guthrie had just explained why Evan killed himself, but Jessie didn't understand what he meant. She wasn't sure if she wanted to understand.

"We suspected you knew," Lise said. "You were the last person alone with Evan. He wouldn't have let you stand in for him. He didn't see things like that."

"That don't make it right," Guthrie said. He turned to face the group.

"I brought this on us because I was incapable of handling my grief," Janek said. "I'm to blame."

"No you ain't. It wasn't like you knew you had a disease, and then irresponsibly spread it around town. You're the last person on earth who would purposely subject other people to suffering and misery."

Guthrie's comment didn't ease Janek's guilt. "I should have stayed in Oregon."

"Erebus would've somehow gotten its claws in you even if you had stayed in Oregon," Lucas said. "And it probably would have gotten its way."

"The boy's right," Guthrie said to Janek. "When you came here, you gave Evan brotherhood and a chance to prove he was worth somethin'."

Lise said, "I wouldn't trade our friendship for anything. Not even if I had known then what I know now. I'm sure Evan would agree."

Janek knew Evan *would* agree. The thought mauled his emotions. He stood up, and after his dizziness passed he paced the porch.

Lise went to Janek and stilled his pacing by taking his hand. He looked at her.

She said, "We have a life again. Let's live it. We'll grow old like we're supposed to. We have a chance to be happy. Don't waste it spending the rest of your days second guessing things."

Janek threw back the whiskey shot he was holding.

"Did you hear me?" Lise said.

He nodded.

"Well?"

"I can't promise." He glanced at the others on the porch. Their attention had drifted from him and onto new conversations. He walked to the end of the porch and lowered his voice to a whisper. "I don't feel right, Lise."

Dread formed in the pit of her stomach.

"I don't know who I am, and I don't care. I should be ecstatic that I'm free of repression, but I'm scared, and I can't validate my life."

"Scared of what?"

"Scared of becoming a victim again. Something about me caused Erebus to prey on me, and I don't know how to defend myself from something I don't understand."

"You honestly don't see it do you? I know without a doubt you've heard it your whole life."

"When my dead family spoke to me, my father said it was because of my strengths. I don't know what those are anymore."

"Your strengths haven't changed. Erebus desired your perfection."

"That's ridiculous. No one is perfect."

"That's a lie we tell each other because we're ashamed of our flaws. You're transcendent for a million reasons. One of those reasons is because you don't compare the things that make you ashamed of yourself to others' weaknesses. You are what you are. You were born transcendent, and you're the most beautiful human being I have ever met."

"Abby said that this morning. I'm the most beautiful person she's ever met."

"Like I said. Women are honest about your perfection. Men won't tell you, but they know. It's unmistakable and threatening. Men manifest the realization of your transcendence in different ways. Evan was unique. He knew, and he loved you from the beginning."

"I don't understand."

"I don't think you'll ever understand. Be kind to yourself, Janek. I've never once seen you be kind to yourself. Evan is dead, and you're grieving terribly. It's no wonder you're confused and apathetic."

"You can't tell me I'm the perfect human being. There are plenty of people who hated me like Emily Hartmann, and people who were part of Niklas' congregation."

"They hated you because they couldn't touch your transcendence in some way." Lise grinned. "Although, I suppose Emily Hartmann got a feel. Now, come on. Let's join in the fun. We could both use another shot."

Niklas passed around the whiskey bottle. They exchanged memories of Evan. They exchanged memories of one another. They talked about the future. For the first time in years, laughter was heard coming from the Sullivan house.

But Guthrie wasn't laughing. He was watching Janek. Janek's bright blue eyes were dull and glazed, and it wasn't attributed to whiskey.

Janek wasn't drunk. He had stopped drinking an hour ago. He was trying to chase the anxiety inducing words he'd exchanged with Lise from his mind, but they refused to leave. *You were born transcendent.* What was he supposed to do with that?

Guthrie knew something horrible was going to happen. He looked at Abigail. She was laughing and talking with Lise and Jessie. He looked back at Janek. Janek rubbed his jaw. Guthrie saw him wince.

"Son, are you okay?"

"I'm fine," Janek said, but he wasn't fine. He was short of breath, and his jaw ached. If he stood up, he might pass out, and he didn't want to scare everyone.

Guthrie whispered to Lise. They got up and walked to the front door. He said, "I'm going in the house for a minute. Janek looks like he ain't feeling good. Watch him and don't say nothin to Abby."

"Okay."

Lise sat in the chair Guthrie had occupied. Lucas and Niklas were talking. If Janek had been part of the conversation he wasn't any longer. She saw the dull glazed look in his eyes. He rubbed his jaw then his upper arms, and then his jaw again.

She leaned in toward him and said, "What's wrong?"

"I'm fine."

"No you aren't."

Sudden pressure in his chest forced Janek to stand up without thinking. Dizziness tried to knock him to the porch floor. He bent over to ward it off, but it wouldn't stop. Dizziness shoved him to his knees and he threw up.

Abigail and Lise ran to his side.

He threw up again. When the nausea subsided, the pressure in his chest eased a little. He wiped his mouth with the back of his hand and tried to stand.

"We're taking you to the hospital," Niklas said.

The pressure in Janek's chest exploded, and he collapsed.

Erebus' abuse had damaged Janek's heart.

Guthrie came out on the porch with the phone in his hand.

Janek wasn't afraid to die, he was afraid it would take a long time.

An ambulance arrived. Paramedics rushed to the porch. Chris Jackson, one of the paramedics who arrived on the scene of Evan's suicide said, "Janek, can you talk to us?"

Janek couldn't talk.

Abigail went berserk. Guthrie and Niklas had to restrain her crazed behavior from interfering with the paramedics. Tremors racked Lise's body. She couldn't cry. She wondered how they were supposed to go on if Janek died the same day they buried Evan.

Jessie couldn't believe she was witnessing this resplendent person die. She was grateful that Evan wasn't there to suffer Janek's pain. She stepped behind Lucas for artificial shelter as he described Janek's symptoms to Chris.

The paramedics hooked an electrocardiogram up to Janek. The machine came to life and a jagged yellow line blipped across the screen. They took his blood pressure and waited for his pulse to stabilize. As the paramedics moved him onto a stretcher, Janek's heart stopped. The electrocardiogram flat lined.

The crushing torture in Janek's chest vanished.

He was walking across a well-manicured expanse of lawn surrounded by towering redwood trees. Janek searched the garden. He was alone. A long time ago, he came close to dying, and he dreamed that death was a lonely darkness from which there was no escape. A terrible shadow had dwelled within that darkness.

The darkness and the shadow were gone. The hollow echo of isolation remained.

He wondered why his family didn't greet him when he passed through the veil. His father promised they would be there. Perhaps, they no longer recognized him. Perhaps, the promise was an illusion.

Chapter 40

"They aren't here because you aren't dead."

"Then why are you here?"

"To make sure you don't stay."

"The pain stopped. How do you know I'm not dead?"

"I can still see your physical and emotional scars."

"If I'm not dead, why am I here?"

"Niklas sacrificed his congregation for this garden. He built it as a place where you could begin to heal and find your way to freedom."

"What garden is this?"

"The garden at the edge of eternity. You don't remember it do you?"

Janek shook his head.

"You have to go back and finish the journey you started. That's the only way you'll heal and remember who you are."

"San Francisco?"

"Aye."

"But you said this garden will heal me."

"This garden is where you begin. You can't stay."

"I don't think I can move on without you."

"You aren't moving on without me. I'll always be with you. I told you that this morning."

"If I go to San Francisco, I'll be alone."

"Is that so bad?"

"I can't leave Abby."

"Take her with you. I know you're in love with her. You just can't see it right now."

"I don't know."

"You're making excuses. Go back to them. They're waiting."

Janek didn't want to go back to the place where pain and confusion awaited him, but Evan was right. He was making excuses because he was afraid. If he didn't move on, he would suffer the rest of his life or end up committing suicide.

"I promise I'll be with you," Evan said.

Janek's horrible chest pain returned, and he struggled to breathe. But he *did* breathe. The garden at the edge of eternity vanished.

"I've never seen that type of damage to anyone's heart. It looked seared as if it was set on fire. There were parts of your arteries that were fused. We put in stints to open the arteries. Your sexual activity and the stress of the funeral triggered your heart attack."

Janek said nothing. He was going to San Francisco as soon as he got out of the hospital. The less he said to the doctor the better.

"I'm releasing you today, but you shouldn't resume normal activity for a week."

Janek looked at Abigail. His eyes begged her to keep quiet.

He had told her what Evan said in the garden. They were moving to San Francisco so Janek could heal, and she would let him do it in his own way. The prospect of leaving her father and Ferndale for the first time in her life should have been frightening, but it wasn't. She would be with Janek.

Lucas, Niklas, Lise, and Guthrie were at the Sullivan house when they returned from the hospital in Eureka. Abigail had said her goodbyes. This was Janek's time.

Lise held her arms out to him, and they embraced for a long time before they let go.

Janek kissed her cheek and whispered, "I love you."

"I love you too," she whispered back.

It scared Guthrie to let Abigail loose in a big world she knew little about with a man who couldn't take care of her. He had kept his fears to himself when she told him they were leaving.

"Get better, son."

"Thank you for giving me Abby," Janek said. "Thank you for everything you've given me."

"Ain't no thanks necessary."

Lucas said, "I'll visit as often as I can. You're going to need a drinking buddy in San Fran."

Janek and Lucas shared a brief embrace, then Janek said, "You're a good friend. I look forward to it. I'll miss seeing you every day."

"Call if you need *anything*," Niklas said. "I can be there in a moment's notice."

Janek offered his hand to Niklas. Niklas took it and gripped it in his big hands.

"I have no words to express my gratitude for what you sacrificed for me," Janek said. "I saw Evan in my garden during my heart attack. He told me you built that garden and why."

"Like Guthrie said, there's no thanks necessary. Take care of yourself. Lise and I will take care of the hotel as long as you need."

They all walked outside to the car parked on the street. Abigail kissed Guthrie then got in the driver's side. Janek opened the passenger side door. He whistled for the cat. The cat trotted to the car and hopped into the back seat. Janek got in the car without looking back. He promised himself that this time, the goodbye would not be eternal.

Also by Salina B Baker

About the Author

Salina is a multiple award-winning author and avid student of Colonial America and the American Revolution. Her lifelong passion for history and all things supernatural led her to write historical fantasy. Reading, extensive traveling and graveyard prowling with her husband keep that passion alive. Salina lives in Austin, Texas and is a member of The Writers' League of Texas.